The Assassin's Quest

Book 4
Of the Paladin chronicles

Dr Neil Port

Dedication:

This book is dedicated to all who pray for peace and strive for understanding. As always my thanks to my wife and family and my 'team' of volunteer reviewers: Meryl, Ralph, Ilona, Shirley and Linda.

Neil Port 2015

Jess Book 4 of The Paladin Chronicles

ISBN 978-0-9873845-6-0

e-ISBN 978-0-9873845-7-7

Published by Neil Port Independent Press, Newcastle, Australia

Proof reader: Marianna Manns (mia.manns@gmail.com)

Print book design and E book conversion: Bhagchand Bhatiya
(ebooksspecialist@gmail.com)

Cover design by: Paul Kimber (mule@angelheartdesign.org)

Map design by Neil Port and Radana Pavelkov
(Nivues@yahoo.com).

All based on Wiki commons templates: see
(Nivues@yahoo.com) for details.

Author's note:

The Paladin Chronicles (books 1-7) are a series. Book 7 deals with events occurring between book 3 and book 4. But each book, by design, can be enjoyed in isolation. This series of books describes a world closely similar to our own from the period commencing three and a half centuries BC. There are also differences, some obvious and some less obvious. The historical aspects are used to provide a setting, but these books are works of imagination. The events described and characters described should not be taken as an historical or accurate account. Any resemblance to any person now living or living in recent memory is purely accidental.

War and battle are not glorious and are not depicted as such. The books of this series are not intended for children.

Many names and terms are *transliterated* (converted into the phonetic equivalent in our alphabet) often with the English translation in brackets. Book 4 and book 5 will introduce a few Persian names and terms. Apologies in advance for any errors in Greek and Farsi grammar.

I have attempted to follow standard rules for capitalisation meaning 'Greek and Gypsy' but 'human and elf' and sometimes 'Queen and Lord' but sometimes 'queen and lord'. I have treated humans, elves, dwarves and svartálfar as species and not capitalised them.

Contents

The story so far

(without spoiling the previous books):

Excerpt from book 3:
The Gathering Storm. Chapter 2: The End

Æloðulf gestured. There was an explosion that threw Hakeem from his horse. He staggered up, ears ringing. Half a dozen of his men were able to stand and make their way towards him. He gathered himself and began to jog slowly to where Æloðulf was. Half way there he saw something that made his blood run cold.

Elana and Jacinta were here! Elana's elves were shooting arrows. Jacinta was running at Æloðulf; a huge black daimôn was stopped just behind her. As Jacinta hit him with her sword, Æloðulf disappeared in a cloud of smoke.

Then there was an explosion near where Jacinta had stood. Hakeem was blinded and stunned. While he was struggling to clear the after image and his ringing ears, a dark figure appeared next to Elana and attacked her. He couldn't see who or what it was. He yelled a warning, but couldn't get there in time. An explosion cleared the hill of anything living; only smouldering bodies and scorched earth remained.

Jacinta was screaming something. The black daimôn had grabbed her from behind.

"Look out!" he cried.

It was too late.

Another blast of heat knocked him to the ground. When he could look up, there was nothing left, only smoke and scorched earth with waves of heat rising up into the air.

The two people he loved more than life itself were gone.

* * *

The Illvættir War: Countless millennia ago there were inhuman sorcerers called the *svartálfar,* Dark Elves. Within them a group the elves called the *Illvættir* (ill breed) learned to summon daimôns. They developed awesome power and long lives but when they did die, they faced losing their souls to the daimôn they had bonded with.

They developed a madness; they believed all other beings of power wished to kill them. Under their leader Æloðulf ('Elf Wolf' meaning 'Hunter of Elves'), they began to systematically hunt down and destroy all other beings of power and then those who might conceive children with magical power.

This was the time of the Illvættir Wars.

The remaining svartálfar developed a number of weapons including a set of spells that could destroy their enemies. They sealed these in the book 'that must never be read', and bound it with protective spells. They sacrificed one of their own, Silver, to be its guardian. The spells were so terrible that the svartálfar decided to accept extinction rather than unleash them onto the world.

As the Illvættir managed to hunt down the last of the svartálfar, they turned to the svartálfar's elvish and any human allies. The elves were only saved by fleeing to the lands of ice and snow, far to the north and west of the world, where the daimôns could not follow. But the world slowly warmed and their refuge was finally breached. It was then that the last of the elves fled to *Anatolē* (modern day Turkey) to seek help from the powerful dwarves that lived in the two great underground cities of Kappadokia. As they fled, they were attacked. The only thing to save them was a mysterious hero wearing magical armour made by the dwarves and infused with forbidden magic. His features underneath the armour could not be seen. He was only ever known as 'the man who never was'. He became the first person of our realm to kill a daimôn. The only other person was Jacinta.

Before the Western Elves could reach Anatolē, a surprise attack all but destroyed the dwarves. It left only their greatest and most powerful city of all, the Deepest, somewhere in the Greater Kaukasos Mountains. What was finally unleashed on that city is unknown, but it is thought that it remains somewhere deep in the remains of that lost city.

The few survivors of the elves and dwarves were only saved when the Illvættir turned on one another.

The Elvish Prophecy: The dwarves bear few children and they never recovered, but after the disappearance of the Illvættir, the civilisation of the elves went on to enjoy a golden age, long and glorious. Two thousand years ago, Ælward, their most powerful sorcerer, foresaw their ultimate destruction. It was he that wrote the Elvish Prophecy, which was to become their last hope. The world was to face not one but two floods, deluges, of savage barbarians. Ælward secretly laboured not to strengthen the elves, but to weaken them. It would force them to ally with humans, not as servant and master, but as equals. It was the only way they would survive the coming of the second horde.

The time of the Aryans: The first great horde was the Aryans. They came from the *Rā* (Volga) River Valley and the surrounding steppe to the east. It was in the *steppe* (vast grass lands) that they developed the new powerful short bows, the spoked-wheel chariots and the bigger horses to pull them. They spread mainly east, out across the vast central steppe of Eurasia and the oasis lands of Central Asia, conquering all they came upon. There were many good seasons and the Aryans became more numerous than the wheat grains in a great field.

Then there came a drought like no other. Starvation stalked the cities and the countryside. The Aryan barbarians began to raid the caravans and farms. Trade ceased, farms became abandoned. Starving tribes could join them ... or fight, or flee. In the end there were whole peoples on the move in wave after wave, in numbers too great to imagine, consuming and destroying everything in their path.

In the wake, many great and fair civilisations simply disappeared. Mighty cities, some of which had stood for thousands of years, lay abandoned in ruins. The light of civilisation had gone out throughout the world. It was the dark ages that signalled the end of the Bronze Age.

The Western Elves stood bravely against the invaders, but they were fatally depleted. They only remain in scattered settlements along the Black Sea's southern coast. The smaller and younger kingdom of the Eastern Elves fared better, the forests and mountains of their home favoured the elf manner of fighting and not the Aryan chariots. The city of mountain and forest, wondrous Elgard, the last great city of the elves, remains.

The Curse of the Elves: The elves have been failing.

They have lost most of their magic and they no longer live longer than humans. Worse, they have fewer children. At the end of book 3, the new Queen, Seléne, prays that intermarrying humans and elves will save her dying people.

Jacinta and the Book that must never be read: Jacinta found the book in the necropolis under the ruins of elvish Troia, killing Æloðulf's daimôn by using the automatic protection spells in the book. Her left hand was injured in the fight. After she realised what she had, she returned the book to a hiding place in the necropolis. The svartálfar were right: the book must never be used.

The Hun and the Daimôn Army: In book 3 of The Paladin Chronicles, the elves and their allies face wave after wave of Hun barbarians. It was reminiscent of the time of the Aryans.

Allied with the Hun is Æloðulf, the last of the Illvættir, Gansükh his pupil and others they have trained to raise daimôns. The use of daimôns led to the apocalyptic destruction of the great city of Darband, the capital of Kohestan, and the terrible events of the defence of Elgard.

The Final Defence of Elgard, the last great city of the elves: The defence of Elgard was desperate. The Huns arrived like a tidal wave, backed by the terrible destruction wrought by daimôns. The elves and their allies were being slaughtered. Only the intervention of Jacinta and the daimôn lord Ba'al turned the tide, but it cost Jacinta and Elana their lives.

Is the Elvish Prophecy fulfilled? If Æloðulf is dead, Elgard saved and the curse of the elves seemingly reversed, surely the events described in the Prophecy are completed.

Yet it speaks of events that have not come to pass:

"Enter the locked room that is in 'No Place' and take its key ...

God's warrior must journey into the Deepest, that terrible place, to find the weapons and armour that are made for the man who never was, nor ever will be, and awaken that which lies within.

Only death will end the one of ancient evil, but he can never be killed. He is the one that no one daimôn, no one living, no one dead, no one made or not made and no one of the races of men can possibly defeat."

Is the Prophecy wrong then, has the ancient war really ended? Or must Jacinta's task pass to another?

Some of the main characters.

Elana: The Great Elvish Queen of prophecy, wife of Hakeem. She is believed to have been killed by a daimôn during the final moments of the defence of Elgard.

Hakeem: The Shantawi Warlord from the desert city of Karsh, a paladin (religious knight) of the Shayva sect, supreme commander of the allies and husband to Elana. He is the great warrior mentioned in the Elvish Prophecy and he led the defence against the Huns.

Jacinta: Their adopted Gypsy daughter and a student paladin. 'The Daughter' mentioned in the prophecy. Her role was the discovery and use of magic, new and old. She was seen killing Æloðulf in the final moments of the defence of Elgard.

It is thought that Ba'al killed her soon after.

Seléne: Elana's younger half–sister and Jacinta's best friend, now the Queen of the Half Elven, the kingdom formed by the intermarriage of elves and humans.

Pericles: Seléne's human husband, now the royal consort.

Silver: The last of the svartálfar; she is bound to 'the book that must never be read' to guard it. She is neither alive nor truly dead.

Æloðulf ('Elf Wolf' meaning 'Hunter of Elves'): The last and most powerful of the Illvættir. It was he that led the annihilation of the other svartálfar, many human šamáns and almost all of the dwarves and elves. He then turned on his fellow Illvættir.

Most were concealed and very powerful. It has taken all this time to hunt down and destroy the very last of his former friends, lovers and pupils. It is thought that Jacinta destroyed him in the last stages of the battle for Elgard.

Ba'al: The oldest and most powerful of all the free daimôn lords. He has taken Jacinta back to the daimôn realm to fight Æloðulf and try to rescue her mother.

* * *

Illvættir: A small group of svartálfar, led by Æloðulf, who learnt to raise daimôns. At death, each of their souls should have been totally absorbed into the daimôn to which they had bonded.

Somehow the Illvættir were able to resist this and slowly take over the daimôn from within, like a parasite. This has resulted in daimôns with the sorcery of both daimôn and svartálfar surviving within the daimôn realm.

Svartálfar: The ancient Dark Elves, powerful in sorcery, now long extinct apart from Silver and possibly Æloðulf.

Paladins: The religious knights of the Shayvist faith. There have only been four previous paladins in all the history of the Shayvist faith. Hakeem is the first in a long time and Jacinta was the second, his student. The Shayvists believe paladins are sent by their God and given a task or tasks. Hakeem's task is leading the defence of the elves and their allies. Jacinta's task was fighting the dreadful magic used against them.

It is believed that Jacinta's task is over and the Illvættir War is finished with the death of Æloðulf.

Chapter 1: Two Journeys

Her grandfather had asked her to go, and she loved her grandfather very much, and so she separated from her tribe at Abydos. They were heading north to Bithynia.

Bithynia, on the north western corner of *Anatolē* (modern day Turkey) in the space of just years has had Lydían, Makedonían and Hun armies riding, marching or fighting across it, backwards and forwards. As it settled into a period of peace and recovery, there was plenty of work to be had and for good pay.

The truce between the occupying Makedónes of Bithynia and the Anatolian allies was holding, though no one fully trusted it. Aléxandros seemed less treacherous than his father and he had plenty to occupy himself with in the West, so everyone prayed and hoped that the peace would hold.

For three silver oboloí the young girl got to share a wagon with a driver, two other passengers and a load of cloth travelling to the Troad. Her father and older brother had gone with her to negotiate the ride. They warned her once again to keep her knife close and handy but they needn't have worried. The route was well travelled and it was patrolled. It was safe enough, even for a single woman.

The driver was a dour old Thessalonian. Her other travelling companions were Lydoí: Magnes, a quiet young tailor, and his wife, Tudo, coming back after their required visit to her family one year after the marriage. Tudo was delightful company and chatting with her made the journey pass quickly.

They had reached the Skamandros River the afternoon before and camped by one of the small villages of the Troad. It was still early in the morning when the driver pulled his wagon to a stop.

"I already told you, he won't see visitors," he reminded her mulishly. "You can save yourself the walk."

She smiled back. "He will see me."

She grabbed her small bundle and hugged and kissed Tudo before hopping down and waving to Magnes and the driver. The old man shook his head as he watched the dark-haired Gypsy girl start down the dirt road to the village.

In the distance the wooden and mud brick hill fort dominated all around. People had tried to visit the man who lived there before, important people, but he wouldn't open the gate and just screamed at them to be left alone. It was a terrible thing, the ruin of what had been a great man.

Finally muttering to himself, the driver called on his team to start. If the Gypsy girl wanted to waste her time, it was scarcely his problem.

It promised to be a warm summer's day, there were few clouds and the air from the meadows was sweet, carried by just a breath of a breeze. The girl found it pleasant to be walking after riding for so long, but travelling didn't bother her. She was still young, and she was born travelling the length and breadth of this land.

The village and the countryside looked prosperous. There was plenty of chickens, goats and sheep and even a few cattle. The fences were in good repair. Their lord didn't neglect all his duties, then. Men, women and children watched her from doorways, windows and nearby fields, but no one tried to speak to her. There was no point, she wouldn't be staying.

"He will see no one, get on your way, girl," the sentry called down.

"He will see me. I am family." She stood outside the gate and waited, hands on her hips, staring up through the shade of her broad straw hat. It took some time before the sentry realised she wasn't going away.

"He'll see no one," the man started to repeat as he opened the gate a crack.

Then he looked at her in shock and swung the gate wide.

"It cannot be! Nikandros! Petros, come quickly! Look! She is alive and has returned!"

The men gathered around her excitedly. It took a minute for her to realise what was happening.

I really must look like her! Well and good.

She told them not to wake him until she was ready. They looked confused and disappointed but nonetheless scurried to do her bidding.

There were only four of them in the fort. They seemed to accept that a major clean-up was inevitable now that *she* had returned. One took her bundle to one of the tents and returned with a great armful of empty wineskins and general refuse.

The man inside the tent woke to a sound of smashing and glugging liquid and men's voices. His mouth was sour and his head pounding. He thought he heard a woman's voice and the men calling out "Lady!"

Was there a woman in the camp?

He struggled to remember when he last changed his clothes or bathed in the sticky heat. He had been sleeping on a mat on the floor and it was hot under the blanket. He threw it off but the sudden movement made his head swim. He sat up with difficulty, trying to comb his dirty, tangled hair and beard with his fingers.

Then he remembered he had been dreaming of Elana and Jacinta. They were travelling disguised as Gypsies. For a moment he remembered and tears came to his eyes.

"They are gone!" he cried out in agony.

Jacinta was standing by the door, scowling at him with her arms crossed.

"They are gone, and it's been all for nothing as far as you are concerned! Just look at you!"

Hakeem realised he was starting to see things!

"Wine!" he roared to his men.

The figure at the door viewed him with contempt.

"There's none left," she said with a smug expression.

Hakeem shook his head and blinked. She was still there!

"Jacinta!" His heart leapt with joy and breath came quickly, his headache forgotten. He looked away and back again and Jacinta was still there, staring at him with a look of revulsion.

"I am not Jacinta, my name is Asha," she spat. "It is only glad I am that my cousin didn't live to see her father lying like a dog in the gutter!"

The ragged man in front of her started to cry. "Not Jacinta!"

Then something permeated through the fog. No wine left? He had two amphorae from Lesbos delivered, when? It was Wednesday last. It should last weeks! His eyes darted to the wineskin hanging from the tent post, but Asha was quicker.

"Let me pour it for you, Uncle," she said with a vicious smile.

She picked up the wineskin and his cup. He could see now she was shorter, more slender than Jacinta. She deliberately poured the wine inches away from the mouth of the cup, splashing it onto the dirt and straw of the floor. Then she turned the cup upside down with a satisfied look on her face. "Whoops!"

She took a deep breath, hands on hips, scowling at him. "You disgust me! I lost both my parents and so did Jacinta. She was so proud of you and look at what you let happen to yourself!"

Hakeem hunched forward, wiping his eyes. "How long?" His voice was rough. "How long will you stay?"

"I *might* stay a year, but only if you prove yourself worthy of me, *Uncle*."

Then the big man started to cry, his great shoulders heaving.

Asha waited patiently. After the fit had passed, she spoke gently.

"Come on, Hakeem, they have breakfast for you. Then you will bathe and change, and then you will start exercising." She caught his look of interest. "No, I won't be joining you. I'm not my cousin. But if I'm to stay, no more wine!" She surveyed his tent, her nose wrinkling with distaste.

"Beer? I can drink beer?"

She looked back at him sharply and was surprised to see he was looking at her sideways with a glint in his eyes. She laughed. "No beer! If I'm to stay, I will have your oath on it."

Hakeem gasped. An oath!

"You're so hard! Are you sure you're not Jacinta? Why an oath? Can't I give you a convincing promise? Something like 'I will try my very best'."

Asha laughed again; she must really look and sound like her cousin!

"You can have breakfast and a bath. Then I'll have your oath in front of me and your men. I may not be Jacinta, but that doesn't mean I'm daft. Come on, Uncle, you may not be running great alliances any more, but there is work for you to do and you have neglected it for far too long!"

"Asha," he whispered, his eyes moist. "Thank you for coming."

* * *

Central Asia

Lake Baikal
Tarim River
Kashgar River
Taklamakan Desert
Fergana Valley
Samarkand
Indus River
Jaxartes River
Kyzylkum
Bukhara
Oxos River
Khiva
Karakum
Amul
Margu
Hari River
Aral Sea
Nisa
Tus
Yaik (Ural) River
Kaspian Sea
Rey

Fifteen months after the terrible events at Elgard

The summer sun baked down in a merciless assault.

The ground was burning, even through the thickest of boots.

The summers had been unbearable since this drought started, but this was the hottest summer in memory. The wind brought no relief. It was like the breath of a furnace, hot and dry.

Many young adults had not in their lifetime seen any rain. Even the toughest desert shrubs and salt-grass were dead or waiting in hibernation for rain that never came.

This was the badlands, the *Kara-Kum* (Black Sands) Desert. To walk in the full sun for long meant certain death both for man and beast.

A man sat in the shade by the small well. His name was Usadhan. He was a *Sakā* (Indo-Aryan), the youngest son of a prosperous trader. While very few travelled in the height of summer, he was an experienced traveller and his business was most urgent.

Still his group were cautious. They were up before first light, they rested in the mid-day heat and then they travelled well into the evening until the light completely failed. They carried spare supplies and water and never strayed far from a source of water. There were many bandits and desperate men now but his was a large and well-armed group.

He had stopped here, a little ahead of his main party, and would rejoin them when they passed. This oasis was only a small stop: one large shop, a small cluster of houses, a spring and a large trough for camels and horses. But he liked it here and he came every chance he got.

The prices were cheaper. He liked the owner, Parvēz, but most of all he liked Vira, the owner's youngest daughter. She had hair the colour of jet, smooth brown skin, fine Aryan features, a lovely smile and a sweet, loving nature.

Parvēz was modestly rich and was honest with friends, though not of course with strangers. He encouraged Usadhan's friendship with his daughter. Even Usadhan's father seemed to be favourably disposed. It would be a good match.

Just at the moment Usadhan was sitting drinking tea and thinking with pleasure about Vira, who had gone to prepare food before she would sit with him and serve him. Vira, like her mother, was a good cook.

The wind had been building all morning, restricting visibility and making it dangerous to travel. If it didn't die down, he might have to weather the storm here. That would not be bad, as long as it was only for a short time.

He thought he could hear the faintest tinkle of bells, from far down the road. It must have been the wind. No one would be out there. The wind was gusting now. It was hard to see.

Then he leapt up with astonishment.

He heard it again! It was clearer, closer, exactly like camel bells! How could that be? Who would travel in this?

As he strained to see between gusts he thought he could see shapes on the road. He screwed up his eyes to try to peer through the dust.

There!

A figure was walking camels in the middle of the heat and blowing dust!

Even the camels, creatures born of the desert, could not tolerate this blistering heat for too long. For a man it was rapidly fatal.

The wind would suck you dry. Become dehydrated and you stop sweating. After that, there is not much time left: your temperature rises, you become confused ... and then you die.

He yelled for Vira to summon her father and his men. No one ran in the summer heat, but soon there were over a dozen adults and many children crowded into the shaded areas to watch the arrival of this mad stranger.

"Get out of the sun!" they called out in Sogdianē.

The stranger stopped in the sun and shook his head. Then he raised a hand to wave to them before taking his camels over to water them. It was three of the local two-humped Bactrian camels known to be stocky and very tough but slower than the one-humped Arabian camels. They drank greedily; the trough level sank visibly. They could drink up to a hundred litres each.

The stranger was tall, medium build, dressed in the pants and shirt like what Usadhan wore, not the loose-flowing robes of those who made the desert their home. His face was covered by a silk scarf with only the eyes showing. The eyes looked like those of a woman! When she pulled her scarf off, he saw it *was* a woman smiling back at him!

She was maybe nineteen or twenty. Her skin was so black it glistened. It had a faint bluish sheen in the heat, unlike anything he had ever seen. She must be from Africa but her features were almost as fine as those of an Aryan.

And she wasn't sweating!

She stood in the heat without obvious discomfort. She was large for a woman and moved with the grace of a warrior. At her waist was an *akīnaka* (Scythian short-sword); she had a quiver on her back and held a compact bow in her left hand, already strung.

She said something incomprehensible, smiling uncertainly. Then she spoke words in a strange Aryan dialect a bit like Hindustani. It shared some words with Sogdianē.

"Welcome!" Parvēz called in Sogdianē.

Three camels, she would be wealthy and she was alone! There might be an opportunity here!

She looked back at him strangely. "Does anyone here speak Aramaic?"

"Welcome, stranger!" Usadhan replied in heavily accented Aramaic. "Let me introduce myself; I am Usadhan and a traveller like yourself. Do you care to get out of the sun?" He finished, somewhat pointedly.

"My name is Jess." The woman smiled. "And I thank you, Usadhan."

She moved into the shade but made no move to sit as yet, glancing back to see how her camels were doing. Their humps (where camels stored their fat) drooped sadly. Their ribs were showing.

"You do not look after your animals." Usadhan couldn't help an unfriendly tone that crept into his voice. Camels were greatly revered in these desert lands.

"The previous owners." Jess shook her head dismissively. "I need to buy feed for them, grain if I can get it, though camels will eat almost anything ... and some flour and tea for myself. Will your friend sell it to me?"

Usadhan nodded and started to translate, but Parvēz was shouting excitedly.

"I know these camels! Three weeks ago a dozen men rode through on camels; they were nasty types — bandits, I suspect. She has stolen everything! She is a thief! Even her clothes were being worn by one of the men. Tell her I know who she got the camels off and they are my camels!"

Usadhan smiled. This would be fun! Parvēz would claim these camels were *his*. Parvēz's two men stood expectantly on either side of him. That meant a lot of money! Even if this thief did not believe him, she was one woman against many men! And a thief could hardly go and complain to anyone, assuming there was anyone left to complain to since the Sakā kingdoms had lost the war with the Hun.

But Jess had an alert look on her face. She moved out of the shade, fitting an arrow to her bow. She didn't understand what was being said but could read the body language and she was no fool.

"He says the camels are his," Usadhan called to her.

"And I say he is a liar!" she said clearly and drew her bow, pointing it at full stretch straight at Parvēz. It was a heavy man's war bow but her hands were rock solid. One of Parvēz's men moved to go forward but she merely shifted her aim and smiled at him enquiringly. He subsided.

"I say your friend is a liar, which makes him a thief. Before I kill him, though, I want to make sure. If he can say what is written under the saddle of the middle camel I won't kill him; I will even give him these camels … or perhaps he is mistaken, they are not his."

After a brief exchange, Usadhan smiled. "It seems my friend Parvēz is mistaken. It was a different three camels that were his.

Will you join me again so we can talk and take tea in the shade?"

Jess shook her head but relaxed her bow and returned the arrow to the quiver.

She stayed watching Parvēz's men cautiously. One of them saw her relax her bow and came at her in a rush. She grimaced as he ran towards her. At the last moment she deftly moved to the side, tripping him and pushing his shoulder down. He fell painfully, face-first into the dust.

"Tell him not to get up!" she commanded, but he ignored her.

She found herself being circled by the two men with knives.

She sighed and walked to place her bow and quiver against a post. Then she stepped back into the centre of the men and waited. She didn't even draw her sword.

Parvēz, Usadhan and the rest watched, fascinated.

At a nod from one of the men, they both rushed her from opposite sides. Jess again moved at the very last minute.

She was so fast! She dodged away and as the men collided she brought her linked hands down on the back of one of the men's neck. As the other tried to stagger up she grabbed his head and kneed him hard in the temple and stepped back.

They lay, not moving. It had only lasted seconds!

She kicked their knives away from their hands and bent over, cautiously watching the men and the crowd, and tucked them into her belt. Then she went almost tiredly over and picked up her gear. When she had lifted her bow and quiver, she smiled sweetly to Usadhan.

"I didn't kill them. Tell your friend if he sells me what I need and doesn't cheat me, I will tell him where I let the other nine camels go free. Give me any further trouble and I *will* kill him and all of you here." She gazed over the people and their houses.

As she paid for her supplies and packed her camels, the rest were impatient for her to leave. Even a share of nine camels was a *great* amount of money.

It seemed that it was only Usadhan who wondered. Who was this black woman? Her fighting ability was frightening. If her supplies came from the bandits how could she be wandering the desert with little or no supplies? And what happened to the bandits? A single woman on foot could not possibly kill a dozen bandits.

Chapter 2: A New Slave, Twelve Sacks of Barley

The civilisation that had grown up in the oases of *Kyzyl Kum* (Red Sands) Desert and its southern sister desert the *Kara-Kum* (Black Sands, modern Türkmenistan) was a wonder to behold.

For millennia, the *Sakā* (Indo-Aryans) and the ones that had lived here before them built strong fortresses and great and wealthy cities. To water their orchards, gardens and fields and cities and towns, they maintained an intricate network of canals (some running hundreds of miles), bringing water from the great rivers birthed in glaciers and snow.

The great mountains described as the roof of the world starve this place of rain but they also give the blessing of rivers to bring life to the people of its oases.

The oasis lands are also caravan stops on the great trade routes stretching across the known world and so they grew wealthy beyond imagining. The Sakā were a clever and industrious people. They were famous for their handiwork: intricate jewellery made of gold, silver, lapis lazuli, and carnelian, tin alloys and delicate combinations of gold and silver. Their libraries, like those of their even more civilised cousins the Persis, were the greatest throughout the human world.

Water, wealth, power, trade and knowledge: and so they prospered. Their temples, homes and public buildings were decorated by the finest marble and brightly coloured tiles in intricate patterns, scenes and calligraphy. Their cities tinkled and sparkled from cooling fountains. Everywhere, it seemed, there were gardens. The well laid streets thronged with people. They even diverted canals of water underground to make cleverly designed sewers for the wealthier houses and public places.

Even after two thousand years, the words of the great *Khordad* (prophet) *Zarathustra* (Zoroaster) still echo across this blessed land. He had called this place paradise on earth.

But what happens to such a place when the heat and drought goes on and on and the rivers and canals begin to dry? What happens when barbarians swarm over the mountains in numbers beyond counting? And what happens when bandits and starving people roam the countryside, killing any remaining traders and farmers? What happens when the organisation with its workers and armies that maintains this vast civilisation, its canals and its secure trade routes, collapses?

The land of milk and honey in the middle of desert, which had given its bounty for countless millennia, showed itself to be fragile.

Many fertile and green valleys had already disappeared; the desert had moved to reclaim them. Even some land that could have been saved was no longer watered, tilled or sown because of the war and trouble.

It was now eighteen months since the catastrophic events of the defence of Elgard and for years before that war and drought had already devastated this land. The same tall stranger walked out of the bad lands. This time she walked out of the nearby sister desert, the *Kyzyl Kum* (Red Sands), and this time she approached one of its great oasis cities.

She paused for a long time, studying the tent-city outside the walls. It was not too long after dawn and a smoke haze from cooking fires still hung in the still air. There were always tents outside these cities. It was where nomads and poorer transients camped and a few poor citizens of the city lived, free of the city tax. But this camp now had a more permanent and desperate air to it. It was filled to capacity and beyond with families that had fled war and drought. They came searching for the tenuous safety of the city and the illusion of hope.

Even from this distance the woman could see not only the tents woven from goat's hair owned by nomads but many other dwellings thrown together from anything that was to hand: palm leaves, mud and brush.

There should have been animals and herds spread out over nearby hills owned by the nomads, but now there were only a pathetic handful of animals, closely guarded.

These refugees were starving here in what had become a place of living agony. They lay in listless hopelessness, watching all that passed with haunted eyes. Their bodies were gaunt and their faces as withered as the crops in the fields.

The dark woman checked that she had easy access to her weapons. She had been given good reason to be wary. Then she shrugged. She needed supplies. Maybe a city with city guards would be safer than the small encampments she had tried before. She led her three camels back to the road and then began her journey down past the beginning of the refugee camp. Regular patrols kept the refugees back from the road and out of the city. The woman wrinkled her nose at the smells of the camp as she passed.

Taking her time, she put a few coppers or a small silver coin in each of the bowls of those elderly or sick who were permitted to beg. She did not understand what they said, but their surprised and grateful looks were obvious.

The walls of the city may have been only made of mud brick but they towered over her as she approached, standing ten times her height. The gate had been built a third as high again, covered with marble and tiles that glittered in the sun. Over the top was a gaily painted balustrade and gallery. She wondered what it was for but it wasn't defensive; the Sakā and the Persis built many things for love of their beauty.

There was a strong guard on the gate, but she had camels so they waved her through.

Beyond the gates, there was a crowd of visitors. Most were Sakā, like Gypsies but not so dark, the women with simple scarves over their heads and the men with Persian style medium square hats and square cut beards.

They seemed to be rich but a closer glance showed their once fine robes were faded and even frayed. Adding to the Sakā, there was a confusion of Chin, *Scyths* (Skythoi), Hun, Persis and even one Greek hurrying by on business of his own.

Just off to one side from the gate there was a large public garden. The entrance was a tall and graceful gate-tower decorated with tile mosaics of storks: storks wading in the water, storks showing the white and black feathers of their wings, storks flying against a blue sky and white clouds and two storks in the foreground guarding their great nest and feeding their young. From March onwards the storks would arrive back from their winter feeding grounds. They were said to bring luck, though luck was not a thing many in this city had seen for a long time.

Jess hitched her camels in sight of the soldiers guarding the gates but still kept one eye on them as she ducked through the arch.

The garden was well shaded from the hot sun by tall shrubs, date palm, trellises and arches covered by grape vines and flowering roses. It had small gardens, lawns, stone seats and walking paths: all of it symmetrically organized.

She saw roses big and small, different coloured lavender and geraniums, rosemary, citrus, cherry and pomegranate, colourful and scented myrtle. The colours of the bushes, flowers and walkways were arranged to contrast each other and were very rich: fresh greens, whites, dusky pinks, terracotta, deep blues, gold and dark reds to name just a few.

Jess gasped in wonder, and as a creature from the desert she was filled with a longing for something she did not understand.

A small fountain bubbled out of a *karez* (small underground canal for water) to form a small gurgling stream through the upper garden. The designers had it turning a tiny water wheel before it cascaded down some shallow steps into series of four ponds, lined with marble and teeming with carp.

So much water! And only for decoration and for the cooling breeze it gave! She let her hand touch the water. The fish seemed unafraid and clustered just out of reach but still curious. Someone must feed them.

In some way this garden was more marvellous than the city's great monuments because it was so fragile. Someone had laboured to keep it alive during all the chaos that followed the Hun invasion.

Nearby was a monument to one of the heroes of the city. He was sitting astride his horse, his sword at his side and his right hand grasping what would have been a spear, long ago removed. His head was nowhere to be seen, presumably lopped off when the Hun had come. There was a life sized bronze statue of a stork. It had been gilded but the gilt had been scrapped off, a bit like the city, the gilt of this jewel of the desert had been scrapped off.

She would have liked to stay longer in the garden, but she needed to get her supplies and this place was very dangerous for her.

Just on from the park was a teeming market place, so she went back to collect her camels and make for that. They had seen black men and black women before though they were not so common this far north. And the Saka had their own warrior women, but they mostly travelled within groups of men. Women were not usually seen travelling alone.

And they certainly had not seen anyone quite like her. She was must have been six feet tall, as tall or taller than most men but she looked fit and well muscled. There was no doubt she was very strong for a woman, and she moved with unconscious grace and power, as if she was prowling the street. She wore linen dyed brown: a loose fitting shirt and trousers. Her gorytos for her bow hanging from her camel's saddle in easy reach, a large knife at her right hip and an *akīnaka* (short sword) at her left. Any who saw her recognised her as a seasoned fighter, secure in her ability to use the weapons in a way that few could match.

Her skin was black with a faint almost bluish sheen and yet her features were fine with ivory teeth. She had frizzy black hair was pulled into two pig tails sitting across her breasts. The whites of her dark brown eyes seemed to flash with a tinge of yellow when she moved in the shadow. She was definitely a striking woman and many paused to watch as she passed.

"Does anyone speak Greek? Does anyone speak Aramaic?"

Eventually a grizzled old man came forward and gestured for her to follow. He led her for almost ten minutes till they reached a taverna near the entrance to a caravanserai. He spoke rapidly to a lady outside and, with a cheerful wave he disappeared back into the crowd.

The lady ducked inside and a young Greek girl, maybe eighteen, appeared. Her feet were bare and grubby, her dress faded and patched. She wiped her hands on a towel, and looked Jess up and down, taking in her black skin and hair parted in the centre platted into twin braids.

"You don't look Greek to me,"

At last! Someone to talk to! Jess felt like kissing her with relief!

"My name is Jess. Who are you and what are you doing here?"

"My name is Pandora. I am from Astakos and it should be obvious why I am here, I am a slave."

Jess nodded; armies had moved back and forward across Bithynia and they had taken slaves.

"You'll get me into trouble with the owner Uvaxshtra if I'm caught talking to you unless you buy something."

"Well, I'll buy something then!" Jess laughed, gesturing to the shop.

But Pandora's eyes narrowed when she saw Jess was wearing a single glove on her left hand.

"Take it off! Take it off now!"

She looked wildly around in case someone had seen it. She moved forward to drape her kitchen cloth over the glove. "Are you crazy? They will kill you!"

"Pandora," Jess took a slow deep breath. "I'm not from around here. I hurt my hand a long time ago in a fight. Are you saying people will try to kill me because I wear a glove on one hand?"

"You're not one of them?"

"Pandora, I don't even know what you are talking about."

"All right." Pandora took a shaky breath. "Back where I come from there is a women's chapter of a religious sect. They train as warriors. The locals call them Amazónes after the Skythian name for fighting women. I'm surprised you haven't heard of them."

Jess looked at her blankly. She shifted her weight and pulled at one of her braids.

"Well," Pandora continued. "When they master the training, they wear a glove on their left hand in honour of their founder, Jacinta. You *must* have heard of Jacinta!"

Jess shook her head. "Pandora, I really am from a long way away. I would like to meet this Jacinta."

"She's dead," Pandora said flatly. "Don't you know anything? Anyway, if men see a woman alone with a glove on her left hand, they see it as a challenge and want to fight them."

Jess's expression hardened, but Pandora was continuing.

"A while ago, a young woman came through here searching for her brother; her name was Katin. She was nice to me. I don't think she was much of a fighter but she wore a glove on her left hand. I think she thought people would leave her alone if she did. I heard in another town there was a large group of men. They raped her and then they killed her." Pandora shuddered.

Jess's expression was unreadable but her voice was cold.

"One day, I would like to meet those men." Then she gave Pandora a conciliatory smile. "I have the other glove in my pack. I can wear a glove on both hands, will that do?"

Jess found another glove and Pandora helped her arrange someone to feed and watch her camels. Then she led her to the taverna to break her fast. There was only one dish on the menu: *khoresht* (stew) made from split peas, served with unleavened bread. The owner, Uvaxshtra, claimed it had mutton in it though this seemed doubtful. Despite that, it was lightly peppered and surprisingly tasty.

Apart from Jess, there was a group of young men sucking hot black tea through lumps of sugar. Jess had time to wonder what it would do to their teeth. A woman was sitting with them drinking salted yoghurt. There were plenty of people walking the streets, but few had money to buy anything, so business was slow. Pandora was able to sit with Jess after finishing her chores. Jess offered Pandora some food and she ate hungrily.

Then Jess leant back to question her. She seemed particularly interested in Jacinta and the Amazónes. When she asked the name of the city they were in, Pandora gave her the strangest of looks.

"You're in the city of *Buxārak* (Bukhara in modern day Uzbekistan). Its name means 'place of good fortune', though I doubt many living here now would describe it as such. The *Xiōngnú* (Turks) destroyed the Sogdianē capital, Samarkand. Until it is rebuilt, this has become the main city for any trade, such as it is. How can you not know that?"

"Pandora, I have been travelling without knowing the language. I mostly keep to myself and live in the desert."

Bukhara lay on the *Zarafshān* (Zeravshan) River, the same tributary to the Oxos as Samarkand, but Samarkand lay upstream to the north and the east. It had the misfortune of lying not too far from the Fergana Valley where the Huns first came after they crossed the great mountains to the east.

Pandora studied her for a while and tried to decide what clever reason Jess might have to lie to her. "You expect me to believe you have been living in a part of the desert that has become so dry even the *Badawiyyūn* (desert nomads) cannot live there and yet you don't know the name of anything, the land, the country or this city."

"I know deserts." Jess shrugged. "I have come from a long way away and I avoid people."

She put a silver *siglos* (shekel) on the table. Pandora still looked doubtful so Jess added another one. Pandora made them disappear.

"How do I get to Anatolē?"

"I don't think you can. The long routes are almost closed."

"I want to find out about Jacinta and her Amazónes."

Just then the owner of the tavern, Uvaxshtra, came up, shouting something unintelligible, and cuffed Pandora hard. A blade appeared in Jess's hand.

"Jess, no!" Pandora pushed her hand down.

She got up reluctantly to follow him out the back and left Jess sitting there. As soon as they got there, Uvaxshtra gestured for her to take her clothes off.

"Hurry up, you slut!" he shouted. "And give me that money that black bitch gave you. Did you think I wouldn't see?"

He raised his hand to hit her again but found his hand caught in a vicelike grip. A knife appeared at his throat and a black girl's face was inches from him, her warm breath on his cheek.

"Tell him, I want to buy you!" Jess said through clenched teeth.

Pandora just looked at her, baffled.

"Tell him!" Jess insisted.

She had a brief conversation with Uvaxshtra.

"He doesn't want to sell," Pandora said. "He set a ridiculous price!"

Jess released him, "I understand the amount. I want him to say in front of witnesses that he is happy with the price."

"But that's almost twice what I'm worth!" Pandora glared at Uvaxshtra, her lip curled in disgust.

"Just tell him I will pay his price."

"Jess, you can't! It's too much money!"

She began arguing with Uvaxshtra, talking rapidly so Jess couldn't follow. He kept shaking his head and smirking at her.

"You shouldn't have been so eager to accept his first price, now he won't come down. He has offered six talantoi of barley as well."

"Pandora, please, just let me pay the man!" Jess held up her hands in frustration. "I don't *want* his barley!"

"But it's all I could get."

Can't you understand that?

"I want him to say he is happy with the price in front of witnesses," Jess sighed. "I don't want him to claim I stole you."

"And why wouldn't he be happy with the price? He's laughing at us." Pandora spat in disgust. "It's lucky for you I got the barley."

Jess followed the two back to the tavern and bought herself her first slave ... and twelve sacks of barley (three times Pandora's weight). She wondered how she would fit them all on her camels, especially if they tried to ride them.

She left her animals (and her barley) at the caravanserai and took Pandora to buy her some clothes. As they walked through the market, Pandora kept gazing at Jess out of the corner of her eye. Uvaxshtra must have thought that she was totally crazy or maybe even she had taken a sexual fancy to Pandora but Jess wasn't acting either way. Pandora simply couldn't figure out what was going on.

"Jess, thank you," Pandora said after Jess seemed to be happy with Pandora's second outfit. "I think you are a bit mad, but what do you want me for?"

"Pandora, I don't need a slave." Jess took a deep breath. "I will make sure you are going to be all right and then I will leave you here."

"Jess, you can't!" Pandora's hands flew to her mouth in terror. "Don't you like me? When you bought me, I was so happy! But you can't just leave me here! A lone woman in this place ... I'd last half a day or less. I would have to go back to Uvaxshtra and beg him to take me back!"

Jess paused to study Pandora's face intently. She was telling the truth.

"If I took you with me, I wouldn't be doing you any favours," she warned her. "I have powerful enemies. I will do my best to protect you but more likely we will both get killed or worse!"

"Where are you going?" whispered Pandora, looking fearful.

"I am making for the Troad," Jess said. "Something tells me I have to go there."

Pandora let out a great 'whoop' of excitement and grabbed Jess and kissed her firmly on the lips.

"Home? You are taking me home?"

Jess nodded grimly. "Yes, but we will more likely die in the attempt."

Pandora danced round making excited noises, repeating 'home' with tears running down her cheeks and stopping from time to time to hug Jess excitedly and thank her again.

Jess sighed.

Even if they made it to Bithynia, what home would her new friend have to return to, after all the wars?

* * *

"Pandora!" Jess said, laughing. "If you 'ma'am' me or 'lady' me again, I swear I'll put you over my knee and spank you!"

"Of course, mistress!" Pandora replied with a mischievous smile as she skilfully navigated the market.

Yes please, Jess!

Jess stood a head taller than Pandora. Her skin was very dark, showing ivory teeth whenever she smiled. Her hair was jet black. Her arms and legs showed strong feminine muscle and she moved with the grace of a dancer. Pandora felt dizzy just being close to her.

Her head was in a whorl of confusion. It made her feel anxious and insecure. Everything was happening so fast and nothing made sense. At first she couldn't believe this crazy black woman was buying her, and why?

And then the last thing she expected, Jess threw her into a panic by trying to set her free! This was not the place for a single woman to survive on her own, but Jess didn't seem to understand that.

It wouldn't be true for Jess, she realised.

She seemed so grim. What sort of experiences had made her this way? She was fast with her knife and confident in how she used it. Maybe she really could live in the desert like she claimed.

Yet she was an impossible paradox: she seemed so competent but didn't know the local language or even where she was, yet she spoke Pandora's native Aeolic Greek with barely an accent.

And she seemed kind. She was treating Pandora well. She didn't have to do that. Underneath she seemed rather shy, but Pandora found she could draw her out and she could be good company.

She refused to say anything about herself. She said she came from a long way off. Her skin was dark, like a Nubian, but her skin had a faint bluish sheen the like of which Pandora had never seen before. And her features were too fine for a full blooded Nubian.

In so many countries a man and woman could not walk together or touch one another in public, even a married couple. The man usually walked in front and the woman followed. But in the habit of female friends everywhere, they started to walk arm in arm or holding hands so they could chat.

At the same time Pandora was puzzling over her, Jess was also puzzling over her new friend.

Pandora's name meant having *all* (pan) of the *gifts* (dora) of a woman. In Greek legend Pandora was said to be the name of the first woman in the world. She was fashioned out of clay by the Gods and endowed with (all the) feminine gifts, to make her irresistible to man.

Typically the Athenian Greeks saw such a beautiful (and hence powerful) woman as being sent as punishment to man (for stealing the secret of fire). Also typically she was said to be the cause of all great troubles in the world when out of curiosity she opened a *pithos* (huge amphora, not a box as some thought) owned by Zeus who stored evils in it for whenever he wanted to curse man.

The Pandora of legend released all the evils into the world ... retaining only 'hope'.

Jess's Pandora was slightly younger, only a year or so. She was slender with olive skin and almond eyes; fine features and lustrous black hair. When she smiled her eyes seemed to twinkle with mischief. Despite all she had suffered she a ready laugh.

She was delightful company. Jess couldn't remember much of her own past, she couldn't remember back to a time when she had friends. She hadn't realised before she met Pandora that she was lonely.

Jess was completely lost in the city and her new friend had to take charge. The main contribution Jess made, apart from money, was adding suggestions when it came to supplies and showing by her body language that these two women weren't ones rough men could bully.

Both women, for different reasons, were keen to leave as soon as possible.

"Not that way," Pandora explained as they left the city. "If you want to go to Anatolē, we need to head for the Oxos. Jess, do you have any idea how *far* this is going to be? With drought and war, law and order has collapsed. It will take at least six or seven moons, likely longer!"

"Not much of a plan, but it is all I can think of," Jess admitted, giggling.

"Well, let's go then!" Pandora giggled in return and led on.

Jess had seemed to be content to let her take the lead.

"Yes, mistress," she said, which made Pandora laugh.

Pandora's heart surged as they left the place that had been her prison for all these years. She was really going home! She shot a look of gratitude to her new friend and Jess smiled kindly back. They began walking their camels at first but Jess planned to teach her how to ride and care for them as soon as possible.

A group of six men on horses passed them.

"Don't smile at them!" Jess snapped.

She stood and watched them balefully as they passed. The message was clear.

Keep away! Try to touch us and I will hurt you!

The men averted their gaze and hurried past. Jess watched them with a satisfied half-smile.

"Jess, I owe you my life!" Pandora cried out and did a pirouette, her arms out.

Jess smiled at her girlish excitement and optimism.

"Pandora, you do not! I don't like slavery and I don't like men hurting anyone who can't protect themselves. Buying you stopped me having to kill that bastard!"

Pandora felt a shiver. "You would have?"

"Why, of course I would have." Jess laughed. "This is better. I would be seen as a murderer and you an escaped slave." She shrugged. "Besides, money is something I have."

Pandora was lost for words for a while and the two walked in silence.

"Who are you, Jess?" Pandora asked. "I mean where do you come from, what are you doing here? I know nothing about you."

Jess sighed and for a moment her eyes held pain. She looked unbearably weary for a moment.

"Pandora, you can come with me but as a friend and a free woman, not a slave. I will not harm you and I will do my best to protect you. As to myself, please don't ask again. There are things about myself I cannot be proud of."

"I'm so sorry, Jess!" Pandora said, taken aback, and her eyes teared a little.

"It's not your fault," Jess smiled to rob what she had said of offence. "Now, you offered to show me some water where we can bathe, and then I will show you how to ride a camel!"

"You would bathe *before* riding a camel?" Pandora asked.

"And after," Jess laughed, "And as often as I can! I like bathing and it's been a long time since I have had enough water!"

Chapter 3: Bathing

"Jess?" Pandora called out as Jess got ready to bathe. "Aren't you afraid of someone seeing you?"

Pandora's heart was racing as her friend casually pulled her shirt over her head and dropped her pants. She opened her mouth to warn her but nothing would come. In an instant Jess was standing there naked and relaxed in front of her.

"There's no one around," Jess replied confidently; she didn't say how she knew.

Pandora felt dizzy and tingling all over. She couldn't believe it! Jess was just perfect! She was black; the faint bluish sheen only added to her magnificence. She was large and muscled. Her breasts were young and firm, her stomach flat and there was a black thatch of hair over her pubes. She moved with such poise and grace! Her hair was tied back in twin plaits; her face was pleasant, feminine but strong.

"You're so beautiful!" Pandora whispered in awe.

"No, I'm not!" Jess laughed, "Now *you,* you are beautiful! I am too big and rather plain ... I know!"

"No," Pandora shook her head. "You're simply stunning!"

"Do you really think so?" Jess asked, delighted, and started to parade naked in front of her friend. Without even realising it, she moved and stood with perfect balance.

"Yes," said Pandora in a strangled voice.

And you have no idea what you're doing to me, do you, Jess?

"Don't men tell you that all the time?" Pandora added, breathless. She suspected her smile looked more like a grimace.

Jess shook her head. No, Pandora thought. She had seen the look Jess had given the men earlier, no one would dare!

"Jess," Pandora asked with growing suspicion. "Have you *ever* let a man make love to you?"

Jess hesitated. It was hard to read her expression due to her dark skin ... and then she shook her head. Pandora was incredulous. Was Jess a virgin?

"What about a woman?"

Jess laughed. "Now I know you're teasing me! What on earth would two women do with one another? Men sleep with other men but women would never sleep with other women! They are not obsessed with such things like men!"

"Of course not," Pandora agreed automatically.

She must have a silly look on her face.

"Well," Jess said brightly. "I'm going to have a swim, but I think you want to wait till after the camel lessons."

"Wait! Jess!" Pandora called out desperately.

Jess paused, the soap and a cloth in one hand and a question on her face. Pandora almost ripped her old dress in her haste to get it off and follow her. This magnificent woman was asking her to come and bathe with her!

"I have a better idea!" Pandora ran up to her. "I will soap you down."

She grabbed the soap and cloth and gave Jess a little shove toward the water.

"Oh, Pandora. You really don't have to do that!" Jess said as she tried to grab the soap back.

She looked at her new friend shyly, touched by her kindness.

"Believe me, I want to!" Pandora said, keeping the soap out of her reach.

I would love to!

"And I'll give you a massage. It's the least I can do after all you have done for me!"

I can't wait to get my hands on that body of yours!

"Why, thank you, Pandora, but only if you let me do it for you afterwards!"

It almost caused Pandora to break out into hysterical giggles. Where had this girl come from, the other side of the moon?

Jess put first her bow and quiver within easy reach but away from any dampness of the natural pond fed by a spring. She put her short sword closer to the water's edge. Then she waded into a shallow section where no reeds grew and rinsed herself and her hair quickly. Her hair was a little frizzy when she shook it out of its ties.

She sat obediently waiting for Pandora and glancing over her shoulder. She couldn't see the uncontrollable grin on Pandora's face.

"Relax, you're too tense!" Pandora complained as she worked the soap over Jess's back and shoulders, feeling the tone of her strong muscles with sensuous pleasure. Jess made an obvious effort to relax.

"You know, that does feel good!" Jess murmured. "But I could do this myself."

Pandora made no reply. She started to soap Jess's arms, how they glistened! She dipped the soap in the water again as she worked. She felt flushed and breathless and she was warm and tingly between her legs and knew she would be wet there too. She had never made love to a Nubian woman before.

"I can do the front," Jess said, reaching out her hand, looking a little dreamy.

Pandora gave her hand a playful slap. "No, I have to do it all, you just relax! Can you put your arms above your head for me for a moment, out of the way?" she said as she slithered around to face Jess's front. "That's it! ... No, I have to do all of it!"

Jess couldn't believe how good it felt. It was so sensuous! But she felt confused; it was starting to feel erotic! Her nipples were erect and her body was starting to tingle. Pandora gave her a reassuring smile, everything was normal. Pandora's own nipples were erect.

Jess stood while Pandora soaped her legs and then washed her off. Pandora told her to lie down on a large flat rock as Pandora rinsed her front and back, lingering on every part of her body.

She was trembling when Pandora had finished.

"Stay there!" Pandora commanded. "You're not going anywhere!"

Pandora raced to the saddle bags and got a bottle of scented oil.

She had Jess lie on her stomach and started to slowly massage her, kneading every muscle.

By the time she rolled Jess over on to her back, Jess was panting and her pulse was thundering but Pandora gave her what she hoped was a distant professional look.

She was concentrating on the massage, not the magnificent body that was receiving it! Of course she was!

When she started on the front, Jess involuntarily sat up. Pandora put her hand on her and slowly pushed her back down.

"You really have to learn to relax, Jess!" she said, giving her a reassuring smile.

Jess smiled back, a little uncertain, and made another visible effort to relax again.

Pandora started to spread the oil on Jess's breasts. It was cool and Jess gasped. Pandora started to massage and give some gentle squeezes to the nipples. Jess's body shivered under the touch.

Girl, you are just so naïve!

Pandora couldn't believe it had gotten this far without Jess understanding what was going on! Jess's body had started to move backwards and forward a little under her hands. Then Pandora moved lower to the wonderful taut muscles of her stomach, and then she went lower over Jess's mound.

She started to move back and forwards with both hands on either side: over the hips, across the groin towards her inner thighs. Tease ... closer, then withdraw.

By this stage, Jess was beyond caring what was going on.

"That feels good!" she whispered harshly.

Pandora slid her own naked body over Jess's and took a nipple in her mouth. When her hand slid down between Jess's thighs, she felt Jess's body go rigid, arching up and quivering. Her pelvis started to move in time with Pandora's stroking.

She smiled down at her and Jess smiled back. Jess stiffened and made a mewling sound and Pandora felt rhythmic contractions.

"Mmmm," Jess laughed in a shaky way after a few moments. "Thank you, Pandora. Is that what you wanted to show me?"

She kissed Pandora on the lips and hugged her naked body. They lay like that for several minutes and then Jess propped herself up on one elbow.

"Now, I promised to return the favour."

"Are you sure you want to?" Pandora asked anxiously.

"Yes," Jess smiled. "I think I'd enjoy that."

She stood up to lead Pandora back to the water.

It only took a few minutes for Pandora to discover that Jess was a very fast learner!

"Whoa, Jess!" said Pandora; she felt more than a little dizzy as they lay together afterwards. "Are you sure you haven't done this sort of thing before?"

Jess stretched across to kiss her and then shook her head.

"And you didn't know what I was doing until the very end?"

Jess looked down, smiling at her face. "Pandora, dear, I didn't know what was going on till it was almost all but over! But towards the end, I stopped caring or thinking. I was enjoying it too much!"

"I think I have just been a very naughty girl!" Pandora said, giving Jess a look of pure mischief.

Jess made no reply, only gave her a dreamy smile.

"Do you think you should punish me?" Pandora asked and laughed.

"Dora, Dora! I don't even understand where this is leading." Jess chuckled with mock exasperation. "I'm sure you will show me some day. But for the moment I am going to have a swim, and I mean just a swim. Then you will have your first lesson on looking after camels. If we don't concentrate soon, we will never get started!"

Pandora had other ideas and Jess couldn't resist a sensuous hug and mutual exploration combined with a long tender kiss. Jess realised every time she looked at Pandora she probably had a silly dreamy smile on her face, but Pandora didn't seem to mind.

Pandora, she thought, all of the Gods' gifts in a woman!

As they were resting in each other's arms half in the water, Jess stiffened.

"Horses, three riders and coming fast. They're not looking for us. They may pass us by."

Jess might be pursued, but no one who knew her would send *only* three men after her and they would definitely try to sneak up on her.

Pandora started to stand up.

"No time," Jess said and pushed her towards the deeper water and the reeds.

She cast a brief, longing glance at her bow sitting nice and dry a little way away from her and then she grabbed the short sword and dove silently under the water. She was gone in one fluid movement, hardly a ripple left behind.

The man in the lead, Utana, pulled his horse up.

"We really have to hurry!" his younger brother, Xshayârshan, warned him.

"I can see a woman's dress!" Utana winked to his friend, Spengha. "Someone is bathing! With a dress like this and the camels, she must be a slave."

"Hello, whoever you are!" Spengha called out. "No need to be shy!"

The three dismounted and cast their eyes over the pond.

Spengha lifted up the dress; there were some man's clothes nearby. "Don't you want your dress back? I have it here for you! Why don't you introduce us to your boyfriend?"

Utana picked up the nearby bow and silently signalled his delight. A water bird took flight and the three snapped to examine where it had come from. They scanned the reeds, then Xshayârshan who had the sharpest eyes pointed to a patch off to the left.

"Well," Utana said conversationally. "Maybe I can shoot a duck for our dinner!" He stretched the bow back.

"Wait!" said a female voice. "Don't shoot, I'm coming out."

"She has a nice voice!" Utana said, grinning.

Pandora started to wade back. She hesitated, squatting in the water, not wanting to stand up.

"Stand up!" Utana commanded. He gestured with the bow half drawn. "We haven't gone to all this trouble without wanting to see you. Let us have a good look."

Pandora stood reluctantly up. Xshayârshan's mouth dropped open and Spengha whistled. She was so beautiful! They all felt swelling in their groins.

"Put your hands up," Utana demanded. "Stop covering your body."

Pandora ignored him, yet she stood there while they took their chance to ogle her.

"Can I have my clothes back now?" she asked.

"No!" Spengha pretended to be indignant. "You haven't earnt them yet, has she, boys?"

Pandora felt a surge of fear.

Utana kept her covered with the bow and gestured for her to come onto the bank. Pandora came forward reluctantly. She was annoyed with herself when she started to cry.

"Please let me go."

"Let her go," said Xshayârshan. He was the youngest.

"Oh, we can't do that!" Spengha couldn't stop grinning. "This lady is going to make a man of you today! Where is your friend, darling?"

"I'm alone. Those were just some clothes I had to wash."

"All alone," Spengha said, as if sympathetic for her loneliness. "Well, it's lucky for you we happened by to give you some company, then."

"Grab her arms!" Utana ordered, covering her with the bow.

Xshayârshan hesitated, then approached. "I'm really sorry," he said.

Pandora was crying freely now as the other two jerked her arms behind her back.

"No one needs to die!" a cold voice behind Utana said. There was a clatter of him dropping the bow. Jess had her left hand holding his chin and the short-sword pressed against his throat; she nudged the bow behind with her foot.

"Another woman! They weren't a man's clothes at all!" Spengha laughed delightedly. "And you aren't wearing anything either. It must be our lucky day! There's no need for that, darling! We just want some fun, that's all."

Spengha left Xshayârshan holding Pandora and slipped around to move closer.

"She's bluffing," he said.

Jess regarded him coldly. She pressed the edge of her blade harder into the flesh over Utana's neck.

Spengha started to circle around, ever so slowly.

"Just stay calm, my darling, we are all going to become real good friends."

"That's far enough!" Jess's voice was hard, cold like ice!

"Just do what she wants!" Utana was starting to look scared.

Spengha stared deep into the black woman's face and smiled. He watched her eyes and body for the tell-tale sign, the slight intake of breath, the slight narrowing of eyes, the tensing of the body, getting ready.

Her expression didn't change. With exaggerated slowness Spengha took another step.

Jess stared at Spengha expressionlessly. Then her arm muscles bunched. She gave a powerful jerk. Blood sprayed everywhere. Utana made a chocking sound as she threw his body aside.

She was onto Spengha with the speed of a panther, stabbing him hard in the stomach, the blade angled up to pierce the diaphragm. He died without a sound.

Then she sprang at Xshayârshan. "Please, I'm sorry!" he said desperately.

She rammed her sword home. His youthful face was almost feminine. His eye lashes were so long and fine. She held him to her, admiring his beauty with sadness until the light went out in his eyes.

"I'm sorry too." She lowered him tenderly to the ground. "You were too young for this."

Then she strode over to Pandora who was scrambling backwards, trying to get away from her. She grabbed her and enfolded her in bloody arms. Pandora struggled to get free and then a dam inside her broke and she sobbed and sobbed, clutching at her friend. Eventually she was cried out.

Jess got up and walked into the water, washing herself carefully and dispersing the blood in the water with her hands. She would leave the bodies where they had fallen but she needed to clean up any evidence that they had been here.

"Can you clean yourself up and get dressed?" she asked Pandora. "Try to avoid more foot prints on the wet sand."

Pandora nodded mutely. When Pandora was finished, Jess led her and the camels back in the direction they had come.

"Do you feel up to leading the camels a little way? I want to cover our old tracks and you need to lay new tracks to show we passed at a distance."

"What about their horses?" Pandora asked.

"Too dangerous to take them, they have water and feed. When their family comes searching they will assume it's a blood feud; it's common enough. If a stranger comes, with some luck he will take the horses and their belongings. Nothing must link us to the killing!"

Pandora numbly led the camels to the cross roads and waited. Jess eventually appeared, walking backwards, crouched low, lightly dusting their tracks with some reeds and blowing on them. She had a small hemp bag over her shoulder.

"The oldest and the youngest were carrying a lot of money," she said as she stood to admire her handiwork. "The sooner we leave this place the better."

"The boy," Pandora said heavily. "Did he have to die?"

Jess turned to face her.

"Dora, *none* of those men needed to die. They were not truly bad men. They were a rich man's sons and you were a slave.

That gives them all the rights and you none. To catch you, was their luck. They wouldn't even consider how you felt about it. Afterwards, you would have to keep quiet. If there was any trouble for any reason, you would be blamed, not them. I didn't want to kill them." She shook her head. "Once I had killed one of them, I had to kill all three."

"You don't care much either way, do you?"

"Not much," Jess agreed. "It was a pity. What else do you want me to say?"

Then Pandora knew.

"You're an assassin, aren't you? You're a paid assassin!"

"I was trained, yes." A flicker of old pain passed across Jess's face. "The ones who trained me died before I could have worked for them, but I would have gladly done their 'work'. I loved them."

"What if I meant to go to those men's family and tell them what you did?"

"They would kill you and then come after me," Jess said simply. "But to answer you, I have a code. You are an innocent, so I wouldn't hurt you. All I have killed have been in fair fights."

"That boy ... was that a fair fight?"

"I *said* it was a shame," Jess spat angrily. "He was armed. Whoever trained him failed him badly. He didn't even try to draw his weapon after I had killed his brother and his friend. It wouldn't have done him any good but *he* didn't know that.

"Now consider this. He was going to hold you down while you were raped and then he would take his turn, do you doubt that? It would be his first 'conquest' and he would be very proud of it. Whilst I doubt they would have hurt you, I can't be sure.

Amateurs can panic and some men feel aroused inflicting pain on those who cannot defend themselves.

"Should I have let them rape you, all three of them? They wanted to rape me too. Did you want me to let them do that also? All I wanted to do was warn them off. I never wanted to kill them, but they gave me no choice. Please don't judge me, Pandora. There are worse things about me. Things that, if you found them out, would cause you to hate me! But what can I do? I have never willingly done evil."

Jess looked at Pandora with pain written all over her face.

"I said you don't have to come with me and I mean it," Her voice broke. She sounded so vulnerable. "If you want us to go our separate ways, I will give you a share of all I have. It will be enough to set you up."

Tears welled up in Jess's eyes and she shook her head, irritated by her weakness.

"Jess, I'm sorry!" Pandora cried, clutching at her friend. "Please forgive me! You have done so much for me! I was in shock that is all."

She dropped to sit at Jess's feet, her face pressed against her friend's legs. Jess squatted down beside Pandora, there were tears streaming down both their faces as the two friends knelt embracing.

Eventually Jess started to laugh.

Pandora smiled uncertainly. "What so funny?"

"If you could see the two of us, that's all; both kneeling in the dust, crying and hugging each other." Jess dragged herself and her friend up and gave Pandora a lingering kiss on the lips. "Come on, we really have to leave!"

"My last question, I will still go with you but I have to know. Are you going to Anatolē to kill someone?"

"Pandora, you may find this hard to believe. As soon as you told me about the Amazónes, I knew I had to go there, but before that I hadn't heard of them at all. The last thing I would want to do is to get into a fight with any of them."

"All right," Pandora agreed.

They smiled at each other and hugged again.

"Perhaps you should teach me some of how you fight!" Pandora said, laughing. "I used to hunt small game with a bow when I was young, but I haven't learnt anything else."

Jess stopped completely and turned to study her friend, intently.

"How serious are you?"

"Not very," admitted Pandora with a self-conscious laugh.

"I will get you a hunting bow and make sure you can use it, but nothing else," Jess said. "Remember that boy? A little training will only get you killed."

"I would be better letting those men rape me?" Pandora joked.

Jess nodded; she didn't understand Pandora was joking.

"Two of them were strong men and the other looked strong for a boy. Unless you could win against such men, the more you fought them, the more they would hurt you.

"I don't think they were bad men. In their mind, they were not doing evil because you were a slave and because of how they found you. They thought of themselves as hunters and you were only prey. Does a hunter feel sorry for an antelope? If you didn't resist too much and seemed helpless I don't think they would have hurt you. I think they would likely feel sorry for you afterwards and give you money."

Pandora looked surprised. "It sounds like you didn't hate them!"

"Why of course I didn't hate them." It was Jess's turn to look surprised. "I told you they were not bad men. Pandora, we need to go."

Away from the waterhole the land was flat and bare. There was no cover as far as the eye could see. No where to hide.

It was crisscrossed by the tracks of nomads. They had left piles of stones as messages to each other but it was something Jess could not read. She led Pandora for half a turn of a glass away from the road, but decided to keep the road in sight. They lit no fire, just drank water and ate some bread and cheese.

Pandora fell instantly asleep. In the middle of the night she woke to see the dark shadow of Jess standing, holding her bow strung with an arrow nocked, pointed down. There was no moon and the earth was black. The sky was filled with diamond stars. In the distance she heard the sound of many men and horses moving along the road.

"What is it?" Pandora murmured.

"Hush!" Jess whispered softly. "Get some sleep."

She tried to stay awake but after everything that happened, she just couldn't.

She dozed off with the image of Jess standing alert yet motionless, watching over her.

* * *

"Good morning, sleepy head!" Jess called out cheerfully.

Pandora opened one eye. It was half-light and Jess had made a small fire from dead *saxaul* (salt bush). She had made some unleavened bread and was frying dried meat in spices. It smelt delicious!

Jess grinned at her affectionately as she stumbled off to relieve herself. Her calves were aching from the unaccustomed walking on the loose soil. By the time she had gotten back and rubbed the sleep out of her eyes and drank some water, Jess served her breakfast on a large slab of bread.

"Jess, I can't eat all that!" Pandora looked at her share.

"Surprise yourself!" Jess laughed.

She had regained her good humour and showed no ill effect from her lack of sleep.

"Did you get *any* sleep last night?" Pandora asked, feeling shame for not sharing the watch.

"Sleep is not something I need a lot of. The road was very busy last night. There were three very large groups of horsemen that passed by, going in a great hurry," Jess replied. "I think we have succeeded in killing the sons of a very important man. For travelling quietly, we haven't made a good start."

Pandora felt a rush of fear. "Should we make a run for it?"

Jess just laughed at her. "Running would only show we are guilty."

Then she gestured to the desert. "I can live in the desert, but not deeper than the nomads go. Getting lost in the deep desert is something neither you nor I would want. Soon they will come to question us."

She pulled a change of clothing for both of them out of one of the saddle bags. She hid Pandora's old slave dress under some rocks while Pandora changed.

"When they come, try to look frightened. You can be the slave woman that I bought at the tavern, so just translate for me. They won't ask my slave directly, that would be rude. We are going to say that we were delayed by one of the camels getting away. It's common enough. Camels like to browse for food, that's why you put bells on them. If they do ask, say we saw three horsemen pass us in a hurry just after midday. You didn't see their faces. If they push, you give vague details of the horses and clothes and the location, not detailed. Can you do that?"

Pandora smiled, amused. "Do you think I'll need to *act* terrified? And don't you think an ex-slave can lie when she wants to?"

Then Pandora looked at her companion in surprise. "Jess, is that a dress?"

Jess looked at her friend, clutching the dress to her, looking totally embarrassed.

"I didn't know you had any dresses!" Pandora exclaimed, delighted. "Put it on, let me see!"

Jess reluctantly dressed for her friend. "I helped a trader who was in trouble and he made a complete outfit, but I've never worn it." She gave an embarrassed cough. "I don't wear dresses."

Pandora watched, entranced as she pulled it on.

It was a loose ankle-length dress of the expensive white cotton from *Aígyptos* with a broad band tied at the waist. It was left white at the waist and over Jess's upper thighs and hips. At the bottom it was dyed with horizontal bands: a double broad band of black at the very bottom, followed by the white of the back ground cloth, then ochre, then white again to finish with a band of black.

Over the top she wore an embroidered red cotton shirt. Finally she wrapped a crimson scarf over her hair and shoulders. Against her complexion it looked stunning! She looked stunning!

"Now I look like a pig in a dress!" she muttered.

"No you don't!" Pandora protested. "You look beautiful. Turn around and let me see! That's it! Now take a pose ... that's exactly right. Now sashay for me! ... Jess, sashay means to glide back and forth moving your hips up and down! Whoa, girl, you are perfect!"

Jess looked embarrassed but pleased.

"Well, Jess." Pandora looked at her with a fond smile. "I'm definitely going to want to get that dress off you later, girl, but for the moment we should move!"

They had not been walking with their camels for long when a group of a dozen horsemen stopped on the road across from them and turned to walk their horses across to them. They were led by a grey bearded man, broad-shouldered and strong looking.

Pandora didn't even carry a belt knife. Jess had a knife tucked into her belt and her quiver over her shoulder. She fitted an arrow but held her bow loosely, pointed to the ground.

Pandora had no trouble looking frightened.

"Greetings, *Kwdy* (Lord)!" Jess bowed, keeping a grip on her bow as Pandora translated. "You do us a great honour to meet us. My name is Jess and my Greek slave here is called Pandora. Please let us offer you and your men some humble refreshment." She gave a command to Pandora, who moved to get a wineskin and dried fruit from one of the saddle bags.

The tribesmen didn't move. They remained on their horses.

"I thank you for your offer, my name is Arshan. Perhaps it should be I who offers you hospitality *as you have left the road and are now on my ancestral lands*." He looked grim. "Yesterday I lost two of my sons. We hunt for their murderers."

"Who would do such a dreadful thing?" Jess asked. She returned the arrow to the quiver and relaxed her hold on the bow, allowing it to slide till it rested on the ground. "Lord, we offer you our prayers in your grief."

"We will find the murderers," Arshan said, dismounting. "Their horses, jewels and weapons were untouched, so it was not thieves. I have enemies, but I didn't think any would dare to act against me so close to home."

Jess looked thoughtful. "It was just after midday and still hot. Three men passed us travelling in great haste. They had horses like yours and were dressed in white such as yourself, but we didn't see their faces. They called out a friendly greeting so they seemed to be in good spirits. They came upon us so quickly that I decided to move back from the road. We are two women, as you can see."

"That was my sons and their companion." Arshan nodded.

Then he raised his voice in anger. "Two women!" he shouted in disgust. "What has ever possessed you to travel, two women alone in these parts and with three camels as well?"

"Uncle, not by choice I assure you. With a bow I am a good shot, though my slave cannot handle weapons," she added.

"Well, the murderers made a mistake," Arshan continued grimly. "They took their gold. My sons were carrying a large sum of money. I wish to examine your money!"

Pandora almost fainted. Jess had taken their money, of course she had! But gold coins were issued by each local king and they were distinctive.

Jess drew herself up! "That you will not, šēr, you insult me!"

Arshan coloured deeply, but he replied evenly. "I will recognise the coins. I need to find the killers of my sons."

Jess laughed. "And you think we did it? Two women, and one who cannot use weapons? Was a bow used?"

Arshan shook his head. "It was a sword. Even for a man it had to be someone very strong, and someone capable of killing three armed men. It couldn't have been either of you, but you are on my land. I will check anyway."

Pandora's pulse was hammering. She knew they were both going to die, painfully.

Jess motioned Pandora forward so they could talk quietly to Arshan. She looked desperate. How was she going to stop him from searching? Pandora wondered.

"My Lord, you asked why I travel alone with just one servant that I bought only recently," Jess whispered urgently. "My family and all my friends were murdered. I only barely got away myself. So as you say, I am a woman alone carrying a lot of money. If I show this in the open, we will have our throats cut. Please show mercy."

Arshan nodded. He clapped his hands and ordered his men to erect a tent.

"I will examine your money alone. Your secret is safe with me. I promise this by my honour."

Jess relaxed and smiled gratefully.

Pandora looked at her in horror.

Jess brought two bags from her camels and Arshan helped her carry them into the tent. Jess felt around in the first bag and produced a large purse. Then she did the same with the second. She reached down the front of her dress and produced another purse and then took a small purse from behind her waist band and passed it across. Pandora had other things on her mind when she watched Jess dress, but she would have sworn before a God that those purses just couldn't be there.

Arshan looked at the amount she was carrying in amazement.

"Princess, please accept the apologies of your humble servant. I will tell my men they need search your belongings no further."

Pandora took a shaky breath of reprieve.

"No!" Jess shouted indignantly. "I would the chance to prove my innocence!"

Then she continued more gently. "Please finish the search, Uncle; we will both feel better. I too had my family murdered. Just please don't say a word to your men about what I am. I travel in disguise and appear poorer than I am."

Arshan nodded. "Princess, you shame me."

Jess waited, looking determined.

What are you doing? Pandora felt like screaming at her friend. She felt like getting her by the throat and shaking her. She felt like leaping on top of her and tearing at her hair and clothes.

Jess gave her a serene look.

Arshan searched the remainder of the saddle bags. Then the three went outside to watch the rest of the search. Arshan was giving orders to his men, but everyone looked discomforted by now. Everyone, that is, except for Jess.

Soon the women's pitiful belongings were strewn on the ground. The princess was hiding her wealth well, Arshan thought. As he expected, his men found nothing.

Pandora was standing, feeling dizzy with a sense of unreality. Her eyes were frantically searching for Jess's sword and the men's money.

"I carry a dagger for personal protection, but don't even own a sword," Jess was confessing a bit shamefacedly. "How on earth could I use one?" She giggled a little at the thought.

Pandora glared at her.

"My Lady, I offer you an apology."

He gave a sharp command and Pandora was impressed with the speed and efficiency with which the men could repack their camels. Herdsmen certainly knew a lot about packing.

"My Lady, I would wish to invite you to our camp, but we are in mourning. The very least I can do is to loan you four of my men to accompany you part of your way."

Pandora was desperately mouthing 'nooo!'

"My Lord, I will gladly accept!" Jess said. "It will make us feel much safer with a murderer loose. No one can say the courtesy of your house is diminished. Please accept this small gift as a token of my friendship."

She gave him a gold ring. Arshan's eyes sparkled as he took it.

He held up his hand. Jess and Pandora both kneeled and bowed to receive the very special *Mazdayasna* (Zoroastrian) blessing that Arshan as a *Pir* (elder) was entrusted to give.

"May Aka Mana, the single and the only uncreated God, watch over you. May you bask in his brilliance and may he keep you from all evil."

When Pandora had a chance to whisper, she fixed Jess with an incredulous sideways glance. "'It *will make us feel so much safer!' Having his men escorting us?*"

Jess chuckled. "Assume each of these men speaks fluent Greek, unlikely though that would be. We couldn't be any safer than being escorted by his men!"

"Where's the sword?" Pandora hissed softly.

"The murder weapon with everyone's blood on it?" Jess looked surprised. "Perhaps I should have hung it around my neck for all to see. If they want to find it, they will have to dive for it. Besides, what good is it to me? Don't forget I can't use a sword." Jess looked smug.

"Are you a princess?"

Jess just looked amused. "I was fostered by a king and queen. They trained me to be a female warrior. I think it was to be an assassin. Before I could truly enter their service they fell in battle." A look of pain passed over her face. "Then some of their enemies came for me. It saved me the trouble of having to find them."

"Jess, I'm sorry about your family." She smiled. "But can I call you 'Princess' sometimes?"

Jess stuck out her tongue.

"How did you get all that money?" Pandora was astounded.

"I met up with several bands of bandits in the desert. I guess I must seem an easy target."

"You stole from bandits?"

"Shhh! No, I didn't steal. They had no further use for it."

"Did you throw the other gold away?"

Jess managed to look deeply offended.

"I'll tell you later. Now hush for the sake of all the Gods! Don't you ever stop talking?"

One of the men walked up to the second camel. He introduced himself to it and whistled; it knelt and sat.

"I think that's your ride, Pandora!" Jess laughed.

Pandora climbed on gingerly. The saddle was comfortable enough though it butted against the sacks of barley hung off the Bactrian camel's second hump.

Jess called out. "Hang on before ..."

It was too late!

The camel lurched back and forward. It kicked its back legs up first and then rocked forwards and then back to stand up. Pandora was almost thrown off, face forward onto the sand.

Jess bent over, helplessly laughing.

She broke a stick off a dead saxaul bush and came to the front of her own camel and jerked its reins once. It obediently sat for her. Then she hitched her dress and climbed on with a practiced movement. Then she gently tapped the sides of her camel for it to stand.

"That's how you are supposed to do it," she called out.

Pandora glared at her and almost missed a handhold as her camel adjusted its stance.

The men roped the three camels together, Jess in the lead, Pandora second.

"It's hardly needed," Jess called out to Pandora. "The camels think I'm an alpha camel."

"You certainly look like one."

"Hold on!" Jess called a warning as the camels took off.

From time to time Jess would glance back at her friend and start laughing again. Pandora's camel was surging back and forwards like a boat caught in the surf.

Or she would call advice. "Relax your body! Don't fight it like that!" And then burst out laughing. She heard the men shouting something to Pandora and laughing ... giving her advice and encouragement, no doubt.

They didn't go very far that day. The men didn't need to be told Pandora would be very sore. When they stopped and the camel settled to kneel, Jess had to lift her bodily off. She could only get Pandora to stagger a few steps before she slipped to the ground. "I'm dying."

She was instantly asleep. Jess paused to smile down at her fondly and then went to fetch a blanket. The men looked uncertainly at Jess and her moribund servant. A female would be expected to cook, but they knew Jess was more than she seemed.

Jess gestured ruefully at Pandora and then solved their problem by going to gather dry bush for the fire. She made a pot of tea and knelt in front of each of the men in turn to serve them.

One of the men unwrapped palm-leaf packets containing chicken, lamb, and small wooden skewers. Well, that was easy enough. Jess removed her glove and sliced the meat. The man helped her skewer it and added spices he had in another packet. He was probably the usual cook.

This campsite had been used before and she rolled a fire-blackened stone against the fire for its surface to heat for bread making.

Her fellow cook brought out vegetables, water, what looked like dry chick peas and dried and salted yoghurt. Jess smiled broadly and shrugged. This caused great hilarity amongst the men. The same man showed her in a laborious fashion with lots of gestures how to make porridge with the chick peas and add yoghurt, spices and vegetables. Once the meat was cooked it was slid off the skewers and combined with the porridge and vegetables and then wrapped in unleavened bread.

They insisted she try the first one with the men watching her face intently. It was absolutely delicious! Her face said it all and the men laughed with delight. Her mouth was watering for more, but she served the men first. She anxiously watched their faces, only relaxing as they all broke into broad smiles and made appreciative noises.

After that, she made more tea and then turned to the left overs. The men had considerately left more than enough for her and Pandora, but just in case, she made some more bread.

The crisis of the evening meal averted, Jess went to wake Pandora and feed her. She could only get her half awake and she kept falling asleep. She carried her a short distance and propped her up against one of the sitting camels and poured a little water over her face.

"You know I hate you, don't you?" Pandora spoke with her eyes closed.

"Of course, you do," Jess said cheerfully. "But I won't let you sleep until you have eaten something!"

Pandora started to chew but fell asleep while eating. After the second attempt, Jess gave up. She forced her to drink some water and then lay her down gently.

Her assistant cook walked over. "Servant?"

Jess understood the word, and made a wry face. He walked back, laughing.

The remainder of meat, bread and vegetables was wrapped in more palm leaves and then a cloth. The chick pea porridge went into a pot with its lid tied strongly on with string and wrapped securely in cloth.

Jess drank some tea and sat for a while with the men to be courteous. There was a lot of miming, smiles and charades. Between the men there was a great deal of laughing and excited talk. Jess wondered if these heavily armed men would laugh after they killed her and Pandora if they ever found out about them. *Probably.*

She smiled back at them in appreciation of the thought.

After a decent period she decided to leave the men to their fire. It was expected that she would join them briefly at the time of the meal, after which women and children would retire to allow the men to talk.

One of the men had set up the tent and two men carried Pandora by the simple method of rolling her onto a blanket and then lifting at either end. She didn't even wake.

Pandora had made promises of what they could do this evening. Jess smiled wryly at the figure of her friend in the darkness. *Not tonight.*

Chapter 4: Kynane

After Chalkedon, the main road east leads to Libyssa, a port city on the northern shore of the Propontis. After Libyssa it becomes a single road which, after a gentle descent, follows the coastal route all the way to Astakos. Between Libyssa and Astakos there is little local traffic. The coastal leg is narrow and deserted of settlements and has several places that are ideal for an ambush.

The men had chosen a small ravine where the road descended to the coast. It had been formed by a small stream flowing to the sea. If their quarry escaped the first trap, they would come here.

What the men didn't know was that they also were being watched. Four women and a man had been tracking them for days. At a nod from the man, the five of them drew back to talk.

"What is it you see, sister?" the man murmured to Anastasia.

The tawny haired girl was the best scout of all of them. She smiled and drew a small map in the dirt.

"Master, as the road descends they have set five archers on each side overlooking the road." She pointed on the map. "The main force is made up of twenty riders hidden at the bottom of the ravine, near the exit. While they may be dressed and armed like Kimmerioi, Kimmerioi they are not. They are too relaxed, laughing and joking, so I think there is a main trap to the west and these men are here just in case of an escape this way. If their prey comes this way they will likely have others chasing them, preventing a retreat. It will form a neat trap."

Entrance to Black Sea

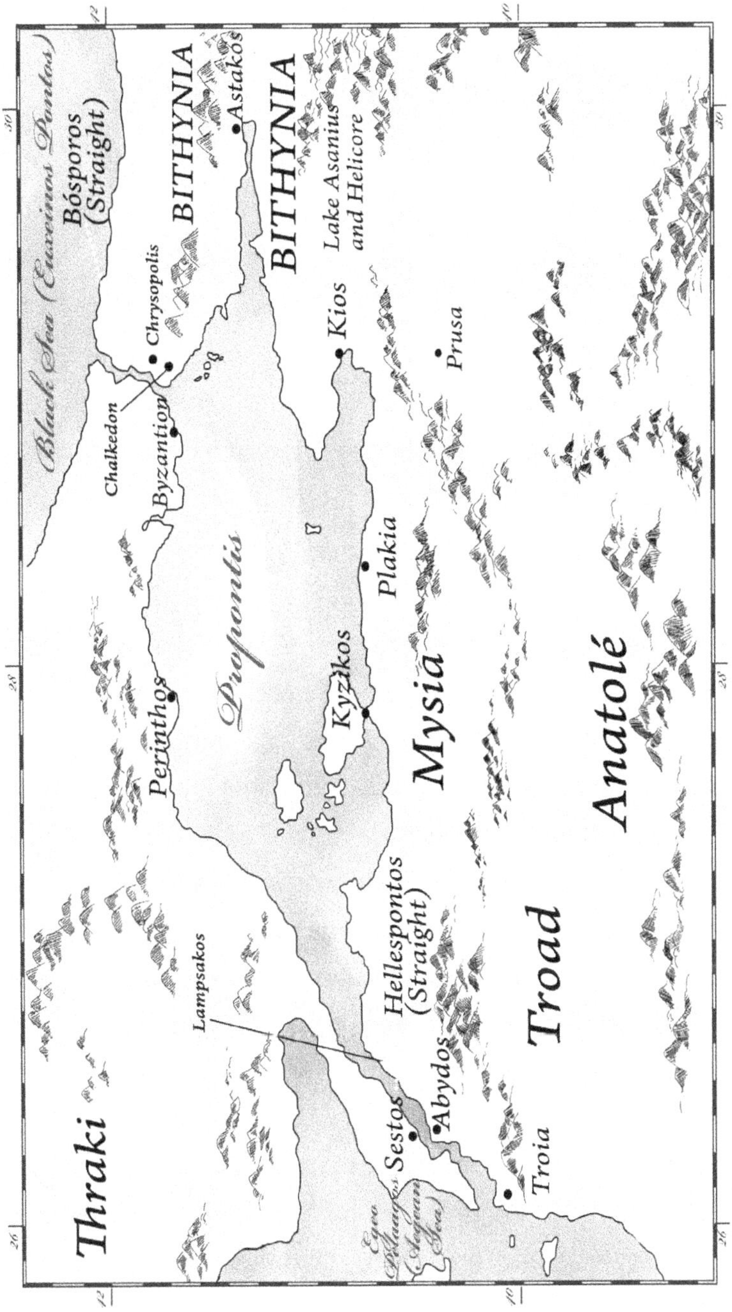

"Very good," the master nodded. "They are not Kimmerioi. How did you guess?"

Anastasia, whose name means 'survivor', smiled at the compliment.

"Kimmerioi raid villages, not set traps. They know the location too well and are too confident of the path of their quarry. This area is deep in Makedonían Bithynia. These men will be Makedónes in disguise. This is one of the endless Makedóne murders. I wonder who the intended victim is."

"Nonetheless, it is not our fight," their master said firmly. "Thirty here and however many are driving the quarry this way. We will watch only."

* * *

They had pushed their mounts to the limit and Kynane paused to give them a moment's rest near a solitary pine tree.

Just ahead the road entered a ravine as it descended to the thin coastal strip. There was a channel made from the local grey stone for a stream that flowed down on the left side.

It was a clear day and the water of the Propontis showed as a light blue in the distance. The grass and forest was already green and lush with the autumn rains, obscuring the twisting ravine and the heights flanking it, making it look overgrown ... and dangerous.

"What do you think might be waiting down that ravine?" Kynane asked Cadmus. "Do you think they would go to all this trouble and not have a plan in case we escaped the first trap?"

"It's you they are after," Cadmus, the leader of her body guard, agreed.

Their enemies were dressed as Kimmerioi, but they had spare horses and they pursued them as if for a vendetta. It was Kynane they were after.

"Well, it's not for ransom." Kynane smiled without humour. "Can you see Aléxandros paying anything for his beloved half-sister, except of course to have me murdered?"

Kynane was with the army near the *Istros* (Danube) when Aristoteles had brought the news. Her mother, Audata, was dead. It was said to be an accident.

Aristoteles suggested she flee to Astakos, where her mother's oldest friend was the military governor. He had arranged passage to Chalkedon for her and the few countrymen who would accompany her.

But Aristoteles had proven not to be the friend she believed him to be. Before they reached the port city of Libyssa, men were waiting. Only a charge by Kynane had allowed the four of them to escape.

Audata, Philippos's second wife, had been his favourite before Olympias. She was an Illyrian warrior-princess and the granddaughter of King Bardyllis. It was she who had trained Kynane, her only child. Mother and daughter had fought in the army with Philippos and it was Audata, more than any other wife of Philippos, who stood up to Olympias.

It was their widespread popularity with the army, especially amongst the older soldiers, and their lack of interest in court politics that had kept mother and daughter alive. At least it had for a while, Olympias had not forgotten about them.

Ten men dressed as Kimmerioi broke cover not far behind them. They were galloping hard on fresh mounts. Their leader gave a whoop of triumph.

"My Lady," Amorantos shouted. "Ride on, we will delay them."

"I'll never run from a fight!" Kynane wheeled to face her adversaries. "If I'm to die, I will die facing my enemies."

Her mare, scenting a fight, began prancing in anticipation. Their pursuers were almost upon them but when Kynane and her three companions charged back at them, it caught them off guard.

Cadmus gave a great war-cry and charged straight for three of the riders. He threw the last of his throwing spears and drew his sword. But as he killed the second man, the third stabbed him hard in the back. He tried to turn his horse to fight the last man, but he was losing strength, his vision darkening.

* * *

"Master!" Anastasia whispered excitedly. "See, the men who are being hunted have woollen leggings, they are Illyroi! The one in the middle is a woman! She wears a breast plate and a long dark dress! See the purple horsehair crest on her helmet? She is an Illyrian warrior-princess! They are fighting back!"

Anastasia, tawny haired and freckled, was born in Illyria and had the keenest eyes of any of them.

The man looked back at his women. For the first time, he felt fear. He trained them and they would have accepted him as their leader in an instant, but he had refused to command them in all matters outside their training.

But having set the organisation of the women up in this way and repeatedly insisting on it, he had created a sword for himself and now maybe it would cut both ways.

"What is it that you wish?" he asked them softly.

They looked back at him excitedly.

Thaïs grinned. "She is the enemy of the Makedónes. We have a truce with them, but how long do you think that will last? You train us endlessly. Here is our chance to put our skills to the test. I say we help her."

Eirene, the eldest and their leader in many other things, nodded, but she looked grimmer than her younger sisters. "This is murder and you know it. While they are distracted, I say we do what we can. We are a weapon. You cannot sharpen a weapon endlessly and never use it. You will only spoil it."

"I can't watch someone being murdered and not at least try to help," Alba, the second eldest, agreed.

The man nodded slowly. They grinned back at him, excited and yet frightened now.

"We will do this properly. If it goes badly and I say run, we will run and no argument. I will deal with the archers on this side first. Cover them in case any become alerted."

The women moved forward and got ready, but the archers were intent on the distant fighting. The master did not make a sound.

* * *

Kleandros, the leader of the Makedóne soldiers, waited impatiently at the end of the ravine. His horse, sensing his mood, was restless. A Makedonían lord, Archelaos waited nearby but behind cover. None of the men had seen a large figure behind them, crouched low as it crossed from one side of the ravine to the other. They were all too focused on the Illyroi who had turned to attack their pursuers. Kleandros decided to leave nothing to chance.

"*Dimoerites* (Corporal) take your squad and see that none escape. It seems our little ambush will not be needed."

The corporal called to seven of the men, smiling with anticipation.

"Come on! Let's show these Illyrians how real men fight!"

He kicked his horse, which leapt forward. As they kicked their horses up the ravine towards its entrance Eirene hissed, "now!"

The four women released their arrows and, as one, they snatched for another. Two men shrieked as they fell; another seemed to struggle to keep control of his horse for a moment before falling off, an arrow in his chest. The corporal seemed to pause and then tiredly slump over his mount.

The remainder riders milled in confusion. One shouted out, "Don't shoot, it's us!"

Three more arrows found their targets. The last horseman threw himself off into the shelter of a nearby horse and scurried for cover as an arrow whizzed past him.

"They have killed our men!" Kleandros shouted, pointing to the ridge. "Get up there and kill them, there are only four of them."

His remaining nine men jumped off their horses and began scrambling up the hill. While climbing they couldn't manage their shields and weapons and near the top their leader fell with an arrow in his chest.

The other men had gained the top and snatched their shields from their backs. They remained under cover and cautiously looked around. They could see nothing. The place was uneven, crossed with gullies, grass and shrubs. It seemed deserted.

"We need to find them!" Orestes, the surviving corporal, shouted.

He sent four men angling inland and led the three others along the ridge to search for their own archers. They moved along a shallow ravine, nervously eyeing the dense shrubs and uneven ground, crouched low with their shields high.

Orestes found the first of the Makedóne archers, his throat cut.

"This happened silently," he said with growing fear. "We will find the others the same. Five men close to each other in the bush, all are killed without a sound. Four bowmen appear incredibly fast and accurate! It's elves! We are dead men."

"How many do you think, *Kyrie* (sir)?" Alketas asked. He was the youngest of the men, barely more than a boy.

"I think five, maybe more," Orestes said. "It would take one of them to kill the men and the four archers to cover him. He must have crossed to the other side to deal with our men there."

"One elf against five men?" Alketas asked, incredulous.

"Confident bastards, aren't they?" Orestes said bitterly. "I think I'd better call the others back. We stand a better chance if we stay together."

Just then there were sounds of screams and a man shouting.

"Dimoerites!" a man called out. "Hesiodos is dead and they have shot Iásōn!"

"Leave Iásōn, it's elves!"

There were sounds of two men crashing through the bush. Alketas, the youngest, stood up to call them over.

"Get down!" The corporal reached up to pull the boy back.

There was a thud. The corporal grunted, dropping to his knees, an arrow in his chest.

The two men burst out of cover, running as fast as they could; an arrow caught one in the back. His companion hesitated and caught an arrow. They could hear Iásōn crying and begging for help. Then his cries suddenly stopped.

The three remaining men sprang up to make a run for it. Almost immediately two were killed. The last threw down his shield.

"Will you allow surrender?"

He felt a punch hard in his chest. From somewhere behind the bushes he heard a woman's voice. "I am sorry."

It was the last sound he heard.

* * *

Kynane and Amorantos grinned at each other.

All their friends were dead. They had killed all their pursuers except two who now hung back. There were riderless horses everywhere.

"Unless I miss my guess, my princess, they will have an ambush waiting ahead," Amorantos said. "I am good in the forest. If we go on foot we might be able to follow this stream back up into the hills. We can live through this yet."

"Save yourself, Amorantos." Kynane smiled at him tiredly. "I could not have asked for a better man or a better friend."

He looked at her sharply. "You're hurt!"

He leapt off his horse to quickly help her down. Her right hand was pressed to her shoulder. Her shield fell to the ground as her left side lost its strength. "Damn!" she cursed, laughing a little.

Kynane allowed him to bind her shoulder as tight as he could. She was bleeding heavily and the blood immediately stained the cloth. By the time he had finished she had no use of her left arm and he had to help her back on her horse.

"Now go, you fool!"

He saluted her with his sword and then kicked his horse to the last gallop it had in it. But instead he turned his horse to the last of their pursuers.

"You always were such a fool," Kynane whispered, shaking her head fondly.

She patted her huge war horse. "Come on Harmonia, there are some men waiting for me. Let's see if I can take one of them with me before my strength fails. It's not very far, girl. At least it better not be."

She sheathed her sword. Her throwing spears were gone and she had lost her shield. She reached back to loosen one of the two Illyrian throwing axes at the back of her belt.

"I wonder if they know about these!" she whispered with the ghost of a smile, and nudged her horse. If only she could stay in the saddle just a little longer...

When she glanced back, she could see more riderless horses, but no sign of Amorantos or her pursuers. She was alone now, at least for the moment.

By the time she got to the entrance to the pass, she felt faint and her mind had slowed. She couldn't understand what she saw. There were bodies of men dressed as Kimmerioi lying all around, arrows protruding out of them. A riderless horse galloped past.

One that was not dead leapt up to grab her horse. She brought her arm behind her and untwisted her body as she threw. She would lose precision but she needed the extra power in her weakened state.

The man screamed as he died, the axe slicing into his collar bone and nearby arteries. Throwing axes are designed to tumble once between being thrown and hitting the target. They require a lot of skill but she had thrown them since she was a little girl.

She felt as if she was struck by lightning. Her vision darkened. When her head cleared she saw Archelaos sitting his horse, his bow in his hand, at a careful distance from her.

"How much did they pay you?"

"They were generous," Archelaos admitted.

Kynane was having trouble staying on her horse. "If you had hoped for some fun first, I'm sorry I will have to disappoint you."

Archelaos nodded in acknowledgement, but he still would not come closer. He knew about her throwing axes. *You needn't worry, Archelaos*, Kynane thought, *anything more is beyond me.*

He took careful aim. Kynane braced herself and heard rather than felt the thud of the arrow.

She looked at him in shock and outrage. He had targeted her horse!

She began to curse him weakly and monotonously. Harmonia swayed and then fell. Kynane cried out in agony as her leg snapped under the animal. The horse struggled to rise before falling back on to her. It felt like her leg was bathed in molten metal. She must have blacked out.

She woke to agony and wave after wave of dizziness. Archelaos had dismounted and was looking down at her as she lay sweating and panting, trapped by the dead horse.

"You never knew I really loved you, did you, Kynane? All those years ... I only wanted you to notice me. But you always thought you were too good for me, didn't you?"

"If this is because you love me, you have a strange way of showing it!" She panted as she screwed her face up in agony. She had broken out into a cold sweat. "You cannot blame me for what I never knew. You also should know about princesses. My views on whom I bed were unimportant. I was property; firstly of my father, then of my brother Aléxandros." *That is, until Olympias remembered her grudge with my mother.* "You only needed to convince one of *them* if you wished to possess me. I would not have been unwilling with you, Archelaos. I had always thought of you as a friend. It was all I could ever offer any man."

Archelaos looked at her in complete surprise. Then his gaze shifted down to the arrow head sticking out of the centre of his chest. He coughed once and dropped to his knees and slumped forward.

A woman's face appeared, looking down at her.

"Who?" was all Kynane managed.

A giant of a man was approaching at a half run, staggering with the weight of a boulder.

Kynane could only whisper. "If you want to kill me with that, you had better hurry."

As he threw it she flinched, but it landed just to her side. The man pushed at it with his heel, hard up against the dead horse. Another woman rushed up to him with an armful of cavalry lances and he began quickly working them between the rock and the dead horse.

"Her war horse is *huge*. It can't be much less than three quarters of a ton," he shouted. "We will only get one go at this! Be careful with her arm!"

Kynane felt four strong arms grab her and the giant heaved. He screamed out with the effort. It was a mercy that she blacked out again.

When she returned to consciousness, a fire had been lit and only one of the women and the man remained. They had bathed her wounds and were cleaning and stitching her shoulder.

The tawny haired woman paused and smiled to see her conscious. "Princess," she said.

She had a pleasant musical voice with an Illyrian accent. Somehow Kynane was amongst friends. "You are awake; if you are in pain, we can give you some herbs."

Kynane gritted her teeth and shook her head.

"I am sister Anastasia," the woman continued as she lifted Kynane's head to feed her a mouthful of water. "I am a Shayvist, as you may have guessed. This man is the teacher of our female order. I was of the Dardanioi tribe in Illyria, the same as you."

Kynane gripped at her hand in wordless gratitude. So she had been rescued by initiates of the new female Shayvist order, everyone called them Amazónes.

"My arm," she asked. "Will it be saved?"

"Of course, Princess," Anastasia said confidently. "We are almost finished."

She knew Kynane couldn't see her leg. It was just as well.

The bleeding from the leg was not as dangerous, but the leg had been crushed and broken in more than one place. It was befouled by dirt and manure from her dying horse and her shin bone was poking through the skin.

Kynane was no fool. While the eventual outcome for her arm depended on whether infection set in, one thing was obvious. "You cannot save my leg."

A handsome bearded face appeared over Anastasia's shoulder. "Try to relax. I haven't turned to your leg yet. We had to attend to your arm first. You were losing too much blood. I had to seal the artery."

Kynane looked at him in amazement. Repair an artery? She had never heard of such a thing.

But the leg ... she grabbed at his arm desperately.

"Thank you, stranger! But please help me. Please take my leg! I lose my leg or I lose my life! You understand that, don't you?"

The big stranger merely smiled gently.

"You will have to trust me, Kynane. I have some skill in healing."

He was a Shantawi, Kynane realised, taking in his darker skin and distinctive clothes. That would explain the connection with the Shayvist order.

"Please," she said faintly as she drifted off.

If they didn't cut off her leg, she was a dead woman.

* * *

She slowly came back to herself.

Her mouth was dry and tasted foul. Strong hands lifted her up and held a cup to her lips. She drank thirstily but had to pause several times to get her breath. They were alone in a cave the size of a one bedroom house. Some light was filtering in. From a crevice she could hear the drip of water into a small pond.

"Stop!" The man laughed. "I'll give you more soon, but not too much at once. Do you need to relieve yourself?"

Kynane nodded. She was big for a woman, six foot and big boned, but she felt herself lifted as easily as a small child, and carried over to a patch of sand. He squatted, holding her by her back and resting her remaining leg over his thigh.

He didn't expect her to relieve herself as he held her, did he?

It was about then she realised she was naked and being clutched against the man's heavily muscled chest. He had a pleasant man smell. She was totally helpless, but she felt safe. She had not felt truly safe since the death of her father.

He was murmuring, "Relax, Kynane. Relax."

Her eyes felt so heavy! She didn't remember relaxing her sphincter but she felt a gush of water from her bladder.

I'm as weak as a kitten and as helpless as a baby, she said to herself as she started to drift off to sleep.

* * *

When Kynane next woke it was night time.

A small fire had been lit and she could smell some broth cooking in a large pot. It was just her and the big man. It seemed that he was the one elected to nurse her. That was strange, a male nurse, especially to look after a woman, especially when women were around, but some men studied the healing arts. This man would be some sort of monk.

"Good! You are awake!" He had such a kindly smile. "I will give you some water and then you must have some of this broth. It is very good. My wife taught me how to make it. "

"You are married?" Kynane asked, surprised. "I thought you Shayvists didn't marry."

"Some of us marry, though most don't." His face was a mask of remembered pain. "My wife is dead."

"I'm so sorry ... I don't even know your name!"

"No, you don't." His smile robbed his words of offence.

"And you're not going to tell me!" she said with a wry smile. "Nor I suppose will you tell me where we are!"

He gestured apologetically. "This place is too useful for us to give its secrets away. But you are safe; we won't hurt you."

"If you wanted to hurt me, there is no way I could stop you." Kynane laughed softly.

She knew she was safe with this strange man. It felt so good to be able to relax her guard and be cared for after so many years of living in constant danger. Soon she was being lifted up in strong arms and given water.

"Can I hold the cup?" she asked.

"It is good to see you getting stronger," the man said with evident satisfaction.

"What?" she said with droll humour. "Now I can hold my own cup! Why, soon I will be so incredibly powerful that I might be able to feed myself with a spoon! Where are the two women?"

"There were four. One has returned to our home. The other three hunt and stand guard. There are several large bands of men combing the land for you. Someone really wants you dead, Kynane! But don't worry, this place is well hidden."

"How long do we stay here?" Kynane asked.

"As long as we need to; it is not safe to leave and you are not able to ride."

"You will stay with me in this cave all that time? Am I your prisoner?"

"Kynane, no. I will use a blindfold when we leave, but then you are free to go your separate way. I suggest you allow us to take you to the Troad, where we can keep you safe and give you time to heal."

"Thank you, I will go with you. Perhaps I can learn to fight again."

"Your leg?" he asked. "It's healing nicely."

"It feels as if it's still there. It's hurting and itching like crazy!"

He looked at her in surprise and then laughed.

"I've just finished bandaging the stump, but we should check what the problem is."

He carried her over to prop her against the rock wall. She felt him expertly undoing the bandage under her blanket. It seemed to be taking a long time for a stump. He must have wrapped it heavily.

"It's a bit of a shock at first, I'm afraid. Are you sure you are ready for it?"

Kynane looked at him steadily. "I am an Illyrian warrior-princess. My great grandfather was King Bardyllis! Show me!"

"I tried to warn you. It's not pretty for a woman to see!"

He whipped the blanket off her right leg, trying not to expose her nakedness too much.

Kynane stared at her leg in shock. A total sense of unreality overcame her. This was a dream!

Her thigh and leg had set straight. She had ugly red scars where the wounds should have been. Otherwise it was completely intact!

The man had collapsed with laughter and was rolling on the ground. He was beside himself with mirth.

Very funny!

Then she chuckled despite herself. His amusement was infectious. Eventually the two of them were laughing together.

"I'm sorry, Kynane, I couldn't resist!" The man chuckled.

She smiled at him. Something told Kynane this man did not laugh very often since his wife died.

"Well, I can hardly claim disappointment!" She chuckled. "But you are not as clever as you think, Hakeem! The healing touch;

only one man I know of could have done all that you have done. I owe you my life and more. I was sorry to hear what happened to Elana and Jacinta. We found ourselves on opposing sides for a good while but I think they fought for all women. I heard you were finished after that, is that when you became a monk?"

"I never stopped being a monk. I might explain paladins to you one day," Hakeem said, still smiling. "I am still the Warlord of the Shantawi, but Anatolē and the elves can manage better without a warlord, despite what they think. If they really need me again, I will be there."

Then he lost his smile.

"Kynane, if I said it was hard for me when my wife and daughter were killed, it would be a niggardly description. It feels as if my heart stopped beating that day. I felt my God had deserted me. Going on has been the hardest thing I have ever done."

"Was it for Jacinta that you took up the training of the Amazónes?" Kynane asked.

"I don't exactly know how that happened," Hakeem answered. "I have a small estate in the Troad and spend most of my time there. After Jacinta was killed, the Amazónes collapsed. Some of them turned up at my gates and then the word got around and more came. Men had turned up for me to train too, including some of those sworn to me. But I sent them elsewhere.

"The women, though, they didn't really have anywhere else. The best they could hope for was being split up and scattered over several of the chapter houses — there were too many for one. And they simply couldn't get the sort of training only I could give them.

"Since then, others have come, not all of them Amazónes. Mostly they are women and a few children out of need, some out of love for what I once was. With so many women surrounding me, I have become the most hen-pecked man in all Anatolē." He gave a wan smile. "Having people depending on me gives me some semblance of life."

"Surrounded by all those women, did you never take another woman?" Kynane asked softly.

"Kynane," he sighed. "I can never love another. If you had ever met Elana, you would understand."

"Oh," was all Kynane could say.

Hakeem looked so sad, so heartbroken, Kynane's heart went out to him.

"Please sit with me," she asked huskily.

The big man moved over to sit down next to her. He had not been able to say this to anyone else. There was something about Kynane that allowed him to share his deepest feelings with her. He took her hand.

"Thank you, Kynane," he whispered.

But she was already asleep.

* * *

Outside a bird called.

Hakeem went to the entrance to the cave and mimicked the call. Anastasia's head appeared at the mouth of the cave followed by the freshly dressed deer across her shoulders. As she eased the deer down she saw Kynane lying propped up against the corner of the cave and smiled broadly. It was the first time that Kynane had been able to sit up for any time, let alone stay awake.

"My Princess, it does me good to see you are recovering!"

"Just Kynane!" Kynane smiled back. "I am no longer welcome in any land that would call me princess. Aléxandros would not welcome me back except to kill me and the last time I visited Illyria, I killed my aunt, Queen Kaeria, in single combat. You're Anastasia, aren't you? I owe my life to all of you, but especially you!"

"Tales of your mother and grandmother were why I wished to train as a female warrior," Anastasia said. "I have brought some clothes for you. It's our field clothes in your size. Your dress was completely ruined, I'm afraid."

"Well, I'll try not to bleed all over these then!" Kynane said with a chuckle. "It's been awkward sharing a cave with this handsome leader of yours and only blankets to hide my nakedness."

Hakeem laughed, "It's been a long time for me too, sharing my quarters with a beautiful naked lady. I don't know how interesting you found me. Every time I started to talk to you, you fell asleep!"

"Perhaps you should give me another chance at sleeping in your quarters." Kynane smiled. "Try to choose a time when my family and childhood friends haven't cut me up into small pieces for dog meat!"

"It seems like we might have a chance to get better acquainted, Kynane!" Hakeem laughed, "Everyone else seems to want to kill you! I don't fully wonder now I have had your company these last few days!"

"Hakeem!" Kynane returned with mock outrage. "You are used to bullying these poor young girls who are sworn to obey you. You are not used to having someone around who is at least your equal and most likely your better! Your girls should be thankful I have shown up to keep you in line!"

Hakeem laughed. "I don't bully you, do I, Anastasia?"

"Yes, you do!" Anastasia laughed back. "You beat us!"

"Hakeem!" Kynane held up the clothes she had been given. "Do you have to dress all your women as men?"

Anastasia broke into giggles at the thought. Their clothes were modelled after elvish scouts and were chosen by Jacinta, not Hakeem.

"I suppose in Illyria you usually crawl through the woods in a formal gown?" Hakeem countered.

"At least I wouldn't be mistaken for a man then!" Kynane replied, amused.

"Kynane," Hakeem let out a sigh, "I could never mistake you for a man, no matter how you were dressed!"

"Why thank you, Hakeem!" Kynane replied, blushing.

Hakeem gave her a frank smile of appreciation. "Your tongue is far too sharp for a start! When are you going to show me how sharp your other weapons are?"

"I could do it now!" Kynane suggested.

She looked pale and drained and suppressed a yawn.

"It's just that you are the only healer, so we wouldn't have anyone to patch you up."

She closed her eyes and was soon asleep.

Hakeem was still chuckling and shaking his head in admiration. "What a woman!"

Anastasia tenderly stretched the blankets over Kynane and made her comfortable. Kynane murmured in her sleep.

"The tradition of the female warrior is very strong in Illyrian royal women," Anastasia said. "She is used to travelling in an army of you men and well used to holding her own against you male bullies!"

"And what about you female bullies?"

Anastasia dimpled prettily in return.

"Still, I hope she stays with us," Hakeem said thoughtfully. "She would be a wonderful addition to your training ... a true female warrior teaching you! And I long for her to show me how she fights!"

* * *

Kynane paced restlessly around the cave; she still limped.

"I'm telling you I'm fit to ride."

Hakeem sat serenely sipping tea. He looked amused.

"Kynane, you are fit to ride when *I* say you are fit to ride!"

Anastasia and Alba sat a little wide-eyed in the corner. They knew that tone. Hakeem didn't use it often, but when he did he always got his way; maybe with Kynane though it would be different.

"I am grateful to you, Hakeem, but I refuse to be a burden."

"You refuse, do you?" Hakeem sounded surprised. "And why do I need your opinion?"

Kynane rounded on him in a fury. "How dare you speak to me thus?" She was trembling with anger. She felt terribly hurt to be reminded of her fall in status. "Maybe I am not a princess any more but I have been a warrior since I was a child."

Hakeem held his hand up and spoke gently, "Kynane, I mean you no disrespect! Amongst the sisterhood and yes, with myself, you will find the name 'Kynane' is spoken with great respect. But I repeat the question. Who are you to insist? Did your healer say you were ready? I didn't hear him speak thus! And who will be the leader of our party, will it be you? Or is the great Kynane completely above following orders? If that is so, you are a danger to all who travel with you!"

Despite these harsh words he smiled gently at her, waiting.

Kynane let out the breath she was holding, ready to make a sharp reply. Her shoulders slumped, defeated. Hakeem seemed so kind and soft; even now his words were gentle.

"*Kyrie* (sir), I apologise!" she said, blushing deeply. "You must think of me as a silly woman. I will have to regain your trust that my foolish words have made me lose. Please don't think I will do anything but obey your orders without question!"

She knew as she spoke these words that, like his Amazónes, she would follow this man into the pit of *Tártaros* (Hell) itself. Hakeem was so unlike any leader she had ever met, so soft and so soft-spoken, and yet she would die for him.

She fell to her knees before him.

"Hakeem, I hereby pledge you my service if you will have it. I will put none before you. By my living or by my dying I will serve you as long as I live!"

"Kynane!" Hakeem was in shock. "There is no need for that!"

But Kynane simply waited, her head bowed. Time started to pass.

"And I Hakeem hereby accept your oath, Kynane, warrior-princess of the Illyrians." He proclaimed loudly, "I will reward your service with my love, my respect and my loyalty in return."

Kynane had given Hakeem her personal oath, something an Illyrian princess would never do!

He stooped over and drew her to her feet.

"There was no need for that, Kynane," he said softly, "No need."

He hugged her and kissed her softly on the cheek. Kynane sighed as he hugged her. She long remembered the feeling of his strong arms around her and her cheek kept tingling where he had kissed her.

* * *

Hakeem had gone to scout and had left Kynane in the company of one of the other Amazónes, Alba.

"And now, Lady, you see how he enslaves us all!" Alba said, smiling.

"I never knew I was going to give him my personal pledge, until it happened," Kynane said in wonder at herself.

"And you'll never regret it!" Alba said with feeling.

Kynane smiled. "You feel it too? Do you find him as puzzling as I do?"

"My Lady, we all do! In my opinion he is the finest warrior there is. To understand him you need to understand that he lives and breathes his Shayvist beliefs. We Shayvists do not like killing, but to protect innocents we will kill without hesitation."

Kynane laughed, "Thank you, Alba, but I am hardly an innocent!"

Alba smiled at Kynane's wry expression. "The manner of your death was little better than murder. Do you want me to continue explaining our leader, or do you want to debate whether the world would be a better place with or without Kynane in it!"

Kynane laughed, "I'm sorry, please go on, Alba."

"Well," Alba continued, "underneath this, and not far underneath, Hakeem is very soft. He has a particular soft spot for women and children. The girls and I have found it simplicity itself to twist him around our fingers. But don't let that deceive you. When he says something about training or safety, he will expect to be obeyed without question. If there is time he may explain, but if he snaps an order in the middle of a dangerous situation, you had better jump and jump quickly!"

"I think that's the mistake I made when I argued with him!" Kynane admitted wryly. "Though never in my life have I been put back in my place in such a gentle way!"

"Hakeem is very protective of any in his charge. We have told him he acts like a mother hen with us. He just laughs at us! Rescuing you was the first time he let any of us get involved in a real fight."

"And he led four inexperienced women against an ambush. All of my enemies killed and none of you even injured!" She paused. "He is very sad, isn't he?"

"My Lady, it breaks our hearts!"

Kynane thought of her father Philippos and his multiple wives. Could a man love a single woman so much?

"He must have really loved her."

Alba sighed and nodded.

"Alba?" Kynane asked with a secret smile to herself. "When we get to the Troad, will you and Anastasia help me get some nice dresses?"

Alba looked puzzled for a minute, and then her face lit up in delight. "You mean?"

Kynane nodded very determinedly. Alba laughed and hugged her.

"There have been so many women who have tried to catch Hakeem's eye, but he rarely even notices. I think most of us wouldn't mind if he showed more interest in us beyond being just his students. But he looks at *you* differently! I think we would be all happy to match him with someone nice!" Alba said.

"I don't know if I would always be described as *nice*." Kynane giggled.

Alba appraised her knew friend. She could hardly be described as pretty in any of the usual ways but she was a magnificent looking young woman, tall and strong. She had an air about her of courage and intelligence.

"This will be a greatest pleasure, my Princess of Illyria!"

She made a mock bow and the women giggled to each other.

Women have their own way of hunting a man.

The prey may be unsuspecting, but he had certainly proven elusive before.

* * *

It was another week before Eirene returned from the Troad to help escort Kynane, and Hakeem pronounced her ready to ride. Thaïs, Alba and Anastasia joined them in their cave, which made it very crowded.

"Your rescue really stirred up a hornet's nest!" Eirene said. "They found your body guard and the men sent to kill you all dead. They found your dead horse with lots of blood stains around it but no body. They knew you were badly hurt and alive or dead, that you had been rescued. They suspect it was Makedónes. Just to keep them busy, we have been laying false trails."

"I would have liked to give you longer to rest, but interest has died down around here for the moment, so we should leave while we can," Hakeem said. "If we come across anything, I want you five to make a break for it."

"Hakeem, we can't do that!" Kynane said in anguish.

"What was that you said, Kynane?" Hakeem looked at Kynane coldly.

"Hakeem!" Eirene turned on him angrily. She was the oldest and tended to stand up to Hakeem more. "Don't be a bully! Just because she has sworn to obey you, doesn't mean you can be cruel. You know she's worried about you! Don't return her concern with scorn!"

Inwardly Kynane cringed. She expected Hakeem to explode in rage. Instead he appeared chastened.

"Kynane, I apologise. Eirene is right. I need to know you will obey me in the middle of an emergency, but I didn't mean to be unkind. Through no fault of your own, it is you that is weak and vulnerable and must be protected. If I tell you to, I want you to flee. The others are going with you to protect you, nothing else. The sisters and I can melt into the forest, but you can't. They will not find me and they will not kill me. Many have tried in the past."

Kynane smiled her gratitude shyly. "Thank you for explaining, Hakeem, and yes, I would be worried for you."

He gave her a reassuring smile.

"Now, do you want me to wear a blindfold?" Kynane asked.

Hakeem had forgotten the blindfold.

"No." He gave her that warm smile that made her feel tingly all over. "You are one of us now."

Alba handed Hakeem a heavy rope.

"Do we have to climb out?" Kynane asked.

"*You* don't," Hakeem replied pointedly. "I will lower you to where we will bring the horses."

"How did you get me into the cave?" she asked, surprised.

"Hakeem needed the exercise!" Eirene commented with a dry smile.

Chapter 5: Bithynia, an Old Friend

In the early part of the journey, Hakeem would not allow conversation except for the softest of whispers. The horses' gear was padded to minimise noise.

This was the most dangerous part of their journey. They were heading due east on one of the lesser roads through the mountainous plateau just north of the usual coastal route to Astakos. It was a fertile and wealthy area and had a relatively large concentration of Makedóne military.

The mountain the Greeks called 'the Mysian Ólympos' after the Greek mountain was several days' ride to the east and south. They would turn towards it once they had given Astakos a wide berth. At this time of the year the mountain passes were clear. They would be safe away from the Makedónes there and could make their way freely to Mysia.

The four women rode a little in front until they found an old trail, overgrown and not used for some time. Anastasia looked significantly at Hakeem, who nodded.

Anastasia turned her horse to a patch of forest. After a while they could hear the soft call of a bird. Alba answered it and made some curious hand movements to the others. Hakeem signalled back with hand gestures and Alba, Thaïs and Eirene melted into the forest.

Kynane and Hakeem were left, seemingly to walk their horses leisurely down the deserted road.

Kynane had travelled with war bands since she was small but she had never seen anything of the like. Hakeem could seemingly wander through Bithynia undetected just on a training exercise for his Amazónes! It made her wonder again why he had never attacked Makedonía in the turmoil following her father's death. With hindsight it would have been a colossal blunder. Aléxandros had wasted no time in consolidating his position. An attack would have simply united all Makedonía behind him.

But everyone expected Hakeem to at least attack Parmenion. Parmenion almost fell off his battlements in surprise when Hakeem and a man called Apollo arrived at his gates offering a temporary truce and desperately needing supplies. Hakeem must have known that when Aléxandros had once again united his kingdom, he would be facing a hostile force with a solid beach head. At the time everyone had believed Hakeem was a fool.

Only in retrospect had it worked out well when the Hun attacked. Was this just luck? She asked him about it.

"It's a very long story. I will tell you, but not while we are travelling." He smiled.

If Hakeem was worried about calmly walking their horses when the whole region was hunting her, he showed no sign of it. They were wandering along a small country road with meadows on either side and finally Kynane could no longer contain her curiosity and nudged her horse closer.

"Lord?" she whispered respectfully.

"Just Hakeem to you, Kynane," he murmured.

"Yes, Master," she replied with a small teasing smile. "I thought we were travelling in secret."

Hakeem looked at her. "We are."

"But," Kynane sputtered, "here we are ambling along in the open, exposed to any unfriendly eyes there might be around!"

"Just you and me, Kynane; we have four others making sure no one takes undue interest in us. I doubt you can see her and for the God's sake don't look now, but Alba is hidden behind that stand of trees in front and to the right. Eirene was in sight just a minute ago on the ridge on the left. I sometimes suspect Anastasia is half-elf, but anyway she and Thaïs are ranging further ahead. In a way, you and I are the bait. But in truth, I don't expect even a spy who sees us will think much of it."

"What would you do if you are discovered?" Kynane asked.

"Then we will see. We can run, hide or fight." Hakeem chuckled.

Kynane looked at him, perplexed.

"You could have taken all this land and yet you didn't."

He spoke patiently. "Kynane, you have asked this before. I told you it was a long story and there is much in the telling. I *will* tell you, I promise, just not here and not now."

"Yes, Master. I apologise, Master," Kynane said humbly.

"Kynane, please don't call me that! You are a princess of both Illyria and Makedonía! I was a peasant and an orphan." He paused. "Frankly, I didn't know what to do when you pledged your allegiance. I was overwhelmed."

Kynane had noticed his hesitation at the time but didn't know why. She thought for a moment he would refuse.

"Please just call me Hakeem," he continued. "I am still the Warlord of the Shantawi, which doesn't really mean a lot in a time of peace. Around here I am only a modest noble in my own right."

"Yes, Lord," Kynane said with the ghost of a smile.

Hakeem made a strangled noise.

"We are in danger yet you put us in plain view. Why don't we hide, Lord?"

"Think, Kynane!" Hakeem looked at her earnestly. "The best place to hide something is in plain sight! We are not a war band. We are a man and his wife going about our lawful business without a care in the world. If we were slinking around in the shadows, then it would look suspicious."

Kynane blushed, "could you think of me as your wife, Hakeem?"

Hakeem sighed, "I meant that as an example, but I'll not lie to you. Second only to Elana you are the most attractive and fascinating woman I have ever met."

"What makes you say that, Hakeem?" Kynane murmured.

Yes please! Tell me more!

"Why, you are in your own right an accomplished warrior! You have a very sharp mind. I don't know anyone I have ever found it easier to talk to."

Kynane pretended outrage. "Those are the qualities you might find in a man! Is that how you think of me, Hakeem? Don't you even notice I'm a woman? I admit I'm not pretty, like some tiny maiden."

Hakeem laughed, "There is no doubt at all that you are a woman! Pretty is not the word, perhaps ... can a woman be described as handsome? You are magnificent! If I had never met Elana I would be proud and happy if you agreed to be my wife," he finished with feeling.

Kynane felt breathless as she stared into his smile and felt his closeness.

"I don't think I will ever marry again," he said sadly. For a fleeting moment Hakeem's face was a mask of pain. "Something is dead inside me."

He shook himself as if to banish a painful memory.

"Kynane," he added, "I am proud and happy that you are joining us. You will be a great boon to the training of the sisterhood. After that, I will introduce you to the leaders of Troia. I have no doubt you will be flooded with marriage proposals till you can't even move! You will find a man worthy of even one such as you. I would be very proud to stand as your family in any negotiation should you ask."

Kynane nodded, but she turned away. It was as if he had stabbed her in the heart.

"That is not needed," she whispered faintly to herself. "I already have found someone, but how can I compete with a dead woman?"

* * *

They had been travelling for three days.

Kynane never uttered a word of complaint, but despite the easy pace they were making, she grew more and more exhausted. At the end of each day she was grey with fatigue and ached all over. She couldn't understand it! She should be able to ride hard all day and still be ready to fight! Admittedly, she had been injured — her leg and arm were still giving her some trouble — but why was she so tired?

Hakeem watched her with concern. They were a day's ride from the start of a mountain trail but at this rate Kynane would never make it over the mountains. He reluctantly decided to change their route; it would leave them in danger longer, but he had little choice.

"About time!" hissed Eirene angrily.

Hakeem had once used the healing power of the paladin to heal her from a serious wound and she well knew the months of crippling fatigue that followed. "The poor girl never complains, but is about to collapse every night! Unless she gets some rest soon, it will take forever to regain her strength, if she ever does! You should never have taken her on a journey so soon! But where can we go now?"

Hakeem didn't like the answer. He had met Omphale at the start of his first campaign in Bithynia. The Makedónes had burnt her village, slaughtered her family and taken her and the few survivors as slaves. At that time, Hakeem had taught the invaders the start of what became a series of bitter lessons. The last thing he wanted to do was to bring his troubles on to her, but what choice was there?

"I know a place."

* * *

Hakeem's scouts had warned Omphale of Hakeem's approach, but it was almost night time when Hakeem led his and Kynane's horse towards the small collection of huts. Kynane had already collapsed.

Outside he was met by Omphale. "So, you bring that devil spawn here?"

But she cried out when she saw Kynane pale and unconscious, slumped over her horse. "What have you done to her, you great big brute? Quickly, bring her in and lay her on my bed."

Kynane didn't even wake as he carried her in. Hakeem looked at her as he laid her down. His forehead was furrowed with concern.

There was only one room in the hut, so Hakeem kept his voice low. "I shouldn't have made her travel so soon; she was almost killed by her family, but there was little choice."

Then he hugged Omphale, and kissed her cheek.

He held her back to inspect her.

"Lady, you are more beautiful every time I see you!"

Omphale punched his chest affectionately. "Liar!"

She was not old, but life had aged her before her time.

"The grief has not left me, I don't think it ever will, but it has eased. I didn't think I would ever say it again, but I am content. Many of the young ones treat me as their own mother with their parents killed, and they are starting to get married and have their own babies." She paused. "You never came back after Elana and Jacinta died."

Hakeem looked away for a few moments, his body stiff with pain. When he looked back, she was shocked to see tears running down the big man's cheeks.

"Omphale, how did you ever keep going? How can I keep going?"

"Hakeem, you put one foot in front of the other, you breathe in and out. And then you do it again and then again." Omphale put her hand on his shoulder.

Hakeem had always been so strong. As a warrior he sometimes seemed cold, but that had never fooled her.

"I love those around me, I must do," Hakeem said. "I would move heaven and earth for them. It's just that I can't *feel* it. I can't feel any joy in living. I feel like I am an actor. Sometimes it makes me feel guilty. People give me their love and it feels as if all I do is *act* for them in return."

"You don't sleep well, do you?"

Hakeem shook his head. "I exercise and mediate and I try to spend time out of doors. I don't drink any more. Asha, that's Jacinta's cousin, would beat me otherwise." He smiled a little. "But no, I don't sleep well."

"It was like this for me for a long time. My heart felt frozen."

"Omphale," he said in a husky worried voice, "I never wanted to bring danger to your people by bringing Kynane here."

"Hakeem! Are you really such a fool? You rescued us and without your help in those early years I don't know how any of us would have survived. Now just shut up and let an old friend repay just a little of what you have given her! It seems for a change, you need someone else's help!"

"I can be a fool, I well know it." Hakeem chuckled, "And yes, I find it hard to ask. Can you hide her for a few days till she recovers? She would be less conspicuous in a dress and a scarf. Have you any spare clothes you can lend her?"

"Do you really think she would fit one of my dresses?" Omphale laughed, "Don't worry! I can make some clothes."

"Can I give you some money?"

"Hakeem, you will really make me angry in a minute! But knowing how you worry, I'll be honest. We are doing well enough. The Hun showed little interest in us and we hide a lot from the Makedóne tax collectors."

Then she asked him the question that everyone asked.

"Hakeem, how could you make peace with them? For a long time we were so angry with you. We felt betrayed. But now many of us are unsure. Much as we hate him, Parmenion is an able ruler. His taxes are not bleeding us and his officials are passingly honest. He has truly laboured to repair all the damage we suffered and to keep order. And now prosperity is returning."

Hakeem smiled. "We need Aléxandros here in case the Hun come back."

Omphale looked sobered by the prospect.

"But when I met you, you seemed to be hiding such rage, how could you not kill them all?"

"The Makedónes were killing, raping and stealing. *Of course I was angry!*"

"I don't think Aléxandros has given up on Anatolē. You must know that."

"Maybe, though I think he is more honourable than his father in keeping truces, and he has more than enough to amuse himself with for the moment. If Jizhu gets his empire in order, he might be back. And while Æloðulf is dead, Gansükh is not, and we don't have Jacinta this time."

"How could we possibly survive something like Gansükh bringing more daimôns back into the world?" Omphale whispered. She looked out of her window involuntarily; the dark outside seemed filled with menace.

"I don't think we could. It almost finished us the first time," Hakeem admitted, and then he sighed. "Parmenion is ruling well. He can protect you better than I can."

* * *

Kynane woke, screaming.

"Lady, you are safe," a kindly woman said, smiling in the faint light from the embers of the cooking fire. "My name is Omphale. I will heat you some broth if you wait."

Kynane looked around. She didn't recognise where she was.

"You're Karian, aren't you? My name is Kynane."

Omphale nodded. "I well know your name, Princess! Your family is not popular around these parts, so I suggest you don't use that name again."

Kynane smiled ruefully. "I am no longer a princess except in name. My family have been busy trying to kill me."

Omphale chuckled, "Well, perhaps there may be a chance for us to be friends after all."

"Where is Hakeem? Are we still in Bithynia?" Kynane asked.

Omphale nodded. "We are in Bithynia, and yes, you are still in great danger. I don't know where the Warlord or his scouts are. They will be watching this place, but from afar. In the meantime you are to rest."

"I could have kept going!" Kynane said in disgust. "There was no need to stop!"

"Of course, Princess. When you first came, I noticed you were so full of energy! It was likely boredom that made you sleep a full day around. This is the second night since you came."

Kynane smiled ruefully. "I suppose I sound foolish to you. They have done so much for me and my body is betraying me, I don't know why. They should be losing patience by now!"

"I don't suppose Hakeem got around to telling you this is a side-effect of the healing he did. As you were close to death it will take months to wear off!"

"So that's it!" Kynane laughed and shook her head in exasperation. "And here I was getting angry with myself! He should have told me!"

"He should have. Hakeem can be just as frustrating as most men I have ever known." Omphale chuckled.

Kynane's face fell. "He is so sad, isn't he?"

"You are in love with him."

"Is it that obvious?" Her eyes teared slightly.

"Probably to everyone but Hakeem. I doubt if you are the first among his women who wished more from him. But I saw how he looked at you while you were sleeping."

"He says he can't love again."

"The man's a complete fool. Good luck, Princess, for all our sakes as well as yours. We need Hakeem. I will pray to his God whom I call Apollōn, to open his eyes."

"Thank you, Omphale." Kynane smiled shyly.

* * *

After her visit to Omphale's village, Kynane felt better, and once she knew the cause of her weakness, she no longer pushed herself beyond her limits.

Now they were making almost a direct line for Mysian Ólympos. On the second day they came upon Lake Askanios. As they topped a rise, the great lake was laid out before them. Kynane's eyes widened at the sight.

"Oh, Hakeem! Can we just stop for a little while, please? It's so beautiful!"

She jumped down from her horse and took a deep breath as if to breathe in the freshness of it all. Hakeem joined her, smiling. Kynane recognised wild hibiscus, laurel and chestnut trees. Scattered around were pines and other shrubs. Down the hill was a well-tended orange orchard and further below someone had a grove of cherries.

Then came the lake: reflecting the light blue sky. There were only a few white clouds drifting up above and they were mirrored on the clear blue water with the mountain range standing behind the lake like its guardian. Dominating all was the mountain the Greeks called the Mysian Ólympos after its more famous cousin from their homeland.

It could be seen clearly: tall, proud and snow topped, reflected in the water.

The mixture of colours —white clouds, white snow, blue water and sky, dark green pine and shrubs and the lighter green of the laurel and the colours of the orchards — was enough to take her breath away, almost as much as the closeness to the man by her side.

"This region was originally called after Skythians, 'Ashkuza' in the local tongue," Hakeem murmured. "You Greeks mangled it to 'Askanios'."

"Hakeem! You can hardly call me Greek!" Kynane laughed. "I am half Illyrian and half Makedóne."

Hakeem smiled back at her. She was so lovely when she laughed. They mounted again and walked their horses on, to the east of the great lake.

After two turns of the glass, Hakeem called for her to halt.

"Don't move and don't touch your weapons," he warned her.

Nothing happened for a little while.

"How long do we have to wait?" Hakeem called out loudly to the bushes.

Four men emerged from the trees. They were Greeks.

"You know, Hakeem," said their leader with a broad grin. "One day, I'll be able to sneak up on you!"

"Is that why you have left the rest of your men in hiding, Nikolaos?" Hakeem laughed back at him. "But you are getting much better. I know there must be five hidden but I can only see one." He turned to Kynane. "This is a scouting patrol from Helicore. Today we are honoured. They are led by one of their commanders no less, probably to check their training."

Nikolaos raised his hand and the rest of his men emerged.

Hakeem raised his voice. "Time to join us, now!"

After moment Anastasia, Eirene, Alba and Thaïs led their horses out of the bushes from behind where the men had been concealed. The four women favoured the men with their sweetest smiles. Hakeem noticed a slight exaggeration in the way they swayed their hips as they walked.

Hakeem and Nikolaos completed the introductions, though Hakeem pointedly didn't introduce Kynane. The three youngest of the women were looking with frank appraisal at the men and they began to smile back.

Hakeem gave the Greeks a baleful glare. *You lot, keep away from my Amazónes!* He didn't want to start losing them to some loutish Greeks just as soon as they started to show promise.

The girls saw his scowl and looked amused.

"Hakeem," Nikolaos said politely, "am I permitted to know the name of this lady?"

He favoured Kynane with a charming smile.

"Her name is Kynane and she is sworn to me. She has agreed to help me train my Amazónes," Hakeem said.

"*The* Kynane?" Nikolaos was astounded.

Some of his men had placed their hands on the hilts of their swords. Hakeem's party made no move.

Then Nikolaos recovered. "Pardon any rudeness, Princess."

Kynane nodded and smiled politely, but waited on Hakeem's cue.

"The lady is under my protection."

Nikolaos looked unhappy. "It will be necessary to escort the princess to Helicore, Hakeem. You know that. I'm afraid my orders are very clear."

Hakeem's Amazónes snatched at arrows and fitted them as they moved away to give themselves a clear line of fire. They still pointed their bows downward. Kynane loosened her throwing axes in her belt. Alba made an apologetic face at the attractive young Greek man she had been eyeing.

Hakeem and Nikolaos made no move towards their weapons.

"Nikolaos," Hakeem smiled pleasantly, "I doubt if your superiors would be pleased if you killed the Warlord and five of his women just to arrest one of our number. Kynane has committed no crime against your prince. Officially there is a truce with the Makedónes, and if that were not so, she is no longer welcome in Makedonía, through no fault of her own. I mean you no discourtesy, but you are far too junior to arrest me, and you have no reason to arrest her. Send a message to your superior and loan me one of your men to escort me by the quickest way home."

Nikolaos thought for a minute, and then nodded.

"Anyway," Nikolaos said, "I expect it would have been these lovely ladies who would be reporting the demise of me and my men, not the other way around."

Chapter 6: Kynane in Love

Kynane was aware they were being tracked well before they reached Hakeem's house. Hakeem and the women ignored it. No one emerged to greet them.

More training, she realised.

As they drew closer, they started to move through well-tended fields and pasture. A number of the workers paused in their labour and yelled out a greeting, which Hakeem and the girls returned in good measure, calling out to many of them by name. They all looked happy and well fed, she noted with approval. Hakeem was a good land lord.

Then a team of excited children burst out from a nearby village like a horde of tiny barbarians.

The rest of Hakeem's party dismounted and waited, so she hopped off, wondering what was going on. Soon they were all leading two or three excited children perched on their horses. A short way on, Hakeem and the others lifted their little passengers down, kissing the girls and ruffling the boys' hair and giving them mock punches.

Hakeem would make a good father, she realised with a pang.

"As you can see, the children are terrified of their fearsome lord," Eirene remarked to Kynane.

The first glimpse of Hakeem's 'house' was impressive. It was a large but simple hill-fort, standing out from the surrounding plain. Surrounded on the summit by earth works — a newly completed mud brick wall had replaced the remains of a wooden palisade — it was not designed to withstand a serious siege, but for anything short of that, it would do well enough.

There was a proper road and entrance at the front and a narrow path at the rear, not much more than a foot path.

Hakeem saw her studying it. "Not as grand as you're used to I'm sure, but well organised and comfortable enough in parts."

"Hakeem, it's more than I expected!" Kynane smiled. "I would be happy never to see the inside of a palace again."

They were challenged at the entrance, very professionally, though Kynane noted the women did not carry swords, just bows and large belt knives. Once past the entrance, they were mobbed! It was complete chaos; mainly women.

Kynane remained on her horse, shy and uncertain, feeling a little overwhelmed by all the strangers. A Gypsy girl was shouting at the top of her voice for people not to bother Hakeem until he was settled. Hakeem took a few strides through the crowd to lift her off her feet and swing her around to hug and kiss her.

Kynane felt a stab of jealousy.

"That's Asha. She is a cousin to Jacinta." Eirene had appeared next to Kynane's horse. "Don't worry, she is betrothed to our stable master. Come down from your horse, Hakeem will be busy for a good while to come. I'll introduce you and find you somewhere to stay. No, they'll take the horses."

Kynane found herself in the middle of a small wedge made up of Eirene, Anastasia, Alba and Thaïs.

"The sisterhood's quarters are at the back. Hakeem rarely goes inside the women's quarters and we have a large weapons practice area near the orphanage."

"Orphanage?" Kynane asked.

"Some orphans sort of ended up here. We keep them healthy and train them. We have been finding relatives and foster families, so we only have twenty left. They are at lessons with Father Lazar, you'll meet him later."

"It sounds like this place runs itself!" Kynane said, a little breathlessly.

"We run it," Eirene admitted. "And we and Asha run Hakeem when he's here. Someone has to! I'll show you the baths in a minute and we will get you settled, but I just have to see people's faces when we introduce you! I hope you don't mind."

They strode past an archery range. Kynane could see the girls were excellent infantry archers and good at unarmed combat, but what about other weapons?

"Girls!" Anastasia announced loudly as she walked past. "Ladies!" She clapped her hands. "I have an introduction to make."

All the nearby women stopped what they were doing and assembled into a loose group, respectfully saluting the four seniors. More started to filter in from inside a nearby building and the ones that had greeted Hakeem were all drifting back.

Anastasia waited patiently till more of them and two more of the seniors came. The seniors could be distinguished by a leather glove on their left hand.

"This lady has agreed to join our senior teaching staff here. She is not part of our faith ... yet."

A lot of the women laughed as they looked at the stranger curiously. Father Lazar and Alba had a reputation for recruiting anyone who didn't already arrive as a Shayvist novice.

Anastasia paused for effect as the women all tried to get a glimpse at the large lady they were told would be teaching them. What they saw was impressive. There was no doubt that this woman carried herself as an experienced warrior, but who was she?

Anastasia held up her hand to still the growing murmur. "I will allow my country woman to introduce herself. There *may* be one or two of you who may have heard her name before." Kynane stepped forward and gave the assembled women a broad smile.

"My name is Kynane —"

That was as far as she got. There were cheers, squeals of delight and whistles. Soon everyone was talking and shouting at once as they mobbed her!

It was very pleasant to be greeted so warmly, but Kynane thought she would need to review the whole program. As scouts, these women would be a close match for a group of elves, but what about with other weapons? How good were they on horseback? And as pleasant as their enthusiasm was, some discipline wouldn't hurt!

(*I'm going to enjoy teaching these women!* she realised as they excitedly jostled her.) Her own training had been very isolating, often surrounded by men and boys. These women had a sense of community and belonging which she had never felt before.

* * *

It was almost a week later when Kynane asked to see Hakeem.

Hakeem managed to see her between a report on sheep breeding, another on the wheat harvest and another on a tract of land one of his retainers wanted him to buy. As Kynane was announced, he rubbed his eyes wearily. He was surprised when

Kynane was followed into the room by the eight senior sisters. He asked a servant to bring tea and forced himself to relax.

"Kynane, I'm sorry! I have hardly seen you since we arrived. I think I have just about caught up and can give you some of my time but in a fortnight I need to go to Karsh and I will be away for a few months. Have you had a chance to look at the training program?"

"Hakeem," Kynane asked looking straight at him. "How serious are you in asking me to help with the training program?"

Hakeem laughed self-consciously, "That bad, huh?"

"Hakeem," Kynane began kindly. "What you have taught is excellent, I've never seen the like of the women for bow skills, woodscraft and unarmed combat. The seniors are fair peltastae. But none have any blade skills worth mentioning. Most can ride a horse but none can fight on one. Discipline is poor and there is no proper command structure. You simply have never taken a firm hand. They may obey *you* but they give the rest of the seniors here a lot of back chat! And we need to think about our seniors beyond being trained and training others. There are not nearly enough opportunities for those who don't want to become full time female warriors."

The other seniors looked uncomfortable, but waited.

"If you want me to help, the only way I can do it is to take over completely and re-organise the whole program. *I* will be in charge and when you help, you will answer to me in all aspects of the women's training."

Kynane waited for the explosion and drew a big breath, ready to shout back.

"I agree."

What? Kynane looked at him in amazement.

"Thank you, Kynane," Hakeem said. "Eirene here tried her best to keep the Amazónes together after Jacinta's death. I have given what I could but I never offered to take over. I want it to be run by women. And unless something major changes it will never be what it could be."

He looked at the other women. "It seems you have the agreement of the others. Let me know what you need in extra weapons and horses. I have a fair bit here, but let Asha know how much you need. I can't buy you elvish swords, but order the best human blades we can afford. I won't have any rubbish coming through my doors. How long will it take you to give me a list of what you need?"

The women relaxed. They had dreaded the confrontation with Hakeem.

Hakeem asked Kynane to stay sitting after the others left.

"Thank you, Hakeem." Kynane smiled. "I was worried you would be angry."

Hakeem laughed softly and walked around to sit on the desk just in front of her chair.

"Why, because you spoke the truth?" He bent forward and took her shoulders and looked deeply into her face. "I am glad to have you. I can't be everything to everyone."

As he looked at Kynane smiling back at him, he felt his breath catch. Without any conscious will his face moved towards hers and they were drawn into a kiss. His arms pulled her up into an embrace. Suddenly he came back to himself and pushed her away. Kynane clung to him; she was surprisingly strong and she grabbed him for another kiss before he could disentangle himself.

"Hakeem!" Kynane whispered urgently. "We both want this!"

"Kynane!" Hakeem replied in anguish. "What am I doing to you? You deserve far more than I can give!"

"Hakeem, I will take whatever you can give me. It's you I love! And you love me too, I know you do."

"I'm sorry, Kynane, I have to ..." Hakeem turned and hurried away, his face averted.

Kynane ground her teeth in frustration and then decided to go to the training yard for a workout. A very hard one!

* * *

Hakeem had gone to Asha in a panic, needing to talk to someone. Instead she was giving him a solid dressing down. "You are such an arrogant pig! You are breaking that girl's heart!"

"I can't give her what she deserves."

"Have you asked *her* opinion on that? There are two people involved in this, you know!"

Fool of a man!

While Hakeem was enduring a tongue lashing, his seniors had gone in search of Kynane.

"What happened?" asked Anastasia, watching Kynane doing an exhausting sword drill she should be avoiding at this time in her recovery.

"He kissed me!" Kynane said in disgust. "He admitted he loved me."

"And?" Alba asked.

"And then he went all noble and said I deserved better, and then he ran away!" Kynane said through gritted teeth.

"Stop exercising!" Eirene commanded. "We need to think."

Just then Asha came hurrying up.

"That man!" she almost spat in disgust. "If I was a warrior, I would be tempted to kill him myself I think."

"How is he?" Kynane asked anxiously.

"I think I have softened him up a bit. He is guilty because he is in love with you. He is guilty he can't give you what you deserve. He is guilty for falling in love after he has lost Elana and now I have made him feel guilty for rejecting you!"

"Oh, poor Hakeem!" Kynane sighed.

"Poor Hakeem, nothing!" Asha countered. "The man's a complete idiot. I had to put up with him after Elana and Jacinta were killed. Now he wants to throw away not only his happiness but yours as well! You have to do something quickly before he talks himself into hardening his stupid attitude. It requires extreme measures, I'm sorry. There is only one thing you can do.

"First, you are still not recovered so we will get you to rest. It's going to be a long night ... at least I hope so. Then we need to bathe you and perfume you and do your hair. Do you have a nice night dress?"

The other women were looking excited. Kynane felt hot in the face.

"I can't do something like that! That's not, er. That's not ..."

"That's not ... nonsense," Asha said briskly. "I know Hakeem. It's tonight or 'kiss' your chances goodbye."

It wasn't true at all, but no one wanted to cope with a lovesick Hakeem over weeks and maybe months to come.

Kynane could hardly sleep waiting for the night to come! She dozed a little and at least got up feeling rested. It was very late when she was offered some food, but she could hardly eat. Someone had found some aromatic soap, and after a bath the girls gave her a massage with scented oil and then brushed and curled her hair. It felt very good and calmed her.

Asha poked her nose round the corner. "He's in bed, but will read for a while. It's important he is asleep and you wake him. Don't startle him awake if you don't want him putting a sword through you!"

The other girls got a severe case of the giggles. Apparently the thought of Hakeem killing Kynane, as she was trying to sneak into his bed, was hilarious.

Very funny! How did I ever agree to this?

Then they dressed her in some thin, red silk night dress that someone had quickly sewn.

"You look lovely in this! But if this works, he may not even notice what you're wearing!" Alba giggled.

Kynane moaned to herself, as they escorted her back to the section containing Hakeem's quarters. She was terrified, as she had never been terrified in battle. Her heart was hammering and her knees felt weak.

"Hakeem, it's me," Kynane whispered.

Hakeem was dreaming of Kynane.

"Kynane?" he queried groggily, coming out of his dream.

Kynane was standing by his bed in the moonlight.

Her gown dropped at her feet and she stepped forward.

Hakeem woke up completely. He gasped; her body was glorious.

"Move over," Kynane commanded nervously.

Hakeem hesitated.

"Are you going to let me in?" Kynane asked, feeling close to tears.

Hakeem jumped back to make room for her. He kissed her hungrily on the lips as she lay down in his arms. She melted into the kiss.

"Kynane, I love you," he whispered softly.

"This is my first time," she whispered, feeling frightened.

"Seducing a man?" Hakeem enquired.

"No!" Kynane gave him what she planned to be a playful punch, but it hit him with a hard thud.

Hakeem grunted. *Oh, no! I've hurt him!*

"You are my first ... ever."

She felt embarrassed and nervous. She was a woman twenty years old and still a virgin.

Hakeem moved back on his elbow and wordlessly kissed her gently on the forehead. His hand massaged her shoulder lightly.

"Do you like me? I'm not too big, am I?" she asked.

"Kynane," Hakeem said softly as he admired her body, "how can you be too big for me?"

He chuckled and Kynane giggled a little.

"You are perfect. Leandros has a statue of Athena naked, it is so beautiful." Hakeem murmured. "To me that is what you look like! Not Aphrodite, but definitely Athena!"

"You think I look like a Goddess?" Tears came to her eyes. "Really?"

Hakeem kissed her on the lips to get her to stop talking, and then pulled back, smiling.

Wordlessly he slid his hand over the muscles of her shoulder to feel skin and her female muscles. Then he slowly ran his hand down to her right breast. Kynane shivered at his light touch. He ran his hand over her abdominal muscles, appreciating their feel.

"Like a Goddess," he said softly.

Then he bent and kissed her breast. His beard was tickling ever so slightly.

His hand was rubbing gently over her stomach and then her hip and then moved to her mound and her inner thigh. Kynane gasped. He started to kiss lower while his hand kept teasing back and forward. Kynane felt her body tingling all over.

He moved so gently. There was no hurry.

She began to flush and pant, and as his fingers found her opening she began to arch back. As she became ready, she felt a mounting urge to have his manhood inside her. Hakeem gently pushed inside; there was a sharp pain, then it was gone. She felt him surging back and forward and she started to move with him. Then they surged together, stiffening in shared ecstasy.

Then she felt Hakeem relax on top of her.

"You're right," she smiled as she felt his weight. "I'm not too big for you. No, don't move!" She wrapped her arms and legs around him. "That was wonderful!" She kissed his neck and shoulder. "Why did we wait?"

Hakeem propped himself up on one elbow, his face inches from hers, and gave her a dreamy smile.

"Kynane," he murmured and wiped a strand of her hair back behind her ear, "I really have no idea, no idea at all."

Chapter 7: Genocide at Khumin

Her daughter, Leila, helped Esther serve the evening meal. It was the usual spiced lentil stew served with flat bread and cups of water.

Things had been hard since her husband had died. Her two sons were not men yet, so with that and the drought they didn't get paid much, but with both of them working now things were becoming better.

Dratha would be returning soon to help his uncle and cousins with their herds. Âthwya, the eldest, was the head of the house now that his father was killed in the wars.

He was apprenticed to the local potter. It wasn't a lot of money but he could stay home to look after her and Leila with Dratha away.

Âthwya and Dratha at eighteen and seventeen were good boys. And Leila, named after her pretty dark hair, was a sweet tempered and loving sixteen-year-old. She was a willing helper with the house and the few crops and animals they had.

Esther was not alone in struggling to make ends meet. A lot of women in the village of Khumin were widows now, and she was better off than some. She had two big strong sons and a lovely daughter.

She was so very proud of them. It was such a shame their father was not alive to see how well their children had turned out. He would have been proud of them, too.

The people of Khumin were *Pahlavi* (Parthian), famous as warriors. It was a tradition for the men to join the Šâh's standing army. They even had their own *hazarabam* (regiment).

When the Šâh went to fight the Hun, many extra men from the village went to help. Only a few had returned.

Esther and Leila sat to join the boys. No, she reminded herself, they were men now.

Âthwya as the head of the house bowed his head to bless the food. *"In the name of God, bestower of all good things, the generous spirited, and loving. Here we revere Ahura Mazda who created the animals and grains, who created waters, and plants who created lights of the sky and the earth and all good things."*

As Âthwya finished, Dratha's dog stood.

His dog was the type favoured by local shepherds: large and muscular, sandy coloured with a black face,. The hairs on his back were raised and he emitted a low throaty growl.

"What's wrong with your dog?" She asked Dratha.

Outside their house, other dogs begun to bark.

Their dog was began barking furiously. That was unheard of, his breed either herded or guarded. When it guarded it maybe growled but didn't bark, not like this. That would only scare the sheep.

Something was very wrong.

All the dogs in the village seemed to be barking now.

Dratha leapt to his feet. Ignoring the dog, he rushed to the window and after a quick look he turned to the kitchen bench. He grabbed her kitchen knife and the goatskin he used for water when he was herding. He pressed them both into her hands. Then he ran to their nearby bedding and grabbed the blanket.

"Mother, take Leila quickly! Hide in the desert!"

His older brother, Âthwya, looked at him in confusion and then his face transformed into an expression of utter dread. He too paused by the window and without a word ran to the box where his father's old sword was kept. Dratha had begun digging through their box of tools. He pulled out a machete and felt its edge. It was kept sharp and he nodded to himself.

Esther stood, clutching what she had been given.

"What is happening?"

"JUST GO!" Âthwya and Dratha screamed together.

"Mother, go quickly." Dratha finished. "Don't take anything else with you. The village is under attack."

Under attack? With her heart pounding, her breath coming fast, she stumbled out of her house. Leila ran after her, a sack of flour and another kitchen knife in her hands. A quarter moon cast a little light.

On the northern road to the village a large number of men were approaching, carrying torches and clubs and other weapons.

Some of them were beating drums and singing as they marched on the village. It was as if it were a party for them!

Those that had reached the edge of the village began banging on doors and shouting for the villagers to come out, calling them dogs. They are Sogdianē. What has gotten into them? They are our neighbours! A handful of villagers were in the street, the rest were hiding in their houses.

"Should we take the dog?" Leila asked.

The Sogdianē men were coming closer. They had a hand held ram made from a log reinforced by metal bands and carried by four men. They bashed in one of the doors and a group of waiting men rushed in to drag a family out, screaming and struggling into the streets. Then they began beating at them with clubs and swinging at them with machetes and swords.

"No, he will give us away."

Heart racing, breath coming fast, she caught at her daughter's arm and pulled.

"Children!" One of the men screamed. "Kill the children! Remove this infestation from its roots."

The devils!

Children were easier to kill. They didn't run fast or fight back or hide well. Many clung to their parents or cried so they were easy to find and a few good blows would finish their little bodies. If you want to exterminate a people, target the children.

Is that what was happening? Is this an extermination?

Mothers with small children would be the next easiest. There were a lot of them with their men dead — and then pregnant women, of course.

She saw a Sogdianē man open the stomach of a woman heavy with child to let her dying eyes watch as he bashed her unborn baby against a rock.

Esther felt cold all over and sick to her very soul. She turned her back on the terrible slaughter of her fellow villagers.

"Follow me," she said to her daughter.

To the side of their village was a dry culvert.

But their neighbours had visited the village at a time that they were called friends. Esther and her daughter didn't even reach it before a figure loomed out of the darkness and clubbed at Esther.

"Well done, son!" a satisfied voice called.

Leila recognised the voice. It was the father of a Sogdianē boy she had liked.

"Dahâka?" she called out. "It's me, Leila, please don't hurt me. Everything has gone crazy."

"Leila!" Dahâka called out. "Father, it's Leila!"

"Just another Pahlavi bitch." His father snarled, looming over her, with his sword raised.

"No!" Dahâka screamed at his father.

It was the last thing Leila ever heard.

* * *

Esther opened her eyes. She could still hear men shouting with joy, and the agonised cries of the wounded and dying. There was the flickering light of flames and the smell of smoke in the air; some of the thatched roofs were burning fiercely.

She felt weight on top of her. She was under a pile of dead bodies; their blood and fluids and manure were all over her. Her head felt as if it was splitting. A moan escaped her lips.

"Shh!" a voice whispered out of the darkness nearby. It was Dahâka, Leila's friend. "They are looking for survivors. I think they will leave soon. Sorry I hit you."

Dahâka had never understood why his father and two older brothers hated the Pahlavi, but then they hated many things. They didn't like him much either. He was the youngest and they said he was soft, just like his mother.

When he used to go to Khumin, people had been friendly to him and he had liked going there. He had eaten in their homes and he had many Pahlavi friends. He especially liked Leila with her shiny black hair, her ready smile and her hazel eyes. She was a year older but she seemed to like him and sometimes he dreamt of her.

His father was furious when he found out he liked a Pahlavi girl. He forbade him to go there again. So it became harder to get away from his father and brothers.

They were big men and he was scared of them. They told him what to think and they stood over him and threatened him. They told him he was stupid and weak, but he was only young, he wasn't even sixteen yet. Only lately had he started to fill out.

Things were hard in his village. No one much had money. Many had no work and seemed sad, but there was a lot of anger underneath. That's when Erezav, his brother's friend, began stirring up trouble. The Pahlavi were doing better, he said. But many had been in the army and had herds; he didn't say that was the reason.

He said the Pahlavi land really belonged to the Sogdianē people. Maybe that was true, the Pahlavi had come from Aryānā a long time ago, but many people here were nomads. Who was to say a land with nomads was owned or occupied?

Then he said that their flocks and houses and everything they had belonged to the Sogdianē people. He said it was time to get rid of the Pahlavi and take back what was rightfully theirs. He said the Šâh had protected them and now it was their chance.

People seemed to forget the Pahlavi were their friends.

Dahâka was scared by the shouting and angry voices; it was like his family all over again. He didn't want to go on the raid but his father and brothers made sure he didn't slip away. They looked at him straight in the face and asked if he was a coward. He said he would come, and then they seemed happy.

For a while, everyone else seemed happy too, banging drums and singing. At first he had enjoyed marching with the men and feeling accepted. But as they came closer to Khumin he became afraid again — afraid of what would happen when they got there.

His father told him to stand in the dark and hit anyone who came from the village, and he never disobeyed his father. But it had been Leila's mother. Leila's family was nicer to him than his own family.

"Leila?" Esther asked.

"One of the men killed her, I'm sorry."

His father had left to kill more people. When Dahâka had found that Leila's mother was still breathing, he had hidden her under her daughter's body and the body of another woman.

"My sons?"

"I haven't seen them, but they killed your dog, I'm sorry. Now keep quiet."

His hand stretched under the bodies and squeezed her hand and put the goatskin of water in her hand.

"They are poisoning the wells by dumping bodies in them."

Then he walked back to join the other men. Erezav was there, looking feverish with excitement.

A few were avoiding looking at one another, looking guilty and frightened now they were no longer carried along in the moment. The people all around were *Behdin* (Zoroastrians). What would happen now when they faced judgement after they died?

Most didn't care though. They were too busy getting carts and loading them up, gathering any nearby goats and donkeys, and ransacking any houses that were not set on fire. Some were still laughing and rejoicing and calling out to one another. Doing this had made some of them feel brave and strong.

"If you want your share, you'll have to get it yourself," his eldest brother called out.

With a dreadful sinking feeling he realised he would have to leave his home and his village. He never wanted to look into his father's face or the faces of his brothers again. He didn't want to see *any* of these people from his village again.

He was only young, so he would need money and supplies.

He started to go into one house before he realised it had belonged to Leila's family. He changed direction and decided to search the house next door. In his mind he could see the face of the widow that had used to live there. He was now going to add theft to his other crimes, but he desperately needed to get away.

He hoped his God would forgive him.

* * *

It was after the midday break and they were back travelling when Jess sat up, alert.

"*Vaysâ (stop)!*" she yelled.

She pulled back on her camel reins and held one hand up to signal to the others. Then she stood high in the saddle and scanned the horizon.

"Pandora, tell them I can smell smoke!"

She grabbed for her bow and quickly strung it.

"Is she sure?" Teispes, the leader of their escort, asked, struggling with his restive horse. "There is a village not too far ahead."

Jess grunted and pointed; they couldn't see the village yet but in the far distance, high in the air, they could see tiny black specks, birds circling.

Jess removed the camel's bells and slipped the rope joining her camel to Pandora's and tossed them both to one of the men.

"Pandora, you stay here."

With a meaningful glance to Teispes, she nudged her camel forward. Teispes looked like he was about to protest, but one look from Jess silenced him.

He nodded to Zavan to follow them.

Jess tapped her camel to speed it up. It made a jerky rocking gait but Jess showed no sign of discomfort. Her bow was ready; her eyes were restlessly scanning the terrain. The two horsemen followed close behind.

Pandora dismounted to sit in the shade while one of the men climbed a nearby hill to keep watch. She didn't mean to fall asleep but she was still bruised and exhausted from camel riding. She was woken by the lookout calling down that they were returning. The afternoon shadows were already lengthening.

Jess was walking her camel slowly back. The two men were trailing far behind her. As Jess rode in, she didn't say anything at all, she just made a fire form the wood one of the men had gathered and got ready to cook.

The men talked quietly amongst themselves. Teispes moved to sit on the edge of their camp and Zavan went to join him for a while, mostly sitting in silence. Finally Zavan murmured something and climbed the hill to relieve the lookout.

Pandora didn't immediately get to find out what was going on. She felt ashamed of not being more help so she hurried to help with the camp.

Jess finally called her over. "See if Teispes wants some tea."

"Jess, what happened? No one will say."

Jess sighed; she didn't look up. "The village was called Khumin. It was a *Pahlavi* (Parthian) village. Most of the villages around here are Sogdianē. The Pahlavi came from Aryānā long ago, raiding. The people around here have long memories."

"You mean after all this war," Pandora had a sick feeling in her stomach, she could feel her chest tighten and her heart beat heavily, "that this was a fight between rival tribes? Haven't they had enough with killing?"

"I wouldn't call it a fight. It was murder, plain and simple." Jess looked at her, her eyes bleak. "The men from Khumin were loyal to the Šâh, he would have protected them. They sent many men to help him fight against the Hun, and they lost, lost badly. With the Šâh dead their neighbours decided it was time to settle old scores. Teispes was the one who followed me into the village."

She poured tea into a cup and passed it to Pandora.

"I have a little wine. I will give it to him later."

Teispes was sitting alone, just staring out over the desert, as the last of the light was fading. He looked up as Pandora approached and she was shocked to see he had been crying. He began to talk as soon as she approached, so she sat down next to him. At first she had to strain to hear what he said.

"I knew your mistress was far more than she seemed. I have heard of women warriors, of course I have, but I didn't know she was one. When I saw her take four arrows in her bow hand for rapid fire, how she rode her camel and how she had trained it, then I knew.

"When we were closer to the village she made us slow. She led me and Zavan off the road to circle around behind a hill to scout out the village from under cover. But we knew what we were likely to find, we could see all the vultures and black carrion birds circling. Whatever had happened had happened days ago; the fires had burnt out.

"Your mistress can't speak a lot of Sogdianē but she said it didn't make sense to her, and I could see why. The Hun might do it to punish a village but there was no reason for them to do that here. They had already won the war.

"But it wasn't the Hun." He shuddered as he remembered the horror of it. "It was their friends and neighbours. It was my people." He held the cup in his hand but he didn't drink from it.

"It was an extermination. Zavan pointed to one of the buildings but we had both seen it already. Out from the village there was a small shop for travellers, really a single room and a veranda. Someone had only just repaired its roof with fresh green palm branches after the fires. Jess was the only one of us with a bow so we rode back to the road and I went ahead, yelling out loudly so they didn't shoot at me. I could hardly hear anything even when I wasn't yelling, my heart was beating so loudly."

He paused for a moment.

"It used to be a village of several hundreds but all we found standing were three men armed with machetes and a woman. They were caring for over a score of injured. Your mistress unloaded all the barley she had and we gave what we could and then she attended to their wounded."

"I didn't know she could do that," Pandora said.

"Well, she can. She knew what she was doing alright. She washed their wounds with water and a little salt," he went on. "The worst that were infected she carefully packed with honey and bandages, they had plenty of honey. The ones with clean wounds, where she could, she stitched with thread soaked in strong vinegar.

"They had been beaten and hacked with machetes. Many had terrible injuries. No few were dying. I don't know how she could stand even looking at them. It was horrible. But she still tried to help each one, even the ones for whom she could do little, still she tried.

"One of the survivors was a little boy, not much more than a baby really. He asked if we had seen his parents but they weren't there. His sister was next to him; there wasn't a mark on her but she just lay there, staring. It made my flesh creep the way she just lay there and stared. They said she hadn't talked or eaten since the attack."

He paused. "That wasn't the worst. Your mistress told me to wait there with Zavan while she rode into the village to search for survivors. I said I would follow her." Teispes drew a shuddering breath. "Before God, I wish I hadn't. You know there was a time when I would have said I didn't like the Pahlavi. What I saw that day will stay with me forever.

"The birds were in great flocks and many of them took flight as we approached. We saw a family of hyenas when we were leaving and some rats but apart from that and the birds, there were no other sign of life. Oh, there were maggots of course, flies were everywhere and there was a terrible stench. I'm a herder; I can handle that sort of thing. Somehow it was the sight of so many bodies and how they lay that was the worst. There were just so many of them! Some were piled up, most were stiff ... so stiff and in such odd untidy positions. It's hard to explain, you would have had to be there to know."

He shook his head and turned to her. "There was too much food even for all those birds. Some of the bodies hadn't been touched. There was an old couple, just like my parents. He had been cut open and his guts had spilled out. She had been stripped naked and her throat cut." A tear ran down his cheek. "This was an old lady and they had cut her parts. I don't want to think what else —" He started to sob, hiding his face in his hands.

"And the children, so many dead children," He gasped as he turned back to her the tears glistening on his cheeks in the failing light. "Did you know that I am a father? There was a beautiful little girl, maybe six. It looked from a distance as if she were only asleep if it weren't for the blood. She was just like my little Adileh. How can I look upon my daughter's face now and not see that little girl?

"They wanted to remove the Pahlavi tribe from our land and they have done a monstrous thing; they have murdered the children.

"Another girl was there, maybe only twelve. They had cut her throat but her dress had been pulled up. SHE WAS ONLY TWELVE!" he shouted, his breath came quickly, his face was flushed with anger; his hands were balled into fists and tears were wetting his shirt.

"How can I come to this land and not remember? How can I see a Sogdianē man in a village nearby and not wonder in my head 'were you here?' How can I look in the face of a Pahlavi and not feel I have guilt I share written all over my face?

"IT WAS MY PEOPLE WHO HAVE DONE THIS!"

Then he quieted somewhat and wiped at his face. "I have seen the face of evil now, and it was a lot like my face. Each of us carries a 'thing' inside of us. Our *Khordad* (prophet) warned us about it, so long ago. He said we, all of us, are capable of doing terrible things when we are told to do them or when we let lust and hatred over power us.

"It is a choice. And he warned us that *Angra Mainyu* (the evil one) uses lies. Lies others tell us, and lies we tell ourselves. We cling to blindness so we can do these sorts of things."

Pandora placed her hand awkwardly on his shoulder.

"Your mistress told me to go out and wait outside for her. She seemed so cold. It was as if she didn't care, but I know that's not true. I don't think of myself as a coward, but I couldn't face any more, so I left and I waited while she walked back in to search that village of the dead. I heard her calling and calling and going from house to house, examining each body. It took a long time and she came back alone. All she said to me was, 'these people were different, but not by much. Is this what you people do to those who are different?'"

"What will happen now?" Pandora asked.

"It's not over; that woman's sons survived. Most people hereabouts don't live in villages, they live in the hills; many of the older ones have been in the army. They will know who the ringleaders are and they will know where they live. They will go after them and many others when they are not surrounded by a big crowd."

"So more killing."

"Yes, more killing, and it won't do any good, it will only feed the hatred, but I can't blame them. They had left or I would have gone with them, even against my own people.

"You women should not be travelling alone."

Jess came up behind them. "There is food if you wish."

Teispes shook his head.

Jess squatted down and clasped her hand on his shoulder. Wordlessly she passed him the wine, all she had, a full goatskin. He pulled the cork and sat for a while with it. Then he tipped it up to drink while Jess turned and walked back to the fire.

Chapter 8: Chandyr

Teispes and his men took them beyond the remaining villages and finally bid them farewell. Jess's fellow cook gave her a small bag of seasoning. One of the men made a small camel charm for Pandora from goat's hair, and made a big deal of giving it to her. It was to remind her of her time riding camels.

It was the third night after they had bid farewell to the men that the pair arrived at an open air caravanserai at the outskirts of Chandyr. Chandyr was a small oasis town on the overland route that ran south and west between the city of Bukhara and Parap, the great river port on the *Vaksu Daryā* (Oxos River).

The Oxos flowed north into the Aral Sea but by a marvellous feat of engineering, a great canal had been cut through the marshes of its delta to join the inland sea the Persis call the *Daryā-ye Khazar* (Kāspian Sea). The people of this land had been good with their canals, but now it would be their Hun masters who would collect the tolls.

Once in the Kāspian, they could no longer reach Elgard by boat. The elves had sunk boats to block the Mt'k'vari River to any boats coming from neighbouring Āzar Pāyegān. Still, if the girls reached Ateshi-Bagavan, the capital of Āzar Pāyegān, they could travel the highland country overland into Anatolē or if it had become safe they could go even go further north make for one of the northern Black Sea ports and take a boat to Troia.

Jess had a knack for languages and she could already make herself understood, but she left it to Pandora to arrange for the care of their camels and a small private stall for the two of them.

Jess wondered if there would be anything beyond chaste sleeping. Pandora had been badly chaffed. She had offered Jess one-sided love-making but that was something she adamantly refused.

Jess helped the men of the caravanserai to unload their camels and stow their gear, with the remaining barley, and then shouldered a small bag so they could explore the town together. Pandora couldn't help but wonder if Jess worried about the rest of her gold hidden somewhere in her luggage. If she was worried she gave no sign of it.

They found some soothing ointment and a Skythian hunting bow for Pandora. Then they followed the sound of hammering, metal on metal. Around the corner from the bow maker, there was an open weapon smith's workshop. One heavily muscled man, naked to the waist, was enthusiastically pumping a great bellows while another man who looked like his twin withdrew a glowing metal bar from a kiln and hammered it on an anvil.

Jess didn't know what was more fascinating: watching the tip of the metal red and yellow with heat being hammered, or watching the muscles working over the men's arms and chests and the sweat running down their bodies.

"A thousand greetings, noble ladies."

Jess turned around, still grinning from watching the sons, to greet their father. He looked just as big and strong, only greyer and not so sweaty.

"He's Persis," Pandora whispered in Greek.

What difference does that make?

"Men from the heart of Aryānā go in for a lot of complicated courtesy." Pandora explained. "Especially towards women, it can get a bit weird, especially if they like and respect you. After all, it is the greatest human civilisation the world has ever seen."

"I want a woman's fighting knife for my friend, and do you have anything better than this?" Jess turned back to the weapon smith and passed her belt knife over.

"How do you use it, great lady?"

"From the front," Jess showed him a standard sabre grip.

"From behind," she held her left hand up as if grabbing someone's chin and held her knife in an inverted reverse-grip across an imaginary throat. That caused him to raise his eyebrows.

"It is big for a woman," he said, considering.

He turned it over and looked down the blade. He felt the edge and balance and spring. Then he held it to his ear while lightly tapping it with a small metal rod. He looked her up and down and finally smiled in appreciation.

"This is a good knife." He took a deep breath. "I do not think any of my humble knives would be worthy of either one of you great ladies."

Jess got ready to leave.

"He's being polite!" Pandora hissed in Greek, pulling at her arm. "It's a compliment to *us* when he says his knives aren't worthy of us."

Jess looked back at her with utter confusion.

"You are too kind," Pandora replied quickly. "I'm sure it is *we* that will prove unworthy of your fine knives. Please show us your worst stock."

They were led to a clean part of the shop. He offered them seats that were of course unworthy for them to sit on while Pandora insisted the seats were far too good for them.

Then one of his sons brought a table and unwrapped his miserable offerings. It was a selection of some of the most gorgeous slender and well-crafted knives Jess had ever seen.

Jess passed over the short and highly decorated ones and chose a long rather plain one from the corner for Pandora.

"Any more of these?"

It had a slender symmetrical double-sided blade easily seven and a half inches long with a handle almost as long again. Pandora's eyes bulged as she saw it.

"My Lady knows her knives; that is the best of this type, but isn't it too plain for your lady friend?"

"It is perfect for a knife-against-knife or knife against someone not armed," Jess explained to Pandora. "The grip on the handle is excellent with a small guard to prevent your hand slipping forward as you stab. It is long and slender to penetrate clothing or leather armour *and* still slip in between ribs. I'll show you how to use it later."

Pandora realised she could draw the knife and warn someone off or bluff them, but if it ever came to using it she would be in a fight for her very life. She might be facing someone who knew how to use a knife in a fight, which she didn't. It was a sobering thought.

"You will need another knife to cut your meat," Jess added.

"Now could you please show me some heavy knives for myself, but bigger than what I have?"

"But you are a lady." He looked distressed. "Such knives are not for women."

Jess stared at him until he broke eye contact. Then she held out her right hand; the calluses were unmistakable. He looked at her in shock. "Please accept the apologies of your humble servant."

"I need a knife heavy enough to parry a sword. And I need a single blade for cutting," Jess explained, making a cutting motion. She turned to Pandora to explain. "A knife doesn't have the weight and leverage, so you can't hack with it like you do with a sword. You have to either stab or draw the blade across your enemy's flesh, a bit like cutting a steak."

"You can parry a thrust perhaps," the weapon smith commented as he gestured to his son to bring their heavier knives. "But trying to parry a sword slash is far too dangerous. You are better off investing in some light armour. Do you throw?"

"No," Jess said. "I do not throw."

The weapon maker nodded. He didn't like people throwing his knives.

Jess finally chose a heavy, single bladed sheath knife. It was longer even than the one she chose for Pandora.

It had a large guard, which was mostly straight but bent at the tips like a back-to-front and elongated 'S'. Jess carefully checked the grip to see if it fitted her hand and examined the wood, and then she grunted and smiled. "Ash?"

The weapon smith nodded with a smile for someone who could appreciate his craft so well. "Yes, and I only use heartwood."

"Let me show you," Jess offered to Pandora. "This is designed for a fight that might involve a sword." She smiled and nodded in acknowledgement to the weapon smith. "Not that you *want* to fight someone with a sword if all you have is a knife. It's much heavier, it has to be. It hasn't got a symmetrical two-sided blade like the knife I got for you or most short swords. There is a front and back.

"The first third of the back, called the spine is thick and blunt to give it strength." She traced her finger along it. "Then comes a short blade that recurves to the knife's point." She demonstrated. "The short blade at the back near the point is for penetration when stabbing but maybe you can do a back slash with it." She flicked her wrist to demonstrate. "Because this knife is heavier it can have a larger guard without having all its balance in the handle."

She moved on to examine the main cutting edge. She ran her finger along the bevel and then took an oiled cloth and carefully wiped the blade before putting it alongside the knife she had selected for Pandora.

"This is a fine knife." She gave the weapons master a look of appreciation. "And I do know how to parry a slash from a sword."

A chill went down his spine.

It was a little bit unexpected in a woman, especially one so young, but this black woman was a master of her art. She was not only a skilled warrior but her knowledge and the first knife she chose showed she was an assassin, the best he had ever met.

It was a privilege to serve her.

"How much do you want for this one?" she asked, pointing first to her knife.

"Your presence is already enough of an honour." He replied bowing very deeply.

"Huh?"

The man held out his hands disparagingly. "*Ghaabeli nadaare* (It has little worth)."

"Pandora, help me! He doesn't want any money for his knives!"

"Not really, but you must have really impressed him!" Pandora whispered. "He is not treating you as a customer, but as an honoured guest!"

"But how can I buy his knives?" Jess was grinding her teeth in frustration.

"In Aryānā it is called *t'aarof* (etiquette)," Pandora explained. "You have to keep insisting on paying him until he finally gives in."

Pandora turned to him. "*Khaahesh mikonam* (I plead with you). We are unworthy of your knives. They are princes amongst all other knives!"

After lots of denials and hedging, he finally nominated a figure. Jess started to pull a purse of silver from her belt. *Well, that's not too much.*

"Wait, Jess," Pandora said. "You have to insist on paying a fifth more. It has become a point of honour."

What?

Pandora finally got a fair price for both knives. Once he decided to treat her as a guest, the dealer would never charge too much anyway, but still the final price caused Pandora to raise her eyebrows. Jess assured her these were serious weapons but to Pandora they seemed rather plain.

Jess for her part felt exhausted by the process. She counted out several silver coins and passed them across. The man inspected each one carefully and even weighed them. Some of the coins from different regions were different weights to the local ones.

He offered her change.

"No thanks," Jess said.

"*Ghadamet ru chesham* (May your footsteps fall on my eyes)," he insisted.

Huh? What? Oh, he is saying he enjoys me visiting him, that's nice.

"Jess, you said that the wrong way," Pandora explained. "Now he thinks you want the change but are only being polite. Now you will have to take it under protest or he will be very offended."

"*Ghorbaanet beram* (I will sacrifice myself for you)," Pandora said on Jess's behalf.

Well, that's one way of saying we like him.

Finally she took the change she didn't want.

Then he seemed overjoyed and offered them tea.

"I would love a cup of tea." Jess breathed a sigh of relief.

"You must refuse it," Pandora advised.

"What?" Jess spluttered. "But I'm tired and I'm sick of all this t'aarof stuff and my throat is hoarse from trying to pay the man!"

"Then you must hesitate when you refuse, that way he knows you really want it. Give in when he offers it the third time."

Jess finally *allowed* his daughter to give her that cup of tea that she was so desperate for.

"Do these people really torture their guests with this?" she asked.

"Most certainly," Pandora said. "It gets even worse if you really are their guest and the closer you get to Aryānā. This is considered a barbaric kingdom compared to there."

How under the Gods could I survive in a place like that?

"I want a long sword but now I am too terrified to ask. He might refuse to take my money again."

Pandora explained her friend's wants, the weapon smith and her trying to outdo each other in professions of humility.

"Lady, I have something to show you because I think only a person like you could truly appreciate it, but I am embarrassed by how much I would have to ask for it," he said.

He disappeared out the back of his shop and returned, reverently bearing a leather scabbard decorated with bronze. He gave it a careful polish with an oil cloth and passed it to Jess.

"When I saw this, I had a moment of weakness. Now I can't sell it and my wife, blessed that I am to name her so, honours me all the time by nagging at me!"

Wordlessly Jess took the scabbard and the sword outside.

The blade was elvish! Somehow the handle had been lost or destroyed but a more than serviceable handle with a fine grip had been substituted. The blade was as new. It had a guard, like her knife.

As she drew the sword, her eyes glittered and a smile came over her face. She could not conceal her look of hunger. The balance, the weight, the length, everything was perfect for her!

She started to go through some routines. She drew her new knife left handed and started to use both: faster and faster. Her hands and the blades became a blur, the sword whistling as it sliced the air. All nearby stopped to watch her, then she stopped, panting a little.

"I'm out of practice!" she said, grinning broadly. "How much is this?"

The big man quoted a figure and walked over to retrieve the weapon. Jess held up her hand for him to stop. He had no idea what it was really worth!

"Jess, that price is ridiculous! It's more than three years of a tradesman's wages."

Jess turned to the owner. "I would be honoured to pay your price. Can I ask you to tell no one about this and can I take a shield of my choosing?"

He looked at her in shock and nodded.

"It is a fine sword!" he whispered.

"Yes, it is!" Jess said softly with a broad smile. She chose a sturdy shield and then carefully made a pile of gold coins. Her purse was noticeably lighter for once.

"I don't want to go through that again," Jess said, wiping the perspiration off her brow as they were walking away. "Though it was nice when he said on behalf of himself, his sons and his daughter, *Cheshmemoon ro roshan kardin* (You have lightened up our eyes). You are right, Pandora, men from Aryānā can be very civilised and courteous."

"Jess, you paid far too much for that sword!" Pandora complained loudly. "But I guess it's your money!"

"Dora, Dora! You're wrong on both accounts. This is an elvish blade, it would surprise you to hear how much this sword is really worth. And it's *our* money. I think it is about time I gave you some of your share."

"I don't want your money, Jess!"

"We are partners aren't we? What about the money we got from the three men?"

"Have you still got that?" Pandora was astounded.

Jess gave her a look as if she was stupid.

"Our camels were owned by bandits, they have several hiding spots sewn into the saddles. We can't spend the big coins yet, but I'll pay you your share in other money."

"I didn't do anything!" Pandora said.

"Yes you did." Jess pushed her gently. "You distracted them! And you sure have been distracting me ever since we met!"

She pushed her friend, then pushed her again gently ... and then pushed her again and again until she got a response. Pandora launched herself at Jess, raining down blows on her while Jess squatted down with her hands over her head. Both of them were laughing uncontrollably.

* * *

"Do you like him?" Pandora asked, curious.

"Dora, you're the only person I want to be with," Jess said flatly.

"But you never said whether you liked men," Pandora insisted.

She was watching Jess closely.

They were in the tavern eating unleavened bread and some form of lentil stew with big mugs of water in front of them. Jess never drank alcohol.

Pandora had caught her watching a handsome young man who was drinking alone but seemed to be spending more time watching who came and went. He was observing them as well, trying not to make it obvious.

To Jess he was gorgeous. He was likely an Avestan (the ancient tribe *Zarathustra* (Zoroaster) came from) and he was dressed in the fashion of a Persian warrior with fine flowing saffron robes embroidered on the edge and a short sword belted to his waist. On his head he wore a short square embroidered *tiyārā* (Persian hat) in white. The gold earrings stood out against ringlets of dark curly hair. He had a short beard and big broad shoulders of a warrior, probably an archer.

"I do, I think! Oh, I don't know!" Jess said with a sigh.

She felt like repetitively banging her head on the table in frustration.

"Don't you ever let up? I'm just working up an appetite for you, I guess."

"By watching men? Do you like watching men, Jess?"

Jess took a deep breath and leaned forward. "Can you keep your voice down a little? I like the look of him, yes. But I don't feel like tearing his clothes off in the middle of this tavern."

"Do you feel that way towards me?" Pandora's eyes were sparkling and she was grinning uncontrollably. "What, right now?"

Jess nodded, blushing.

"My rash is better," Pandora said, still smiling.

Then she looked down and lost her smile.

"Jess!" she hissed, "where's your other glove?"

"Oh, oh!" Jess put her left hand under the table. "I must have left it at the weapon smith's. I'm not used to a glove on my sword hand. I was distracted by my sword," she said, touching the new purchase she was wearing at her hip. "I have several spare right hand gloves back in our luggage but I really need to buy some designed for a swordsman."

Someone had noticed she wore one glove. He was making his way a little unsteadily towards them. "You think you are smart, don't you, bitch!" Jess felt some of his spittle on her face.

He leant forward to bring his face close to hers. He was dirty and unshaven. He reeked of body odour, beer and sheep. Jess considered saying something, but he was a drunk; it would only make it worse.

She looked away. Why was a woman in pants with a sword and a single glove such a problem for these men?

"Oh, so you're not talking! You think you're better than us! Dressed like a man, screwing this bitch here! Do you know what we did with the last one of *your* kind?"

"No," Jess swung back to face him. Her left hand closed around the hilt of her knife and she shifted in her seat, getting ready.

"What did you do to the last one?"

"She was only a girl dressing up like a man! She couldn't fight any of us! She was begging for it. Me and the men, you see, we gave it to her, see? We showed her what her place was." He gave her a nasty leer. "She cried just like a girl in the end." He smiled.

Jess smiled at the man. "Was it all your friends that did it? How many of you are there?"

The man looked surprised by the question. "Twelve of us, we each had our turn!"

Her knife was out of its sheath, still concealed from the man standing over her. Her hand had closed over the hilt of her sword. She leaned forward, her body tensed as she began to slowly work the bench back. All thoughts of avoiding trouble had gone.

"Why don't you show *me* my place?" she asked sweetly.

The handsome warrior that had been watching the two of them appeared behind the man and grabbed his shoulder. "Leave them alone or you will answer to me!"

All talk in the tavern stopped.

This man was a very different proposition to the one that was harassing them! He moved with the power and grace of a trained warrior.

Oh my Gods! Jess thought. He had such lovely brown eyes and such a warm deep voice.

Well, it was very nice to be looked after! She relaxed back and favoured him with a grateful smile. The sheep herder decided better of it and left hurriedly, muttering to himself.

Jess tried to project her most winsome smile. "Well, thank you, stranger, for rescuing us! What is your name so we may thank you properly?"

It was already an immodest thing for a woman to ask his name, but she couldn't very well invite him to join them without knowing his name.

He leaned forward, flushed with anger. "I'll say this to you once and once only. Don't come around these parts dressed like that unless you are looking for more trouble than you can possibly handle! Leave this place, leave it now!"

So much for the gallant rescuer!

He spun to leave. Jess needed information and she needed it fast. "Wait, stranger!"

He turned back slowly, as if he had been given an unwanted burden.

"As you can see, I am from far away," she said in a placating tone. "How I dress is common for women where I come from. This glove," she held up her hand, "is because I have wounded my hand and it is not a pleasant sight. I know this is a great problem but I don't fully understand."

The man nodded and sat down with a sigh.

Everyone in the tavern started to gossip and point to the three of them. Jess and Pandora were tagged as prostitutes now. They seemed to be good at attracting attention wherever they went!

Travelling with a man would help. Perhaps this man may be for hire.

He looked at her left hand in the glove. "Show me!" he demanded.

Jess had not even shown Pandora her left hand! She hesitated and then pulled off her glove. She held out her hand. But her head was averted, ashamed. It was black like her skin but looked dry and dead with a sickly green tinge and dull red highlights.

He returned her hand.

"Can you use it?" he asked.

Jess demonstrated, opening and closing her hand. "It is strong, far stronger than my good hand, but it is slow and clumsy. I'm trying to practice with it as much as I can. It is getting better."

"How did this happen? Your hand has not been burnt by anything natural!"

"My family had enemies." Jess shrugged. "One had arcanc power."

"Your family is dead," Pandora added.

Jess nodded recognition.

"Lady, I am sorry for my earlier rudeness. My name is Iraj. This is a curious coincidence. Jacinta, the Warlord's daughter, also injured her left hand. It was in a battle with a daimôn."

Jess felt a chill, as if someone walked over her grave. Jacinta, there was that name again!

A daimôn? Had Jacinta survived an attack by a daimôn?

"In honour of her memory," Iraj continued, "the women of her order who achieve mastery wear a glove on their left hand. We Aryans have women warriors, but not everyone accepts them. You do understand that any woman claiming to be a skilled warrior and travelling without a man is a challenge to all low born men?"

Jess slumped in her seat. "I'm afraid I do. Thank you, Iraj. It seems you have saved me from serious trouble."

"Can you use that sword you have?" Iraj gestured.

"I am still alive." Jess shrugged. "Iraj, we are travelling and I think if we had a male escort it might help us keep out of trouble. Are you a mercenary?"

"I am, but I am not for hire. I had a young sister, her name was Katin. We were very close, perhaps too close. My father promised her in marriage but she wanted to be a warrior like me.

"She ran away and came in search of me, dressed as a female warrior. She hoped it would keep her safe. It only got her killed. I have followed her trail here and now I will find her killers!"

"I would like to go with you, Iraj, when you meet those men," Jess said softly.

She stepped on Pandora's foot ... hard.

"No!" Iraj said. "You don't know what they did to her before she died! Leave here! This is a very bad place!"

He stood and left.

"Maybe we should leave?" Pandora suggested.

Jess was staring at her hand. With a nod she tossed some coin on the table.

"I don't want you mixed up in any of this. Let's go back immediately. Even this tavern isn't safe."

As they got back to their private stall at the caravanserai, Jess stood opposite to Pandora and took her hands. She kissed her lightly and looked closely into her face. "I want you to stay in the caravanserai tonight; it's guarded. You'll be safe here."

Pandora looked at Jess with horror. "Jess, you're scaring me! You can't be thinking of looking for those men! Don't even joke about such things!"

Jess sighed, "I am going to scout around, yes. I have certain *advantages* in the dark. If I'm not back in the morning, take all our possessions and find Iraj. I don't care what you say to him or offer him, make him take you away from here."

Pandora clutched at her friend. "Jess, no! You heard the man! There are too many of them!"

Jess kissed her gently. "I'll be careful."

Pandora clung to her, terrified. "Jess! Why are you doing this?"

Jess firmly disentangled her friend's hands. "That girl was brutalised and murdered simply for wanting to be what I am."

"Jess, don't leave me!" Pandora called urgently as Jess stood. "If you really love me, you won't go!"

"Pandora, I do love you!" Jess turned and took her bow, looking at Pandora sadly. "You can't know how much you mean to me. But there are things about myself that I just can't help."

Then she was gone.

Pandora threw herself down and started to cry.

"Jess!" she screamed into her blanket. "I hate you!"

Jess kept to the shadows as she snuck out of the caravanserai. She had an almost overwhelming desire to run and hunt the desert creatures of the night.

Not tonight. Tonight she had other prey.

She lay her sword, her quiver and bow on the ground. Then she took off her clothes and undergarments and wrapped everything carefully and buried it under rocks near a shrub, and covered her tracks. They were there in case she needed them in a hurry later. All she would take was her knife. She wore a dark waist band, otherwise she was naked.

It was very dark now. In the dark she could see clearly but only in black and white. She felt a fullness above her nose; it wasn't just her sense of smell that got sharper, she could feel the energy traces left by humans and animals. As she had said to Pandora, she had certain 'advantages' in the dark.

She smiled, setting off, following the trail left by the man they had met at the tavern.

He had stopped to piss on the dirt. Jess paused, bending over to thoroughly sniff the area.

Then she crept on.

* * *

Manuschithra got up and staggered over to relieve himself again. It was his turn to watch over the flock. The other men of the young men's camp had finished their drinking and were asleep.

He felt irritated by the events in the tavern. There were two women this time that had scorned protection of men. He was going to show them what real men could do with women, but that bastard had intervened.

He thought back to when they caught the other bitch, riding by as if she owned the road. Now that was fun! They soon had her crying and begging for mercy. She hardly knew how to use the weapons she wore!

"Was it fun killing Katin?"

For a moment he thought he imagined it, a woman's voice, calling out from the darkness. He strained his eyes but could see nothing, he hadn't regained his night vision from staring at the fire.

The voice was in front and he didn't hear anyone circling around him, but a powerful hand caught his chin from behind and a huge knife pressed hard against his throat. It made him arch up on his toes to ease the pressure.

"Don't move, speak only in whispers. I asked you if it was fun killing Katin."

It was that bitch from the tavern! He could feel her naked body pressed against him back but every nerve in his body was focused on the knife at his throat.

"I didn't know her name," he said desperately.

"Those men near the fire, are they the ones who were with you? Were there any here that didn't join in? Or any that joined in that are not here?"

"No, it was all of us. It wasn't me alone!"

Jess jerked him back, her hand clamped over his mouth. She tore the knife hard across his throat. His body struggled for a while and then convulsed. When it was still, she lowered it carefully to the ground. Some of his blood ran down her stomach and trickled down her thigh.

"Thank you," she whispered.

"Manuschithra, is that you?" a sleepy voice called out.

"Come, look!" a gruff voice called.

His cousin wondered why Manuschithra sounded so strange, but got up and shuffled over to where he called. There was a shape lying on the ground in the darkness.

He made an 'urck!' and a gurgling sound as Jess slid the blade across his throat.

This knife really is worth the money, Jess smiled.

Three men sat up. "Did you hear something?"

Shepherds are light sleepers.

"Over here!" a strange voice called out in the darkness.

Aiwi-xvarenah drew his sword. He was their best tracker. He motioned to the other two and melted into the shadows. The other two started to kick the others awake and motion for silence. They built up the fire and lit torches. Somewhere in the darkness a man cried out in agony. There was an animal snarl ... then silence. The darkness surrounding felt like a physical thing, pressing in around them.

"It's a lion!" Ankasa, the eldest, told them.

"I don't think so," Vara, his younger cousin, replied, surveying the darkness.

Some of the big cats had become desperate with the drought, but they didn't come this far into the desert. And they hunted at dawn.

What was out there? Two of the men with swords drawn went in search of Aiwi-xvarenah, calling his name. One was Vara's older brother. Vara had doubts they should be doing that but he wasn't the eldest so he couldn't say too much.

"Be careful," was all he said.

Ankasa got the others ready with slings, throwing spears and torches. Then they went together. They found the three men lying not far from each other — with their throats torn out. The night stank of blood.

Vara screamed and dropped to his knees when he saw his brother. He lifted his body and hugged it to him, keening his grief. The rest stood around, stunned into disbelief.

Ankasa clasped him on the shoulder. "The time to mourn is later, let us kill this beast first."

But if it was some animal, why didn't it kill one man and disappear into the night, dragging its prey? Why kill three and leave the meat? On the other hand if it was a raid, they would have been attacked in force by now and it would be planned for closer to dawn so their attackers could drive the sheep off.

No, this would be one or at the most just a few and Vara was beginning to suspect what it was. They shouldn't have hurt that girl; he knew that, even though he had joined in with the others.

Ankasa formed them up in a line, holding torches; everyone looked frightened. They started to move along the ground yelling at the top of their voices and beating the bushes to drive the animal from cover. The ground was uneven with hollows and rocks, just too many shadows. The light from their torches kept dancing up and down as they walked, and the shadows seemed to leap and move.

There was a lot of ground to cover and they had to separate to go around palms and shrubs. One man hung back, *let the others take the risk.* A dark figure rose up behind him. The sound of him dropping his weapons couldn't be heard above the men's shouting.

Ankasa glanced back to see a dark figure down low, flying through the trees.

"Panther!" he cried, pointing.

"No, it's like a man but I don't think it's human!" Vara yelled. "Careful, there may be more of them! Hey, someone else is missing!"

The remaining seven men gathered in an uncertain group.

A throwing spear came sailing out of the darkness. A man screamed as it took him in the chest.

"The torches are making us targets!" Vara realised.

"Back to the camp!" Ankasa yelled.

Only five made it. One man was left wounded. He screamed out in the darkness for help. And then, abruptly, his voice stopped.

Vara's breath was coming rapidly now, his heart was racing. He couldn't see anything much in the darkness. He thought he saw movement near one of the date palms. Another throwing spear came sailing from that direction. His friend standing next to him screamed out in agony.

Without another word, Ankasa broke and ran in the opposite direction. He was fast for an old man, but something dark rose from the ground and moved with frightening speed.

The three remaining men crouched as low as they could, seeking cover. From the darkness, where Ankasa had fled, a woman's voice called out.

"Was it fun killing Katin?"

Then Vara knew. "It's a demon!" He screamed in horror.

One of the old Gods, a daēva, had sent a demon to claim their souls.

"I told you," he muttered, almost to himself. "We should never have hurt that girl."

It was too late now.

Another spear flew with inhuman accuracy. It was as if a bull had rammed him in the chest at full speed, goring him. Vara fell to his knees, his hands feebly trying to pull it out.

The last two desperately cried out to Ahura Mazda to send angels to protect them. They shouted and clapped their hands to frighten the demon away. A black figure ran at them and leapt with an animal scream of rage.

Chapter 9: Pandora

Jess carefully watched the sleepy guards patrolling before sneaking back over the wall into the caravanserai. Her hair was still wet from washing but she had dressed and recovered her weapons.

Pandora sat up as she returned.

"Are you still awake, Dora?" she whispered hopefully. She remembered Pandora's earlier offer, was she still interested?

"Jess, you killed those men," Pandora said, her voice dull with horror.

Jess made no reply.

"What are you?"

Jess's shoulders slumped. "I'm sorry," she said tiredly in the darkness.

"I'm leaving in the morning," Pandora said.

"Not here!" Jess cried out in fear. "Please not here, Dora. It's not safe."

"Am I safe with you?"

It felt like Pandora had slapped her, did Dora really think so little of her?

"Please don't leave me, Pandora." Jess sounded lost. "I love you. I need you. I would never hurt you."

"Then tell me the truth."

Jess hesitated.

"I can't," she whispered. "You'll only hate me worse."

"In the morning, then," Pandora said. "In the morning we go our separate ways."

Pandora lay down but couldn't sleep. Every time she looked she saw Jess sitting motionless on the edge of their bedding. A few times she heard muffled sobbing.

The next morning Jess seemed detached and businesslike. They moved around avoiding looking at each other.

Jess would keep two camels, which was only fair. She talked a lot about how she had divided the supplies and what Pandora would need to do. Pandora found she couldn't listen. Her heart was aching too much.

Jess was giving Pandora a large amount of money.

"Jess, I can't take all this money. It's a fortune!"

"Take it unless you want to be a slave again or sell yourself on the streets," Jess told her. "You have to use it to live the rest of your life."

Pandora looked at her friend. "Do you think we will ever meet again?"

Jess walked across to her and gave her a chaste kiss.

"Why do you even ask that? It was you that said you would go a different way. Maybe it's true, you are better off without me."

Pandora had thought they would talk more. All that happened was Jess asked her to stay with her several times. She repeated her demand to be told the truth and Jess seemed resigned.

There was a lot to do. And then it was time to part.

Pandora felt a sense of panic then. She couldn't believe Jess was letting her go, just like that. Jess noticed Pandora seemed to be dragging out the farewell.

"Pandora," she said tiredly, "I have to leave here quickly, and you know why that is. Please come with me. It's not safe for you here. But if you're not coming, I have to get ready to leave."

Pandora nodded. "It's goodbye then."

She turned and started to leave.

"Goodbye, Pandora," Jess whispered softly.

She wanted to say more but she just sighed and watched the only person she loved in all the world walk out of her life.

* * *

Pandora made her way into the town looking for another place of lodging. She couldn't stand the thought of staying a second night in the room they had shared. She would spend a second day here and then she would travel to Anatolē a different way.

At first she couldn't bear the thought of meeting Jess on the road. She knew she wouldn't be strong enough to ever leave her if she did. But the further she went, the more her heart longed to turn around and run back to her.

She looked around but Jess wasn't following. There was only a crush of strangers going about their business. She suddenly felt very lonely and scared. Why not turn back?

Later, she wished she had.

* * *

Jess quickly paid and readied herself to leave.

She tipped handsomely so everyone was smiling at her. Before she left, she went in search of Iraj. He had booked a full room to himself and he looked at her quizzically as she pushed past him and carefully closed the door.

"You have to leave and leave now," she said without any preamble. "Last night, the men you were looking for were all killed. I don't know how many enemies they had, but you were asking about them, so you will be the prime suspect." She held up her left hand. "And I am included. We were both seen together and we weren't very quiet about it."

"You didn't have anything to do with that, did you?" Iraj looked at her curiously.

"And how would I kill twelve armed men?" Jess snorted with amusement.

"Who said anything about 'twelve'?"

"Look," Jess said. "Don't jump to any conclusions. My offer still stands. I need to hire a body guard. I need to get to Anatolē."

"Jess, I'm suddenly a man on the run and Anatolē is the other side of the world!"

"Just what you need," she said crisply. "Name your price."

"I get the feeling you are a very dangerous person to know, I want half a silver mina a month!"

"Whoa, you have a high opinion of yourself! That's almost twice the usual."

Iraj started to say if she wanted him for any less she needed to tell him the truth about herself but she held up her hand to stop his reply.

"Agreed. I'll pay in advance, if that's all right with you of course."

She dug a gold coin and passed it across. If she tried to pay him in silver it would not be much less than 300 grams. He did think well of himself.

"I'll meet you about three kilometres beyond the city, I recommend we leave separately," Jess finished.

"Is your friend coming?"

"No." Jess's expression was impossible to read. "She made the decision to stay another day and then leave and travel to Anatolē by a different route."

"That's not good."

"Yeah, tell me about it. I told her it's too dangerous." She shrugged. "She's a grown woman."

Just then they heard a man come galloping in. He was shouting at the top of his voice. Iraj and Jess exchanged a significant look. "That's your news, if I'm not mistaken. Thanks for warning me."

"This place just got a whole lot more dangerous for both of us. Act surprised. Leave big tips. I will wait for you, but not too long." She turned to leave.

"Why?" Iraj asked.

"Look, Iraj. I never said I did anything!"

"All right, you didn't do it."

Jess chuckled. "That's better!"

"But if you ever did do such a thing, why would you?"

Jess paused, her eyes looked moist. "If I ever would do such a thing, I would have done it for Katin." Her voice was gruff. "Katin and others like her."

"But why?" Iraj persisted. "You didn't know her!"

"No, I didn't," Jess said, and gave him a level look. "And I'm sorry about that, because now I never will."

"I'm sorry Katin never had the chance to know you, either," he said softly.

Jess bowed her head. "Thank you, Iraj, that helps. I'm not feeling very good about myself at the moment. They would have killed you, you know."

Iraj nodded, she was right.

With that she was gone.

* * *

Pandora was certain that Jess had left their room last night and killed a large group of armed men. She was a dangerous killer and held many secrets. Pandora's head told her she needed to get as far away from her as she could.

But Jess had been so kind to her, and Pandora had fallen in love with her. She didn't expect Jess would let her go so easily. She expected her to break down and explain what was going on with her. She seemed so sad, but resigned, as if she felt it was inevitable.

It made it hard to talk about.

Jess didn't want to talk about it because she was in so much pain, Pandora realised with a stab of guilt. Then Jess had to hurry, and before Pandora knew it, it had happened.

Only then did Pandora feel what she had lost. She had been a slave, now she was leading a camel with a small fortune in gold.

What are you doing, girl? How can you let someone like Jess get away?

She didn't understand what kept her walking, away from Jess, away from the caravanserai.

The main road diverted to meet the town that had grown up around a fresh water spring so there was no single main street, more an irregular maze of laneways.

Who ran this place? There seemed no one who took responsibility: no prince, no town council, no law. As she walked further from the caravanserai, she realised she was being watched. Men and women stood to watch her from windows and doorways. Those going about their business and children playing would stop and stare as she passed.

People began to call out, and if she turned to look she could hear the sound of laughter. She considered getting her bow down from her luggage and stringing it.

She realised she should turn back and head for the caravanserai. There were guards there and the owner would help her to employ some guides who could be trusted. Just as she was about to turn around a well-dressed older man hurried up to her.

"Lady!" he said urgently. "You shouldn't be wandering here on your own! This place isn't safe."

There were groups standing around staring at her and he yelled at them to go about their business. They turned away; this man had some authority here!

"My name is Ashô-paoirya, I have a shop here. Foreigners call me Ashô."

Pandora let out the breath she was holding in relief. She gave him a grateful smile. "Thank you Ashô, my name is Pandora. I am a little lost I guess. I was looking for somewhere I can stay the night and then I plan to go on my way in the morning."

"The caravanserai is the best place, I think," Ashô-paoirya said. "Or there is a wealthy lady who has fallen on hard times who takes travellers in. Her house is magnificent but staying there is not cheap." He looked Pandora up and down. "I'm not sure if ..."

"Oh, don't worry!" Pandora assured him. "I have enough money!"

"Well, I'll take you there, then!" Ashô-paoirya declared. "But surely you're not travelling on your own? Where's your family. Don't you have any friends?"

Pandora shook her head. "I'm travelling alone."

"That won't do!" Ashô-paoirya fussed. "You don't seem to be carrying any weapons."

"Just a knife, I have a bow in my luggage," Pandora admitted. "I'm not a fighter, really. I hope to hire a guide and maybe one or two guards for the journey."

"How then did you get this far?" Ashô-paoirya seemed surprised.

"I was travelling with someone, but we parted this morning."

"I think I understand." Ashô-paoirya gave her a sympathetic smile. "He tried to take unfair advantage of you."

Pandora nodded ... something like that.

"Well," Ashô-paoirya decided. "Don't you worry about a thing. My house is not far, you can leave your camel with my servant. Then I will take you and arrange a guide. You must leave the bargaining to me. Then we will see you settled into comfortable quarters."

He gave her a fatherly smile.

Pandora felt overcome by his generosity. "Ashô, you are too kind!"

"Nonsense!" Ashô-paoirya insisted. "It's all decided then, it will be my pleasure."

Pandora felt a great load had been taken from her shoulders.

She realised she shouldn't have told a stranger that she was alone and had money and could barely defend herself, but she somehow felt she could trust this man. Besides, he was a merchant, with a nice house, and he obviously commanded respect here.

After getting the camel settled and giving the servant some money for grain, Pandora followed the man as he went in search of a guide. She had a bag which mostly contained the money Jess had given her which she slung over her shoulder.

"This man is very good," Ashô-paoirya was saying over his shoulder. "I knew his father. But he lives in a very poor area of town. Here! Let me help you with that!"

Before she knew it, she was following this man through a maze of back streets and he was carrying all her money!

It seemed to be taking forever and Pandora started to suspect they were doubling back. This place was not so large! Had he deliberately gotten her lost?

He had separated her from her animal, her bow, and her money. Now she was following him through dark and narrow alleys. She started to feel afraid.

Ashô paused and gave her a reassuring smile. "Sorry to take you a round-about route, but believe it or not, there is a temple at the front and we needed to avoid people coming and going. It has a nasty reputation."

"I can take my bag, now," Pandora offered.

"Not at all, not at all!" Ashô insisted. "Now stick close to me and you'll be safe enough, but this is a poor area."

He started to climb a ladder that led to the top floor of a huge mud brick building.

Pandora heard some chanting from the temple carrying faintly. There was the smell of aromatic smoke in the air.

She wondered whether she should just run and let him have her camel and her money but she told herself that she must be imagining things. She realised Jess had already left and she had no way of finding her.

Ashô led her into a small dark room. There were four people on the floor, shapes in the gloom and two doorways closed by curtains. Ashô gestured for her to go through one.

"It's just next door."

"Look," Pandora said. "I think I have made a mistake."

Ashô-paoirya turned slowly.

His face transformed into a smile.

He was greatly pleased.

"Yes you have, young lady! Yes you have!"

It was then she noticed someone behind her, cutting off her escape. She snatched at her knife and tried to back up against a wall. The man struck her hard on her calf with a cudgel. She collapsed screaming. He reached down and twisted her arm cruelly, taking the knife. He didn't bother to hold her, he just stepped back.

Two women rose to take positions at either side. Pandora was boxed in. They needn't have bothered. She had no use of her leg. All she could do was half sit, rubbing it and glaring at them. She was caught so easily!

"I really need to thank you," Ashô-paoirya said, greatly pleased with himself. "I can't believe you are so stupid! Now we have you, an extra camel and this." He hefted her bag.

"You're slavers," Pandora said in bleak realisation.

Ashô-paoirya and the two women started to laugh.

"Slavers!" said one of the women. "Is that what you think we are?"

Ashô-paoirya hushed her, but he was still chuckling. "Where did you get this?"

He held up her saddle bag.

"It was given to me!" Pandora said.

One of the women bent over to look at her face, smiling down at her. When the blow came, Pandora couldn't even dodge away. She saw a flash of red light and blackness across her vision. Then the woman lifted Pandora's chin up and smiled at her again and struck her back-hand; a ring cut her cheek. A drop of blood began to run down her chin.

"When the master asks you a question, you answer truthfully."

"Enough, Hvôvî," Ashô-paoirya chuckled. "I'll let you have your fun with her later."

Hvôvî patted Pandora's head and gave her a proprietary smile.

"No need to lie," Ashô-paoirya said with a bored look on his face. "You are a harlot and from the weight of your saddle bag, you served a prince. You stole from him and left in a hurry. That black woman was helping you but you have had a falling out, probably over money."

He smiled at her. "So you see, we know all about you. It's very fitting you have come to us here! Our God helps us in many ways!"

A God?

Pandora felt a terrible chill. She was upstairs from a temple!

And they weren't slavers!

"Please," she began, trembling. "Please let me go! My money and my camel you can have it all, just let me go!"

"Now she understands!" Hvôvî laughed in glee, "This will be great fun!"

"Pandora, you have nothing to bargain with," Ashô-paoirya said, almost kindly. "I already have your money and the camel. Do you seriously propose to give me what is already mine?"

"I have friends, they know I'm here," Pandora tried desperately.

"We know about your friends, and when you separated from them, we couldn't believe our luck!" Ashô-paoirya smiled. "That Nubian woman and the man you met have already fled. Someone raided a camp of shepherds and the whole tribe is out hunting them. They won't get far, they may be dead already."

She felt as if a knife had stabbed her heart. Jess dead! A single tear ran down her cheek but she wiped it away. She didn't want these people to see her cry.

"We have a great honour for you." Ashô-paoirya continued, "We will present you as a bride to our God, Aēšma. A harlot, so young and beautiful, he will shower you with many blessings. The transition, I'm afraid, is painful."

He actually believed that to be a human sacrifice to his God was an honour.

Millennia ago Zarathustra had taught that the ancient blood thirsty Gods were really daēva, working in the service of the evil one, Angra Mainyu. The ancient good Gods were archangels working in the service of the one true and good God, Ahura Mazda.

All Pandora could remember of *Aēšma* (Aeshma) was that he was depicted as a blue giant with clawed feet and the head of an elephant with great ivory tusks. She didn't know why he was supposed to be the arch fiend in service of Angra Mainyu but she had an awful feeling she was going to find out.

"How long have I got?" she asked.

"The ceremony for your conversion will be on the fifth night from now," Ashô-paoirya said with something like pity in his eyes. "There is another, but she is older and sicker. She is unsuitable and will be given to our sorcerer to increase his powers over the dead."

Pandora felt a leaden feeling inside. "I'm sure she is ever so apologetic for being unsuitable. I am so happy to be chosen in her stead."

Ashô-paoirya looked at her sharply.

"Oh, I see you are trying to joke! You need to be taught proper respect for our God."

Pandora felt herself being grabbed from behind. Hvôvî was approaching with the eager smile on her face. She tried not to flinch.

* * *

Pandora was kept in a small cell. There was a barred window in the door and a slot for food and water. It overlooked what seemed to be the workshop for their sorcerer/priest. Hvôvî and the other woman were his assistants.

There was one other woman in the cell but she seemed to sleep most of the time. She looked half fed, her hair was grey and matted. When Pandora gave her water she swallowed listlessly and mumbled a few incoherent words. The cell stank of urine, faeces and sweat.

She tried to think how to escape, she tried to sleep, but all she could do was lie, listless with despair. Her leg was aching and her face was bruised and swollen.

That evening the two women and the priest came to take the other woman away.

Hvôvî gave Pandora an unpleasant smile. "I get to use the knife on both of you. Yours will be in our temple. It will be quicker, I'm afraid. I have to show your beating heart. Hers has to be slower and more painful to release her full power."

Pandora looked at her in sick horror. She was going to die here. Jess was probably already dead.

An hour later, she could hear the old woman scream. It seemed to go on and on. Then it got weaker and changed to moaning, interspersed with cries of anguish, and then it stopped.

Pandora drank some of the tepid water. She couldn't eat. She couldn't sleep. The hours dragged on till dawn.

After dawn the priest came into her cell to examine her. The women stood behind him as guards. He wore a leopard's skin over a loin cloth but had painted his body with white ochre and exaggerated his eyes with black paint circles. His hair was a tangled mess dusted with some sort of white powder. His eyes looked feverish as he studied her.

She cringed away from him as he moved forward to touch her. He didn't speak at all, just touched her and stared at her and then left, grinning.

She expected a visit from Hvôvî but it didn't come. She lay and tried to doze again, terrified and sick at heart. It seemed to take forever but the night eventually came. After this night there would be two others, and then she would die.

With nothing to do, she looked through the bars of the window into the workshop. A half-moon had risen. She could see the priest and his two women assistants making potions by lamp light. They had brought a pot filled with what looked like clotted blood. The priest was muttering to himself.

The workshop had large windows to let the breeze in. The nights were turning cool this late in the season but they had left the wooden shutters open and long coarse curtains drawn back. Little of the cool managed to penetrate her cell.

The half-moon came out from behind a cloud. She looked at the window and then looked back. One minute she wasn't there. The next minute she was!

Jess!!

Pandora bit her tongue to stop herself from crying out with joy.

Jess gave her a tiny wave of acknowledgement. She was completely naked, just wearing a black waist band and a tie for her hair. She wasn't wearing her glove.

She looked gorgeous sitting in the window, like a panther in the trees. The only weapon she had was her knife inserted into her waist band. She was outlined by moon light but would be invisible in the shadows.

"You have made a big mistake," Jess said conversationally, to the priest and his assistants.

She sat on the window ledge, dangling one leg casually down. They jerked around in surprise.

"What say you let my friend leave with me?" She gave them a small smile. "And then I might forget about this."

"You won't be leaving either!" the sorcerer cried, muttering something, and he pointed to the window.

Jess jumped down in a crouch. There was a hum of power and the air across the window started to shimmer like ripples on a pond.

The two women had drawn their knives and they moved to circle Jess from either side.

Jess moved like a cat. She punched the quiet one hard in the stomach with her knife. The woman screamed and died quickly. The sorcerer tried to aim a silver staff at Jess, but Jess had already moved.

Hvôvî screamed and dropped her knife as Jess twisted her arm, slipping behind to hold her. Jess's knife pressed against her throat.

"Let my friend go or I will kill her!" Jess warned.

The sorcerer just shrugged.

Hvôvî started to say something but Jess jerked the knife hard across her throat and threw her struggling body away from her. The sorcerer aimed his staff. There was a loud explosion and fire licked at the mud bricks. Jess rolled out of the way.

"That was easy so far!" Jess said with a cheeky grin. "Now just you!"

She danced across and kicked him hard in the stomach.

It felt like she had kicked a tree trunk with her naked foot!

The sorcerer watched her with amusement as she hopped and limped about cursing. He wasn't affected in the slightest.

There was a pounding from the locked door. The noise had woken the residents of the house. The sorcerer screamed at them, he wanted to do this himself. The distraction gave Jess the instant to dodge as he slammed his heavy staff at her. She appeared next to him again, balancing awkwardly on one foot and tried to shove him but it only made her stumble backwards. He was immovable.

Pandora watched with her hand in her mouth.

Jess dodged a fireball and broke a chair over his head; he wasn't affected. Jess was starting to tire and she hadn't hurt him at all.

This is not going well!

Jess went to duck to one side but her foot slipped sideways on some blood, causing her to fall. The sorcerer smiled and pointed his staff straight at her.

Pandora screamed.

Jess shrivelled into a ball, with only her left hand held up. When the smoke cleared, she raised her head and looked at her hand. Her face broke into a smile of delight. She stood up, holding her left hand out in front of her.

"I never knew it could do that," she said brightly, as she limped towards him. "That should prove handy, don't you think? Do you want to see what else it can do?"

It was then that Pandora realised what had happened. Jess's hand had been hit by sorcery in the past; it must contain some sort of spell.

But why was she naked?

The sorcerer looked frightened for the first time. He lifted his staff over his head and tried to bash Jess with it. But she was already too close; he couldn't get any power into it. She caught the staff with her right hand and pushed her left hand towards his face while he struggled to snatch his staff back.

The air around the sorcerer started to shimmer. Her hand was cancelling his protection spell! There was a momentary struggle and his protection shield dissolved with a small 'womph!' and Jess touched his face. He shrieked and staggered back; silvery fluid started to run over his cheek.

"It doesn't do that on normal people," Jess said.

She pulled the staff from his hands and threw it across the room.

She grabbed his clothes with her right hand and drew her left hand back. Grunting with the effort, she punched him hard. The edge of her hand hit his throat with a sickly crunch.

The sorcerer gripped his throat and began making 'whooping' sounds, and waving his hands about as he tried to get air. He began turning a dusky red.

Jess took several limping strides to the window and, after a struggle, pushed her left hand through the barrier with a small 'pop!' Then she limped and hopped back as fast as she could and, ramming him with her shoulder and giving him hard jabs from her knife, she herded the struggling man towards the window.

As he hit against the window frame she ducked to lift his legs and push him through.

"Look out below!" she called.

There was a faint 'Hey!' from below and the sound of a body hitting the road below.

"Make sure he's dead!" she hissed softly.

Jess turned with a look of immense satisfaction and raised a bar to open the door to Pandora's cell. Then she looked in consternation. "It needs a key!"

Just then the banging and questions started again outside the locked door. Jess tried to grumble something low to mimic an irritated male voice. It didn't work! It only caused the people outside to begin throwing themselves against the door. It was a very stout door reinforced with metal but it wouldn't last forever.

"Around her neck, I think!" Pandora pointed to Hvôvî's corpse.

"It would have been nice if she told me that *before* I cut her throat!" Jess grumbled to herself as she limped over. She was moving better already. As she rolled a chain over the head, Pandora had a vivid image of the dead woman opening her eyes and grabbing Jess's hands. She shuddered at the thought.

The men outside had found something to use as a ram. The door was still holding, but not for long. Jess quickly moved back to the door to the cell, dropped the slippery keys, and the fumbled to get them in the lock.

"It's starting to clot," she grumbled to herself. "If you had told me before I killed her, I could have ..."

Just then she finally got the door open ... And was almost knocked over by Pandora throwing herself at her crying and hugging!

She gave Pandora a fierce hug. "Not much time, sorry, where are your things and the money?"

Pandora shook her head.

"It's not important, I really mean that. *You now,* you are important but I didn't go to all this trouble just to get you caught again."

Jess reached up and gave one of the curtains a sharp tug. She was showered by a heavy cloud of red dust but it didn't give.

She gave it a furious heave ... and was buried under the curtain as it came away. After a struggle she managed to poke her head out between bouts of coughing and sneezing.

The sound of hammering on the door was getting louder; the wood was starting to give way.

Jess gave another sneez and then threw one end of the curtain out the window. Someone below began coughing. Then she braced herself ready to let Pandora down through the window.

"Over you go!" she instructed, "And don't scream!"

Scream?

Someone caught at her feet and Pandora let out a small 'squeak' in surprise. She ended up in Iraj's strong arms.

"Don't scream, it's me."

He led her over to his two horses. "Can you ride a horse?"

Pandora shook her head.

"Of course not, that would be too easy. Don't worry, speed won't help us now."

He passed Pandora a heavy black garment and helped her into it. Only her eyes showed.

It would be suffocating in the heat.

"It's a local custom; it allows young women to pass more safely in dangerous places by concealing their beauty," he explained. "They are looking for a man and a Nubian. In that outfit, you can pass as a local and Nubian you obviously are not! I will lead your horse and do all the talking. Try to look shy."

"What about Jess?"

"She's coming a different way."

"Iraj, why is Jess naked?" Pandora asked, puzzled.

"She was attacked by a wizard, it affected her," he said ambiguously. "Being without clothes and without her glove gives her ... advantages."

"Yes, I saw that! That sorcerer tried to hit her with some sort of spell and her hand, the left one, countered his spell."

Iraj looked at Pandora. "That man that Jess threw out the window was their chief sorcerer?"

Pandora nodded. "She was wonderful. You should have seen her!"

"So much for sneaking quietly out of town," Iraj muttered. "There was possibly only one group left from these parts that aren't trying to hunt us down and kill us. And what does Jess do? Well, why not go and kill their head priest?"

All he could see were Pandora's eyes. They were sparkling with love and excitement. Iraj sighed.

They were stopped several times till the men of the village passed the word: 'let the man with his wife go'.

Chapter 10: Jess, the Truth

The vigilantes had marked where Pandora and Iraj were to spend the night, so the 'married' couple would not be disturbed. It was a ruined hut well out of town. Tomorrow they would go to where Jess and Iraj had left the camels.

"Can I come in?" a soft woman's voice called from the darkness outside.

"What is the password?" Iraj called back, grinning.

"Iraj! Don't be ridiculous!" Jess hissed. "It's me, Jess!"

"Wrong password!" Iraj called back. "You know the arranged signal."

They heard some muttering out in the darkness.

Eventually Jess's voice replied with a sigh. "The night is black but I am blacker."

Pandora and Iraj were overcome with giggling as Jess stalked in. She was completely naked except for a waist band but she held her head high, with an air of offended dignity.

Iraj sat with his mouth open in shock as she turned to speak to him in the flickering candle light. She was magnificent!

Six foot tall and large, muscular and lean. Her stomach was flat, even her stomach muscles showed. Her breasts were fair in size rather than large, but stood proud and erect.

Her unruly hair was pulled back in twin plaits. Her teeth flashed ivory against her dark complexion.

"Can I have my clothes, please?" Jess asked humbly.

Iraj shared a look with Pandora.

Clothes? Now, I'm sure we put them around here somewhere!

Iraj couldn't tear his eyes away. His manhood was as hard as a rock.

"Clothes!" she pouted.

She put her hands on her hips and stood with her feet astride, frowning at the grinning pair. Then she stamped her bare foot. It hardly made a sound in the sand on the floor.

"Clothes!" she insisted.

Iraj reluctantly opened a bag and stretched out his hand with her pile of clothing. She jerked it out of his hand and actually turned her back to take her waist band off and get dressed. The view of her back was just as good as the front.

"There should have been a counter to your silly password," Jess grumbled as she got dressed. "Something like 'and I'm an Avestan pig!'"

"But you're not an Avestan, and why call yourself a pig?" Iraj asked.

Pandora and he broke into laughter. Jess sighed and squatted down with a look of all-suffering on her face.

"What happens now?"

"They'll be out searching in earnest now; first the raid on the tribe and now the raid on the town. Pandora tells me you seem to leave a trail of dead bodies wherever you go."

Jess looked at the pair smiling at her. She felt deeply hurt. She felt bad enough about killing people. She certainly didn't like to be reminded.

But it all seemed unfair. She had been attacked twice in the desert by bandits and once she had to rescue a single traveller. Since she met Pandora, she had to kill men twice to rescue her. The latest mess was one Pandora walked into, despite warnings from Jess!

The time with the shepherds ... well, admittedly she went looking for trouble, but she just couldn't stop herself and it was better than Iraj getting himself killed!

Iraj was continuing, "I don't think anyone will see you two as the cause, but you are linked to the killings and that will be enough. They will chase you and they will try to get you to confess. Then they will kill you. Does anyone know which way you intend to go?"

Jess nodded. "We told Arshan, the leader at the last place we were at."

"The one whose sons you killed? I think we should veer north and then head the less travelled routes. I don't think I'm charging you enough, Jess."

"I'll try to get her to kill less people next time," Pandora giggled.

Jess stood up, tears in her eyes. "Pandora, I will give you enough to set yourself up somewhere. I will pay Iraj to take you to somewhere safe." Tears started to run down her cheeks and she took a shuddery breath.

"You two need to stay away from me, for both of your sakes! You may not believe it, but I am sorry. You don't have to sit in judgement of me; I hate myself enough already! Maybe if those men catch me it will be a good thing. It's just that I d-don't m-mean t-to be evil."

She lost control and with a sob burst out of the hut.

"Damn!" Iraj said. "You had better go to her."

"She said ..." Pandora sounded unsure.

"And you would listen, now?" Iraj was incredulous. "Pandora, right now your friend needs you more than anyone has ever needed you in all your life! Go to her!"

Pandora ran outside. She looked round anxiously but couldn't see anything in the light of the half moon. Then she followed the sound of muffled sobbing. She sat down and took her friend in her arms. Jess pulled away.

"I'm sorry, Jess. Please don't talk like that!"

Jess turned her back on her, huddled into herself in her misery.

"Jess, I love you!" Pandora started to cry herself. "You are good and kind and you have saved my life."

In the darkness she sensed more than saw Jess turn to her. She was hiccoughing and sniffing.

"What did you say?"

She sounded like a lost little girl.

"I said I loved you," Pandora said. "I want to be with you. Please don't talk about us separating. I'm sorry. I just seem to keep hurting you. It's just that ... I don't know who and what you are."

Iraj appeared on the other side of Jess. He sat and put his arm on her shoulder. She didn't draw away.

"You really have to tell her!" he advised softly.

Jess gasped, sitting up straight. She turned to him. He couldn't see her face in the darkness.

"You know?"

Iraj nodded. "I guessed there was something about you, and now I realise what it is. It doesn't make any difference to me, may the one true God have mercy on my soul. Tell her or I will."

Jess looked away in the darkness. "I can't," she shuddered.

"Do you want me to?"

He felt her nodding jerkily, again and again.

"Pandora, your friend here ... I would be proud if she were my friend too. Your friend is a changeling."

Pandora sat there in shock. The words echoed in her mind.

Your friend is a changeling.

"Come on!" Iraj pulled Jess up to walk the short distance to the hut. But the Jess who was as sure footed as a cat, the Jess who could run faster than a man, could only stumble. Her friends had to half carry her, one on each side. When they got back, she flung herself in misery to the floor. Her head was bowed in shame.

"Now you know." Her voice was harsh. "Now you both know. A word from you, either one of you, and every man's hand will be turned against me. They will hunt me down without mercy. I will have nowhere to hide."

She looked up at them, her face a mask of anguish and pain.

"I woke ... I don't think woke is the right word. I came to some sense of myself ... a year and a half or more ago. I already had memories of living in the desert maybe for months, eating the snakes and small animals that come out at night." She shuddered. "I was an animal. The only thing I had was this."

She took off an object hanging around her neck on a thin metal chain and handed it to them.

"It looks to be some sort of key," Iraj murmured. "I have never seen anything quite like it."

"The chain is very strong; it looks like a dull type of bronze but a metal smith said he didn't know what the metal was." Then Jess continued on; her voice was toneless. "For a time I ranged, naked in the desert. I was not in the form you see before you. I could abide the sun and heat and sand storms better than its own creatures. I enjoyed the hunger of the hunt. I hid from men, a complete animal, maybe worse.

"Then knowledge of people and language began to return to me more and more, but little of my own past before the desert or how I got there. I began to spend more time in human form and gain control over the change. It is harder though at night, especially under a full moon.

"When I felt I had enough control, I came upon a camp of men in an oasis. There were ten. I was naked, without clothes or possessions or weapons. I tried to say I had been robbed and beg their help. I guess I was a woman walking naked into a camp of single men. I don't know what they said, but they laughed and made fun of me. They grabbed me and gathered around.

"I was enraged. I changed, and when I change I can be inhumanly fast. I can still hear their screams. I can still taste their blood in my mouth."

Jess paused for a while.

"When I regained control I was surrounded by bodies horribly torn. Their clothes were torn and bloody from where I had worried at them in my anger. It is something that I don't wish to remember.

"I stayed there for a period. Then I dressed as best I could in what I could find and took supplies, their money, some weapons and one of their horses and I walked. The horse died. There was nothing I could do for it. Near another oasis, I was attacked by men riding camels." She paused. She didn't say what happened to those men.

"So I took three of their sturdiest camels and this time followed the tracks. I stopped at a small oasis to buy food. I was attacked again but that time I didn't kill anyone.

"After that, I was afraid of people. I lived for a while longer in the desert until I felt confident that I had control over myself. Then I came to Bukhara where I met Pandora. Pandora, I love you!" she cried desperately. "You make me feel human."

"You said your parents were killed," Pandora prompted.

Jess nodded. "I have very faint memories. They are like smoke in my head. As I try to grasp them they fade away."

"What can you remember of your family?" Pandora asked softly.

Jess shook her head. "It seems the more personal details are, the more they make me human, the harder they are to grasp. I was human once, I think ..." Jess's voice trailed away.

"Jess," Iraj said firmly. "You are human as far as I am concerned. Do you think you are cursed?"

"Of course I am cursed." Jess laughed. "If you ask whether it was a curse that did this to me, I think so. I have a strange ghost of a memory of fighting a powerful wizard. It was in a very dark place deep under the earth. He seemed young and pale and red headed. That's how I got this." She held up her hand. "I can't remember but I must have managed to kill him. Maybe it was he who cursed me.

"When I met Pandora she thought I was an Amazōn. I dress like them, and I wear a glove on my left hand. I don't have false modesty but even before I became a changeling I don't think many female fighters could match me. The Gods give us messages. As soon as I heard it, I knew many of the answers I seek lie in the Troad."

Pandora inched up to her friend and took her hands and as an answer kissed her hungrily on the lips. "I will come with you, Jess," she said huskily.

"It will be morning soon and we will have to leave and find our camels or the only place we will be heading for is a 'beheading'." Iraj smiled crookedly at the lameness of his joke. "Jess, I am proud to have taken service with you. I don't see you as evil at all. I would like you to see me as your friend. I did not mean to hurt you but if we are to be friends you will have to understand I *will* tease you."

"So will I!" said Pandora, giving her friend a hug.

"So don't take everything I say to heart, please. Now I still think I could have asked for more money!" Iraj said with a self-conscious grin. "But don't you dare offer it now or I will be very offended!"

Jess laughed. Her eyes were glittering with gratitude.

* * *

That very night an old man, a senior maguš of Mazdayasna, awoke and lay in the darkness wondering. In his dreams he had seen a face. She had seemed to be a Nubian but something told him she was not. And he had heard words that echoed in his mind: *Your friend is a changeling.*

What it meant to him and his people he didn't known yet, but he intended to find out.

* * *

They kept to a minor route with only small villages and oases interspersed with long stretches of desert.

"They are expecting us to get river transport at Parap," Iraj said. "I suggest we cross the Oxos at nearby Āmul instead and take the overland route across the desert to *Margu* (Merv). Our route from there will depend on what information we get from other travellers."

What the three friends didn't know was that that particular hunt had quickly died away. It was only the third morning after the death of the blood priest that Ashô-paoirya and several others were found with their throats cut.

The small township had long lived in fear of the devil–worshiping cult but there were still some good people left. They set up a town council; they employed town guards, and asked priests of *Mazdayasna* (Zoroastrianism) to return to their town to cleanse it.

The dead sorcerer could only have been killed by an even more powerful sorcerer. The shepherds seemed to be have killed by a demon, probably summoned by the same great one to punish them for killing an innocent girl.

No one in their right mind would want to catch up with this great sorcerer who had come to dispense justice, for whatever reasons of his own.

But there were others hunting for Jess that they knew nothing about. A great maguš was searching for a certain dark woman, a changeling, whose face had appeared to him in a dream. Another of great power, Tishari, was looking for the killer of Horkan, the blood priest.

But neither was having any luck; Jess also didn't know it yet but she carried protection from the far sight. It obscured her and those around her.

* * *

Jess was somewhere off in the desert scouting. Iraj and Pandora were leading the two camels and his two horses along what looked like a rarely used trail.

"Do you mean to tell me that when you *didn't* know about Jess, you couldn't stand it?" Iraj asked. "Now you know she is a changeling, it's perfectly all right?"

Pandora laughed and shook her head. "Iraj, you must understand that I am a woman. I'm not even supposed to make sense *all* of the time."

"That is something I would never get away with saying."

"I can't explain it, myself." Pandora laughed again. "I loved Jess as soon as I met her, but there was too much I didn't know."

Pandora saw a distant unmistakable figure coming towards them. "Here she comes."

Jess flashed them both a fond smile as she trotted closer.

"I found a hidden cistern with water; I can find forage for the camels, but finding feed for the horses in the desert is a problem."

"Lucky we have the barley," Pandora suggested.

Jess had almost a supernatural ability to locate the hidden sources of water. If anyone was very good at finding something, people said they had 'sniffed it out'.

Iraj wondered, could that be her secret?

Jess saw him giving her a quizzical look. "Is anything wrong, Iraj?"

"No," Iraj shook his head and gave her a reassuring grin. "Nothing at all."

* * *

"The desert, once you know it, is so lovely," Iraj murmured as they drowsed by the fire. Jess had cooked for them again. Neither Iraj nor Pandora could really cook and Jess seemed to enjoy it.

They had been travelling for two weeks since Pandora's rescue. They had found a spring with some grass and were spending a few days to allow the horses to regain their condition.

Camels can go for long periods without water and food. They grow shaggy coats in the winter and store fat in their humps separate from their body for the heat of summer. Their bodies also had many ways of storing and conserving water.

They can eat almost anything and their upper lip is split so they can strip and eat thorny plants. If food is short they can eat meat, leather ... or sometimes, they say, their owner's tent!

But horses are creatures of the grassy steppe. They need plenty of good water and roughage from grass, not just grain.

This small oasis wasn't big enough for full time occupation but someone had taken the trouble to dig out a pond at the base of the spring and there were small clay pipes that drained any excess water into a small irrigation system that fed a couple of dozen date palms and some grass.

Climbing was another thing Jess could do very well so Iraj had set the girls to gather dates and set them out to dry as supplementary feed for later.

These few days' rest were a pleasant interlude and Jess realised, as she bundled up the left overs, that she had never felt this happy in all her recent memory. Pandora, now that she understood, seemed to be freed of something. There was no doubt about her love for Jess.

Iraj had fitted in as if they had been three friends since childhood. He was an exceptional man. He had accepted her as a changeling immediately. He was quieter than Pandora, but just about anyone else Jess knew was.

He had a quick intelligence and a surprising sense of humour when you got to know him. Most of the time his sense of humour was firmly directed at teasing Jess in an affectionate way! He was muscular, handsome and *did* have a smile that made Jess feel weak at the knees!

Though Jess didn't like what she was, both her friends seemed to accept her and like her no matter what and that helped so much!

Now they were watching the twilight as the stars started to come out; the moon would be up soon. Jess studied her left hand for a while.

"As soon as Pandora told me about Jacinta, I felt this strong connection with her. I am hoping that in the Troad I can find a clue as to what I am."

"When my sister got killed, I found out all I could about Jacinta," Iraj said. "Apart from you being black and older than she would have been, there is a remarkable similarity between the two of you." He rubbed his beard thoughtfully. "What if Jacinta's task was not finished? Her God would have sent someone else, don't you think? Maybe that is you, Jess. Gansükh is still alive. It was he who trained the other daimôn raisers and he is guarded by a daimôn lord."

"I am an assassin, a good one. You think I have been sent by *a God* to kill someone?" Jess laughed. "You think that is why I'm similar in some ways to Jacinta? I thought even Gods hate my kind."

"How do you know? Have you met any lately?"

Jess had to smile at that.

"Jacinta acted like she was much older but she was only fifteen when she was killed. She would be just over seventeen if she had lived. How old are you, Jess?"

"Over nineteen, I don't know how I know but I feel certain about that. I had been living in the desert for a couple of months when Jacinta was killed. Could her God choose me to replace her even *before* she was killed?"

"Who knows what Gods can do?"

"I can't fight a daimôn lord."

"Jacinta's hand was struck by a daimôn blast. Somehow it meant her hand had some sort of magic."

Jess looked at her left hand and opened and closed it slowly. "My hand worked on the demon worshipers' magic." Then she gave a sad smile. "But me, sent by a God? Iraj, that is ridiculous."

"Do you think Jacinta could do what you can do?" Iraj asked quietly.

"No, I suppose not." Jess laughed softly, "If my hand can attack daimôns I would be much deadlier than Jacinta ever was."

She sat for a while, looking at her hand as she opened and closed it.

* * *

"Tomorrow night's the full moon," Pandora reminded Jess the next evening.

They were resting by the fire.

"Yes," Jess replied. "The stars look so bright. They seem close, as if you can almost touch them. I find the desert so beautiful at night. Even in this form, I can see better than you in the darkness."

"What's it like?" Iraj asked curiously.

Jess hesitated; she felt a surge of shame. But her friends accepted her. If all she had to do was tolerate their curiosity she could cope with that. Well, she supposed she could at least.

"I see things in black and white in the dark and colour during the day," she answered. "But still very clear. In the brightest glare, I feel something flicker across my eyes." She gestured to her eyes. "My sense of smell becomes very sharp too. I can feel a fullness here," she touched her forehead just above her nose, "especially as I change."

"Don't you feel restless?" Pandora asked.

"Pandora, I can hardly wait for some answers to all this but I am a hunter, I can be patient."

"Not restless about that, are you listening to me, Jess? Tomorrow is the full moon!"

Jess looked at her friend suspiciously. "In answer to your question, you don't have to tell me about the full moon. I can feel its power over me. I *was* trying to put it out of my mind. That is, as long as my best friend doesn't keep reminding me!"

"I would like to see, that's all!" Pandora said wistfully.

"Pandora! That's cruel! You know how I feel about it, and you want to watch me change? Like I'm some sort of freak show for you!"

"No, Jess!" Pandora said, giving Jess an encouraging smile. "It's not cruel at all! I'm really trying to be kind to you!"

Jess waited, favouring Pandora with a very old fashioned look. She waited for Pandora to explain how humiliating her was kind. How was asking her to expose that part of herself that she was totally ashamed of, the part that would likely cause the maximum disgust in others, was being kind to her!

"Jess," Pandora started, "remember how you felt about anyone finding out you were a changeling?"

"I felt awful! I was ... I still am, a *thing*," Jess said softly.

"And then we both found out! How did you feel then?"

"You both gave me the greatest gift I could ever have been given." Tears started to run down Jess's cheeks with strong emotion as she recalled. "You knew, and didn't find me disgusting. I could share what I was with my friends. It was as if a great burden was lifted from me. I am very grateful to both of you."

She sighed. She could tell where this was going.

"So," Pandora said sitting forward, "if we see you after you have changed then you can feel better about that too. The fact that I am curious is beside the point, really it is! Besides, it's a safety issue. If we know what you look like, we won't attack you and can help you and not be so scared. And, well everything! What do you think?"

Jess took a big breath. "I think you are winsome and devious, Pandora. And I think I have been around you too long. You can say the most preposterous things and they are starting to make sense to me! And you, Iraj?"

Iraj looked a bit embarrassed. "Sorry Jess, you're the first changeling I have met. I would be lying if I said I wasn't curious."

Jess sighed, "I'm the first changeling I have ever met, too!" She laughed a little self-consciously. "To tell the truth, I don't know what I look like exactly. I know I'm black like a panther, but I don't grow fur. My limbs get very strong with claws, my teeth are sharp and my jaws powerful. I'm about the same size as I am now, just four footed and a different shape. Lately I can remain partially human and change back and forth more quickly. So I can run with paws and as soon as I stop, I can use my hands. So far the only weapon I can use without fully changing back is my knife."

"Is that why you are such a good warrior?" Iraj asked.

"I don't think so. I have certain advantages, even in human form. But I 'know' I was trained as a female warrior before, and a very good one."

Jess could feel her resistance crumbling in the face of Pandora's arguments. "I don't want to take off all my clothes for a full change. You wouldn't give them back to me last time!"

Iraj and Pandora smiled in unison at the memory of seeing Jess naked.

"I couldn't help it," Iraj confessed sheepishly. "You are a magnificent woman, Jess! I'm only human, after all! I feel hot and dizzy even thinking about it."

"Do you really think I look good?" Jess looked at him shyly.

She couldn't suppress a smile.

"Good isn't a strong enough word!" Iraj breathed out heavily and flashed her a broad smile.

"Pleease, Jess!" Pandora asked in a wheedling tone.

"You won't give up on this, now you have started," Jess said, and shook her head in fond exasperation. "Will you, Pandora?"

"I'm a much nicer person when you satisfy my curiosity," Pandora replied sweetly.

"All right," Jess agreed, gritting her teeth, "I'll do it. But you must understand I feel very exposed, changing in front of my friends, and I'm terrified I will disgust you."

"Oh well," she sighed. "I may as well go all the way!"

She turned her back and pulled her shirt off, dropped her pants and then took off her under-clothing and put it in a neat pile. To force herself over any shyness, she deliberately twirled naked in front of her friends, while Pandora and Iraj made appreciative noises.

"I suppose I just should ... just ..."

"Jess! Just do it!" Pandora settled down to watch her friend intensely.

And Jess changed. The being they saw looked at them curiously but didn't otherwise move.

After about ten minutes, Jess changed back. She crouched, bent over.

"Oh," she groaned, hugging herself. "It was so hard to resist that! All I wanted to do was to run into the night and hunt. Can I have my clothes?"

Iraj was so stunned, he just automatically handed them over. He had gathered up her clothes and had every intention of teasing her for them but that was all forgotten.

"That's not what I expected," he said slowly, looking towards Pandora.

"Nor I," Pandora agreed, speaking slowly.

"I wasn't disgusting, was I?" Jess asked anxiously.

"No, you weren't," Pandora said slowly. "Though if I didn't know it was you and if you came on me from out of the darkness I would have been frozen with terror."

"I must say, I didn't think smaller ones existed," Iraj said thoughtfully. "Pandora's right, I wasn't scared because I knew it was you, Jess."

"What did I look like?" Jess asked, confused.

"The yellow eyes looked rather cute," Pandora said helpfully. "And the small pointy ears, but your teeth were so sharp and really needed a clean! Your jaws looked strong enough to crunch through my arm."

What am I supposed to make of that? ... not disgusting at least. Strong, sharp teeth she expected but yellow eyes? ... cute??

"What animal form did I take?" Jess asked.

Pandora looked back at her and gestured helplessly.

Iraj wordlessly took a pan and carefully poured water into it and put it close to the fire.

Jess transformed her face only.

"Oh," she said in shock. Hands flew to her face. "I'm a daimôn!"

"A small cute one," Pandora added.

"You know," Jess shuddered a little, "I don't know how I could have coped with it if I didn't have the two of you." She crawled over and took her two friends in a loose hug. "As much as I hate to admit it, you were right, Pandora. Once you two had seen it, I feel better about it. Though I don't think you wanted to see it just for me. Curse you and your curiosity, Pandora!" She shrugged helplessly. "I'm a daimôn!"

"A small cute one!" Pandora repeated helpfully. "At least small, as far as daimôns go!"

Jess shook her head. "I can't believe you just said that!" She chuckled despite herself. "Tell me, Pandora, in your vast experience ... how do daimôns 'go' exactly?"

Soon the three were gently laughing.

I'm a small cute daimôn, Jess thought ... one the size of a huge panther, capable of running down a man and tearing his throat out! One capable of killing a dozen armed men.

Chapter 11: Iraj

It was the evening after they had left the oasis. They had made camp early just up from the floor of a dry wadi.

"You tell him!" Jess hissed to Pandora.

"No, I have to gather some brush for the fire."

"No you don't, you know I collect the brush so I can build the fire just the way I like it. You talk to him, you're better at this sort of thing."

"No, you tell him. You like him, I know you do!"

"Pandora! That only makes it worse."

"Jess, you aren't afraid of anything."

"You know that's not true, Dora. Please don't make me do this."

"And how long do you think you can put up with this problem, then?" Pandora gave her a sly smile. "I won't be long."

Jess made a growling noise in her throat as she walked back to prepare for their evening meal. As she settled down, she glanced across at Iraj. He was repairing a leather strap. Damn that Pandora! How *did* she let her friend talk her into things so easily? She wiped her hands nervously on a clean cloth.

"Iraj?"

"Mmm," he said. His tongue was sticking out the side of his mouth as he worked.

That would be a bad habit in a fight.

She watched him for a moment taping the leather punch with the hammer. He was using thick waxed hemp as thread and was double stitching everything. She liked watching him work with his hands so strong and sure. She bit her bottom lip, wondering how to bring it up.

"I suppose you don't know that Pandora and I are, well we are ..." Jess stopped, at a loss.

"Lovers?" Iraj suggested.

He carefully put the leather strap down and looked up. If Jess could have, she would have flushed beetroot. "Blur, er, wha ... how did you guess?"

"Jess, you may have been born yesterday, but I wasn't!" Iraj smiled to rob his words of offence and picked up his strap again.

Jess walked over and sat down next to him and suddenly threw her arms around him and kissed him fiercely on the lips. Iraj almost stabbed himself with the needle.

"Er, that was nice! But what was that for?"

"That's because you are the most wonderful, incredible man I have ever met! Both of us have been too nervous to mention it. So you don't mind if we sometimes need a little, er, privacy?"

Pandora appeared out of nowhere, not having to pretend to be busy collecting brush wood. All she had was a twig.

"And you two have been waiting for over two weeks because you were afraid to ask me?" Iraj broke out laughing.

"And you knew anyway and didn't care!" Jess finished for him.

They had been desperately restraining themselves, or trying to be quiet, or trying to sneak time together. It was so frustrating.

"So, some privacy at times," Jess repeated. "Trying to hide it from you has been killing us."

"I will be discreet," Iraj said with a perfectly straight face.

Jess thought for a second and then gave him a little shove. He almost stabbed himself again.

"Now what is that supposed to mean? You'll be discreet! You're starting to sound like Pandora! I said privacy. Surely you're not curious, are you?"

Pandora giggled.

Jess gave her a sharp look.

"Curious isn't the word. I think I'd better stay as far away as I can. Having you two making love in earshot would be torture for me!"

Now Jess *and* Pandora were curious.

"Tell us!" Pandora begged.

"Don't you know?" Iraj shook his head. "You are both absolutely beautiful. Even the thought of you making love to each other drives me wild with desire!"

"Oh! I didn't know that." Jess was surprised. "I don't understand!"

"Jess," Iraj said patiently, "you are a woman and may not feel exactly the same way as a man! Besides, I suspect our mischievous friend here has only just begun your education!"

Pandora looked thoughtful for a moment, then her eyes sparkled and a mischievous smile started to spread across her face.

Jess caught the look.

"You!" she ordered, pointing to her. "Don't even think about it! There is absolutely no way I am going to have an audience! If you want me, *absolutely* no audience! Now if both of you will excuse me, I suddenly feel in a hurry to cook dinner! If you are really nice to me, I might even hunt for fresh meat first!"

Jess was as good as her word.

She looked anxiously at her two friends for approval of what she had caught and cooked.

"No!" Iraj smiled his reassurance. "Really, that was the finest snake I have ever tasted!"

"Yes, me too!" Pandora agreed. "In fact, it is the only snake I have ever tasted."

Iraj burst into chuckles. That was exactly what he had meant.

"We have some left," Jess offered anxiously.

* * *

It was only the afternoon on the fourth day out from the last oasis. Jess had found a hidden cistern so they made an early stop to allow Jess to prepare the family of lizards she had caught that day.

"The larger animals aren't this far into the desert," Jess said, sulky in the face of all the teasing.

"I'm going for a little walk," Pandora said with a secret smile after they had all eaten.

She was carrying Iraj's hunting bow and a small bale of hay for practice.

"Do you want someone to check your technique?" Iraj called out.

"No, thanks," Pandora answered. "I just want to practice what you have shown me."

"Not too far, dear," Jess said automatically.

Iraj looked at Jess, who was pouting a little as she finished wrapping the left over lizard meat.

"Jess, it actually did taste good the way you cook it, thank you for hunting," he said gently.

Jess flashed him a smile and carefully washed her hands, and then looked about nervously.

"We have enough water, Iraj. Do you want to bathe?"

Iraj nodded. "That would be nice. I'll do that first thing in the morning before we set out again."

"If you like," Jess said shyly, "I could help. Anything you want me to do."

Iraj looked a bit puzzled. "Thank you, Jess. But I'm sure I can manage."

Jess paused and knelt next to him. "We have been riding a long way."

"Yes?" Iraj replied, starting to realise Jess was behaving very oddly.

"You must be very sore; if you like I can give you a massage." Jess looked at him hopefully.

"Jess," Iraj asked. "What's going on? And where is Pandora?"

Jess wouldn't look at him for a moment. She muttered something about Pandora. Then she looked up at him, humiliated.

"Iraj, I'm sorry. You must know how attracted I am to you!"

"Jess!" Iraj said, looking at her incredulously. "Have you been trying to seduce me?"

Jess looked away. "Bad idea!"

She gathered herself, ready to rise and make a shame faced retreat, but Iraj caught at her hand. "Jess, please sit down."

She sat and waited, looking confused and embarrassed. "I'm sorry, Iraj."

"Well, I certainly am not! You surprised me, is all." Iraj gave her a smile. "I'm not sure this is a good idea. What about Pandora?"

Jess looked at him earnestly. "I would never hurt Pandora! She knows I am attracted to you from when I first saw you." She paused. "It was her idea!"

"Jess," Iraj laughed, "that almost guarantees it is a bad idea!"

Jess managed to chuckle; Iraj was putting her at her ease. At least he wasn't disgusted at the thought of making love to her!

"Jess," Iraj continued, "I get the impression you don't have a lot of experience with such things."

How can you guess?

"Pandora was the first," she whispered reluctantly.

Iraj looked surprised. "The first woman?"

"No," Jess shook her head, "the first!"

"Jess! Where on earth have you been?" he gasped.

A look of pain passed over Jess's face, her eyes teared.

"Jess that was a silly thing for me to say, please forgive me!" He turned her face to him and wiped her tears gently with his hand. He kissed her lightly on the lips, more like brushing her lips with his.

"Here, I'll show you how it goes for everyone else *but* Pandora!"

Jess got quickly undressed and sat up straight, like a student, all ready to be instructed.

Iraj had to struggle not to laugh.

He moved closer to her and bent over and gave her one of his gentle kisses on her lips. She responded but kept watching him closely, wondering what was coming next.

"Relax." He smiled at her. "We are good friends, don't forget, there is no pressure."

She smiled back at him uncertainly.

He bent to kiss her again and this time she grabbed him and kissed him hungrily, she reached behind him and loosened his hair from his warrior's tie and ran her hands through it and then kissed him on the neck. It tickled, making him feel dizzy. She began running her hands over his chest, he could feel her heart racing, her breath coming faster as she pressed herself against him.

"Whoa," he said, a little breathless himself. "You're a fast learner!"

"That's what Pandora says."

"Jess, let's just both forget about Pandora for the moment. Why don't you lie back and let me do this slowly."

He eased her down, slipped off the rest of his clothes, and kissed her again as he ran his hand down from her shoulder. When he found her nipple she gasped; it was hard and erect. He ran his hand over and over her breast, luxuriating in the feel of it. Then he turned his attention to the other side.

He started to work down over the taut muscles of her stomach and then started to tease her mound and move back and forwards going lower. He could feel her moist and ready.

"Can I touch your manhood?" she asked.

"Jess, of course you can. But if I discharge you will have to wait till I am ready to get hard again and there is less strength each time. It's best not to waste it too much."

Jess looked amazed. "You can't do it twice?"

"Er," Iraj was having trouble thinking as Jess was cradling his testicles in one hand and was lovingly stroking his penis with the other. "I think I can do it twice," he whispered harshly.

"That's nice, isn't it?" Jess said, studying his face intensely.

"The answer is yes, but I think you should stop now."

The tip of his penis was releasing fluid.

Jess seemed to be intrigued and kept stroking until Iraj grunted, tensed and lost control.

"I'm sorry," he apologised.

"I'm not!" Jess said. "I've never seen that before!" She squatted facing him, grinning.

"Now we wait," she announced.

Iraj had no trouble with a second time but he had more control. He slid himself inside Jess and she moaned as they started to move together. Then they clutched each other tightly in shared ecstasy.

"How did I do?" She asked anxiously.

Iraj had to laugh.

"Jess, you were brilliant! I think that was maybe the best I've ever had."

Jess held him inside with her legs and arms wrapped around his body and kissed his chest over and over. "I'm glad," she murmured. "I want to keep you inside forever!"

She gave his buttocks a little tug towards her pelvis.

"Are you sure Pandora won't mind?" Iraj asked.

Jess stiffened.

"Oh, no!" she gasped. "What a fool I am!"

"What?" Iraj was a little alarmed.

"Pandora promised not to watch!"

With a sigh she buried her head on his chest, her shoulders slumped in defeat.

"And you believed her?"

Jess smiled helplessly and pounded her head a few times into his chest in mock exasperation. Then they both began to laugh.

"It was worth it, just to get her permission!" she whispered, grabbing some of his chest hairs with her fingers.

Chapter 12: Trap in the Desert

They couldn't be that far from the Oxos.

They had expected to have reached irrigated land by now but all they had found was yet another deserted village and endless stretches of parched land. This village would have barely been enough for a couple of dozen families. There were a few small houses made of mud and brush, with fences of mud and rocks to keep herd animals out, or in.

Bits and pieces of rubbish were lying around: fragments of wood and pots, traces of ancient dung, amphora and mats of woven palm leaves. More ominous was the remains of what had been home-made tents, made ragged with the winds.

"These people would not move on and leave their tents," Iraj said grimly. "Whatever happened here, how long ago was it do you think, Jess?"

Jess seemed to sniff the breeze. "Less than a year."

She slowly walked over to a large mound of rocks and sniffed again. "Some of them are buried here."

She dug around in the sand at her feet and brought out a broken chain link.

"Slavers," she said, scanning the horizon. "They hid the fact they had been here, why would they even bother doing that?"

They spent a few moments standing near the mound, scanning the surrounds and thinking of the people that were buried there.

"The only reason I can think of is that their base is not too far away," Iraj finally suggested. He paused.

"I think we had better get off these back roads."

Pandora and Jess both nodded together.

Before they left Jess found the remains of a small herb garden. It was shaded and there were four clay water-pots buried up to their necks each with a small stone to seal them. Around them was some oregano still clinging to life. Jess drew some water from the well and lifted each stone and carefully filled each pot.

"What are you doing?" Pandora asked.

"Being a bit silly I guess." Jess admitted, chuckling a little. "I am watering this garden. It seems the least I can do because I am going to take some of this oregano. These pots are unglazed. The roots wrap themselves around the pots and form a seal so they only take the water as they need it. It's very efficient."

"Jacinta's father taught her all about the desert," Iraj remarked, admiring the micro watering system.

"I *lived in* the desert, Iraj." Jess frowned. She didn't like him harping on about Jacinta which he sometimes did.

She began to pluck some of the leaves and lay them out. "These are good for stews and can be used as a medicine."

"Medicine?" Pandora was surprised. "Teispes said you helped with the injured at Khumin, do you know about herbs as well?"

"Yes, I do. With oregano you can make tea for runny noses, poor appetite and women's problems."

"Jacinta's mother was an elf and taught her a lot about healing," Iraj added.

"Iraj!" Jess stood up to face him, planting her hands on her hips and screwing up her face. "Stop comparing me to Jacinta! A lot of assassins know about herbs, some fighters know about healing wounds, it's not so unusual.

"Someone returned after the raid and tended this garden," she added, changing the topic. "Oregano is good in a drought but it shouldn't still be alive. I wonder what happened to them ... maybe the slavers came back."

* * *

"What do you think?" Iraj asked his two companions.

From the hill where they had sought cover they had a good view of the desert fortress. It sat on a low hill of grey and yellow sand and rock. Its mudbrick walls were squat, maybe six meters high, with crenulations for archers. There was a rounded tower at each corner and on their side was a gate protected by a single gate tower. It was more than enough for bandits and raiders, but would not hold against a small army and a determined siege.

There were a scatter of mud brick houses outside the fortress but most of the settlement was inside walls, so the fortress had been built before the town came into being.

Not far away was low lying land, the wide slash of green showing that some of it was irrigated. A good number of camels and sheep were grazing down there.

They didn't see anyone patrolling the walls, most of the sentries would be in the gate house then but there was what looked like a work party clustered around a well making mud brick, using buckets to irrigate young date palms and fruit trees and either some grain crop or grass, they couldn't tell.

"I doubt the slavers would attack such a fortress," Pandora said. "We could get news."

Jess sucked her lip thoughtfully and said nothing.

Iraj read her thoughts. "There is another reason why slavers may not have troubled this fortress, Pandora."

"We will run out of feed for the horses soon," Pandora reminded them. "We are in danger of losing them."

Jess screwed up her face in a grimace.

"This is the only place we have found," Pandora insisted.

Yes, that's exactly what worries us.

"I'm tempted to go in alone," Jess said.

"That would be inviting an attack," Iraj said. "No, we will go in together."

Iraj was in charge of their security ... so the decision had been made. They hid most of their possessions in a shallow cave and began their approach. They were still some distance away when one of the men supervising the workers looked up and went running inside. After a few moments a prosperous looking Persian rode out to meet them.

"*Khosh amadid* (welcome)." He greeted them. "My name is Bagabuxsha but foreigners call me 'Baga'. My shop can provide you with accommodation and any supplies you need. This is a troubled region, but you will feel very safe and comfortable in Dilkor, our fortress is very secure."

Pandora shivered, he somehow reminded her of Ashô-paoirya from Chandyr.

"We are pleased to meet you, Baga, but unfortunately we won't be able to stay," Jess said with a pleasant smile. "My name is Jess. This is my servant Pandora and our guard Iraj. All we need is supplies for our journey at a reasonable price, especially feed for our animals and some flour."

"Could we get some tea, mistress?" Pandora asked Jess with a straight face.

Jess glared at her.

"That we certainly can do," Bagabuxsha said enthusiastically, rubbing his hands. "Women cannot carry weapons in our town. You will have to surrender them at the gate."

"It is normal where I come from," Jess said, giving him her sweetest smile. "My servant only carries a hunting bow. If you insist, we will ride on."

"No, no!" Bagabuxsha said. "That will not be necessary! Just unstring your bows and keep them in their *gorytoi* (holsters for short bows). You too, sir."

Iraj and Jess exchanged a glance. Iraj gave a faint nod but he looked unhappy. Bagabuxsha waited while they all unstrung their weapons.

"Where are you from?" he asked Jess.

"I come from the Kush, the one the Greeks call Aithiopia, are you familiar with that region?"

"I'm afraid not."

That's what I was hoping for, because neither am I.

They passed several thin looking people labouring away.

"Your town has a lot of slaves."

"Yes, things have been very bad with the drought. Our slaves are luckier than most. At least we can find work for them."

Their generous benefits may have included plenty of work but it didn't seem to include a lot of food. As she looked at them, Jess felt a chill. Most of these had come from nearby villages, others would be chance travellers.

They had found the slavers.

She glanced back the way they had come. There were a dozen armed men on horses casually following behind.

Bagabuxsha ushered them through the town gate. There were three bow-men in the gate tower and two warriors attending to the gate. Another three men waited just inside. The gate was closed as soon as they and two of the following men entered.

"I insist you ladies allow me to offer you refreshments in my small taverna while my stable hands help your man attend to the animals," Bagabuxsha said with a cheerful smile.

"That would be delightful," Jess replied.

She didn't sound delighted.

"This is a trap," Pandora muttered in Greek.

"Yes, it is," Jess murmured, while giving Bagabuxsha an engaging smile. "Just act normally."

They left Iraj with the men. At the tavern door Bagabuxsha took Jess's long sword and both of their gorytoi before allowing them in. It was not unheard of being asked to remove weapons before entering a tavern but 'Baga' seemed to have a one track mind as far as separating them from their weapons was concerned.

The only other person in the tavern was a small lady in one corner playing a *veena* (like a sitar). She was dressed in a saffron sārī trimmed with a thin edge of lace. She wasn't much bigger than a twelve-year-old with the light colour and fine features of a northern Indian, an Indo-Aryan. As they entered, she began singing.

Jess stood for a moment, entranced by the pure tones of her voice and the lingering notes of the veena, sweet and melodious.

"She sings like a nightingale!" Pandora said in Sogdianē.

"Enchanting, isn't she?" He motioned to a bench behind a table. There were several stools and tables scattered over the floor, business didn't seem to be too good; assuming of course that their real business was running a tavern.

"We are lucky to have her here. Why don't you relax and refresh yourselves while we organise this?"

"She is singing in one of the other Indo-Aryan dialects," Jess whispered in Greek. "I think it is Hindōstānī."

"Do you know Hindōstānī?"

"No, I don't, but I know an Aryan dialect a lot closer to hers than Sogdianē," Jess whispered back. "How do I know it? I have no idea."

Jess made sure Pandora was on the inside of the bench, she was on the outside.

The manager of the shop stalked in. He was a giant of a man, also an Indian. He leant one of the heaviest swords Jess had ever seen against the wall, within his easy reach. It was a two handed s*hamshīr* (sabre: curved, single edged slashing sword). It would be terrifying to face but even in the hands of such a big man it would be too heavy. He would have to concentrate on circular slashing movements.

"More victims for you to drug?" the small singer asked him bitterly.

"Just keep them entertained. Don't forget you owe us money."

"I don't want to make money this way."

And neither of you expect me to understand what you are saying, do you?

Jess thought longingly about her bow and sword, which were at the entrance. Bagabuxsha was in the way, his sword sheathed. He was not expecting trouble yet.

"I am going to make a move," Jess murmured, swivelling slightly in her seat. "When I do, get under the table and stay there, no matter what happens."

Without warning she lunged at Bagabuxsha, snatching at her belt knife. He wasn't a trained fighter and made the elementary mistake of trying for his sword. Jess was too close for him to use it and he died with a gurgling shriek. His sword dropped in a clatter.

"Look out!" the Indian girl yelled.

Pandora screamed.

The big man had grabbed his shamshīr and was closing the distance with remarkable speed. He gave her no time to grab Bagabuxsha's sword, so she would face him with only a knife. With a great yell, he gave a wide roundabout swing, hard enough to take her head from her shoulders.

Jess ducked underneath it and spun, grabbing a stool and throwing it, all in one motion.

It hit him hard in the chest but he showed no reaction, his chest and arm muscles bulging as he gave a downward swing strong enough almost to split her in two. Jess dodged to the side; the sword struck the hard flooring sending up a cloud of dust.

This man may be as strong as a bull but he has no skill.

Jess's thigh muscles strained as she sprung back. Before he could swing again, her left hand grabbed his blade a third of the way down from the handle. He looked at her hand holding his blade in disbelief and gave it an experimental tug but the weight and leverage was against him.

"Didn't know I could do that, did you?" she asked as she reached across and sliced down hard on his hands.

He screamed with rage, dropping the sword and clutching his bleeding fingers. Then he made a mistake. He staggered back, raising his hands protectively to his chest.

It gave Jess space to swap hands and try to use the shamshīr one handed. She dropped it in disgust and stepped over it to stab him hard in the chest. He shrieked with rage and agony. There was no chance to retrieve her knife as he fell. His weight drove the knife in.

She had to heave to roll him over and then put her foot against his chest to work it out. "Erk, what a mess."

Outside there was the sound of running feet.

"People coming!" Pandora warned.

Jess leapt across the room to grab Bagabuxsha's sword, just as the door burst open.

Pandora didn't know much about swordplay, but she did know that one person didn't last long against multiple assailants and Jess was facing six of them.

The first man was dead before he realised it. The second man got a deep slash to the thigh. Jess danced back a few paces.

The four remaining men were shouting excitedly at one another but they only got in each other's way. The one in front tried a low jerky thrust. Jess deflected it with her knife, her wrists crossed as the tip of her sword sliced across his throat.

She quickly sheathed her knife to pick up another stool, her eyes never leaving the three uninjured men. They were trying to come at her in a three pointed pincer movement. The fourth man with the wounded thigh was hopping across to join them.

She kicked a stool in the way of the man on her right and swung the stool she was carrying straight into the man in front. The man on her left came in for a thrust to her kidneys.

She dodged forward, letting the momentum of her throw continue to spin her body around to chop at his sword arm. He screamed as her sword connected with a meaty "thunk".

Even Pandora could see that their enemies were not skilled and not used to coordinating in a mêlée. They were fighting in a jerky fashion, thrusting only and pausing with their blades held ready.

Jess danced around and in between them, wielding her blade, smoothly, confidently, slashing and the occasional thrust, quickly dodging back and forwards. Pandora could see her use her foot and blade work to open up her opponents for a counterattack.

She ducked behind the man with the injured hand, grabbing at his shirt with one hand. She kneed him at the back of his knees and rammed him forward. The man in front was forced to catch his friend in an awkward embrace; Jess thrust hard through a gap in the tangle of limbs.

Then she ducked around both of them with the speed and ferocity of a tiger, swinging her blade hard at the neck of the man with a wounded thigh.

There were two men left alive, one unhurt.

The one with the injured wrist had climbed off his dead friend and was holding his sword awkwardly with his left hand. His right wrist was bleeding heavily. Watching the other man, she moved in quickly and stabbed him in the chest. He flailed his hands in front as if trying to block her sword with his hands.

It left one man alive and unwounded. She smiled at him as she moved in, like a wolf stalking its prey.

* * *

We are in serious trouble, Iraj had thought as soon as they had entered the front gate of the fortress.

He had turned to study the three men, Yoishta, Dratha and Frânya, with a terrible sinking feeling. They were to take him to the stables. It was the first time ever that Iraj had seen stable hands wearing leather armour and carrying cavalry swords to work in the stables.

The slavers were only using a fraction of the strength they must have but the odds were still completely overwhelming. They were obviously used to doing this and didn't expect too much trouble from one man and two women. His mind was racing, searching for a way out, but they were trapped and outnumbered.

He decided not to start a fight near the gate where the numbers were even worse. So there was no choice but to allow Bagabuxsha to take the girls off somewhere and he would have to follow these men to the stables.

The stables were only a short walk from the gate; the entrance was through a walled-in courtyard with a large barn making up one wall. As they entered the courtyard and closed the door, Yoishta broke into a friendly grin.

"It has been a hot morning, hasn't it, Iraj? Can I offer you a mug of beer before we start?"

"I'll attend to my animals first if that is all right with you." Iraj gave him a friendly grin.

What's in the beer?

"I would be more than happy to join you after that, thank you."

There was a veranda off the barn and a large water trough. He led the horses and then the camels over to drink. The three 'stable hands' didn't seem to be about to offer to help.

"Do you have any wheat-hay or oat-hay?" he asked.

Yoishta looked at Dratha. Dratha looked at Frânya.

"Most certainly!" Frânya said cheerfully, indicating several bales in the corner.

Iraj didn't move. "Ah, Frânya, you know that is wheat straw, cut and dried *after* the seeds are harvested." *I'm actually sure you don't know that.* "And you know I want wheat *hay*, harvested green with the seed heads still attached and then dried. My animals haven't been eating well lately and that's what they need."

Yoishta and Dratha looked puzzled. They obviously had never worked in the stables, nor had they ever had their own animals.

"I think I know where that is kept," Frânya offered and disappeared through the door to the outside. As the door opened and closed, Iraj noticed several men were waiting outside.

Well, I'll be cursed if I am going to be taken without a fight.

He turned back to his horse and removed its saddle. The saddle was of Sakā design, two leather cushions with a pommel and cantle and leather fastenings: girth, a crupper and breastplate to keep it in place. It made it heavy enough for what he needed.

Underneath was a felt saddle-cloth red and adorned with stylized horse motifs.

"Can you help me with this?" he called over his shoulder.

He lifted it off, saddle blanket and all, and turned around. As the two men came up behind him, he threw it at them with all his might.

He whipped out his short sword and stabbed one in the hollow above his breast bone, leaving the sword sticking in him. He fell on the other with his knife, his hand over the man's mouth to stop him crying out. Just then he heard a man cry out in agony in the distance.

Iraj leapt to his feet, his face splitting into a delighted grin. "Jess!"

She was not only alive but she was causing their enemies trouble.

There were shouts from outside the door and the sounds of running feet as the men outside took off to join the fight. Iraj ran to the door to help her, short sword in his hand just as Frânya came through in the other direction, almost bumping into him.

They froze for a moment, looking at each other. Frânya had a bale of hay on his shoulder and a look of confusion on his face. Not for long. He threw the hay at Iraj and drew his long sword.

Iraj had a short sword and no shield. He was facing a man in leather armour wielding a long sword.

He turned and ran.

If Frânya hadn't stumbled over the hay, he wouldn't have made it. But by the time Frânya caught up with him, Iraj had whipped his saddle blanket off the ground and draped it over his left arm.

Frânya tried a clumsy thrust. Iraj spun to deflect it with his blanket and Frânya's sword became snagged on the blanket. With a smile, Iraj threw the blanket over the man's sword and danced in to stab him hard in the chest. Frânya died, bleeding all over the horse blanket. What a shame.

He liked Frânya ... and it was his favourite horse blanket.

He quickly restrung his bow and grabbed two quivers.

Now, where have they taken Jess and Pandora?

In the distance another man screamed.

* * *

"Jess?" Iraj crept in, crouched low.

His bow was strung and an arrow nocked. And then he slowly stood. There were eight men dead in the modest tavern. Pandora was climbing out from under a table looking very pale.

"Did Jess, er ...?"

"No," Pandora said. "But I've never seen anything like it."

Jess was over in the corner squatting down by an Indian girl whose eyes were staring at her wildly. She tried to smile at her in a reassuring way. The effect was spoilt by the blood dripping from Jess's hair.

The girl slid across the floor trying to get away from her, shuddering violently.

"Hello," she tried. "My name is Jess, what's yours?"

The girl only stared at her.

"Can you tell us how to get out of here?" Jess tried again.

"Rohana, my name is Rohana, but they'll kill me if they think I helped you."

"They will think that anyway, Rohana," Jess said. "You had better come with us."

Rohana realised it was true. Bagabuxsha liked her singing. The cook and manager, Chiranjeevi, was a cruel man but he had protected her. She would be sent to work ... and she couldn't work.

"I can't."

Jess reached out a bloody hand and gently lifted Rohana's hands to inspect them. The swollen fingers, the dusky blue lips.

"You're dying, aren't you, Rohana?"

Rohana nodded.

"Come with us then, and die a free woman."

"I'll slow you down."

Jess smiled as she stood. "Then we had best make sure they don't follow."

"The eastern gate," Rohana said. "There are five guards. Most of the town is working on the irrigated land today, beyond the west gate. I would like to come with you but I can't."

"It's decided then." Jess smiled. "Iraj, take Pandora and Rohana to the horses, I will meet you there. Give me ten minutes, no more."

"They will be ready for you, Jess," Iraj warned.

"They won't be ready for *me*." She smiled as she lifted her gorytos. "You don't mind me doing this, Pandora?"

"I only wish I could help."

Jess's face burst into a happy grin. "You just did." And then she was gone.

"She isn't human, is she?" Rohana asked.

"What she is, is our dear friend," Iraj replied. "She said she would look after you. I don't think she can lie about that sort of thing."

They took Rohana's meagre possessions in a small leather bag, a few sārīs, blouses and underclothes, a hair brush and her veena in its own case. Iraj left the door to the courtyard open and had Pandora keep watch. He found another saddle blanket and quickly loaded the animals, and Pandora found a few bags of grain.

Then all he could do was pace, his heart pounding, reminding him of the time that was rushing by. He felt like he was trying to hold his breath. Should he leave now? But how could they possibly get past the town gate without Jess?

Then from over at the gate house he heard shouting. A man screamed out. He expected one of the town citizens to sound the alarm but maybe they had learnt to keep in doors when something like this was happening.

There was a soft whistle and Jess's head appeared around the corner. She was leading a donkey laden with supplies. She had cleaned up her hair and face, though her clothes were still blood stained.

"Sorry it took so long." She smiled. "There was more than we expected. They had plenty of supplies though. I left some sacks of grain near the fort's gate."

She lifted Rohana onto Iraj's spare horse and mounted behind her.

"I often faint if I overdo things," Rohana said.

"Don't worry," Jess said. "I have studied healing."

That got a laugh.

As they rode through the gate, there were dead bodies all around. Jess was in front with Rohana, but she became breathless and dizzy so Jess had to slow the horse to a walk.

"I'm slowing you down."

"And I am not going to leave you. Don't worry, I don't think they will follow us."

"These won't," Rohana said softly to herself at the sight of all the dead bodies.

She had seen Jess kill people so very easily. She knew she wasn't fully human. And now she was riding on a horse, settled comfortably in the arms of a deadly killer.

"How did you get caught?" Jess asked.

"I am easy to catch. I was born with a bad heart. I came looking for work as a singer two years ago. I have gotten sicker this last year."

"You have a hole in the heart. Too much pressure for too long has started to damage the vessels inside your lungs. That's what happens towards the end."

Rohana nodded her understanding. "They used me to distract travellers so they can catch them more easily. A lot of the ones they have caught have died already. They only have less than two dozen now. Luckily I don't eat much."

Rohana felt a dull pain in the chest like a great weight pressing in. She struggled to breathe, the world seemed to be darkening.

She woke up to find they had stopped for the night. It wasn't even dark. A small camp fire was burning and Jess trying to soften smoked horse-meat by boiling it with a little salt. As Rohana watched she poked it with a knife.

"Oh, you are awake," Pandora greeted her cheerfully from the other side.

"You don't seem to understand, I'm only going to slow you down!" Rohana insisted.

Tears came to her eyes. "We didn't get far enough!"

"Don't worry." Jess seemed unconcerned. "I've got to go back in once it's dark anyway. I want to see if I can rescue the others."

"What?" Rohana asked. "Are you insane?"

"That's what we have been trying to ask her," Iraj said heavily. "And she won't even let me come."

"Iraj, someone has to look after Rohana and Pandora," Jess said. "Besides, I can sneak around better on my own."

Pandora gave her a sulky look.

"I'm sorry, love," Jess apologised. "It's like a hunger, driving me."

"Jess, you can't fight a whole village," Pandora said, looking upset.

"*That* would be difficult," Jess admitted. "But all I have to do is enter a heavily guarded fortress and rescue a couple of dozen people from inside its walls. And I will have a big advantage."

"What's that?"

"They won't be expecting me."

* * *

Twenty-four men lay on the dirt floor of the stone warehouse that had been their prison since they had been captured. Most were too far gone in hunger and exhaustion to talk or move. Their jailors kept a great torch in a sconce just outside the door. It gave the prisoners some light through a crack in the door and the small window above.

Frashaoshtra crept over to whisper to his brother, Geramig.

Two years ago Frashaoshtra and Geramig had been part of a small party of traders who had stopped for supplies. They were lulled by Rohana's singing and the food and drink had been drugged. Only Geramig and Frashaoshtra were still alive.

This had been a small garrison town. After the defeat of the Šâh, all order had collapsed. Phraotes, the oldest of the *Dah-bashi* (commanders of ten), had murdered the commander and had found a way to profit from the chaos. He made slaves of anyone he could catch or any who opposed him. But he didn't sell his slaves. All around were too many starving people with the drought, and there was no market for slaves.

Instead he put them to work: building, irrigating and looking after his stolen herds. At first the slaves were promised freedom if they worked hard. It did make them work harder. They didn't believe it but they had no other hope. None were ever freed.

By keeping them exhausted and weak from hunger they became easy to manage and cheap to keep. They had bread in the morning and a bowl of thin soup at midday.

Refusing to work or being unable to resulted in a public hanging. Even a simple illness would be a death sentence. A great deal of them did die. At first it didn't matter. Slaves were of little value and there were lots of undefended villages nearby.

For a while they had made many of the town's petty criminals their guards and armed them with cudgels. With few exceptions they were the cruellest of all jailors: arbitrary punishments, beating the slaves for fun, throwing their food on the ground and molesting any of the women.

Geramig was determined he would escape, but first he had to survive. He forced Frashaoshtra and any who wished to follow him to save some bread for later in the day despite their hunger. That way they weren't too weak to work in the afternoon.

He taught them to weave little cages for rats and feed them scraps, sneak milk from the herd animals, steal grain, plant a few seeds and water them in secret, make loop snares for catching lizards and rats and bait small traps with scraps. They ate anything they could get: plant roots, lizards, rats and even insects.

They caused no trouble. They avoided looking at the guards to cause offense. They obeyed immediately and spoke politely. They especially made sure they were favourites of any of the townsfolk or guards who helped the slaves in small ways.

After a while the supply of slaves slowed. And then it stopped. There used to be a lot more of them, but they kept dying, especially the women, unless they could get one of the guards to protect them.

Finally the slaves got better treatment. Sometimes there was meat in their soup, especially if someone died. After a while the local criminals were forced to join them. The two most sadistic ones were found dead the next day and there was meat in the soup for several days after that.

There were only a couple dozen prisoners left now. They had long lost any hope of escape, but survival had become a habit.

"Why do you think they made us stop early?" Frashaoshtra asked.

"The guards said the town was raided. They took that *Hindu* (Indian) bitch."

"She was a prisoner too," Frashaoshtra reminded him.

Geramig only grunted with disgust. As far as he was concerned, it was she that helped catch him.

"Why would they take her, though? She's sick," Frashaoshtra asked. Geramig only shrugged.

Outside there was a muffled cry. Geramig's head jerked up. He motioned for all the other men to keep quiet. For many moments there was nothing. Then there was a loud thump as if the door had been kicked.

Again silence.

A man's voice outside called out the name of a guard. Then a noise like a choking, wet cough and then something falling softly in the dirt.

Frashaoshtra saw the look on his brother's face.

"Forget it. No one is coming for us."

There was a noise like a large animal sniffing around the door. Time passed, and then the light started to dance; someone had removed it from its sconce. It moved lower and then went out.

They heard the familiar sound of a bolt sliding. The door opened cautiously, a dark figure appeared in the doorway, well back in the shadows. A voice came out of the darkness.

"Can all of you walk?"

"You're a woman!" Geramig said in shocked realisation.

"Last time I checked. My name is Jess. Are you in charge? I have six swords and six knives."

She entered then, dragging a bundle wrapped in one of the guards' coats. She dumped it with a metallic clutter. "I have two camels, two horses and a donkey waiting just outside the town, but we will need supplies."

"We can't fight or run carrying sacks of grain," Frashaoshtra said.

"I only have time to talk to one of you," Jess said. "Choose who it will be. But all I really want to know is if you want to come with me or not. The guards, I can take care of."

"Talk to me, Geramig, and yes, we are all coming. How many of you are there?"

"Just me, but I have others waiting outside."

"Just you? Are you mad?"

"I think so. Let's get those supplies. Not too much water, I can find that. Leave the guards to me. Oh, and watch your step."

There was a dead guard, naked, near the doorway. Jess was wearing his clothes and carrying his weapons. There were several scattered humps in the darkness.

"What are you?" Geramig whispered in fear.

"What I am is an assassin, the best I know of," Jess said, a little out of breath. "These people annoyed me, so I came back."

"Lucky for us," Geramig said softly. "Unlucky for them; there can't be many who can do what you have done."

"I don't know of anyone else."

The store room door wasn't locked; that meant a patrolling guard. Jess gave Geramig a meaningful look and while they filed in to get supplies, she disappeared into the darkness.

"She's not human," Frashaoshtra warned him.

"I don't care," Geramig growled in reply. "I would follow a demon from hell if it would get me out of this place."

As they came out bearing sacks of grain, she reappeared. She didn't seem concerned, and she wasn't out of breath any more.

"I'll meet you at the east gate."

"They normally have eight people guarding it, two awake."

"Let's hope I only have to kill two of them then." She grinned. "They are not well trained you know."

"They will come after us," Geramig said. "They will want their slaves back."

"How many?"

"Fifty-eight guards and some villagers will help."

"It's less than that now, but it's still more than I had hoped."

* * *

Arxa, Phraotes's second in command, stood on the battlements of the fortress the next morning. He was deep in thought as he surveyed the surrounding land.

The Kyzyl Kum was one of the driest places on earth. He couldn't remember when they last had rain. Apart from what they had irrigated, everywhere he looked was rocks, clay and sand (yellow and red) with sparse salt bush scattered about and some rank grasses.

Thousands of years ago, the people of this land had first built the great canals; some ran hundreds of miles. But Dilkor was too high for the canals. So for Dilkor they had brought water from the nearby mountains. It allowed them to irrigate some of their lowlands, but the lowlands had too much salty land which only soured when irrigated. It wasn't enough.

With the drought there were fewer merchants and nomads and some of the oases had run dry. Dilkor had lost its reason for being; it had become a forgotten outpost in the badlands. Only the worst of soldiers were ever sent here.

After the death of their Šâh, the supplies stopped and Dilkor should have died too. Phraotes had seized control and somehow, he made it work.

Instead of killing anyone who opposed him, he came up with a brilliant solution: work them to death. He had fought the drought and the desert. He made his captives water good land higher up using hand buckets and watering cans. Now his men had enough, they even a good life, but they needed their slaves.

Uvaxshtra, one of his *Dah-bashi* (corporals), approached him. "As you already know, Šēr, Bagabuxsha brought three travellers inside the fortress, a man and two women. Their leader was a black woman, as tall as a man. It was the usual plan: split them up, separate them from their weapons, drug them and capture them. It should have held no risk to us and resulted in no damage to them. Instead they somehow killed Bagabuxsha and Chiranjeevi and fifteen of our men. Then they rode out of the gate, taking that Hindu singer with them."

"Why would they take her?" Arxa asked.

"I don't know. Then last night we got raided. We lost all our slaves and another eight men, killed in silence. I don't even know anyone who can do that sort of thing."

"There are rumours of an attack near Chandyr. A sorcerer was killed and a group of shepherds who were attacking women."

"And you think this is connected to what happened here?" Uvaxshtra asked. "No, Šēr, I think this is a group of mercenaries, cursed good ones. Those three were scouts and maybe there was a dozen more. They must have opened the gates somehow and caught our men by surprise. All we have found is the tracks of two horses. Maybe they split up and the smaller group isn't even covering their tracks."

"Take four men and chase those down while I keep looking for the main party. If we don't find our old slaves we had better not give Phraotes any reason to choose us instead."

Uvaxshtra's party, counting Uvaxshtra, had two mounted bowmen and three lancers but none of them were the crack troops the Sakā were famous for. Several miles on they passed a deep ravine. They were too focused on the tracks they were following to see a dark figure step out just behind them. Jess had six arrows in her bow hand, and one already nocked on her bow-string. Only the finest archers could use the rapid fire technique. If you had asked Jess where she had learnt it, she couldn't have told you.

She only knew that at this range she wouldn't miss.

* * *

As the morning wore on, Arxa and his men were no closer to tracking down their escaped slaves. They had found a bloody hand print on the wall outside the slave's quarters. There were the tracks of a large animal outside the fortress wall. At least two of the guards seemed to have had their throats ripped out as if by a large animal. One of the villagers had thought she saw a dark shape running low down, through the shadows.

Arxa wasn't about to tell his men that what they were facing may not be human. Uvaxshtra hadn't returned. He wondered if he should have sent out a small party, it was only the tracks of two horses but who was riding those horses?

* * *

It was mid-morning when Jess returned with Geramig and Frashaoshtra from the trap they had set.

She joined Raj who was looking out over the fortress. Their main party was hidden in caves. The ambush this morning was to discourage the slavers from sending out small parties so it was harder for them to mount a search.

The next step was going to be more difficult.

"When we leave here most of us will be on foot and they will know roughly the path we will have to take," Jess said. "To stop them moving against us in force, we need to damage them more."

"Just what I was thinking," Iraj agreed. "Unfortunately it looks like they are expecting something just like that."

Down below, men were inserting unlit torches into sconces in the walls and gathering piles of brush for camp fires. They had armed the villagers with spears and had them patrolling the walls.

"They mustn't know how few we really are," Frashaoshtra murmured. "We won't be able to sneak around so easily with all that light."

"We?" Jess raised an eyebrow in query.

"Yes. We are coming."

"Tell them, Iraj," Jess whispered urgently. "Tell them that I'm better by myself, you know why."

"Jess, I have no idea what you are talking about." Iraj tried to look innocent. "Besides, I'm coming too."

Jess wanted to snarl at him.

"You need us anyway." Geramig smiled at her. "We can show you where to find Phraotes. If you can kill him their organisation will collapse and we can show you the fort's weakness."

Jess turned slowly to him. "The fort's *weakness*?"

"Yes, it's simple, really," Geramig explained. "If you can find a good enough well or underground spring inside a mountain you can run a channel under the ground from high up so that when you reach the lowlands the water comes out at a height. It means you can irrigate more easily."

"That's interesting," Iraj said blandly. *So what?*

Jess screwed up her face, thinking. "It's just like running an aqueduct from higher up a river before the river drops. That gives you water pressure for irrigation and for your city, even fountains if you want, except in this case it is all or mostly underground."

Iraj looked at her quizzically. *What was this leading up to?*

"It is very hot here in summer," Geramig added. "The wind blows a lot of dust and sand."

"So keeping the channel under the ground as much as possible is better." Jess paused. "And you're going to tell me they have done this for Dilkor."

Geramig grinned at her and pointed to the low mountain range in the near distance.

"Ah, I see," Iraj burst out into a wide grin. "There is a water channel leading from an underground spring somewhere under those mountains straight into the fortress, all underground."

"The main channel is used to irrigate the lowlands," Geramig said. "They have a side channel to the town, yes, but the town is higher than the lowlands so the channel feeds a series of wells inside the fortress. The channel itself has ventilation shafts at regular intervals so that workers can climb down and clean it and repair it, which is why I know about it. They only let their most trusty slaves do that but one day a slave tried to escape along the water channel. The guards simply rode horses to the next shaft and killed him easily as he emerged."

"And," Jess said very slowly, "you will tell me that no one has thought to put a heavy grill set in rock across the channel as it enters the town."

"Yes, they have thought of that," Geramig admitted. "But I am told it is made of iron and it is old and rusty."

"You thought about using it to escape," Jess realised.

"Yes, but I was never given the chance. It would be fitting if we could use it to break in."

When Geramig and Frashaoshtra showed them the ventilation shafts for the underground water channel it looked for all the world like a row of mine shafts, all in a line across the floor of the desert leading towards the town.

The dirt from each shaft had been heaped around the mouth, causing a shallow dimple with the access hole in the centre.

"How deep are they?" Iraj asked as Jess and he bent to examine them.

Jess peered down. "Not deep here, six feet at the most; it will be less at the start of the plain but deeper under the fortress."

"With all the water I won't be able to take my bow." She looked unhappy. "If all we can use is bladed weapons, I will need your help after all."

"You're not going to ..." Iraj asked.

"No, I'm not, Iraj. Have you forgotten you have invited an audience to this little show tonight?" She sighed. "How many are coming?"

"All of the former slaves would, but there are only ten that I would judge fit enough. Of those, Geramig and Frashaoshtra are good with a sword and two others are experienced with thrusting spears and we have four that can use slings. You can't deny their right."

"Slings? At night? This will be just great." Jess spat down the shaft. "You and me and ten half-starved men; none have fought together before this. Barely half have any training and all of those are out of practice. The rest are inexperienced and poorly disciplined. Not to mention we will be outnumbered by fully fit troops by more than three to one. Have you got any good news?"

"Yes, I have. It won't be your problem. They have elected me to lead them. Geramig will be second in charge."

He made sure the ventilation shaft and his horse were between himself and Jess. He tried to dodge but Jess was onto him with lightening speed. "Now, Jess! It's nothing about you being a woman. They are scared of you."

What? How dare they be?

She realised she had Iraj by his shirt. She loosened her grip and patted it back into shape.

"And they think you are not human."

* * *

"This may take a while," Geramig observed to Jess.

Crawling on your hands and knees through a narrow tunnel half way across the plain and then cold chiselling through an iron grate while trying not to make too much noise? Yes, it just might.

"Oh well, we may as well start." Iraj sighed. "Jess, can you go ahead and open the grill? We will join you as it gets dark, so we don't have torches in the channel going in, but we won't attack before middle watch."

Jess was tempted to make a suggestion to their great leader that was anatomically impossible.

Instead she managed a "Yes, šēr!"

Anything you say, šēr!

Her sarcasm would be wasted on the other men waiting.

Once she had calmed down she had realised she wouldn't be good as a leader. She tended to want to go off and do things all by herself rather than co-ordinate the activities of a group. But it didn't stop her from still feeling annoyed.

She crawled closer to the fortress before disappearing down one of the ventilation shafts. Because of the water she wore a short shift, without underwear; thankfully no one was following close behind. Her sword was strapped over her shoulder in an improvised baldric.

She had a hammer and cold chisel tucked into her belt, rags to try to muffle any chiselling as well as a packet of food to snack on while she waited. The floor of the water channel was lined with stones but the roof and sides were packed earth. It was rough, irregular and narrow, no more than a crawl space. The dark between ventilation shafts was not a problem for her and she was not in the mood to be worried about the others who were following at dusk.

Setting out on all fours, it didn't take much time for her clothes to be soaked with icy underground water, her food packet and rags to be soggy and her knees to be bleeding and stinging from the stones. Here and there some lucky tree roots had found the water just so they could trip her and bark her shins. *And* she was thoroughly fed up with catching the hilt of her sword on the roof. She took it off her back and pushed it in front of her, trying unsuccessfully to keep the expensive scabbard dry.

The grill when she finally reached it was a series of wrought iron bars hammered and jammed into a patch of heavy underground rock. Leading up to it was a wide section with a higher roof and a deeper floor to allow a black smith to set up an underground forge.

At least she could stand up into a half crouch and stretch and rub some of the gravel out of the cuts on her knees and elbows.

The iron was heavily rusted and flaking apart. They should have used bronze. To repair it now they would have had to block the channel and drain the area. Dilkor must have had some sort of importance at one time, but no one was going to do that now.

Jess bent over close to the rusting barrier and smiled.

"Forgotten about you, haven't they?"

* * *

Phraotes jerked awake.

He couldn't have been asleep all that long. It must be middle watch. It would not be the first time he had missed sleep to check on the sentries. He eased himself out of bed and put on his slippers. Firuza murmured in her sleep.

He smiled. Since he had taken over Dilkor, he had been a much better soldier than he had ever dreamed possible. And he made an excellent commander: the village was prosperous and his men well looked after.

Before going out to check on the sentries, he buckled on his single edged *kopis* (machete). A kopis was really half a weapon and half of a farmer's slashing tool, hardly an officer's weapon but it was what he was used to and he felt comforted by the familiar weight.

He stepped out and waited a minute, looking around. Arxa had suggested that they were facing something supernatural, Phraotes wasn't sure he even believed in daēvas.

The best protection against them was said to be prayer. Somehow he didn't think that would work for him. Heroes like Rostam, Tahmûrath or Jamšêd bested them with wrestling or trickery. After that, it was said, they became faithful servants. Now that would be handy, having a daēva as a servant! Mostly they were supposed to stand nine feet tall on clawed feet with horns and a tail. Very handy indeed!

Several of the torches had burnt down, leaving patches of darkness. There was no moon. A night time breeze caused the lights and shadows to dance.

Did he hear a noise? Had something woken him? He glanced behind. The breeze rustled some dust and dead leaves. A cloth curtain sighed as it drifted against a window sill.

He saw a sentry patrolling further along the street and made to walk that way, trying to resist the urge to hurry towards the reassurance of some company.

The town seemed otherwise deserted. That was strange. He had put extra guards on. He glanced behind again, straining his eyes to see in the shadows. In the distance a man's voice was raised in query.

He turned back to call out a friendly 'salaam' to the soldier. The man didn't reply, just stopped and turned towards him.

"Who are you?" he called out, moving closer, putting his hand on the hilt of his kopis. The man just stared at him.

Or behind him.

A powerful arm grabbed his chin from behind him and tilted it up. He felt a sharp pain as a knife sliced into his throat.

* * *

It was morning and Geramig found Jess pouring Rohana some herbal tea.

"You do this as well?" Geramig laughed. "I heard you bandaged and stitched some of my men."

"I see nothing funny about that, Geramig." Jess said.

While Rohana sipped her tea, Jess poured oil on her hands and squatted to massage the fluid from her legs, ignoring him.

"Yes, well er, you know what I mean." Geramig blushed. "We honestly have never seen the like of you. I was there when you killed Phraotes and some of the others, you are very fast."

"If you want to kill someone, you don't want to stand around waiting."

"I would have liked Phraotes to suffer a bit first."

"It's not a game, Geramig."

"I have offended you. At least you are not a daēva."

Jess just shrugged. Geramig looked a little taken aback.

"I heard you're planning to leave tomorrow. I think that is for the best."

"I'm taking my choice of two of the five horses from the men I ambushed," Jess said, glancing his way. "That will give us a horse each, plus my two camels. Keep the donkey. And I want a heavy bow for my friend Pandora. We will need supplies, and Iraj and I deserve a share of any money you found."

Geramig hesitated. "I suppose that's fair."

He didn't sound too happy.

"Be careful on the road, Arxa took off this morning with a dozen men. The rest of the soldiers left the gates open and threw down their weapons. People are asking me to stay and take over."

Jess looked up in surprise. "Are you even considering that?"

"I spent most of the time here dreaming of escape." Geramig took a deep breath. "But it's hard not to think we own some of what we have worked so hard for. This town is prosperous, it will require hard work but I don't know that we can find better. Not the way things are at the moment. I will ask the worst to leave but anyone half decent can stay. We will try to forget the past and start anew."

"Good luck to you then," Jess said politely. "Don't forget to repair the grill."

As Geramig walked away, Rohana bent over to study Jess's expression.

"If he said 'thank you' I must have missed it. Do you want me to stay here too?"

"Don't worry about him," Jess shrugged. "No one wants my type around, except when they need me of course, then it's different. Do I want you to stay? For my part, no. Travelling may bring your death closer, but if you do come, I can look after you. I promise you will die amongst friends."

"I would like to come." Tears came to Rohana's eyes. "I like travelling. If I'm to die, I'd rather die travelling. There is absolutely nothing for me here. I just don't want to be a burden."

"You will be a burden, but it is one that I will gladly bear." She stood and wiped a tear from Rohana's cheek. "You're coming with us. I want no more of your arguments."

She pulled a face and they both laughed.

* * *

"Geramig was here this morning," Rohana was telling Iraj when they were alone. "He virtually told her to leave. She didn't say anything, but I could tell it hurt her. I'd rather deal with Jess any day than with Geramig."

"You are a shrewd judge of character, then." Iraj smiled at her. It made her feel flushed.

"I can't run and I can't fight back, so I had to be good at reading people and trying to make them happy." Rohana looked into the distance. "It started with my mother. She was not an easy woman. My father and I were close. It was him that was the musician. When he died I got free transport on caravans by being an entertainer."

"That was a brave thing to do, with your heart and all."

"All I can do is watch people doing things I can't, that and play my music." She giggled. "So I like travelling, seeing new things. Jess says she wants to take me, but what about you, you and Pandora? It is asking a lot of you. "

"You're not so big. I think we can handle you without you causing us too much trouble."

He gave her that smile again that made her feel weak all over.

She looked at the handsome Avestan, his broad shoulders and muscular chest, his dark curly hair and beard, his ready smile, and his deep, gentle voice. She felt a terrible sense of loss for something that she could never have.

"She's sad, isn't she? Jess, she is very sad underneath."

"Yes," Iraj replied, "yes, she is."

* * *

Before they left, Frashaoshtra came to see Jess, who was massaging Rohana's arms and shoulders.

"I've found someone who will sell you *opion* (opium). How much do you need?"

Jess gave a shaky sigh of relief. "About as much as I can get, I think."

"Then I will take you to her," Frashaoshtra said. "Jess, I want to thank you for what you have done for us. I am not ready to leave or I would have taken it as a privilege if I could travel with you, if you would have me of course. Geramig can be a hard man but he has kept us alive."

"Why do you need so much opion?" Rohana asked Jess.

Jess wouldn't look at her for a moment. "Er, towards the end you will get breathless, fighting for every breath."

"I am very much afraid of that time," Rohana said quietly. "I didn't want to tell you. I didn't want to be a burden. It's just that it's hard to be brave sometimes."

"Opion will ease the fluid in your lungs. More importantly it will calm you and stop your body fighting so hard towards the very end. Unfortunately that means—"

"I know what it would mean if my body stopped fighting so hard to breathe," Rohana said quickly. Tears came to her eyes. "Thank you, Jess."

"I just didn't want you to think ... er, you know, if you found out about the opion. I didn't want you to think ... that I was trying to, well, I would never do anything like that without telling you." Jess couldn't seem to find anywhere to look.

"I would never think that of you, Jess," Rohana said softly.

"Well, er, thank you, Rohana." Jess's voice was hoarse and her vision blurred with her own tears. "Oh, and thank you, Frashaoshtra. Sorry to be so emotional. It just means a lot to me is all."

* * *

By their second day travelling Jess was alarmed that Rohana seemed so sleepy. They were taking it slow. Jess had insisted

Rohana ride with her, in her arms. Jess felt her heart burning for the young woman, if only she could breathe for her.

She didn't want to worry anyone else by saying anything, but the girl could hardly stay awake. It wasn't fainting at least, it was sleepiness, and she did seem to sleep comfortably and wake in good condition.

Maybe it wasn't too surprising. Rohana didn't just have a bad heart and fluid, she was also badly out of condition from any form of exercise. If it wasn't for the sleepiness and being plagued by constant chest pains, the small Hindu woman might be seen to be coping better than Jess had ever expected she would.

By the fourth day it was obvious to everyone that Rohana was better. Her colour no longer had the dusky tinge of blue and she seemed less breathless. Perhaps it was being out of doors. Perhaps it was being amongst friends. Maybe it was Jess's obsession with doing anything and everything to help her. Jess didn't expect it to last. But it gave them a little more time and for that they were grateful.

Rohana even managed to sing a third song for them when they stopped for the evening. Her three new friends sat around the cooking fire and listened in awe.

"I've just never heard anyone with a voice like yours," Pandora said. "And you play like the Goddess of music herself. I can't sing anything like you, but can I sing along sometimes?"

"Of course you can, and if you teach me songs of your home, I will sing them, too."

"My home?" Pandora's eyes sparkled in the firelight. "You would sing Greek songs? How about you, Jess? ... Oh, I'm sorry."

"You may as well know, Rohana. Something happened to my memory. I don't remember my home and I remember very little of my past. Maybe I'll say more about it later. It's a long story." Jess managed a smile. "Or maybe I should say it is a rather short one. And I think most people would pay me not to sing."

"Can you dance? The way you move."

"Dance? Yes, I can dance very well, at least I think I can."

Jess, what has happened to you? Rohana wondered.

"Jess, I *am* feeling much better, is it the tea you are giving me? Have you used it much before?"

"Rohana, many things I just *know*, but where I learnt them, I don't know. I don't think I have any real experience looking after someone like you. It's all theory and not much of that. As far as the tea is concerned, I don't think it is supposed to be this potent."

"Jess, you killed eight men within only moments of when I first saw you."

"It was fourteen, er fifteen," Jess said. "Some you didn't see and then there were more that evening. Rohana, I'm not proud of what I am but I would never hurt you or force you."

"Jess, I know that's true." Rohana laughed, "I have met a lot of people who have frightened me, but nothing like you. Now I know you would never hurt me. I know you have secrets some of which you may not want to share, but is there anything I need to know about you, *right now*?"

Jess went very quiet.

"I think Jess likes you," Pandora suggested.

"That's nice, I like her very much."

"No, I mean I think Jess *likes* you."

"Well, I do," Jess muttered, refusing to meet Rohana's gaze. "But not like you, Pandora."

"Oh!" Rohana's hands flew to her mouth. "I must say that wasn't what I expected you to say."

"I would never push," Jess said. "You are very pretty and your singing is like that of an angel. It makes my heart feel like soaring. I think we all feel that."

"You and Jess?" Rohana asked.

Pandora and Jess looked at each other and then back and nodded in unison.

"How does Iraj fit in?"

"Iraj is a wonderful man!" Jess said. "He fits right in!"

"Jess? ... Are you a threesome? Is it that that you want me to join?"

"Why of course we are, and we love the idea of you joining us."

"Jess, I simply can't do that sort of thing!" Rohana was horrified. "Anyway, I am not well enough."

"Rohana," Pandora said softly. "I don't think Jess knows what a threesome is, let alone a foursome."

"Why of course I do!"

Then Jess paused and looked puzzled. The three of them were grinning back at her. "What's a foursome?"

Pandora pointed to each of them slowly and deliberately.

"Iraj and three women?" Jess asked in shock. "What, at the same time?"

No, no, no, I couldn't do that!

Iraj was looking smug. Jess screwed up her face and poked her tongue out at him. Pandora had a far away look on her face and a faint smile.

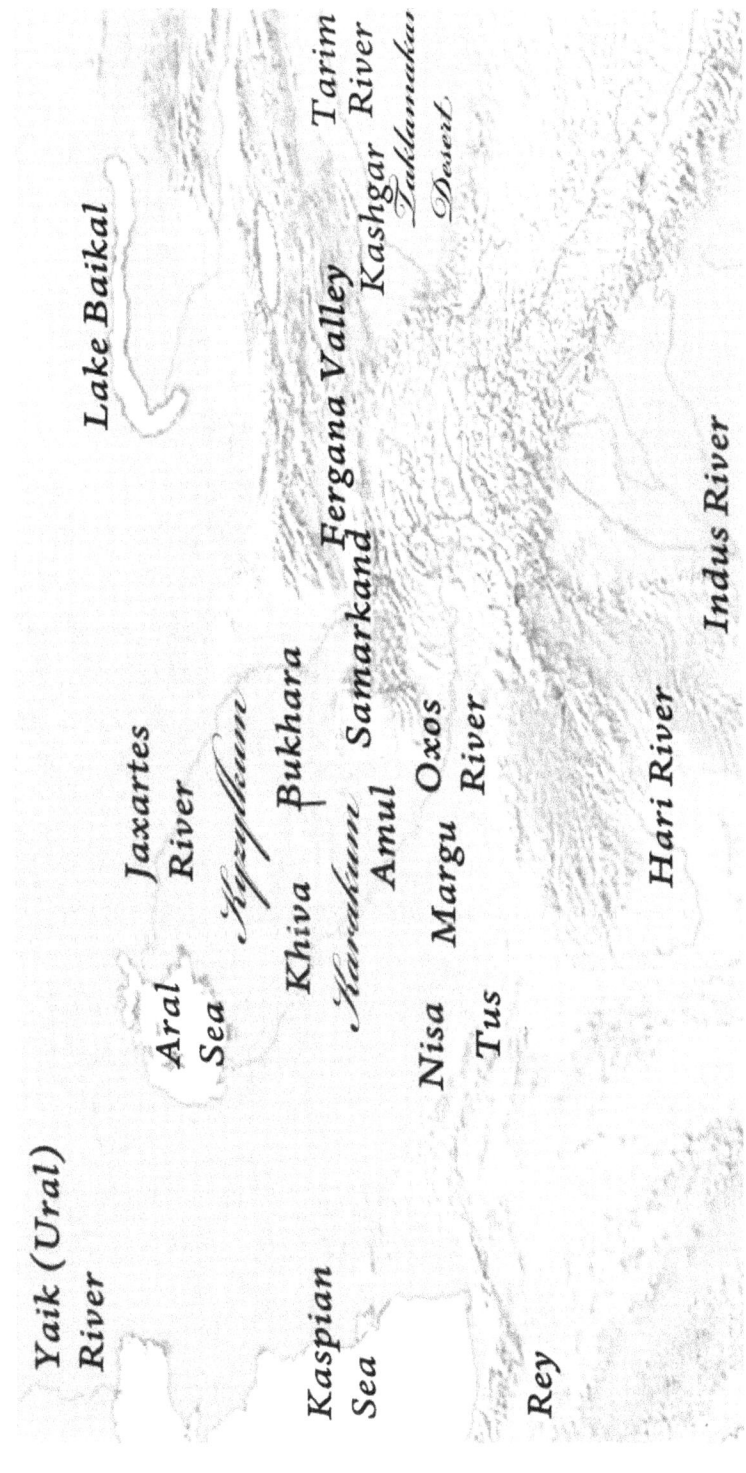

Central Asia

Chapter 13: Āmul, the Dancer

Jess couldn't believe it when Rohana asked to ride one of the horses, at least for a short while. She had only ever been led on a horse or travelled as a passenger before.

She laughed at Jess's concerns. "Jess, I'm going to die. There are so many things I can't do. I may as well have some fun. Thank you for caring for me, really, but I don't want to be wrapped in your fine lamb's wool all the time."

She was right, Jess knew. She may as well die happy. Iraj and Jess hopped down and moved their packs around and fixed the saddle and then Iraj took Rohana for her first riding lesson.

Just how hard can it be to let go, and not feel anxious? Jess asked herself. So far the exercise seemed to be doing Rohana good. They were walking the horses so it would not be too strenuous, not much more than riding as a passenger with Jess, as long as they took it slow enough.

Still, she watched from a distance, gripping the reins of her horse, frowning and chewing on her lip. Pandora moved closer and they stretched out to take each other's hand while they watched Rohana laughing and Iraj teasing her.

She had felt called to take Rohana, just like she felt called to journey to the Troad, and to rescue Pandora and the slaves from Dilkor.

As she watched she realised that no matter how this girl died, it was going to hurt. It was going to hurt a lot.

* * *

Rohana took a deep breath and laughed again.

"We should get a pony," Iraj teased. "Something for a twelve-year-old."

"Iraj, there are plenty of small women!" Rohana laughed. "I'm sure you'll find I am more woman than *you* can handle."

She hadn't laughed like this in a long while. She couldn't remember feeling so free and she had these three wonderful friends, especially a handsome man.

She ignored her chest pain. She hoped that this was what took her in the end, her heart going suddenly like a ruptured muscle, not slowly, drowning in fluid, fighting for every breath.

She also ignored the terrible feeling of tiredness and Iraj and Jess's demands that she should rest. She was going to die, she would get plenty of rest then!

She wondered what it would be like to be carried held by Iraj, rather than Jess. It would be so nice if she could lie back in his strong arms and to have his deep voice murmuring in his chest. But as a real woman, not as an invalid or someone close to the size of a girl.

Eventually she couldn't keep awake any longer and she was passed back to Jess, almost unconscious.

"I want to ride again!" she said almost as soon as she woke.

Jess pulled her around to face her. "Are you sure?"

"Yes, but I would like to eat first."

She had woken in Jess's arms feeling happy and full of restless energy ... and she was hungry.

Jess called a halt to feed her some dry figs and goat's cheese and left over stale bread soaked in wine and water. Then Rohana mounted and urged her horse up front so she could ride with Iraj again.

* * *

It was late on the morning of the sixth day when the travellers topped a hill to get their first glimpse of that paradise called the Oxos River Valley. Here it was a good 15 kilometres wide. Far in the distance they could see the great river itself.

"It's *huge!*" Jess gasped.

"The river is no longer at the height of its full flood but it gets much lower when winter comes to the mountains." Iraj told her. "This is one of the narrow stretches of the river but it is still *twelve stadia* (almost a mile and a half) wide. At other points in maximum flood it can be as much as *a parasang* (a league, three and a half miles) wide with many of its islands flooded. You can't wade across now and it's too far to swim the animals, so you have to cross by barge."

In the near distance were field after field of golden wheat, soon it would be harvest time. In the lower parts Jess could see swamp-land and reeds and in the north of the valley was a forest. Close to the river was mainly willow and poplar and further out was oak and elm. Between the willows and poplar her keen vision showed her a glint of water.

Of course, the forest must rely on seasonal flooding and ground water rather than rain which rarely came here, and the flooding would bring a load of silt washed down from the mountains.

"The river is very muddy," She commented.

"Up in the mountains its flow is very swift," Iraj told her. "I know where we are now. And it can't be much more than a moon till the *Galla Bayramy* (harvest festival)."

"You harvest your wheat in summer, later than elsewhere?" Jess asked.

"Yes, we do," Iraj said. "It is all irrigated so we don't have to plant around seasonal rain like they do in Anatolē and elsewhere. The river comes from the melting snow and ice in the mountains. It flows most in spring and early summer and that's an ideal time for grain to grow. During the harvest time, almost everything grinds to a stop. Shops shut and government buildings close down. Everyone has a relative or friend they want to help, or they have a small plot of land or they want some extra money. But it is hard work in the heat for not much money." He laughed. "I was born only a few days' ride from here and I tried it over a couple of summers."

He pointed to where the road they were following led east, parallel to the river.

"We have to follow that road to the main crossing."

"Let's go then." Rohana called, kicking her horse up to a trot.

"Rohana!" Jess shrieked.

"Jess!" Iraj shouted a warning. "Don't try to catch her, you'll only spook her horse."

"Slow down, Rohana!" Jess cried out helplessly, her hands in her mouth.

"I'm going to beat you all!"

Rohana was laughing like a crazy woman as she raced her horse down the slope to be the first to reach the valley floor.

* * *

On the northern bank there was an outdoor market and a shouting aggressive crowd of ferrymen. Jess felt more than a little overwhelmed.

She was happy to hang back with Rohana and let Iraj and Pandora go to battle over the cost of getting them across the river. Iraj had done this dozens of times and Pandora absolutely loved bargaining.

Once they were across the river, Jess and Rohana waited with the camels near the docks while Iraj and Pandora entered the city with the four horses to find accommodation.

The three women would stay at Āmul while Iraj visited his family to bring them the terrible news of his sister's death.

Āmul had been an important town on the western bank of the Oxos and might be again. It hadn't been fully restored after an earthquake and it had been overtaken by the more energetic township of Parap upstream and across the river. So Āmul was better than Parap for somewhere that the young women could lay low.

Back across the river was the road leading to Bukhara where Jess had first met Pandora. On either side of the great river, parallel to each bank, were the river roads.

Khiva, the capital of what had been Xvairizem, lay down-river (north and a little west) at the start of the vast marshes of the Oxos delta. The Oxos mainly drained into the Aral Sea but a canal had been dug to link it to the Kāspian.

They had originally planned to go north on the Oxos by boat but now they would be taking the overland trip west to *Margu* (Merv), the great oasis city, still in the hands of the Persis.

Jess and Rohana waited on a couple of boxes in the shade, idly watching the boats plying up and down and back and forwards. Close up the Oxos looked even muddier. Jess was engaged in cutting up a watermelon, using her knife in her left hand, and there was a small pile of melons at her feet.

"Jess!" Rohana laughed. "You don't have to pamper me. You are like a mother hen with one chick and I love you for it, but is this part of my treatment?"

"No." Jess looked a bit embarrassed to be caught fussing. "I'm sorry."

Then she giggled at the description of her as a mother hen. "It's just that you must try these melons. This region is famous for its melons ... and carpets."

"Maybe I can eat one of their carpets too. I don't know why I am so hungry all the time."

"Your colour is better, there's no fluid around your ankles, and you are breathing better. At first I could feel a thrust over the left side of your chest below your breast and then a vibration which got louder and louder, but now that has gone."

"And I thought you were interested in my chest for other reasons."

"No, no!" Jess surged up. "Rohana, I would never ever do that! Please believe me!" Her eyes grew moist.

"Jess, dear Jess. I'm only teasing."

"Oh ..." Jess sat down, a little uncertainly. "I'm not good at understanding when I am being teased."

"That's what makes you so much fun to tease." Tears came to Rohana's eyes. "Jess, in such a short time you and Pandora have become such dear friends to me."

"And Iraj?" Jess smirked.

Rohana actually blushed. "Er, like you have said, he is a lovely man."

Jess turned serious. "Rohana, Iraj isn't spoken for and he likes you."

"I think he is just being kind," Rohana said, blushing again. "Sometimes it seems more, but I am going to die. I wouldn't want to do that to him."

"What I'm saying is I think the hole in your heart might be closing. That's why the noise got louder like a whistle and then stopped as it closed. That can happen with children as they grow but I didn't even know if it could happen in an adult."

"You seem to know so much. Who taught you?"

"I don't know. It's so frustrating to have no personal memories. If you ask Iraj, he'll start telling you about a dead Gypsy girl."

Rohana looked at her enquiringly.

"It's his pet theory about me, I'm sure he will tell you about it soon enough, but the point I'm making is you seem to be getting better." Jess sighed. "But I don't understand it so I don't want to give you false hope."

"Hope?" Rohana for a moment was uncharacteristically bitter. "It's been a long time since I had any hope, Jess."

They were silent for a while.

"Jess, why do you cut fruit with your left hand?" Rohana asked. "You seem right handed."

Jess looked at the knife in her left hand. "My right hand is for my sword," she showed the hilt of the sword on her left hip and then turned her hips to show the empty sheath for her knife on the right hip. "My left hand *should* be for the knife but while my left hand is very strong, it is clumsy. I try to practice with it as much as I can because I do most of my killing with a knife. You have no idea how irritating it is to use your knife in a fight and have to change hands when you draw your sword."

Cut throats with your knife and then change hands to kill more people with your sword?

"No, I don't," Rohana agreed. "Jess, you don't seem to get angry much, at least not with your friends. My mother was angry all the time."

"You should see me with bullies." Jess laughed self-consciously. "I wish I could stop that. It gets me into trouble all the time. I am trying to hide from my enemies but it's as if I get on top of the tallest building and scream out to them 'here I am!' I wouldn't have wanted to do it any differently, but what happened in Dilkor was a disaster for me. There must be people searching for the killer of the sons of the sheik and that group of shepherds and the blood priest. If they hear about Dilkor it's as if I have hung a sign around my neck and walked the streets ringing a bell and yelling out 'it was me! It was me!'"

Rohana giggled. "If you were trying to travel quietly you are not doing a good job, I'll grant you that."

"Excuse us, great ladies." They were interrupted by a girl, maybe nine.

She was very thin looking, dressed in rags and had a grubby face. She had an equally grubby six-year-old boy in tow hanging back shyly. "Can you spare a few coppers?"

"Don't give them any." A nearby stall holder called out loudly. "You will have a whole pile of them on you. A lot of them have handlers who take most of it off them."

"No money," Jess said. "But I'll feed you if you are hungry."

The girl considered that for a moment. Then she nodded warily. Jess left Rohana to eat watermelon while she organised bread and vegetable *khoresht* (stew) at the stall.

Ten of the local street rats appeared from out of nowhere. They had the fine features of the Persis, most had darker hair and skin but two had brown hair and one girl was even blond and blue eyed, having some blood from one of the northern tribes.

They eyed her suspiciously but when she left them alone to eat squatting in the dirt, and walked back to Rohana, they relaxed. She didn't want anything in return.

"For some of them this is more food than they have had all week, but they still eat slowly," Jess said.

An ancient grizzled water seller appeared, his orange hat was lined around the rim with tassels and beading. His wide grin showed only the stumps of three teeth. He had a large leather skin slung over his shoulders wrapped in a cloth which he kept wet to cool his water (and himself). Across his chest he had a row of bronze cups strung like military decorations.

Jess called him over and they had a few cups of his cool water. He walked briskly away as an *arban* (small contingent) of Hun horsemen rode up.

The urchins scattered in all directions except for the little girl and her brother. They couldn't get away quickly enough and ended bailed up in a corner.

"They've probably been stealing," Jess muttered as her hand flew to the hilt of her sword. She began to stand up.

"Jess, no!" Rohana said. "Let me handle this."

She lifted up her veena onto her lap and frowned in concentration as her finger flew over the strings, striking up a lively rhythm. Then her clear voice burst out singing ... in Hunnic, no less. Jess found to her surprise that she could understand a few of the words.

The men surged over; the girl and her brother were forgotten. They stood in a semi-circle, all smiles, and began clapping and singing in time. Jess hesitated and then joined in the clapping.

Hunnic music had a lively beat and strong rhythm and Rohana set up a nasal second counterpoint on the veena to the main tune. Her singing became high pitched with a slight guttural twang in the back of her throat.

Whatever it was, it was just perfect for her impromptu audience. One of the older Hun men had tears in his eyes.

Rohana went on to sing four of the lively ballads. For the last two she put her veena aside and brushed her long black hair back and began to dance as she sang: arms out, swaying and turning, swinging her hips, gesturing and rocking her head and shoulders, her eyes sparkling.

"Enough, Rohana!" Jess laughed.

Rohana glared at her for interrupting and then looked confused. She sat down, flushed and a little breathless. "Sorry, I completely forgot about my heart. I don't know how. I was really enjoying that!"

"So I noticed. How do you feel?"

"I have never felt better in all my life!"

The leader's name was 'Roua'. He asked Rohana in halting Sogdianē if she was staying long in the town. "You play at Tashkent, best in city. I have much influence with owner Marspend."

He had assumed they were travelling minstrels! Jess searched her brain for a polite excuse. She was distracted as the men took up a collection of coins.

"Thank you, Roua, we'd be delighted," Rohana said. "I will definitely go and talk to him first thing tomorrow."

She gave him a cheery wave as he walked away.

"WHAT!" Jess spluttered in disbelief. "'We'd be delighted,' she says! 'I will definitely go and talk to him tomorrow,' she says! What about us trying to hide?"

"Oh, Jess, a group of lady entertainers is the perfect disguise." Rohana gave her a smug look. "No one would look for a rabid killer in a group of lady musicians. It's better than you leaving your trail of dead bodies behind."

Rabid?

"Jess, you said you can't resist certain things," Rohana added. "Well, I can't resist an audience."

"A bunch of Huns?"

"They were very appreciative," Rohana showed her small handful of silver. "I doubt anyone here can do Hunnic music like I can. I am very good, you know. Besides, Roua *was* rather handsome, don't you think?"

Jess felt like slapping her own forehead with frustration.

When Pandora and Iraj arrived not long afterwards to collect them and have their share of watermelon, Jess was still quivering with outrage.

"Singing at a tavern, can I help?" Pandora asked.

"It sounds like a perfect disguise," Iraj agreed. "Er, but it is Jess's decision."

"Absolutely not!" Jess said firmly. "We need to be inconspicuous for once."

Iraj was more interested in Jess's theory about Rohana's heart.

"I would have said it can't happen in adults, but there is so much I don't know," Jess told them.

"It's you," Iraj said.

"What do you mean?" Jess turned to Iraj. "It's me?"

"The more I find out about you, the more things I find you have in common with Jacinta."

Oh no!

Iraj explained his theories about Jess and Jacinta to Rohana. "I think Jacinta's task isn't finished and her God has sent Jess to finish it," he concluded with satisfaction.

"Iraj thinks I am some sort of poor second choice to a dead Gypsy girl," Jess explained. "If I never hear the name Jacinta again, I'll be very happy."

"Which is why you are going to the Troad, I suppose."

Jess looked at him sharply, and then she sighed with a sheepish grin.

"All right, but I think I was alive and in the desert *before* Jacinta got killed. So her God called me before she failed. Besides, what does this have to do with Rohana?"

"The elf queen, Elana, was an elvish healer."

"Oh no, please, Iraj! I am not the first assassin to know about herbs."

"What you *do know* is absolutely amazing," Rohana whispered. "It is more like elvish knowledge."

"Please, don't encourage him!" Jess moaned. "I've never even met an elf."

"That's it!" Iraj said, clapping his hands. "Now I know! Hakeem and Jacinta were paladins, religious knights. They had the healing touch. I think Jacinta's God has nominated you as her replacement and has given you some of her abilities."

"*Me*, a religious knight? Come on now." Jess laughed. "It would be handy to have a healing touch, but I can assure you I don't!"

"Are you sure?" Iraj looked at her intently.

He rolled up his sleeve and with a dramatic flourish produced his knife. Before they could stop him he had sliced his forearm.

"Iraj!" the girls shrieked in unison.

Blood began dripping on the ground.

"Jess, heal it!" Iraj's eyes had taken on a feverish excitement.

"I can't believe you just did that," Jess muttered.

She grabbed his arm, her hands slippery with his blood, and frowned in concentration. Then she strained hard, darkening and holding her breath. The only thing that happened was that she managed to look constipated. Blood continued to drip onto the sand.

She let her breath out with an explosive sigh.

"Pandora, can you bring that spare cloth from the saddle bag so I can bind this genius's arm?" she asked. "And bring a tent hammer so I can hit him over the head a few times."

"Maybe you need practice." Iraj looked embarrassed as she bound his arm.

Of course, I really think the other girls would be happy to cut their arms too.

I hope this stings.

* * *

As they led the camels back to the inn, Pandora kept excitedly jumping on Jess's back and hugging her. "Pleease Jess can I perform with Rohana! Pleease!"

Jess tried her best to ignore her and walk on, but it was hard with her girlfriend jumping all over her and grinning excitedly into her face.

"All right," she eventually said through gritted teeth.

I know I am going to regret this.

"Yes!!" Pandora shouted in Jess's ear, half deafening her.

When Jess looked up to see Rohana sitting on the camel and trying not to burst out laughing, she gave up on any pretence of dignity. She threw the reins of the camels to Iraj and allowed Pandora to jump on her back. They went running down the street. With Jess running around like a (black) circus pony and her girlfriend on her back crying out with delight and waving one hand in a circular motion, they managed to get a fair number of startled passersby to stop and watch.

* * *

Jess didn't know that in Margu there were two different groups searching for signs of her.

"Did you find something, master?" Vanâra, his senior acolyte asked as he helped Tishari to sit up.

"There has been an attack on Dilkor led by a dark woman." He paused to smile at Vanâra. "And some have accused her of being a daimôn changeling."

"If she is part daimôn, she will join us." Vanâra said excitedly. "Chandyr, Dilkor … it is Margu that she is headed for! Our God has finally answered our prayers."

"That she is part daimôn is only a rumour at the moment." Tishari cautioned him. "But there is more … I cannot locate this woman by far sight. As you have guessed, she must be the one from Chandyr, the one we are seeking. Come, let us pray that she is coming to us."

* * *

"No," Marspend, the owner of the tavern, said to Jess.

"I don't need you as a guard. My customers would laugh at me if I hired a female guard." He looked her up and down. "Can you dance?"

Jess thought for a minute. "I can dance, but I would need practice first."

"Good," Marspend gave her a smirk. "I have the perfect outfit in mind."

* * *

Jess took a big shaky breath and tugged at her pony tail.

She only had a few days to practice. And Rohana didn't help at all. She kept varying what she played in complex ways. She said that it expressed her mood.

And Jess really *should* have checked what sort of outfit the owner of a tavern had in mind before she had agreed to wear it. A drop of perspiration ran down her ribs.

Rohana started with a playful prelude: nasal and resonating. Then she started to sing, not words, just tones. Pandora joined slowly with the beat of the drum.

Jess felt like wiping her hands on the flimsy silk outfit. How did she ever agree to this?

She experimentally shook her ankles to hear the bells. Rohana's veena began to talk to itself, in a complex introspective way. Jess walked nervously out from behind the curtain. The room was dimly lit, most of the men looked up and then idly went back to their conversations. With this many men in the semi-darkness, the room was hot and smelt of beer and male sweat.

"Take it off!" one of the men right at the back screamed out.

The veena began to establish a soft dominant rhythm and the drum joined in; Jess began to rock and sway to the music.

"Don't worry about dancing, just take it off!" the same man yelled out.

After a moment Jess forgot where she was and started to enjoy herself. She lifted forward on one foot, the other stretched out behind her, and in time with the beat spun gracefully to the floor, pulling her arms in, head bowed.

Then she threw her arms out, her back arched as the silks floated around her.

Rohana picked up the pace.

Jess began to leap and kick and twirl, bells tinkling but not too fast yet, her superb muscular control holding her in perfect balance as the beat got faster. She dove into a forward roll and sprang up into the air, her hands stretched out.

The noise of talking began to subside.

The beat got faster and stronger. It became insistent and primal, beating on the walls. A hush fell over the audience as Jess lifted the first veil, big enough to cover her body, and threw it up into the air

Her breathing was quick, sweat trickling down her face.

She broke into a grin.

The music got faster and she strutted and stomped in a semi–circle, making the ankle bells jingle louder, nodding and pointing to each group of men in turn, a woman challenging each one of them, their masculinity, with a knowing, breathless, half smile.

Then she spun and dropped to the floor. The music slowed for a moment and she rose on one leg and hopped into the air, one leg balanced out behind her. Another veil floated away and one of the tavern guards scurried to retrieve it.

Then the rhythm really picked up, urgent, commanding. Jess began to clap and skip across, bells jingling, to slap her hands loudly on each table, one after the other. The men began to clap in time. She was breathless and sweating freely. She spun and leapt, another veil came away.

Soon I'll be dancing naked!

She rolled sideways and turned it into a forward somersault all in one movement and then leapt again. She felt all the men's eyes on her now, the heat of their bodies, their lust. It was such a delicious feeling.

There was a group of men sitting in a corner. Amongst them was a boy, maybe thirteen. His eyes were huge. He couldn't take them off her. She let another veil fall and danced across to him, smiling just for him. He flushed, crimson.

The men around him laughed and teased him, slapping his back. She put her hands on his shoulders, moving in time with the music. Her breasts bouncing gently as she swayed and his hands gravitated towards them.

"That's the way, little brother!" The man next to him laughed.

She moved to sit in his lap, arms around his neck, and kissed him on the lips; his hands seemed glued to her breasts as she kicked her legs up in time to the music. Then she was gone, leaving him clutching at a veil.

One of the patrons got up a little unsteadily. She danced around him and he tried to dance clumsily in time. He lunged for her, she tripped him but then caught him before he could injure himself and lowered him to the floor. She kissed his hair and got up to continue to dance as the tavern guards helped him back to his seat.

"No more," one of them warned. "Let her dance."

The music was faster and faster and now Jess was pushed to keep up.

The last veil dropped. The men surged forwards. The tavern guards drew their cudgels. Jess ducked for the stage door, laughing as she pushed a bolt home.

Everyone stood to cheer; the stamping and clapping and whistling was deafening while Jess leaned against the inside of the locked door, panting and laughing.

* * *

"There is a wealthy patron to see you," Marspend said.

He looked at her, still in the flimsy outfit minus several veils, and obviously liked what he saw.

Jess used a towel to wipe her forehead. "I'll get dressed."

"No, leave that outfit on. If you play this right you can make some real money."

"I don't do that sort of thing."

"I told him that, but he still wanted to see you. I think he is really rich."

Well, she would enjoy putting this 'really rich' man in his place. Did he think she would do anything for money?

Well, apart from dancing nearly naked to a roomful of men, that is.

A handsome Sakā man was shown in. His clothes were modest. By his bearing he was of noble birth.

"My name is Kaeva."

That wouldn't be his real name.

"And this is my friend Syavash."

His 'friend' eyed Jess guardedly and then glanced over the small changing room, looking for concealed threats. He took up a post in a corner where he could cover any entrance points.

Whoever Kaeva was, he was in hiding.

"My name is Jess. How may I help you?" She favoured him with her sweetest smile.

"My young brother Hvâzâta was quite taken with you."

"The boy?" Jess sputtered. "Is that what this is about? Was it he who asked?"

Kaeva coloured. "He is too shy for that. You will be well paid!"

"He didn't seem so shy when I was dancing. A virgin! Kaeva, I must say I'm tempted, but I have to say no, I don't do such things for money."

"A pity," Kaeva bowed. "We really did enjoy your dancing, though. Will you be here tomorrow night?"

"Yes, I will." *Most definitely!*

When he left there were five silver sigloi on her dressing table. Jess lifted them up, and held them to her cheek, a smile on her face.

* * *

"Where are my clothes?" she asked.

"You look fantastic in that outfit," Pandora said breathlessly. "Doesn't she, Rohana?"

Rohana nodded. "It almost makes me want to switch to girls."

"Really?" Jess paraded back and forwards and spun around in front of her two friends. "Won't Marspend want it back?"

"You are supposed to take it home and wash it. I sent your things back with a maid who was going that way. Come on,"

Pandora coaxed, passing her the veils she had discarded. "It's only a short way."

"You can't expect me to wear *this*, surely?"

"I'll make it worth your while," Pandora said with a suggestive smile.

"Oh, all right then," Jess said, taking a deep breath. "Where's my weapons?"

Pandora gasped; her hands flew to her mouth in dismay.

"Pandora, don't tell me you have disarmed me in the middle of a border town and left me dressed like this!"

"You can't blame me!" Pandora protested. "I was excited thinking of you in that outfit ... You can have my bow."

Jess looked like she was considering strangling her girlfriend.

"Keep it, but string it and fit an arrow," Jess said between clenched teeth. "With the mood I'm in I think I might just break it over your head."

Rohana passed Jess her belt knife.

Jess held it up. It was a third the size of her own belt knife.

A toy belt knife! Great, just great.

"Thank you, Rohana," she managed, her voice sounding strangled.

"It's only a short way," Rohana said, encouragingly. "After all, what could possibly go wrong?"

* * *

Jess stalked through the dimly lit streets muttering to herself. Her two chastened friends followed close behind.

There was a full moon. Pandora had an arrow fitted and was scanning the buildings, the shadows, the roof tops. She was making a point of showing how alert she was.

"'You look fantastic,' she said," Jess muttered. "'Where are my weapons,' I said. 'Here, have a toy knife instead,' she said."

"Do you know how chilly it is dressed like this?" she called back to Pandora.

Pandora and Rohana thought it best not to answer. It had been warm in the crowded tavern but it was spring in the desert, still chilly in the evening. Another thing they hadn't thought of.

At least it seemed quiet, Pandora thought.

They were most of the way to their inn when Jess slowed and motioned them into the shadows.

"What's the problem?" Pandora whispered.

"It's *too* quiet," Jess whispered. "Many of the houses aren't showing any light."

They could see their inn but Jess stayed, watching and listening and sniffing the breeze. She eventually stood up. "Whatever it is, it's not about us. I think maybe one of the local gangs have set a trap for someone, nearby but not here."

Just then they could hear the distant sounds of a man screaming and men shouting.

"Rohana, go on to the inn," Jess ordered. "We are going to see what it is, don't worry, we won't get involved. It's not our fight."

She led Pandora, crouched down, in the direction of the fight.

A small group of men were being set upon by a large group. They had retreated into a blind alley. They must have expert swordsmen as they were holding their own even though badly outnumbered.

"That is Kaeva there!" Jess cried out in dismay. "Oh no! His young brother is on the ground and he is hurt!"

"Who?"

"Kaeva, that nice Sakā man who wanted to buy me to have sex with his brother." Jess explained. "There are two archers on that roof. Do you think you can get them if I distracted them?"

Pandora felt a thrill of fear. "Do you think I'm ready?"

"I do, but we have to hurry. They can't hold out for much longer and they are trapped in that alleyway."

Pandora slung her bow across her shoulders. Jess gave her a savage kiss and hoisted her up. Then Jess sprinted down the alley, running up a stack of boxes for a flying leap into the fight.

Sailing through the air with her silk dress streaming out behind her, she looked like a vengeful (black-bodied) butterfly. She landed just behind the attackers and rolled.

Local men, not Hun, so it's nothing official.

One of the archers shot at her but she ducked into the shadows. He screamed as he tumbled from the roof. The other archer looked around wildly but didn't sight Pandora.

Jess scurried in low, slashed one of the hamstrings of an attacker and stabbed another in the calf. She had a sword by the time several of the men turned to face her. It was not a moment too soon; another of Kaeva's men had fallen and they were hard pressed.

Jess ducked in and out of the darkness, leaving another four men dead or injured on the ground.

As she came back into a patch of moonlight the last archer stood up. Distracted by a man trying to circle around her, she wasn't watching him and an arrow punched her in the back hard enough to knock her to her knees and make her cry out. Her left arm went useless and the dagger fell somewhere on the ground. She only barely managed to hold onto her sword to stab the man in front of her.

Pandora appeared on the roof. "Jess, get out of the way!"

Jess had to lean her weight on the sword.

She dragged herself painfully into the shadows and Pandora began firing at the remaining attackers. Having lost archer support they gathered their wounded and fled.

Jess stumbled over to Kaeva and Syavash. Everything seemed to be rippling in a strange way.

"*Jess Khánum* (Lady Jess)!" Syavash called out in shock.

If Jacinta can do it ... She fell to her knees beside Hvâzâta and collapsed forward, reaching out with her hand.

* * *

Jess opened her eyes to see Syavash sitting on the edge of the bed, grinning at her.

She couldn't move.

"Are you going to explain to me how we ended up being rescued by a pair of dancing girls?"

"Rohana is an entertainer but Pandora and I aren't," Jess admitted.

"*Really*?" Syavash said mildly.

"I have enemies." *Just don't ask me who they all are, I only know some of the many, many, recent ones.* "And we are travelling in disguise."

"You make a wonderful dancer and fighter, but if you are trying to travel quietly you are doing a terrible job. Are you an assassin?"

"Yes," it seemed useless to deny it. Between herself and Pandora they had killed how many men? Syavash looked cold. He leaned forward and placed a dagger at her throat.

"And who have you been sent to kill?"

"Syavash, if you wanted to kill me now, I can't stop you," Jess said. "I am not hired to kill anyone and if you think I came to kill Hvâzâta and Kaeva you are a lot crazier than you look ... Have you tied me up? I can't move."

She was half sitting and partly turned on her right side. Her weight was on her right arm. Her left arm was bandaged against her chest. She tried to roll over but there was excruciating pain in her back.

Syavash put the knife away and hugged her forward, packing pillows behind so she could sit up comfortably.

"We owe you our lives, but I had to ask. You are in our new hiding spot. Pandora and my men have gone to pick up Rohana and your belongings. And I haven't tied you up. You were shot in the back, remember? It shattered your shoulder blade but didn't penetrate your lung."

Jess moaned in pain and disgust. Then something occurred to her.

"Did you dress my wounds?" She was naked under the sheet.

"Jess, I saw you dance." Syavash gave her a smirk.

Jess felt the blood rush to her face. "Can I get dressed, please?"

"Your outfit is ruined. Pandora said not to give you any clothes or you would only try to get up."

"Everyone keeps hiding my clothes!" Jess pouted.

"Really?" Syavash smiled at the memory of her naked body. "I wonder why."

Chapter 14: The Šâh of Xvairizem

"Argh! What is this?" Jess tried to turn her head away.

Pandora climbed astride her. She grabbed her chin with one hand and firmly tipped the contents of the bronze spoon into her mouth. "It's *opion* (opium) dissolved in wine brandy, and there are other good things in it too. I'm supposed to give you a spoonful every four hours if you need it."

"Wal I done need id." Jess screwed up her face, looking for somewhere to spit it out. "Is bidder, can you mix id wid honey?"

"Just swallow it or I'll hold your nose and cover your mouth."

Jess swallowed. "Awk! Doesn't this stuff cause you to vomit?"

"Hvâzâta didn't complain, but of course his dose was half yours."

"How is he?" Jess asked.

Pandora's face fell. "They got the arrow out but it pierced his lung. He shouldn't have lived this long."

"You know that thing that Jacinta was able to do, you know the healing touch? I tried it with Hvâzâta."

"Did it work?"

"I don't know, I passed out."

"If you could do what Jacinta could do, you could heal yourself and fight the medicine."

"I'm not Jacinta." Jess was having trouble keeping her eyes open. "Maybe she couldn't do it either, thay jus said she cud."

"What did you say?"

"May bee thed jus sed—" Jess tried to talk clearly. "Whad you gib me?"

She heard Pandora mutter that it shouldn't work so fast.

The next thing she knew she was dreaming.

"You have to pray." A young Gypsy girl, tall and muscular, was standing in front of her. Jess couldn't see her face clearly.

"Pray to whom? And for what?"

"If you want to heal somebody you need to pray to our God. You know, the one you can feel inside yourself."

"You're Jacinta! What is your connection with me?"

"I'm just in your mind." Jacinta seemed to smile. "I can't tell you anything you don't already know."

* * *

It was still dark when she woke. Her vision jerked as it adjusted to the darkness. If she had a room to herself, it must be a big place, a noble's house and not too many people around. At least she was being treated well. There were some advantages in saving people's lives.

She needed to get up.

She couldn't.

Syavash had bandaged her arm securely to her chest. Every effort was agony. She couldn't lever herself out of bed. She clenched her jaw and reached deep inside herself for that 'something' that helped her block the pain.

Moving her legs crab wise she managed to slip one hip off the couch. She still hadn't turned so she had to continue on until she got her other hip over and let herself slip down till she was almost squatting against the bed ... which moved backwards a little. It almost resulted in her falling; she would have been sprawled, helpless on the floor.

She rocked forward and managed to stand. Wave after wave of agony stabbed through her. She had to bite her lip to prevent herself from calling out. No, she wasn't Jacinta, she couldn't heal herself. Then she remembered that strange dream.

Damn Syavash for tying her arm up! Damn Syavash, damn Pandora! They bossed her around and they did things to her without even asking! She smiled. It wasn't really their fault she had a fractured shoulder blade. It was nice having people caring for her.

When she was in the desert she was bitten by a snake which she was trying to catch for food. She was alone. That was bad, really bad.

Well, first things first. She found a heavy glazed pot under the couch by clever method of kicking it with her naked toes. At least it was empty.

As she limped around waiting for her toes to stop hurting she imagined Syavash holding her up, naked while she peed. Hardly erotic! Was she attracted to the handsome Sakā who had threatened her with a knife?

Yes, she was.

Her pot had disappeared under the couch, of course it had.

She had to hook it with her foot somehow. Eventually she managed to position it and painfully lowered herself down. Unfortunately when she finally got into position she gave a deep sigh of relief. Slumped over, all she could do was wait for the waves of pain to pass.

When she could relax she could feel a thin stream running out of her and hear a faint tinkling sound. Of course, there was no cloth to wipe herself or clothes to wear! Oh well, her nether-regions would dry in the warm air of the house.

She poured herself several cups of water one handed and drank her fill. Then, grabbing the linen sheet and wrapping it around her, she padded out into the house.

The door from her room led into a larger room used as a dormitory with several men and a small fire which had burnt down. Rohana and Pandora were lying on the floor.

Rohana was the only one awake. She looked like she hadn't slept much and had been crying.

"He's dying," she said. "Most of them have left him to let him get some sleep."

Jess hurried as much as she could, following a light showing down a corridor. She saw a large man move out of the room before she got there. He didn't seem to see her in the dark.

Kaeva was asleep in a chair. Hvâzâta was a small figure lying on the couch. His body bathed in sweat. His lips were dusky in the poor light. His breathing was laboured and was starting to have pauses followed by shuddering gasps. She reached out to take his hand. His pulse was faint and racing.

The room smelt of death.

There is no time, he is dying! Pray, Jess, pray!

Would a God even listen to something like her? How does one pray to a God?

Surely it doesn't have to be in a lot of words. A God would know. She bent her head, closed her eyes and ... concentrated.

Pray!

She felt sweat trickling down her forehead.

In her mind she could see where the arrow had penetrated the lung. He hadn't been wearing any armour and it had passed through, fracturing his ribs front and back. The bleeding had stopped but there was too much blood in the chest cavity, filling it, pressing on the lungs so he couldn't breathe. She needed to drain it.

Pray!

Her mind merged with his wounds. She felt herself opening the wound at his back to form a flap. It sealed when he breathed in but pushed a little blood out every time he breathed out. Slowly, bit by bit, the blood began to pump out, a thin trickle.

The room was darkening and starting to spin.

She hung on to the bed to steady herself. She still needed to check if those blood vessels would start bleeding again once the pressure came off. No, they had sealed.

Now for that rib; good, it wouldn't be pressing on the lung.

Someone shouted. There was the sound of running feet. Jess was grabbed. She was completely helpless and felt herself lifted and flung against the wall. Agony shot through her and darkness claimed her.

A hard slap woke her, she tasted blood.

"Careful, Zhubin," Syavash warned. "She's no use to us unconscious."

Zhubin pressed a knife hard against her neck. He was furious; he was trembling with a barely restrained desire to cut her throat. She was in so much pain it was hard to know if she cared.

"You don't need a knife. If you want to kill me all you need is a pillow."

In the other room Pandora was screaming, then her screams cut off abruptly.

"Kill her," a tall man suggested. He was one of the swordsmen from the fight in the alley.

"A simple thank you would have done."

She tried to block the agony. She needed to think, her life (and the lives of her friends) depended on it.

Syavash shook his head. "Tell me what you and your friends are doing in this city."

I am a daimôn changeling and I carry a dead Gypsy girl inside me. I have been selected to kill someone who is guarded by a daimôn lord.

"What have you done with my friends?"

"Kill her and her two friends," the tall one said again.

Jess was beginning to dislike him.

"What were you doing with the boy?" Syavash asked. "You had your hand on his throat. Were you trying to kill him?"

"Sure I was, after I and my friend rescued him and the rest of you. First I dragged myself over to kill him in the alleyway by bleeding all over him. When that didn't work, I came here without a weapon to strangle him one handed by laying my hand on his throat and wrist in my weakened state."

The guard put more pressure on the knife at her throat.

"All right, all right," she said quickly, "I might have healing magic. I wanted to see if I could make it work on him."

"You *think* you *might*?" Syavash gave a nasty laugh. "What sort of story is that?"

"Leave Jess alone," a faint child's voice came from the corner.

The men surged over to look at Hvâzâta.

Jess was ignored.

"He is awake, his breathing has eased," Kaeva said.

"I still say we should kill her and her friends," the tall man sounded disappointed.

"Not if she can help Hvâzâta." Zhubin sheathed his knife and gently lifted Jess, cradling her against his strong chest as he carried her back to her bed.

First throw her against the wall, then hold a knife to her throat and now tuck her into bed. These Sakā men really needed lessons on how to treat a lady.

He put a chair down near the door and sat to guard her, whether to prevent her escaping or from being hurt by one of the others wasn't clear.

Kaeva appeared at the doorway. "I'm sorry about our men. They are very protective of Hvâzâta. We should be thanking you, not hurting you. You don't know who we are, do you?"

"Please don't tell me," Jess said weakly.

Kaeva moved closer and kissed her on the cheek.

Maybe that was a good sign, she hoped it was. It was hard to tell with these Sakā men.

She just couldn't keep awake any longer, her eyes kept losing focus.

* * *

It was night time when she woke again.

She must have slept the whole day.

Rohana and Pandora were curled up on the floor. Jess tried to move, the pain was less but she couldn't suppress a faint moan. Rohana sat up.

"Rohana! I am a danger to anyone who comes near me."

"Jess, what are you talking about?"

"Whatever Jacinta was fighting, it's not over."

"Jess, you are not making sense. Was it you that healed me? That chest pain, was it you healing my heart?"

"I don't know. I wished so hard for you to get better, is that a form of prayer? Though it wasn't anything like what happened when I healed Hvâzâta. But that's not important now. I have been sent to finish what Jacinta started, I know that now." She tried to sit up and couldn't, damn! "I bring danger to everyone around me. We have to split up. I can't stay here."

"Jess, don't talk like that or I will get really angry with you! We are your friends, if you are in some sort of trouble we will stick by you."

"Rohana, I think I am in about as much trouble as I could possibly be in. I have to take up where Jacinta left off."

"Oh that! Pandora and I had already worked that out. What do you have to do?"

"I don't know."

Just then Kaeva and Syavash heard them talking and brought a lamp in. Kaeva replaced Rohana on the bed and bent over to kiss her, his tears wetting her cheeks. Then it was Syavash's turn. As Syavash went to straighten up Jess desperately grabbed at his vest.

"Syavash, please! I am bringing danger to everyone in this house. I have to leave."

"What's she talking about?" Syavash asked Pandora.

"I'll tell you as soon as I have given Jess her medicine."

Pandora had a look of determination on her face as she measured the dose into the spoon.

She straddled the couch and pushed the spoon to Jess's mouth, grabbing Jess's chin. Jess tried to struggle, she pressed her lips together as hard as she could.

"Could you give me a hand holding her, Syavash?"

Syavash leaned forward.

Jess opened her mouth to protest but Pandora took the chance to tip the medicine in and clamped a hand over Jess's mouth. The determined look on Pandora's face told Jess that resistance was futile.

"That's not fair! Awk! You forgot the honey."

"It is supposed to take half the turn of a glass but it seems to be much faster with Jess," Pandora said conversationally as she eyed her patient with smug satisfaction. "All we have to do now is wait."

Jess poked her tongue out at her grinning friend. "How is Hvâzâta?"

"It seems you have saved my brother again." Kaeva eyed her up and down. "Now what trouble are you girls in?"

"Just me, and I am so sorry! If the Hun knew I was here they would send their men to kill me. I am bringing danger to all of you."

Kaeva looked at the earnest look on the girl's face and ... he burst out laughing.

"Whaz so fuddy?" Jess was struggling to talk clearly, her eyes felt so heavy.

"It shouldn't work so fast but Jess *is* a little bit different to the rest of us." Pandora giggled.

"Maybe we can take some of that stuff with us when we leave," Rohana suggested.

"Done oo dare. Gan you tage dis bandarge orv of me?"

"What's she saying?" Kaeva tilted his head slightly.

"She's thanking you for your offer of protection and saying she is happy to stay with you here until she is better," Pandora said.

Jess stopped struggling to speak, mainly because Jacinta had appeared, standing amongst them. Her facial features were clearer now. "I told you it would work."

"I keep passing out."

"That's because you are hurt. It will get better. Your shoulder will heal more quickly than normal but you need to learn how to *actively* heal yourself. For that you need to understand about energy and healing."

"They don't seem worried about the Huns."

"Of course not, Hvâzâta is *Šāhzādeh* (Prince) Kûrav. Didn't you pick that up while you were healing him? *Šâh* (Shah) Āfrīg had two sons."

"Who is Āfrīg?"

"Jess, Āfrīg was the Šâh of this whole country. Don't you know anything?"

"Hold on, you said you were only in my mind and you only knew what I knew."

Jacinta ignored her. "Āfrīg got killed fighting the Huns. That means Kaeva is Parvēz.

"Jess, we are in the house of the true Šâh of Xvairizem."

* * *

Jess woke up at first light.

Pandora was asleep on a mat on the floor. She woke when Jess stirred.

"Good morning, can you take this bandage off me *please*? My shoulder doesn't hurt anymore."

"You're lying."

"Yes I am but I'm completely helpless bandaged like this. Please."

After being unwound from the bandage and using the pot, Jess went with Pandora and Rohana to check on the young prince. The boy was sleeping. She closed her eyes and concentrated. No signs of infection, but he had lost a lot of blood.

Syavash led her to two men with stab wounds. They were easier to heal. At least she didn't pass out, not quite, but Pandora and Rohana had to help her back to her bed. Her use of her shattered shoulder wasn't much better even without the bandage.

It was only a few hours, this time, before she woke again. Parvēz was sitting by her bed side.

"Šâh Parvēz," Jess made a futile effort to rise.

"How did you know?" Parvēz gently pushed her back into the bed.

I'm haunted by a dead Gypsy girl.

"When I healed your brother I got his name, *Šāhzādeh* (Prince) Kûrav. It was a matter of guessing who you would be."

"Pandora tells me you believe you have been sent by a God to finish the task that Jacinta had."

"It seems so, but all I have are guesses. I don't know a lot about Jacinta."

"Jacinta was only a young girl when she was killed but she, more than any other, saved the world from daimôns. With her gone and Gansükh still alive the world has no defence against them."

This had to be some sort of sick joke, it had to be.

Could a God have a sick sense of humour, sending Jess, a changeling *imitation* daimôn to fight *real* daimôns?

Parvēz noticed her expression. "Jacinta, Hakeem and Elana were the central figures in the ancient Prophecy of the elves. Jacinta's role was finding magic old and new. There was a book of forbidden spells of the extinct svartálfar hidden in the catacombs beneath the ruins of elvish Troia. She was carrying the book when her party was attacked by a daimôn sent by the great enemy Æloðulf. She was bathed in daimôn fire —"

The room disappeared.

Parvēz disappeared.

She was fighting the sorcerer in a dark place deep beneath the ground, or was it really the sorcerer she was fighting? Her family and friends were about to be killed. She was frantic. Then there was an explosion, and it was all fire and pain.

Her mouth was opened and her chest was straining, a high pitched noise filled the air. She realised she was screaming. There was the sound of running feet and Pandora was holding her, rocking her, stroking her hair and kissing her.

All she could do for a long time was sob. "I'm sorry."

"No, *I'm* sorry," Parvēz insisted. "What happened?"

"I don't have memories about myself, a few fragments only," Jess said. "When you told me about Jacinta being attacked by the daimôn, something similar happened to me." She held her hand up and Pandora pulled her glove off for her. She showed him her hand.

"For a moment I was back there, being hit by a blast of wizard power. It was horrible."

Parvēz was astounded. "Your hand is just like what they said about Jacinta's. Does it sparkle in the dark?"

"If it does, I won't be too surprised, but I don't think I want to know." Jess shuddered. "I'm sorry. I'm more than a little fed up of being like Jacinta."

He looked at her.

She sighed, defeated, "All right, can you tell me more about her?"

Parvēz looked at her anxiously and then slowly resumed his story. "The daimôn fire did something to her hand. It retained the ability to attack daimôns and spell weapons and they stayed spelled for a few weeks at a time. That's how they protected Elgard against the daimôns."

Jess looked at her left hand. "It doesn't attack daimôns, at least I don't think it would, but it did help me fight against some other magic."

"Jacinta had her own daimôn lord called Ba'al," Parvēz continued. "It helped her kill Æloðulf, but then it turned against her and killed her. A lot of people thought it was the last battle of an ancient war against the daimôn raisers."

"Apparently not, I have to go to the Troad and find out what it is I am supposed to do."

"That is something that I have found puzzling," Parvēz said. "The Prophecy mentions a room in a place called 'Nowhere', and armour and weapons in a place called the 'Deepest' and it also says Æloðulf will never be defeated. So when Æloðulf was killed before the other parts it seemed that the Prophecy was wrong."

"Maybe he isn't dead." Rohana shuddered.

Jess yawned. She was having trouble staying awake.

"You need rest," Parvēz said. "Do you want to eat something first?"

Jess nodded. "Thank you, please, I'm so hungry I could eat an old riding boot."

They began filing out.

"You are so beautiful," Syavash patted her foot before he left. "It would have burned my heart to kill you."

And you Sakā men say the nicest things.

But when Pandora came back with bread and stew Jess was staring into space, silent tears running down her face. "Do you think Jacinta's God threw me scraps of memories copied from a dead girl? Maybe it doesn't matter with something like me."

"Jess, don't you talk like that or I'll fetch your medicine! Firstly, it is *your* God too and he gave you the healing touch. He wouldn't give you something like that if he didn't love you. You may not have much of a past but I don't care."

"I may not have much of a future either if Æloðulf is still alive."

"The point is that you have people who love you." She paused. "I know just what you need."

"Not more medicine!" Jess protested.

"No, not medicine." Pandora gave her a mischievous look. "Me."

"Pandora! I'm injured, I can't do much."

"I'm not injured." Pandora laughed, putting the broth away.

Chapter 15: A Šāhzādeh (Prince)

Pandora was right, Jess thought as she woke. She was surrounded by people who loved her. And Pandora also knew just what Jess had needed to cheer her up. She had had an uninterrupted sleep, no dead Gypsy girl.

Normally she didn't sleep this much but she wasn't surprised that it was dark when she woke. Her vision jerked a little as it adjusted. In the dark all she could see was shades of grey except for the figure that was standing at the foot of the bed dressed in an exquisite red dress.

It was Jacinta. She looked younger and Jess could see her face clearly now, if this was what Jacinta really looked like.

"That's a lovely dress."

"Thank you, Jess. It's an elf dress; Seléne gave it to me when I was fourteen."

"I'm sorry you had to die so young."

"Oh, I haven't died. I'm just lost. I don't know where I am or how to get back. I wanted to tell you how to heal yourself. It's not a lot different from healing others but to stop you getting tired there are special sources of energy you have to use, you have lots of spare energy inside you."

"Daimôn energy," Jess snorted in disgust. "Jacinta, is it me who has to help you? I know you don't mean to haunt me, but I'm a little sick of feeling like a pale imitation of you."

Or a dark imitation.

"That's perfectly all right, I am leaving you now anyway."

"Wait!"

But Jacinta was gone.

* * *

Jess woke feeling refreshed and almost free of pain.

It had worked just as Jacinta had said and Jess had no shortage of energy to use. She regretted telling Jacinta to go, but didn't know how to call her back.

As she walked into the kitchen wrapped in a blanket, Šāhzādeh Kûrav was sitting by the stove and Syavash was making him a large omelette. The young prince was looking very pale and tired.

"Your Imperial Highness," Jess bowed.

"Jess, please use our new names," Syavash asked.

"As long as I can still do this." Jess moved closer to hug and kiss the boy.

"I will make it a royal command." Parvēz laughed, coming in from behind her. "As long as I can have my share."

Jess took that as a challenge and threw her arms around his neck and gave Parvēz a lingering kiss on the lips, pressing her body into his arms.

"If I may, I will stay till Iraj returns and I'm sure Hvâzâta is well enough. But after that I must head to the Troad."

"Thanks for saving my life again," Hvâzâta said. "And I really liked your dancing."

Jess ruffled his hair and gently touched his cheek.

She looked at Syavash. "Is it safe here?"

"Not really. As soon as Hvâzâta can travel we will have to smuggle him into Aryānā, but it will mean we are moving away from our main supporters."

"I will be going to Margu, then I was thinking of heading for *Tus* (Susia) or Nisa at the start of Aryānā."

"I think Nisa would be safer."

"After crossing Aryānā we will head into the desert to Babylṓn, then Taḏmôr (Palmyra), then the Aramaic town Hamath and finally Tarsos and the Kilisian gates into Anatolḗ."

"Be careful crossing the deserts and isolated regions. Always join the big caravans. The old trade routes are no longer safe for small bands. There are a lot of desperate people since the wars and the drought."

"I've certainly noticed that," Jess said quietly.

* * *

When the men led Iraj into the courtyard he was mobbed by the three women.

"This is nice," he laughed.

"We missed you desperately, all of us did," Jess said.

Rohana smiled at him, her eyes sparkling, but she hung back a little.

"Well I see you haven't been able to keep out of trouble. Do you have any idea who owns this house?" Iraj laughed. "All you had to do was keep low."

"I don't think Jess knows how to keep low." Pandora laughed, hugging him.

"Rohana, I brought you flowers," he said, calling her closer. He lifted a large bunch of roses from behind him: white yellow and red.

"Why, thank you, Iraj." Rohana blushed as she took them.

"I just saw them for sale and knew you liked roses. I hope you don't mind."

Iraj watched her smell them, to make sure she really liked them. Jess exchanged a glance with Pandora.

No flowers for us.

But they just smiled. It was *so* good to have Iraj back!

* * *

Rohana was sitting in the garden tuning her veena when Iraj came over and sat down close to her.

"I have missed you, Rohana."

She felt like fainting. She was finding it hard to concentrate on her veena and it gave a discordant note. He reached over and took it off her and put it gently to one side.

The kiss, when it came, made her feel as if her heart had taken flight. When he finally released her, she gasped for air as she stared up at his handsome face.

"Are you feeling breathless?" he asked with concern.

She laughed and threw her arms over his neck for a fierce kiss. It felt like she was kissing him with her whole being. Then she pulled away, in a panic.

Oh no, w*hat have I done?*

"Iraj, I cannot be with a man. Because of my heart, being with child would kill me."

"I don't think that is true any longer," Iraj said, tilting her face towards him and kissing her again. "But you can be with a man and not become pregnant."

"Iraj, I *want* to be with you," she said breathlessly. "I want to be all of a woman for you, not just a heart cripple."

"Have you asked Jess?"

"What?" Rohana sat up.

"Have you asked Jess if you could have children?"

"Would she be able to tell?"

"How would I know? Have you asked her?"

* * *

Jess had Pandora seated, brushing her hair, enjoying its silky smoothness. Eventually she gave up and threw the brush on the bed so she could nibble at her ear.

"Jess?"

"Mmm, mmm," Jess was giving her lots of kisses, tiny pecks on her neck.

"Are we becoming an old couple?"

"WHAT?" Jess sat up, bolt upright. "Dora, as far as my memories are concerned I am only a couple of years old. How under all the Gods could we become an 'old couple'? And what is an 'old couple', anyway?"

"You've never bought me flowers," Pandora said. "We have passed a lot of flower sellers and you haven't bought me flowers."

Oh, oh.

"I bought you watermelons."

"That's not the same."

I want to have sex with you. I don't want to be having this silly conversation.

"Dora, if you wanted flowers all you had to do was ask. I'll buy you flowers tomorrow."

"It's not the same if I have to tell you."

"Why not?" Jess started to get irritated. "You end up with the flowers either way."

"If that's the case, I may as well buy them myself."

"Well you can, you have your own money from the tavern and if you would let me I would give you a share of the money from Āmul." Then something occurred to Jess. "Oh, that reminds me I asked one of the men to get that scented oil you like. I just haven't given it to you yet. And I got you some of that Persian scent. It's made *from* flowers at least. I knew you were running low."

"Presents?" Pandora gave her an excited kiss. "You brought me presents?"

Not really, you were running low and the men were going to the market.

Jess got up and rummaged around in her belongings for the little pots. Pandora kissed them and then kissed her and tugged her forcibly to the bed. After a little while, Jess wondered what a bunch of flowers might get her.

After that they were much too busy.

* * *

"How did the visit go?" Jess asked Iraj when she was able to get him alone.

They were in an inner courtyard. Iraj was sitting on a stone bench and Jess was perched just above and behind him on a short wall, dangling one of her legs in the air and the other on the back of the bench.

"Not good," Iraj said, looking up at his friend. "My father would not admit it but he feels responsible for what happened to Katin. They had a big argument before she ran away. Arranged marriages are normal in this part of the world like most other places and a daughter should obey her father. Jess, he looked *old*. I've never seen my father like that. It's as if a light inside of him has gone out."

"Iraj, do you need to go home?"

"No, I'll stay with you till the end of Aryānā. I'm being well paid after all."

Jess laughed. "I think you are earning it."

"I'd want to do it anyway."

Jess smiled at that. "I missed you. I will miss you."

"I'll miss you too. My family wanted to know about Katin's killers, I told them they were dead but I said it wasn't me and I couldn't tell them what happened. It's going to be awkward though: they know I'm working for you and they are going to hear about Dilkor. While Chandyr is further away all sorts of rumours will eventually make their way here."

Jess smiled. "Rohana is the latest to say I leave a trail of bodies behind me wherever I go. I don't mind your family knowing, but the more people who know a secret the harder it is to keep."

Iraj stepped out to arrange something and Rohana entered as if she was waiting outside for the chance to speak to Jess.

"Jess? Do you think I can live a normal life with my heart?" she asked, settling in the spot Iraj had just vacated, leaning against Jess's leg.

"I don't know for sure, but I think so."

"Is there any way you can, you know, tell?"

"Erk!" Jess hit her forehead. "How silly I am! When I healed, er 'Hvâzâta', I found myself looking inside at his injuries. I never even thought to try it on you."

"Can you check me down below too?"

"Rohana, have you got something wrong down below?"

"No, Jess, but I'm a small woman. I was never able to even hope that I could have a normal life. Now I am going to live, but can I be a real woman? Can I carry a baby for Iraj? Can I deliver a child? Can I live long enough to be a proper mother to my child?"

Jess slid down onto the bench and put her arms around Rohana and hugged her fiercely and kissed her cheek.

"Just keep quiet while I concentrate." She closed her eyes.

"There is no hole in your heart and your heart is strong. Your lungs have recovered. I didn't expect that, I can't sense any wrongness there at all. You are small but your pelvis is nice and broad for babies. That is why your bum wiggles so nicely when you walk."

"Jess! Have you been admiring my bum?"

"No! Well, er ... well, maybe." Jess would have flushed if she could. "There can be no guarantee against something going wrong with pregnancy and delivery, you know that, but there is no reason for you not to have babies. A lot of Hindu women are small like you."

"Iraj wants to marry me," Rohana confessed, blushing. "Should I say yes?"

"What do you think?"

"Yes, yes!"

Iraj appeared. Was he waiting just outside now?

"What are you two talking about?"

"I just asked Rohana to marry me and she said yes." Jess laughed and leapt up to hugged him and kissed him fiercely. "I think there was something you wanted to talk to Rohana about. I'll be back with Pandora and the others in a little while. This, we need to celebrate!"

* * *

They waited half a day's journey south of Āmul to join the big caravan.

Syavash had made all the arrangements and paid the usual fees. The guards nodded acknowledgement as they slipped in, unremarked upon by most of their fellow travellers. Groups were still joining and leaving from time to time. It was a large and well organised group with several hundred camels.

A surprise was waiting for them that evening when Frashaoshtra came searching for them, leading the *jack* (male) donkey from Dilkor. He was travelling with some people he knew to Margu, but he joined their camp fire for some of Jess's cooking and to bring them up on events in Dilkor since they left.

Rohana had been teaching Iraj how to play the veena. She loaned Pandora the drum she had bought in Āmul and they all stayed up late around the fire making music and singing some of the old tunes that Iraj and Frashaoshtra knew.

As he was leaving, he took Jess's two hands in his to thank her. "Jess, you have given me my life back. I will never forget you or your friends. Once I get to Margu I have family and connections. I should be able to open a small shop and settle down. If there is anything I can do for you, please let me know."

Little did they know as they drew closer to Margu that a warrant had already been issued for Jess's arrest by the *Dastur* (head priest). He was the third most important man in all the Zoroastrian faith.

If she went anywhere near Margu a trap was waiting, and he was not the only one desperate to find her.

Chapter 16: Margu (Merv)

"Mainly Persis," Iraj said as they rode past. "And a few Hun."

Margu in the west and its surrounds were in the hands of the Persis. The cities along the Oxos in the east were in the hands of the Hun. The desert land in between had seen the greatest empire the world had even known in a desperate fight for its very life against a brutal, implacable foe.

The heaviest blow had fallen against the Transkaukasos region to the north of Aryānā, but this was the eastern front. If the war against the elves had succeeded the Persis would have found the Hun on their door step both in the north and the east.

With the death of Mòdú Chányú the fighting had faded into a wary peace, at least for a time. Eventually one side or the other would decide it was time to settle it once and for all. Then the Persis and Hun would face each other again.

For the moment this land in between lay abandoned. They had passed oasis after oasis, burnt out villages and farms and the sites of old battles, some great and some only skirmishes. Now it was only inhabited by dust and sand and the skeletons of the past.

What they were passing now had been the site of old ambush. It looked like a small Persis patrol had gotten the worst of it.

The bodies had been picked clean by birds and other scavengers. Anything of value was long gone. It was just bones and scraps of clothing flapping in the wind, half buried in the sand, and a few skeletons of horses covered by scraps of grisly leather.

But each of these sad remains had once been a warm breathing person or a loyal animal.

The war had taken everything from these people and their trusting animals: their life, their hopes and their dreams.

* * *

"Pandora, take Rohana further back please," Jess ordered, stringing her bow as she saw the dust of armed horsemen approaching them from a distance.

It proved to be a large patrol out of Margu. After some initial wariness and a bribe changing hands, the caravan had officially entered Persian territory.

They were even given a small escort for the early part of the journey. The merchants and their guards relaxed and Pandora rejoined to point out one of the junior lieutenants in their escort.

"I've already seen her." Jess laughed.

She was a horse archer, a truly stunning young woman: fair skinned, dark brown eyes and hair the colour of jet. She wore a black keffiyeh decorated by silver beading, a loose red tunic over leather body armour, leather trousers and full riding boots.

"I didn't know the Persis had women in their army," Pandora said.

"They do," Iraj said, riding beside Rohana. "All Aryan and Mazdayasna nations have female warriors. She is from the Lur tribe. They grow up in the saddle and are known for their horse archery."

"I'd like to see her shoot," Jess said wistfully.

"She looks so young and energetic," Pandora said. Her mouth was almost drooling as she watched the young woman. "She rides so well!"

"Look how she commands her men!" Jess said, her eyes sparkling. "Do you think she might join us at our camp fire tonight?"

"She won't be interested in either of you." Iraj laughed. "You didn't see the way she smiled at her captain."

Later, several times that afternoon, they heard Iraj chuckling to himself ... for no apparent reason at all.

* * *

The Murghāb River was fed by melt waters from the great mountains to the east. It started young, and brave and strong as it entered the Kara-Kum Desert.

Somewhere in the long, dry and lonely stretches it became tired. It failed to reach the Kāspian or the Aral seas, petering out ignominiously in lowlands of salt marsh and small brackish lakes, drying in the sun.

Before it died, the river birthed a rich delta region and it was there that Margu, the great city lay.

On the way to the city they had already passed many wealthy towns, villas and farms interspersed with desert where the land wasn't irrigated.

This delta had been host to civilisation for thousands of years, the cities and towns having been forced to move several times in their history as the sluggish delta changed course.

To their left was a dry barren hill rising out of the plain, flat but sloping on top with a saddle in the middle. It was huge, dwarfing the great caravan strung out across the plain. The highest point was at one end, crowned by the remains of some undefined structure looking like a great wall but likely the side of a collapsed building.

"Further to the west, they call them 'tells'," Jess said, pointing to it. "It's the remains of an ancient city. They build the city on a hill for defence but over centuries dust, garbage and building rubble accumulate and raise the ground level. The newer parts of the town are built on top of the debris from the older parts so the city builds up its own mound over time. The river probably changed course or it became too high to cart water and this site was finally abandoned. It doesn't rain here often but it does rain and much of the buildings are mud brick. It finally melts like a child's castle washed over by a wave."

"Jess, you amaze me." Iraj twisted in his saddle. "I have ridden past this and climbed over it but never really thought about what it was beyond being a handy lookout to catch the first glimpse of Margu.

"We call it *Tepe Mouru*, (Mouru Hill). Mouru is the name of a wondrous city described in the oldest of our legends from the time of Zarathustra. Maybe this is where it once was. Well, if it is here, then there is not much left of fabled Mouru. Come and I'll show you the lookout."

There were two roads to the top. One angled up to where the tracks of countless visitors had worn the saddle in the middle over many hundreds, maybe even thousands, of years. The other followed a somewhat steeper path to the ruins at the very top. They left their camels with a friend from the caravan and Jess kicked her horse to take the steeper path at a run.

"I want to see what those ruins are."

"Whatever for?" Pandora moaned.

"This way!" Jess called out, galloping ahead.

Iraj took Rohana up the gentler way to the more usual lookout. Several miles across the plains, past some ruins, they saw it: Margu, the great fortified city.

"Everything is so green!" Rohana said in surprise.

"We Aryans certainly know how to irrigate." Iraj smiled, nudging his horse closer to hers.

"So much is gardens," Rohana said with delight. "Gardens, right here in the desert!"

Even in the distance Rohana could pick out trees of every type: palm, of course, and fruit trees, olive, pomegranate, pear, quince, walnut, fig and grapes on orderly trellises and the red flowers of pistachio. But there were also tall trees for shade and decoration: cypresses, junipers, ebony, rosewood, oak, tamarisk, ash and meadows and gardens.

"Don't you people eat much?" she asked.

Iraj laughed. "They have plenty of farms as well, but we Mazdayasna love our gardens. We believe the world has been corrupted. If we practice good thoughts, good deeds and good speech we will be led to live in Paradise in the afterlife. In the meantime we love to try to build a paradise on earth.

"The very word 'paradise', one of the names for *behesht* (heaven) comes from our word for garden, 'pairi-daeza'. There is a legend, that centuries ago the King of Babylon, Nebuchadnezzar, built great hanging gardens to please his *Māda* (Median, Persian) wife."

"That is so romantic!" Rohana said, her eyes sparkling. "That a man would love a woman so much he would build a wonder of the world for her. Much better than building a beautiful tomb, don't you think?"

Iraj laughed. "It is only a legend. Some say it was in Nanwa (Nineveh) and it was the Assyrian king Sennacherib and his Persian concubine. He was said to have an inscription carved in stone at the entrance to his palace. 'For Tashmetu-sharrat, my beloved wife whose features the Mistress of the Gods has made perfect above all other women, I built a palace of loveliness, delight and joy.'"

"That is so lovely." Rohana sighed. "Would you build such a thing for me if you were an emperor?"

"Of course! Mazdayasnas don't go in for burials and tombs. What we do is —"

"Iraj! I know what you Mazdayasnas do for funerals. I'm trying to be romantic."

"I could collect your bones afterwards, I suppose, and put them in a nice ossuary. Some people do that at the one year anniversary. Then I could visit them."

"Iraj, will you stop that?"

Iraj leaned across to pull her to him, half out of the saddle, for a kiss. Just then Jess and Pandora rode their horses down, showering them with a cloud of dust and sand.

"We couldn't see much," Jess said, disappointed. "There were lots of shards of pottery lying around and some sort of building but it is mostly collapsed. It might have been the wall of a palace."

"Or a cow barn," Pandora said in disgust. "Why do you like old buildings and ruins so much? I can't believe you made me ride all the way up there just to look at shards of pottery."

"It couldn't have been a cow barn, Pandora."

"Jess, did you even look at Margu?" Rohana asked.

"Yes, I did," Jess said. "The city has a good wide moat and a fortified castle at one end. The walls stand maybe 25 metres up from the hill, all with crenulations, towers and sally ports. They look thick but they are packed earth faced with mud brick. Modern siege weapons would make short work of them, well eventually they would, and how could they have enough men to man such massive walls? The city must cover 20 hectares at least. The walls are for the city tax, or raiding tribesmen. They would be no good in a proper siege. Oh, the irrigation is incredible, but they seem to have overdone it with gardens."

"Jess, there is more to a city than its military and the commercial aspects."

"Huh?"

"See what I mean?" Pandora called across to Rohana. "My girlfriend is so romantic! Stick to Iraj; at least he buys you flowers."

* * *

Half way to the city they passed a squat octahedral building with a single azure dome. There was a low wall around it and a tall decorative tower at the gateway (one of the features of Persian architecture). The decorative entrance-tower had blue, light-blue and white tiles organized into geometrical patterns and the older cuneiform (wedge shaped) Persian letters, all still in good condition.

"It is a tomb of one of the Šâhs from before Kūruš (Cyrus the Great) took this region," Frashaoshtra said. "It is rumoured to be cursed. Grave robbers have tried to break into the crypt but they have found nothing and later they all died."

"Serves them right!" Rohana said with a toss of her head.

Not much further along was the irrigated land and the road became flanked by fields. From a distance, the city seemed to be on some sort of military alert. Warriors could be seen manning the gate and nearby walls and there were patrols coming and going.

Frashaoshtra led them to the eastern gate, the gate of Zāl (named after the legendary Persian albino hero). There he hugged Iraj and shook the hands of the girls before bidding them farewell and going on his way.

The guards were very interested in Jess. They were asked a lot of questions, and had to unload their animals and everything was checked. Eventually after more than the turn of a glass they were waved through.

"What is going on?" Iraj asked one of the locals as they were let go. He was an old man, standing idly to watch people come and go.

"Don't you know?" The man paused, thinking how to explain it. "The new emperor has ordered the arrest of our *xšaçapāvan* (satrap, governor) several months ago." He turned his head to spit. "Now that we have peace with the Hun we can get back to our favourite sport of fighting amongst ourselves."

"What? This is right on the border!" Jess looked outraged. "How does he dare leave such an issue unresolved for so long?"

The man laughed. "He has no intention of arresting him. Our satrap was appointed by the vizier, Bagōas. That's who the emperor really wants to challenge."

"Has the satrap or the vizier submitted?" Rohana asked.

"No," the man said. "Open warfare has not yet been declared but they say the satrapies of Egypt and Babylonia would join them in revolt. Our satrap is out shoring up support. If I were you, I wouldn't stay here too long. There has already been one attempt on Bagōas's life."

"Why did they take such interest in my friend?" Iraj asked.

The man shrugged. "They are doing that to anyone who looks different."

They thanked him and went in search of Shaheen, Syavash's contact in Margu. He was a local grain merchant (and spy for the old Šâh of Xvairizem). His shop was close to the (southern) Jamshīd gate so they had to pass the great central square.

If Jess was not impressed with mud brick fortifications it would be very hard indeed *not* to be impressed by the great city itself. It had suffered less than many other oasis cities. Not only was it very rich, everything about Margu was *huge*.

As they walked, leading their animals, Iraj tried to explain a little about the politics of Pārśa, the Persian capital that the Greeks call *Persépolis,* (city of the Persians).

"The last three emperors have taken the name *Artaxšaçrā* (Artaxerxes, 'perfect king'): Mnemon (Artaxerxes II), Ochus (Artaxerxes III) and now the latest Arses (Artaxerxes IV). Ochus lived well into his eighties and was a great general. He died just under two years ago but towards the end of his reign it was his vizier, *Bagoi* (Bagōas), who was the real ruler. Bagōas was the head eunuch and was one of Ochus's best generals and most capable administrators. As you know, kings prefer eunuchs."

"It is a horrible thing to do to a young boy!" Jess shuddered.

"It is for slave boys who show special ability." Iraj shrugged. "It gets them into royal service. Gelding young boys makes them loyal when they grow into men: the gelding makes them less aggressively ambitious, they have no dynasty of their own and they cannot rule without a king behind them.

"Anyway, Ochus's father, Mnemon, was said to have over a hundred sons. Ochus had most of them killed when he took the throne. He didn't have as many sons himself but he lived such a long time that his best sons rebelled. So he had to put them to death. When he did die, the faction loyal to Bagōas elevated the youngest son, *Aršan (Greek* 'Arses'), to the throne and had the other surviving sons killed. It's not even been two years now and Aršan is already moving against Bagōas. He is backed by ambitious men with grudges against Bagōas."

"What a mess," Rohana said.

"Yes, it is," Iraj admitted. "All anyone can hope for is that one kills the other before it breaks out into civil war, especially with the Hun sitting on their door step."

A little past the markets, they found themselves passing the high walls of a private garden and house. They couldn't see inside but they could hear the sound of running water and loud bird-whistles high pitched, with silvery trills.

"Is that a nightingale?" Rohana asked.

"Yes it is, though a nightingale cannot match your singing," He gave Rohana a look of pure love. "Your voice is a gift from God. It is the male that sings to find his mate. Tonight I will sing for you, Rohana."

Pandora thumped Jess in the middle of the back. "Why don't you say such things?"

"You want me to sing?"

"No, but some dancing just for me would be nice. You know the type of dance where you take your clothes off."

The main public square was, like everything else in Margu, huge and rich, dwarfing the people inside it standing around and walking backwards and forward across it.

It stood at a cross roads of six streets spreading out in a star. One end, east for the rising sun, lay open. The other three sides were occupied by three enormous buildings that had been built over many centuries. The entrance to each was up marble steps and through giant ornamental portals far higher than the buildings themselves, rising maybe as much as a hundred metres to the sky and flanked by tall delicate spires. The walls were honey combed by large doors, back set into arches to look a bit like caves but all three of the great buildings were completely covered by mosaic tiles: gold, black, dark blue, and ivory. The roofs rippled with smaller domes.

They entered through a corridor of matching fountains, flower gardens and olive trees. The public square was mainly open space, paved by giant geometrical mosaics in large symmetrical squares. As they reached near the centre of the square, Jess paused, to drink in the sight.

"Ah, now you are really impressed." Iraj said pointing to one of the buildings. "These are philosophy schools. The schools of Margu are famous throughout the known world. We call these public squares *rēgistan* which means 'sandy place'."

"I have never seen anything like it." Jess admitted, her eyes sparkling and darting here and there, trying to look at everything at once. "Please, can we stay and explore, maybe for a few days?"

"No," Iraj said. "This place is too dangerous."

"I would have liked to go inside." Jess said, disappointed.

Iraj didn't realise just how dangerous Margu was about to come for them.

Rohana grabbed his arm. "I thought I just saw Firuza near that group of men over there."

"Who is Firuza?" Pandora asked.

"Firuza was Phraotes's lover from Dilkor," Rohana said. "She started as a slave and became the second most powerful person in Dilkor. She wasn't the worst of them, but she lived like a princess. She has good reason to avoid us, let us just hope she does."

"She'd be a fool to advertise her presence," Iraj agreed. "But she also has reason to hate us. The sooner we are back on the road to Nisa the better I will like it."

They met Shaheen in a small office at the back of his warehouse. He looked worried. Maybe he always looked worried. He talked for some time about how difficult things were but all he said could have been summarized by "everything is dangerous and unsettled, leave here as soon as you can."

Following his directions, they made their way towards a small caravanserai near the south gate. A guard patrol passed them, moving the other way. As they reached a small public square, Firuza was there talking to a Mazdayasna priest. She disappeared down a small street of crowded stalls as they approached.

The priest had a felt turban, a plain brown coat over his white robes and bare feet. Hanging from his turban was the cloth that all the Mazdayasna priests wore: across their mouth and nose to prevent any saliva from contaminating their sacred ceremonies. He signalled to a small troop of town guards and its leader stepped into their path.

"I am *Dah-bashi* (Corporal) Behrouz of the city guard."

His name in *Farsi* (Persian) meant 'good day' but it didn't suit him. He had the look of a man who didn't smile a lot, maybe at funerals. Jess had a sinking feeling as he eyed her closely.

"Are you Jess Khánum? I have a warrant for your arrest under suspicion of being a changeling and I am to arrest Pandora *Khánum* for aiding you."

Rohana and Pandora froze in shock. Jess looked for escape routes without seeming to, another troop of soldiers across the square had paused to watch what was going on.

"This is ridiculous!" Iraj protested.

The corporal was unmoved. "The accusation has been made and there is a warrant. She will be questioned by the Dastur himself and appear before the *Atash Dadgah* (religious court)."

"What about that lady you were talking to?" Rohana said loudly. "She was involved with the slavers at Dilkor."

"That has nothing to do with us," the priest said.

"You think so? They were capturing travellers including several from this city. I think she escaped with some of their money."

"If we find her, we will question her," Corporal Behrouz reassured them. "In the meantime *Mobad* (Teacher) Asruta," he indicated the priest, "has a warrant for the arrest of Jess Khánum."

"Wait a minute!" Rohana stepped in front of him. "You can't arrest Pandora then! She is happy to give a statement, but you can't arrest someone as being an accessory to something that is unproven. You said yourself that she is not mentioned on the warrant."

"Ignore her!" the priest demanded.

"No, honoured Mobad," Corporal Behrouz said. "I think she may have a point. All we have is a suspicion that she may be involved in what is currently only an accusation."

"You have been ordered to co-operate with us!" The priest replied angrily.

"I'm sorry I have to take this matter to my *Kuipan* (superintendent of police)."

The corporal and his men were only doing their duty. Jess couldn't bring herself to kill them, just for that. Besides, she was trapped in the middle of a city on military alert in broad daylight. She would be unlikely to be able to escape and any resistance would only get her friends killed. It looked like she would have to go quietly. She passed her weapons to Iraj.

The corporal and five of his men got ready to take Pandora, her arms bound, with Iraj and Rohana. The rest bound Jess's hands behind her back and took her with the priest in a different direction.

"Don't worry, Jess!" Iraj called after her, "We will come for you."

The guards took Jess to an older part of the city, where they were met by five priests who took over. As they walked on even Jess began to realise they were headed in the wrong direction.

"This isn't the way," she said.

With her hands bound behind her she couldn't duck as one of the priests swung a cudgel at her head.

"Careful," the head priest growled. "We don't want to have to carry her. It would arouse suspicion."

They pushed her down a narrow alleyway and through an overgrown entrance. It was a ruined manor house guarded by four large statues of winged lions with man-like heads in a row, complete with the Persian square beards. Beyond that was a covered corridor painted with frescoes of war, killing and rape.

She was not being taken to a religious court.

They hurried her through a room painted with images of fearsome beasts and then down two flights of wooden stairs into a basement. There was a narrow corridor with a number of rooms opening into it. She could hear the sound of water.

They had reached the sewers below the city.

She was pushed through a room with a large wooded table. It was stained dark and smelt of blood. Swords were pointed at her as her bonds were removed and she was prodded into the next room where there were six women prisoners sitting on a bench along one wall. The door slammed shut.

There was another locked iron door on one wall of the cell from which the soft sound of water flowing came. The only ventilation was slits in the two doors leading to the blood stained room from which she had just come and to the sewer. There was a sanitary bucket shared by the women. Flies were buzzing backwards and forwards. It was hard to breathe in the small crowded room with the stench from the bucket. The room darkened as their jailors closed the next door as they exited the blood stained room.

* * *

The duty corporal, Bêndva, remained seated, studying a wax tablet as Iraj, Rohana and Frashaoshtra were shown in. As soon as Frashaoshtra received the message that they were in trouble, he had hurried across the city to help.

"You were correct in saying there are no charges against the Lady Pandora," Bêndva agreed, looking up. "We will allow Lady Rohana to attend her while we organise for her release. Please accept my apologies on any inconvenience caused."

That was easy, *so far.*

As Rohana was escorted out to see Pandora, Iraj leaned forward.

"Thank you, *šēr*, but we also want to make enquiries about our other friend."

Bêndva looked as if he had bitten into something sour. "Are you aware of the allegations against her?"

"She has committed no *crime*!" Iraj interjected. His hand flew to the hilt of his akīnaka but it had been surrendered at the door.

"The *Dastur* (senior priest of the city) himself issued the warrant," Bêndva said. "When the issue is sorcery, he has every right to question her. If you wish to complain you must submit a deposition, it will cost you five sigloi."

"What?" Iraj spluttered.

"Plus the cost of a scribe. We will refer it to the Atash *Dadgah*."

"Who looks at them then there?" Iraj asked.

"One of the Dastur's subordinates."

Iraj's reply was interrupted by the door bursting open. A large beefy man in leather armour strode confidently in. He looked to be in his late fifties. Bêndva almost knocked his chair over in haste to stand up and salute.

"I hope you are giving these people every co-operation, Bêndva? Good. Good."

"Who's that?" Iraj whispered to Frashaoshtra.

"Someone who doesn't have to knock, maybe?" Frashaoshtra suggested.

"My name is Bahadur," the man said in a loud voice. "I am the *Kuipan* (superintendent of police). You need to come with me; we have to see the Dastur immediately. Your ladies are *juddin* (non-believers) and cannot come, but they will be taken to my home. They will be safe there."

"Safe?" Iraj asked.

"Yes, when you protested Pandora's arrest you likely saved her life. I'm sorry, but we have to hurry."

"What about Jess?"

"I am really sorry," Bahadur repeated, looking grim and shaking his head. "Your friend is in great danger. We will tell you more once we get there."

As they were being shown out Pandora was waiting near the entrance looking very pale. Rohana was standing nearby.

"Iraj, I hear Jess is in some sort of danger," Pandora said.

Someone was passing Iraj his sword.

"We will do all we can for your friend." Bahadur said, "But there is not a moment to lose."

"Just get her back," Pandora called to them as they hurried past. "Just get her back."

After a hurried trip, almost jogging after Bahadur and his men the whole way, they were bustled into a large audience chamber in the temple. They were hardly seated when an elderly priest burst in flanked by a large contingent of temple guards. He held a large ceremonial mace the height of a staff in his right hand.

Iraj, Frashaoshtra and Bahadur automatically dropped to their knees and bowed their heads. "Holy one," they murmured in unison as he gave them his blessing.

This was Dångha, the Dastur (Holy Father) of one of only three great fire temples. He was the third most powerful man in all of the Mazdayasna religion.

"This is very serious," he said as they sat.

"Holy one, we want to arrange the release of our friend," Iraj said respectfully. "Frashaoshtra here will bear witness that she helped rescue innocent men in Dilkor."

"I know about Dilkor," the Dastur's expression was hidden by his *padan* (priestly mask), but his voice hard. "Do you deny the accusations against her?"

"It is only gossip," Frashaoshtra said.

Iraj was silent.

"Can she be released to my care?" Frashaoshtra continued. "My family has a good name."

"That would not be possible." Dångha leaned forward.

"In any case, we do not have her."

* * *

Four of the women in the small cell were prostitutes who had been trying to avoid the city tax and two were petty thieves. The woman sitting next to her was called *Niloofar* (water lily).

"I'm accused of stealing a purse, but it was planted on me," she explained. "Just because I have been caught before no one will believe me."

The rest of the room's occupants explained they were unfortunate victims of various misunderstandings too.

"I've never heard of this place," *Niloofar* added, twisting her hands over and over. "And there are stories of women disappearing."

You are right to be worried, Niloofar.

There was a scream outside and another woman was thrown in. Jess looked down at the face of the newcomer.

"Hello, Firuza."

Firuza threw herself at Jess, scratching and trying to punch her. Jess just held her hands by the wrists. Firuza wasn't very big and she wasn't really hurting her. Eventually some of the other women pulled her off and Firuza crawled over to sit as far away from Jess as she could get.

It wasn't long after a man in the uniform of the city guards took Firuza away for questioning. It seemed to take a long time. They had to carry her back, a guard on either side. Jess moved over closer, and some of the others looked at her curiously.

"What happened?"

Firuza's face was badly bruised and her lip was bleeding. "They wanted to know about you. I couldn't really tell them much, and then they wanted to know where I keep my money. These aren't normal guards, are they?"

"No, Firuza, I'm sorry but they are not. I have a little ability at healing and if you allow me, I will ease your hurts."

"You would do that for me?"

Why not? We are going to die here anyway.

"Of course I would." Jess gave her a gentle smile.

* * *

"You don't know where Jess is?" Iraj leapt to his feet in fear and anger.

"Calm yourself," Bahadur asked. "Sit down and allow us to tell you what we *do* know and what we are doing to try to find her."

The Dastur took up the story. "When Ahura Mazda, the spirit of *aša* (goodness), created the world it was perfect. Angra Mainyu, the evil one, brought *druj* (evil, corruption, the lie, destruction, sin) into the world."

Iraj scowled at him. He didn't want a religious lesson at this time!

But the Dastur was getting to the point. "When our people were strong we, the keepers of the sacred flame, were also very strong. Now there is chaos everywhere and enemies we thought we had destroyed long ago have returned. I first saw Jess in a dream. She has been hidden from my far sight but I have managed to follow her through omens and other signs. I now know she is one of the most important people in an age and that our greatest enemy is also hunting her."

"Chandyr!" Iraj whispered.

"You know about that too, do you?" Dångha asked in surprise. "Jess faced a powerful sorcerer, a priest of *Aēšma* (Aeshma) of the bloody mace. Aēšma is the most powerful of all the *daēva* (false gods)."

"She broke his neck," Iraj admitted.

"She should not have been able to do that. She isn't fully human, is she, Iraj?"

Iraj sighed, the tension all drained out of him. "No, she's not, Holy One." He felt he had just condemned his friend to death.

"I already knew that, so I issued a warrant so I could question her but the priest who carried it was waylaid and murdered."

"The priest that took her was an imposter?" Iraj cried in anguish.

The Dastur nodded, looking grim.

"Women have begun disappearing. We suspected blood priests had come to our city, but capturing your friend from the city guard is their most audacious act yet."

"Jess hurt them badly." Iraj gave the Dastur a sad smile and his eyes misted. "She tends to do that sort of thing."

"They will want her to join them," Dångha said. "With her they would be near invincible."

"Jess would never do that." Iraj shook his head determinedly. "She only ever fights evil."

"You think well of her."

"Holy one," Iraj rose to his feet. "If she needed my right arm, I would cut it off for her. If she needed my eye, I would pluck it out. If I had to give my life for her I would gladly do so and count myself blessed. I am honoured beyond my worth to know her. Does that answer your question?"

"Holy one, I don't care if she is human or not." Frashaoshtra joined him in standing. "She saved me from a living death as a slave, me and so many others."

"Well," the Dastur said quietly. "She has two good men who are willing to speak out for her, at possible risk to themselves." His smile robbed the comment of any threat. "But if she doesn't join them, they will kill her."

"We know where they were last seen and there are only a few places they can be," Bahadur added. "But if my men will be facing priests of Aēšma, we will need your help, Holy One."

The Dastur held up the ancient mace. "This is the mace of *Mithra* (once seen as the ancient God of justice, now seen as the greatest of all the archangels). The minions of Aēšma cannot stand against its power."

"Can we come?" Iraj asked.

"Yes, we might need you to identify your friend."

Identify the body.

Jess, no! Not Jess!

* * *

They took another woman away.

First two guards came in and pushed Jess up against the wall. One held a knife to her throat, the other poked her torso with a naked blade. Then two others came for the woman.

Firuza and another woman led the others in an attempt to prevent them taking her. They almost overpowered the two guards with their bare hands but the men beat them back with cudgels and then dragged the woman, screaming and trying to hang on, away.

The women lay there, bruised and bleeding, listening in horror to the screams of agony and terror from next door. Many of them put hands over their ears and bent their heads. Many had tears in their eyes.

Eventually the cries subsided into moaning. Then they stopped. There was the sound of men moving about, a door opened on iron hinges and there was a soft splash.

Then they came for Jess.

"Just let them take me," she said.

Anyway, the fight had gone out of her companions.

Two men waited with drawn swords, while another two men chained her hands behind her back and hobbled her ankles.

As they led her through the room next door, one man was wiping blood off the table. These were death priests. They used the energy a tortured victim released at the time of their death to feed their magic power. Sometimes they bound women to their God in death as his 'brides'.

She was led through another room to where a man was seated comfortably behind a desk. He was dressed as a simple scholar: a white turban, a white vest showing under a brown robe. He had a beard trimmed short, a rather thin face and a pair of the coldest eyes Jess had ever seen. He rose as she entered and bowed. The guards waited just behind her.

"Ah, Jess Khánum, I have waited a long time to finally meet you. It is a great honour. My name is Tishari."

"Forgive me for not greeting you as I would wish," Jess said politely, glancing meaningfully at the chains on her feet.

Behind him was a life sized marble statue, Greek. It was of a young man, heavily muscled and handsome, naked but for a Greek helmet. His hair was short and curly and he was beardless. He was standing holding a shield at his feet and a spear in his hand. The wall behind him was pink, *white wash and human blood, very pretty.*

It had a quote from an epic written in black ink.

'Rejoicing in bloody wars; fierce and untamed, he is the one whose mighty power can make the strongest walls shake. Mortal-destroying, defiled with gore, pleased with war's dreadful and tumultuous roar. Human blood, swords and spears delight him. He loves ruin, the savage fight, furious contests and avenging strife. He visits misery on human life."

Jess got a feeling of terrible revulsion. It was Ares, the Thraki God of War!

Tishari saw the direction of her gaze.

"I like to think I have made quite a study of Greek culture."

It was strange. He could smile and still look so cold.

"We do not make images of our God, but it is hard not to admire the beauty of Greek sculptures, don't you think?"

"You worship Agin," Jess whispered, in understanding. Agin the brutal Skythian God of War; a picture of a great mound and the life blood and limbs of captives poured and thrown over an iron sword came to her mind.

"We prefer the more civilised name, Aēšma. It was you at Chandyr, wasn't it?"

So this is the God of that bastard in Chandyr. It figured, whatever you called him: Ares, Agin or Aēšma, he was a mad and brutal God.

Jess's expression gave him his answer.

"If you designed the perfect warrior what characteristics would you choose?"

The question took Jess by surprise. She moved restlessly for a moment, her chains clanking. Was Tishari just as crazy as the God he worshipped? It might be better to humour him, especially as Jess was the one bound in chains.

"Er, let's see; strong and tireless, brave of course, skilful and loyal."

How am I doing?

"My God can give you all these things and more!" Tishari leapt up in enthusiasm and gestured to the statue. "You are already a great warrior. Join us and we can make you stronger than you could possibly imagine. You will be invincible."

"But doesn't your God delight in bloodshed for its own sake and the rape and murder of innocents?"

The furious look Tishari gave her suggested he didn't like awkward questions. *Perhaps I should just keep them to myself.*

"Aēšma is the God of War! Of course he delights in war. He cannot be judged by the worthless emotions of puny mortals. He can give you real power! Join us and we will make you even stronger and your heart completely fearless."

"Fearless ... and without compassion," Jess replied. "That helpless woman you tortured to death, is that the sort of thing your God tells you to do?"

And why can't I keep my stupid mouth shut, like around about now?

"He is a God!" Tishari was outraged. "Those women are whores and thieves, by their death they will join HIM in honour."

Jess realised she would rather side with the whores and thieves. *What does that say about me?*

"You remind me of those snivelling Mazdayasna dogs."

She definitely wasn't handling this well.

"You are mortal and can be killed," he warned her.

Now, why would there be any doubt about that?

"Ha! I see you are curious about what I know! I know *who* you are, I know *what* you are and I know what happened to that Gypsy girl. Without you she can't return. It is all rather amusing really."

"And you are going to tell me, just because you are such a dear, dear, man."

He looked at her puzzled and then he burst out laughing. "Oh, I see. Join us, knowledge and power can be yours for the asking."

"Why don't you have someone take these chains off so I can give you my answer properly?" Jess gave him a sweet smile.

Tishari strode over and slapped her hard across the face. She tasted blood.

"You are wasting my time and time is something I no longer have. The city is crawling with men and priests looking for you. I didn't expect that. Of course they will probably kill you when they find you, but it wouldn't do for us to take a chance on that, would it?"

Margu seems such a friendly place.

"No time to do this slowly, I'm afraid."

One of his acolytes offered him a long and slender knife on a red silk cushion.

"Jess!" Jacinta's voice shouted in Jess's head. "He is going to cut your throat! Get him to throw you in the sewer instead! All you have to do is slow your body down."

"Jacinta, is that you? I don't know how to slow my body down."

"Then take a deep breath and let me do the rest."

"Just as long as you don't throw me in that filthy sewer!" Jess screamed, shuddering violently. She tried to look terrified. It wasn't too hard.

Tishari's smiling face moved closer. She tried not to upset him by spitting at him or lunging at him with her hands bound behind her back. Instead she cringed away, trying to look defeated. Maybe she was.

"What a good idea! The water and cold will weaken your daimôn nature and drowning is an excellent way for you to die, as slowly as we can hope for under the circumstances, with your body fighting for air."

He gestured to his acolytes, who took turns to fondle her breasts and jam their fingers up her vagina while one of their number cleared the way to the sewer.

"I'm going to kill you, you know," she whispered to them conversationally.

One of the men twisted her nipple cruelly. "You have to live to be able to do that."

One man hit her over the head with a cudgel. She really wished they would stop doing that.

Then they shoved her back to the other room. The iron gate to the sewage canal was open. There were a few stone steps down to it and a narrow boat waited in the canal.

That's when they all heard loud banging on the door.

"Open up in the name of the *Dastur.*"

A priest's smiling face came close to hers.

"Unless they have brought a ram, which I very much doubt, it will take a long time for them to get through that door, it is very solid. It is time you simply do not have."

She didn't answer. She felt her mind slowing down, serenity floating through her.

They shoved her hard at the canal. Hobbled by the chain, she missed the steps and crashed face forward onto the stone surrounds, leaving a smear of blood and loosening a tooth.

The acolytes followed her down. They kicked and shoved at her body till it tumbled over the edge. She was blinded by the splash as the dark water closed over her head. She twisted and squirmed so she would sink onto her back.

Her eyes clicked in. She could see the surface rippling above her, bubbles still rising up to it. Up there she could breathe. It may as well have been on the other side of the moon.

The boat rocked as the men climbed inside. She got poked in the face by one of the oars and then they were gone.

"Open up in the name of the *Dastur.*" It was faint, and very far away.

All she could feel was a burning, irresistible urge to open her mouth wide and suck in a deep, deep breath.

* * *

The Dastur was not too old to ride. In fact he was an excellent horseman. Iraj found himself careening through the streets of Margu following the Dastur and the Kuipan, Bahadur. Four Mazdayasna priests and a dozen city guards followed closely behind, yelling themselves hoarse for people to get out of the way.

He wondered if the priests and the city guards engaged in regular horse races, the way they rode. His own borrowed horse seemed completely out of control but his own heart was burning for Jess so he let the animal have its head.

Apparently they had been moving closer to an older section of the city as they narrowed the search area. Then there was a frantic message. The blood priests had been sighted.

The small party arrived outside the old town-house in a clatter of hooves. As they arrived, four men ran from the cover of building.

"Dah-bashi!" Bahadur yelled out commandingly. His corporal and six other men smoothly turned their horses to give chase.

The rest of the men threw themselves off and hurried after the Dastur, Iraj and Bahadur. They burst through a gate, past some winged lions with human faces.

"Hurry," the Dastur said from just behind Iraj and Bahadur.

Normally Iraj would suggest a cautious approach, but he found himself barrelling madly down a corridor covered with images of violence.

Three men jumped out to stop them, Iraj and Bahadur barely paused. They punched their akīnakes savagely into the men and threw their bodies aside while the Dastur hit the other man over the head with his staff.

"That's what it's for," the old man said with a broad smile; he seemed to be enjoying himself tremendously.

They burst through another room. Bahadur seemed to know where he was going, down stairs to a heavy locked door. Bahadur kicked at it and rattled the handle.

"Open up in the name of the *Dastur*."

The Dastur caught up, panting and clutching at his chest; Iraj grabbed his mace.

"That is over three hundred years old!" the Dastur protested while trying to get his breath. "You can't just use it on a *door*."

"You can use it on people," Iraj said. "As you said, it was made for this."

A few solid blows and the hinges began to loosen. Then Iraj rammed the precious mace through a gap in the door and gave it a wrench. The door sprang open.

"We have missed them," one of the guards cursed. "Let's see if your friend is in the cell."

"The sewer!" Niloofar and Firuza were screaming over and over. "They threw her in the sewer!"

Iraj followed the smear of blood on the stone and leapt into the water. He immediately felt a body at his feet. One of the guards jumped in next to him and they struggled to lift the weighted body up and onto the floor. Jess's head lolled lifelessly, foul water ran from her mouth.

"She is dead!" Iraj screamed in anguish. He felt like he had been stabbed in his heart.

"Not yet, but very close," the Dastur said hurriedly. He nodded to his priests. Two of them rolled her, another jammed his finger down her throat to hook out any mud and slime. Then they began violently pushing up and down on her chest. Water oozed from the corner of her mouth, her body spasmed and they quickly rolled her on her side. She whooped and vomited and coughed weakly.

"I don't think she will survive," one of them said.

"Please don't hurt her," Frashaoshtra pleaded.

"It *would* seem a shame to go to all this trouble just to execute her," the Dastur agreed.

* * *

"You are awake."

She was propped up sitting. Jess ineffectually waved her arms in an effort to sit up further.

"No, just lie back. You had foul water in your lungs. We didn't expect you to survive, you still may not."

The Mazdayasna priests with their knowledge of corruption and how to combat it were the greatest healers in the human world. From next door there was the sound of chanting and running water.

"Something about this place feels so wonderful," Jess whispered tiredly. "It's as if healing is in the very air."

"That is a strange reaction for one accused of being evil." A vigorous looking white haired old man had entered the room with two attendants. It was as if he were waiting next door for her to wake. All three were dressed in brilliant white. They had the cloths hanging from their turbans covering their mouths that all the priests wore.

These are the real thing, Jess realised.

"I am Dångha, the Dastur of this temple. I have been waiting for a long time to meet you. You have proven, shall we say, elusive?"

"Thank you for saving my life, Holy One. The other women with me ...?"

"Are safe, unfortunately the most senior of the priests of the Aēšma-daēva escaped. One of the women, Firuza, was involved with the slavers of Dilkor. Perhaps the punishment I give her should be particularly harsh."

"Please, Holy One, show mercy. She was only a slave girl trying to survive. Please let her go."

"What about falsely accusing you of being a changeling? That is a serious matter, surely, is it not?"

Jess sighed. "Firuza is speaking the truth, I am unclean. I shouldn't be here, I cannot presume to call you Father."

"I see." Dångha's eyes burned into her. "She has retracted the accusation, saying she was forced to make it by the false priests."

"She is lying to protect me," Jess said. "Please forgive her."

"I thought you two were enemies, but here she is trying to protect you and you put your life at risk for her. Don't you find this all a little strange?" His eyes seemed to penetrate into her very soul. "Daughter, are you prepared to confess to me and accept my judgement?"

"I am, Holy One." Tears came to her eyes. "I have no right to ask this, but please spare my friends. Their only crime has been to show me kindness, kindness beyond what I deserve."

"You stand accused of being a changeling. Is that true?"

"Yes, I am part daimôn. I try to resist what I am, I am sorry to be evil."

"Would you work for truth, honesty, loyalty and courage? Or would you tell lies and support corruption and destruction?"

He drew himself up. "Tell me!" he demanded.

She felt the compulsion to answer. "The truth of course! All those things! And I like to bathe, you can ask my friends."

Dångha seemed to be resisting a smile behind his padan. "Are you ready?"

"To confess?" Jess sighed as if she were lowering a great burden from her shoulders. Such was the air in this place and the stare of the high priest that she knew she would tell all she could. "I wish to, great one. Can I tell my story from the beginning?"

After a nod from the Dastur, she continued.

"I think I was attacked by a sorcerer, it was he that damaged my hand I think, but the memory is very faint. I think it was he that put a curse on me that made me a changeling. Almost two years ago now I woke to an awareness of myself in the desert. I was not human; I ate small animals, snakes and lizards that came out at night. Slowly I seemed to recall the things that belong to humans but almost nothing about me as a person, who I was."

Then the long questioning began.

Why did you buy a slave's freedom, someone you had just met? Why did you kill the three men who were to rape your friend when you could have gotten away? Why did you kill the men that killed Katin, when you didn't even know her? Why didn't you attack the town guards when they came to arrest you? Why did you risk your life for people you didn't know?

At that Jess struggled up. "Those slavers were destroying those people's lives."

"Were you angry with them?"

"I don't feel I have a right to judge people, but I felt a great hunger to stop them, yes. I can be very destructive when I fight."

He made no reply to that.

"Weren't you invited to join the worshippers of Aēšma; didn't they promise you great things?"

"But you don't understand! They were going to torture and murder those poor women. I was bound by chains but all I wanted to do was to get free so I could attack them.

"Oh, I don't feel like that here," Jess said, looking around.

"Perhaps that is a good thing." Again the Dastur looked like he was smiling behind his padan.

"You think you were attacked by a sorcerer." He changed the topic.

"Yes," Jess held up her hand. "I think so."

"And you say you have the power of healing?"

"No, šēr, that power belongs to a God; I am not worthy of having such a power myself."

Jess felt herself dozing. "Are you going to kill me, now?"

"I believe you have told me the truth, at least the truth as far as you know it." He gave her a sad smile as if he pitied her. "We Mazdayasnas do not judge beings by what they claim to be. We judge them by what they say and do I believe you are one of the farohars, a fravashi or guardian angel, sent to our earth."

"Fravashi?"

"Yes, our God Ahura Mazda does not act directly in this world. To defeat the *druj* (falsehood and destruction) he needs humans to choose to follow *asha* (truth, righteousness and proper order). That is why corruption and unclean spirits can have no power over us in our temple.

"But other battles must be fought with other weapons. There are the six great *Amesha Spentas* (archangels), then there are the *yazata*s (angels) and beneath them are the farohars (plural)."

"You believe I am a guardian angel?"

"I do, most fravashi come from the essence that Ahura Mazda has put in all things to guide their evolution: both animate and inanimate. Most of the fravashi we know are attached to human souls as guides and to some extent protectors against the spite of daēva.

"But a few fravashi are different, created out of the substance of heaven itself and working to complete and preserve God's plan for heaven. Those fravashi can be chosen to descend in human form. That is what I think you are. It is a great honour to be chosen, but it is also a great trial."

"So you think I am a *fravashi*." Jess had to smile. "I apologise, *šēr*, but I wouldn't call myself an angel." She covered her smile. "I do now believe I was sent by a God but I am unworthy; it was supposed to be Jacinta, only she got killed."

And yet she still talks to me.

"Maybe I was made in a hurry, which is why I don't have proper memories."

"Angels are not always gentle when they have to fight our enemies." Dångha looked amused. "And as unworthy as you feel, there is only one true God and he does not make mistakes. I fear the indications are that you have been chosen to face something infinitely terrible. While a *juddin* (a non-believer) is not normally allowed in our temple, I think it will be safer for you to stay here while you recover and we hunt these conspirators."

"Thank you," Jess began to cry. "It feels so wonderful to be here."

"I certainly don't think something truly evil would think so." He smiled. "You were destined to come here; I saw this in a dream. Tomorrow we will talk again."

Jess couldn't keep her eyes open any longer.

* * *

Jess woke to daylight, the chanting and the same priest watching over her.

Her nose was blocked, her mouth dry, she ached all over and her head was pounding. She couldn't get enough air and could feel her lungs bubbling and rattling as she breathed. She was overcome with a bout of coughing till she was exhausted and her head was spinning. She weakly spat a glob of thick yellow mucous into a shallow bowl that the priest, whose name she later found out was *Dārayava(h)uš* (Darius), passed her.

"That is good!" he remarked with satisfaction.

She lay there, too weak to move.

With a call from Darius, two burley priests bustled in and quickly rolled her on her front, head down, and positioned pillows underneath. Then they cheerfully beat her to death with their open palms.

She was draped, head tilted down, naked and helpless, hawking up phlegm. They exited, leaving her slumped over the cushions like a stranded fish.

"That is much better, isn't it?" Darius asked after they left.

Jess tried to scowl but couldn't get her eyes to focus.

"Your body is wonderful. Normal bodies do not produce phlegm to clear the infection until the third day at the earliest."

And I thought you were going to say my body was wonderful for other reasons.

"I think you might live after all," he decided. "If so I will lose some money on a bet, but not too much. I didn't think you would survive when we washed you down."

Jess couldn't remember this particular group of men washing her naked body.

He moved closer to feel her forehead.

"A temperature, but not too high." Then he felt her pulse. "Oh, very good! Now take a deep breath."

It set her coughing again.

"Better and better," he remarked with satisfaction. "We use this room if any of our priests get sick with the fever. Sorry you won't be allowed to move into any other areas of the fire temple with all that corruption in your chest."

What a pity, I really wanted to get up and dance around right now.

Perhaps Dångha spent all his time waiting just outside her room. As the door opened to let him through the chanting sounded briefly louder. The scent of sandalwood and frankincense wafted in as he moved near her bed.

Jess tried feebly to grab at a blanket. The strong hands of his two assistants rolled her over and lifted her up in the bed and lay a blanket over her nakedness.

"Sorry we cannot allow your women friends to attend you here."

"Being attended by the famous Mazdayasna priests is not something I can complain about, Holy One." Jess gave a weak smile.

"Later we will perform a purification ceremony for you with fire and water."

"You use fire a lot in your ceremonies, *šēr*," Jess remembered.

"Ah, must I tell you a little of our religious politics? You may be surprised that belief can have politics as well, but it is so.

Zarathustra was a great reformer. He lived to the north and east of here. Since his time our religion has slowly incorporated beliefs of the past and added new beliefs. When our beliefs reached the Magi, the priestly caste of the *Medes* (a tribe in Persia), they met an influential and educated hereditary priesthood. The Magi worshipped the ancient God Mithra as their major God, we see him now as the greatest of our archangels. They also worshiped the four holy elements: ateshi (fire), badi (air), abi (water), and heki (earth). We Mazdayasnas may have conquered the Magi with our beliefs, but they conquered us with their rituals. We would never admit that many of our rituals have their roots in fire worship."

"But I find hearing it so restful!" Jess protested. "I can never remember feeling so safe and comforted."

"It is not just the content, it is the tone," Dångha agreed. "We call the chanting a manthra."

"It moves me strongly," Jess whispered.

"As it does me, it has special power over the druj and daēva."

"I don't fully understand your beliefs."

"Not fully understand?" the Dastur smiled. "Nor do I, but this part is simple: when our God created the world it was perfect. The Angra Mainyu brought corruption and lies into it. The duty of all of us is to fight the druj until the time of the final battle of good and evil and the final judgement which will restore his creation."

"The blood priests are your natural enemies. I should have realised that."

Dångha nodded. "Our great Khordad Zarathustra said to reject all Gods who do not work for good. It is why we call ours 'the good religion'."

"The Greeks think you are sorcerers."

Dångha laughed. "I suspect if they came here they would want to burn our books like all the other conquerors, but the Greeks have a fascination with mystery cults and anything purported to be from an eastern religion: astrologers, horoscopes, the philosopher's stone, alchemy, or fountains of eternal life. If you want to make money just go to *Hellás* (Greece) and write fake scrolls. The Greeks will buy them. They call our imagined sorcery '*magikos*', after the *magâunô* (Magi)."

"Yet you have a power, and you have wisdom," Jess whispered. "I can feel it."

"Our greatest power is the power of prayer, and the help that our God sends us," Dångha said. "And now our God has sent one of his soldiers to help us, but I think you need to rest for now."

* * *

She had a restless night, woken by breathlessness and seemingly endless bouts of coughing. Her whole body ached. One minute she couldn't get warm, no matter how much she shivered; the next minute her body was covered with drenching sweats. She lay, in the darkness, longing for the dawn.

Dawn brought the heat of the day. She lay there coughing, weak, feverish and headachy ... and she found she was longing for the cool of the night.

Not a good way to live your life, Jess.

Darius strode in looking energetic and cheerful. "Good morning."

She looked at him with bleary eyes.

"Are you ready for your chest percussion?" He rang a small bell.

"No!" Jess said weakly, shaking her head.

The two muscular priests came in, grinning at her broadly. Now that she could see them they were built like wrestlers.

She cast about for a means of escape but they were onto her. They lifted her and rolled her over as if she were a small child, jamming great cushions underneath and pounding them into position. Then they began to play her chest as if they were drummers and she was a wooden drum at a mighty celebration.

They wore wide grins. The fact that very little phlegm came up didn't dampen their enthusiasm.

"She may not need much more of this," one of them remarked a little regretfully.

They left her draped and gasping over the pillows in case that very last bit of elusive mucous might be hiding somewhere in the bottom of her chest.

Jess wondered what they did when they didn't have her to bash around. Perhaps they punched bulls unconscious or broke rocks barehanded.

Darius gave her a few moments and then felt her forehead and pulse and gave a satisfied smile. "You are better."

Jess was instantly asleep.

* * *

Rohana sat in the room she shared with Pandora, watching her pace. Iraj was staying in the guard's barracks nearby and came every day to escort Rohana out, but for Pandora it was judged to be too dangerous; so poor Pandora was confined to the superintendent's house.

Pandora didn't cope well with boredom at the best of times. Now she felt she was going insane. She also desperately worried about Jess and was missing her terribly.

Rohana offered to stay at home and keep her company but Pandora insisted she spend time with her man, while she had the chance.

"Iraj says he hasn't been able to see Jess. He has been so worried about her, we all have. She almost died, even after they rescued her, but we should be able to visit soon," Rohana told her. "The Dastur knows she is a changeling, he won't discuss it in any detail but he assures Iraj she isn't in any trouble from him or the temple."

"Are you going to join the Mazdayasna?" Pandora asked, changing the topic.

"I think so," Rohana said. "Iraj is taking us back to his parents' home, at least for a while. With what Jess has been paying him he could stay and buy his own herd. I hope he does. I have just found him, I don't want him going off somewhere expecting me to stay at home and wonder if he had gotten himself killed somewhere." She smiled. "That doesn't sound like me. I would become a camp follower."

They both giggled at that. Female 'camp followers' of a group of soldiers had a very bad reputation.

* * *

It was four days later that Iraj escorted them into one of the small gardens of the temple that was open to the general public. Unlike most Persian buildings, fire temples (by tradition) were built to look plain. This one, though, held one of the three eternal fires and so it housed a large religious community.

They waited in a pleasant garden of grass and flower beds. A nearby stand of cypress pines had coloured wish-ribbons tied all over them. A small fountain tinkled in the background.

Jess had to be assisted in by two burley priests who left her on a stone bench. She slumped forward. A blanket was draped over her shoulders despite the heat. She had lost a lot of weight. Her skin looked a muddy colour, probably as close to pale as she ever got.

"You're looking well," Pandora said.

That got a wan smile.

"Most of the senior priests were sure I wouldn't survive. The Dastur made a tidy profit from betting against them. They should have known better than to bet against him."

"They know you are a changeling," Pandora said. "Surely you didn't admit to it?"

Jess nodded weakly. "I expected to be killed."

"Are you a prisoner?" Rohana asked.

"No, nothing like that." Jess laughed. "The Dastur believes I am one of the *fravashi*s, a guardian angel. There are supposed to be a large host of us. To be chosen to descend to the earth is said to be a great honour and a rare one." She smiled, embarrassed. "Oh and *fravashi*s are known for their fighting prowess."

"A guardian angel!" Pandora was delighted. "My girlfriend is a guardian angel!"

Iraj stood and gave her a solemn bow.

"*Arda Fravash* (Holy Guardian Angel)," he murmured.

Jess was shocked to realise he was absolutely serious and not teasing!

"I must say I knew it had to be something like that. It is a great honour to know you."

She didn't know what to say. "Er, thanks Iraj."

Iraj pointed to a carving on the wall. It looked like the winged sun: a disc with a bird's tail and two great horizontal wings. Standing up from the circle side-on was the figure of a Persian man with a beard and a Persian hat. In his left hand he held a ring. It was the most famous of all symbols of Mazdayasnaism.

"That is the male version of a *fravashi* but more of them are female."

"I don't care what you think I am, Iraj, as long as you don't stop treating me as your friend," Jess said. "I need my friends."

They hugged her and kissed her in turns, which brought tears to her eyes.

"Can I call you 'holy one' sometimes?" Pandora asked.

* * *

"She survived!" Tishari spat.

Tishari had spies in the fire temple, which had allowed him to trap Jess, but he had no need of them. In Margu people everywhere could talk about nothing else: *Blood priests serving Aēšma, a desperate hunt by the town guard and senior priests, women rescued from a dungeon and a Nubian sorceress dragged from the sewer, more dead than alive.*

It was the sort of story that would fuel gossip and legends for many years to come.

The rescued women prisoners had confirmed that not only did the sorceress have the healing touch but it was she that had helped free Dilkor from the slavers and Chandyr from the blood priests. They had a good description of her and her companions.

No one knew the origin of this mysterious lady but there were many that were more than happy to invent details.

"I'm sorry, Holy One," Vanâra, his senior acolyte, said automatically.

"Cold water *should* have been one of the worst things for her." Tishari stopped pacing. "It *should* have taken too long to find her." He gave one of his cold smiles. "She *tricked* me."

It had all started in Chandyr. Someone had killed Horkan. A little earlier some shepherds had been found killed and they suspected a supernatural creature. Horkan had been one of their most powerful sorcerers, he was virtually invulnerable.

Try as he might, Tishari could not trace who or what had done it. There was something out there, something very dangerous that was protected from his far sight. He couldn't see where it was, but he could tell where it had been.

It wasn't until she acted again in Dilkor that he found out what he was facing. A daimôn changeling, and even in human form she was a formidable fighter. And who knew what magic power she had as well.

Used properly, she alone would turn the battle against the Mazdayasnas. A daimôn, she would obviously want to join them. When he finally met her, something had happened to her memory and she had tried to wall off her daimôn self from her human side. Her power would be immense if all that was released. All she had to do was join with Aēšma. She could not, she would not, refuse.

And yet, incredibly, she had! She carped on about innocent victims of war. He remembered her look of loathing. Surely a daimôn wouldn't worry about such things? And now to make it a complete disaster, not only had they *not* managed to kill her but she had formed an alliance with his worst enemies.

One day she would come looking for him.

"We cannot trace *her* or the people with her, but as soon as they leave her protection we will be able to track them. She is soft-thinking and will come to their rescue. Then all we need to do is think of a way to kill her."

* * *

Jess was able to walk now. She was getting better every day.

She had ways of healing herself, but something told her that accessing her daimôn energy was too dangerous whilst her human side was so massively depleted.

Today she was dressed in a white gown supplied by the priests but wore a short blanket over her shoulders, and she was hobbling slowly back and forward in front of the seated Dastur.

"You recovery is remarkable," Dångha said. "Are you always this restless?"

Jess flashed him a grin. "I am used to training most days. I also have a strong feeling I should leave as soon as possible."

"You are nowhere near recovered enough."

"Soon I will be able to use the healing power on myself, but I have been too ill so far."

"If you insist I will give you an armed escort as far as the pass through the *Koppeh Dagh* ('Heap' Mountains) into Aryānā. I can also give you letters of introduction but beyond Aryānā I have little influence."

"You have already done so much for me, Father," Jess said, kneeling in front of him. "This place feels like a home to me."

"In a way, it is your home. You will always be welcome here."

"Thank you, Father, but I don't think my fate is to remain in a place of quiet contemplation."

"We sometimes have our times of excitement, Jess."

Jess gave him a small smile and then frowned. "I feel a growing sense of unease. I know I need to hurry but I do not understand why."

"Then you must leave, truly. I hear Gansükh has made plans to train more daimôn summoners."

Jess shivered. "Hasn't he done enough?" She looked at her hand. "I don't think this will destroy daimôns."

"You sound sure."

"I can't be sure, of course I can't, but I am part daimôn. Jacinta isn't dead, she is lost somewhere. Apparently I am the one that has to help her to return."

"Then perhaps that will be your next task."

"For that I have to go to the Troad. And something is telling me that I have to hurry."

Chapter 18: Seléne, Queen of the Half Elven

It was not long after the second anniversary of Elana and Jacinta's death when the carriage was sighted. It was unannounced; there was no letter, no forward courier, just the coach and a large escort.

Kynane had only had a day's warning from her scouts. She waited nervously on a seat in the shade while the lookouts on the wall reported its slow progress. It wasn't hard to guess who it was. A royal elf coach, escorted by five hundred warriors; half elf and half human!

It was the new queen of the half-elven.

Most of the escort camped a short way back and the coach proceeded on with a hundred of the elite royal guard.

Kynane had been overjoyed to be pregnant. Hakeem's first child! Now with not much more than a month to go and with the weather increasingly warm, she was wishing it would all end. She was sleeping poorly, her back hurt and the baby kept pressing on her bladder! And now she had to play hostess to an elf queen in the rustic fortress of a minor noble!

While he hadn't said so, the Hakeem who was afraid of nothing was absolutely terrified of meeting his sister-in-law. At the last minute he had gone off to meditate. He would need to hurry if he would be there to greet the queen in person.

"Alba!" Kynane yelled out. "Tell Hakeem to come here *now*! He can't expect me to meet her on my own! Take a sword to the coward if you have to!"

Asha appeared at her side and put a supporting hand on her shoulder. Kynane put her hand over Asha's and bent her head to kiss it in gratitude. She didn't know how she could have survived without the young Gypsy woman helping her run everything.

The narrow zigzag road up the hill almost defeated the great royal carriage but the coach man certainly knew what he was about. Anastasia assembled the honour guard of Amazónes. Kynane's heart swelled with pride when she heard the loud challenge and reply and the sound of the fort's doors thrust widely open, followed by the first of the queen's escort clattering into the courtyard.

As the coach came to a stop, one of the elf men leapt down to smartly open the door and Anastasia's voice was heard shouting a loud command. The women warriors dropped to one knee and drew their swords in a salute. Kynane awkwardly went down on one knee as Queen Seléne stepped from the coach.

She was dark haired, which was unusual for an elf, but it was the lustrous silky hair of an elf. She had the extraordinarily fair skin, pixie ears and the superhuman beauty of an elf maiden. As Kynane saw her, she realised how beautiful Elana must have been.

"My Queen," Kynane greeted her. Asha had to help her get back up.

Seléne's eyes narrowed as she looked Kynane up and down. "So it's true!" she hissed. "And who is this?" She glared at Asha.

She didn't wait for a reply. "Am I to be insulted by my brother-in-law who doesn't bother to greet me? It seems he has forgotten his original family and found a replacement one!"

Kynane paled at the insult.

"Asha is Jacinta's cousin, as you may have guessed," said Hakeem, coming up from behind Kynane. "She is not here as a replacement. She was sent here by the Gypsy king shortly after the death of my family. If it were not for her, I would have drank myself to death."

"Am I not your family too, Hakeem?" Seléne stood facing him. Her back was ramrod straight and her head held proud, but her voice cracked with hurt and tears started to roll down her cheeks.

Hakeem bowed his head in shame and fell to his knees before her. "Little sister, I am sorry."

"You never replied to my letters, you never visited. I waited. I gave you time, but you never came. Did I not lose a sister too? Did I not lose a dear friend? My kingdom was all but destroyed; I did not have the luxury of running away and hiding like you did. I could have done with you then. Now perhaps I see why. This *woman* has replaced my sister in your heart. She will give you a child whereas Elana never could."

"Seléne, I'll not hear a bad word spoken of Kynane in my hearing," Hakeem said carefully as he rose to face her. "I have done you a great injury, but Kynane and Asha are blameless. If all you have come for is to judge them then you can turn around and go back."

There was an angry murmur from the elf escort. The Amazónes started to move apart to give themselves space and to fit arrows to their bows.

"Halt!" Hakeem called angrily. "They are guests! Seléne, I love you. I will always love you, but I couldn't face you! How can I make you understand that? You once said to me when you thought Pericles was dead you couldn't go on. Well, I lost Elana and Jacinta both. Can you understand now? Each long night, every single day all I could do was think of what I had lost. I couldn't eat, I couldn't sleep. I don't know how I could even draw breath. Getting out of bed was like climbing a mountain. Food tasted like ashes in my mouth. Death would have been welcome. I couldn't bear to see anyone. I had nothing left to give.

"After that, I got better and I could pretend. I could pretend to be alive, pretend to be interested, pretend to smile for those that needed me. I was like an actor in a poor play. But my heart inside was a block of ice. Then I met this wonderful lady who bears my child. She loves me and I love her. Not as much as I should, because something deep inside of me is dead forever.

"I meant to write, I myself can't explain why I didn't. I meant to visit but the thought of facing you and those memories filled me with panic.

"I have failed you. Can you ever forgive me?"

Hakeem held his arms out to Seléne, his face full of pain, asking for forgiveness. Seléne, queen of the Half Elven, moved a few uncertain steps forward and then with a small cry launched herself into Hakeem's arms. He held her for a long time, kissing her and crying. Then she pulled back a little and slapped him as hard as she could across the face.

"I'm still angry with you!" she said.

Then she kissed him. And then she slapped him hard again and then hugged him, crying for a long time, and then she punched him weakly in the chest.

Finally she pushed past and reached a hand out to Kynane.

"Kynane, I'm sorry. I love this brute and he refused to have anything to do with me! I should have never said those things about you."

"My Queen, I never knew or I would have pushed him," Kynane said. "It's no excuse but in truth lately we have hardly seen him ourselves."

"I can think of one time you saw him," Seléne said with a wink.

Kynane looked at the queen in shock ... and then they both laughed, a little warily.

"Kynane," Seléne said, "I have the two royal princes and my daughter asleep in the coach."

"The twins AND your daughter?" Kynane exclaimed in delight. "You brought them here? I want to see them! My Lady, we can put your staff and guards up here but we have no quarters suitable for a queen!"

"Don't worry, Kynane!" Seléne laughed. "The first time I met Hakeem he had me locked in his dungeon, or at least my brother's dungeon and I thought he had come to torture me!"

Kynane's eyes lit up. "That sounds like a great story!"

"Well, if you will put up with me for a little while I'll tell you that one and a great many other stories about this useless man we both love!" Seléne smiled, taking Kynane by the hand. "Come and see my babies, the boys are three years old now. They can be a handful when they are awake, especially together, but when they are sleeping, they look like angels."

As they passed by, Hakeem called to Seléne, "I'm such a fool, Seléne! Thank you for coming. It feels so good to see you again. You don't know how much!"

Seléne looked at him and sniffed. "You *are* a fool, Hakeem! If you had allowed me to, I could have given you ease and it would have helped me too. I'm still angry with you, but you know I'll forgive you."

Kynane had her arms linked with Seléne. "She's right to be angry with you, Hakeem."

"I went more than a little crazy after Elana and Jacinta were killed," he said. "You understand that don't you, Seléne? I forgot how much I love you and the others."

Seléne stopped and went back to kiss the big tribesman softly on the cheek. Then she walked back to Kynane and linked arms with her as they went to peek at the sleeping royal babies.

* * *

"Oh, Seléne!" Kynane laughed, holding her aching sides. "If you make me laugh any more, I will have my baby now! I'm sure I must have wet myself with this baby riding so low!"

"It's true, Jacinta told me herself!" Seléne's facial muscles ached with laughing so much. "She was telling the Gypsy shop owner that she was Hakeem's slave and he would beat her if she didn't get a good price! When Hakeem kept telling her to buy an expensive scarf the man got suspicious. Jacinta almost had apoplexy when he went to talk to Hakeem. She really did think he would beat her!"

"Seléne, I don't know how to thank you!" Kynane said, clutching at her hand. She had tears from laughing and gratitude in her eyes. "When I had first met him, he was so sad. No matter how hard I tried, I couldn't rid this house of a shadow hanging over everything. Since you have come, he can talk about Elana and Jacinta and remember the good times. I think he has finally started to heal."

"I should have come sooner! I should have known when he was avoiding me that he needed me!" Seléne said. "But I felt so hurt and angry and I was so busy all of the time."

"I think rather that you have come just at the right time. Any sooner would have been too soon!"

"Oh, Kynane!" said Seléne, showing her dimples. "You're starting to sound like Hakeem! They are not getting to you with their Shayvism are they?"

"I hate to admit it," Kynane nodded with a smile. "But they are. I am going to join the sisters before I give birth. If I have a daughter I would love for her to become the first born daughter to a sister. Hakeem wants a son so much ... maybe we can eventually have both."

Seléne moved closer to Kynane and kissed her on the cheek. "Elana would have liked you, Kynane. I know we are going to be good friends."

Kynane caught Seléne's hand and kissed it. "Seléne, I feel we have been friends for a long time already."

* * *

They were watching Asha sitting on the grass minding the three-year-old twins. Seléne's youngest child Helénē (named after her dead aunt) was asleep.

There was fierce competition between the women of the fort for minding the children but Seléne had put her foot down about too many strangers.

"How can you tell them apart?" Hakeem asked Seléne about her twins.

"Hakeem, that's easy!" Seléne teased. "The one closer is Biôrn, he's the first born, and that's Úlfr."

"Biôrn, the bear, and Úlfr, the wolf," Hakeem translated.

Seléne nodded. "The names of ancient elf heroes from the old lands; we elves believe that the child inherits the quality of the name they bear."

"Elana, the shining one!" Hakeem whispered.

Seléne looked at Hakeem sharply, but he was smiling fondly at some memory.

"Hakeem, I want you to marry Kynane," Seléne said firmly. "I want you to marry her while I am still here."

Hakeem jerked out of his reverie and looked at Seléne in surprise.

"My sister is dead," she said bluntly. "She would have liked Kynane. I didn't know what to think when I heard you had taken another woman and that she was with child." Seléne smiled. "I realise now that this is right. Elana would have wanted you to marry Kynane, you know she would. I think you owe it to her memory, as well as to both of you." Her voice was thick with emotion.

Hakeem broke into a broad grin. "She might refuse!"

Seléne snorted. "If she had any sense, she would!"

"It's a shame we can't invite some of her family," Hakeem said.

"What? So they can kill her on her wedding day?" Seléne laughed. "No, Hakeem we are her family."

* * *

In honour of the visit of the queen, the marriage ceremony was cut short. It would have normally lasted a week. Hakeem and Kynane exchanged plain gold engagement rings in a small ceremony and then everyone gathered for a celebration.

The next day all the women gathered around a wool-blanket, even Seléne. By tradition all the females old enough had to contribute to making the honey-moon blanket, even if just by a little bit of sewing.

Mostly it was a chance for the women to have fun together, but with a fort full of Amazónes they had to take it in turns. Some were sewing, cutting out tassels, tying the blanket off, dying wool for decoration, all coordinated by Asha.

By local tradition, no one was allowed to pass a positive comment about the bride or groom without pretending to spit, to ward off the evil eye. Shayvists didn't believe in the evil eye but most did it anyway, deliberately passing compliments about the bride, their wedding outfits and the groom ... just for fun of pretending to spit. Ptou! Ptou! Ptou!

The marital bed was prepared and decorated in Hakeem's quarters so Hakeem had to sleep somewhere else.

On the morning of the wedding, the bride and groom had their respective baths and the groom waited in the impromptu chapel while the bride was escorted to him by a procession of smoking torches (even though it was a daytime wedding.)

Hakeem wore a pure white keffiyeh bound with a black 'iqāl, circled twice. His beard was neatly trimmed. He wore a black Kaftan embroidered with gold cloth at the neck and edges, over a simple white shirt and pants.

Kynane wore a white vest embroidered with flowers over a colourful silk blouse. In the somewhat rustic traditions of the Illyroi she had a petticoat under a full skirt, with an elaborately embroidered and tasselled red apron and sash over the top, all loosened to accommodate her ballooning belly.

Over her hair she wore a red wool scarf and around her neck was an exquisite filigree necklace in gold, a gift from Seléne.

"I Hakeem," his voice rang out strongly, "before all here present and in presence of my God, Apollōn, take you, Kynane, as my wife. I will love you, honour you and cherish you for all the rest of my days."

"And I, Kynane." Her voice was softer, almost shy. Tears were in her eyes. "Before all here and in front of Apollōn, take you, Hakeem, as my husband to love you, honour you and cherish you for the rest of my days."

Father Lazar paused meaningfully. "The union of a man and a woman is holy in the eyes of both God and man. What God has joined, let no man or woman tear asunder. I now declare you as man and wife joined. You may kiss the bride."

Hakeem turned smiling to Kynane, who looked at her man with love in her eyes.

"BANG!" The ground shuddered, dust cascaded from the ceiling, and cracks appeared in the walls. "Earth quake!" someone shouted.

One of the elf guards burst in, "My Queen! My Lord Hakeem! We are under attack. A great daimôn has appeared inside your fortress!"

Hakeem took two strides and struck the alarm gong.

"Alba! Androcles! Get as many troops on horses as you can. They can't catch horses. Take the children, the queen and Kynane away from here in any way you can. Make for the river. These things can't stand water.

"Eirene and Kleon! You're in charge of the rest of the evacuation. Get as many people out of here as possible. Spread out, it can't get all of us."

He turned to Anastasia and the remaining elf commander, Theseus. "Anastasia and Theseus, gather your weapons and troops. We will try to delay it! Chares," he beckoned to the youngest of the Amazóne seniors, "in my room there is a large box. It contains a single throwing spear. It is Jacinta's, left from the catacombs. Let us pray its magic still holds.

"Where's Sophie and Daniel when we need them?" He shouted out to no one in particular.

Pandemonium broke out as people ran to their tasks. Someone passed Hakeem his sword and a shield. He was still dressed in his wedding finery.

Kynane grabbed at him. "Hakeem, what are you going to do?"

"Love, you carry our child! They say you can't fight a daimôn, well we will see, we will see!"

He kissed her fiercely and ran to the door.

"Fire arrows," he shouted. "Let's see if fire arrows work better! I wish we had water cannons."

As he cleared the door, he paused for an instant.

Then he could see the daimôn.

"Ba'al!" he screamed in a rage. "Murderer! I will send you back to whatever hell you came from."

But Ba'al seemed hurt. He crouched on the ground, clutching at his side.

"Hakeem!" he shouted. "I came to parley, not to attack!"

He crouched under a shower of arrows. He was covering something with his body.

"Hold your fire!" Hakeem bellowed.

He had to repeat the order till all firing stopped.

"Jacinta lives, but she is lost to me," Ba'al yelled.

"What lie is this?" Hakeem demanded. "I saw you engulf my daughter."

"She and I journeyed far and fought many battles together. I have brought Elana back with me, don't shoot or you will hit her!"

Seléne and Kynane, who were being hurried past, froze.

"Be careful of Elana, she will not remember you for a short while. She has been in the daimôn realm too long and was beginning to turn. I was attacked and am too weak, I cannot stay."

He started to flicker in and out, then he faded and was gone. Lying on the ground, unconscious was what looked like a small daimôn, dark with yellow hair.

"That is Elana," Seléne screamed. "Don't let anyone hurt her! It will take a few moments before she returns to normal."

"Everyone stay well back!" Hakeem commanded. "For God's sake don't shoot, no matter what happens!"

In front of their eyes the black was fading and the features were moulding back into those of an elf. Hakeem held back until he was sure.

"It *is* Elana!" He sheathed his sword and cast his shield aside.

"Careful," Kleon warned. "The daimôn king is the master of lies! It might be a trap."

"Elana!" Hakeem called.

It was her! She was thin and worn, her hair dry and coarse and her complexion tanned.

Hakeem ran to her side. "Elana!"

She struggled to sit up and he steadied her.

"Elana, are you all right?"

Elana made an animal snarl and opened her eyes. They were glowing yellow. She grabbed his wedding jacket and stood up, lifting him, and *heaved*. Hakeem was thrown into the air to crash into a pile of wooden crates, which splintered under his weight.

"Careful, Hakeem! Don't hurt her!" Seléne shouted urgently.

Hakeem got up, holding his side. Wincing, he limped slowly back towards Elana.

"She's not herself, Hakeem!" Seléne repeated. "Don't hurt her."

Just then a voice shouted in Hakeem's head.

"HAKEEM! YOU'RE NOT UNDER ATTACK!"

"Thanks, Sophie," Hakeem thought back at her. "You're a little late with that. Can you turn the volume down a little?"

"Sorry, Hakeem," the elf child-seeress apologised. "You know it's is almost impossible for me to get through to you. Ba'al isn't trying to attack. He was returning Jacinta and Elana. They were never killed, Elana was captured and taken to the daimôn realm by Æloðulf; Ba'al and Jacinta followed to try to rescue her. But don't try to approach Elana for a few moments, whatever you do. She may attack you!"

"Thanks, Sophie! But where's Jacinta?"

"I don't know. Ba'al was taken by surprise and attacked just as he left the daimôn realm. He was carrying Elana and Jacinta inside himself. He was thrown off course and they were in danger of being lost in the region of nothingness between the two realms. Jacinta stepped out. She did it to save Ba'al and Elana."

"Where is my daughter?" Hakeem demanded loudly.

"I don't know, Hakeem. She is lost in the realm of nothingness. It is made up of the stuff from which the universe is created. It doesn't exist in space or time."

"Can't Ba'al find her?"

"He will try. He loves her you know, but I don't know how anyone or anything can search that place ... and he is injured."

"Can you and Daniel search?"

"Daniel will do what he can from here. I will see if I can work the far seeing mirror and I will search the libraries in Elgard first and then I will come to you, but Hakeem I'm not sure we can even survive in that place let alone search, even Maerwen. We have already contacted Silver but Jacinta is lost and we don't know what to do."

Hakeem fell to his knees and screamed, a great cry of agony.

Elana was getting herself up. "Seléne, is that you? Praise the Gods! Where's Hakeem? Where's Jacinta?"

Seléne rushed to cover her sister's nakedness.

"Seléne, is that the twins? Who is that lady that is pregnant? She is carrying Hakeem's baby girl!"

Hakeem was too numb to sort out all that had happened in his concern for Jacinta. He was in too much turmoil to feel the joy of Elana's return. Then he realised he was about to have a baby to another woman he loved and had just married her!

Elana had been pronounced dead. An empty coffin had been interred in her family crypt. Her sister was crowned the queen of the Half Elven. What were they going to do?

* * *

It was the third night after Elana's return.

Kynane had withdrawn to the Amazōn quarters. She had refused to sleep in Hakeem's bed on their wedding night. All the happiness, all the excitement of marrying the man she loved had turned to ashes. Hakeem had tried and tried to get her to talk, but no matter what he said she said their marriage was over.

Eventually, Elana asked Asha to accompany her to talk to Kynane. She waited at the door to Kynane's room. "Can I come in to talk?"

Kynane was loading some clothes into a saddle pack.

She looked at the elf waiting in her doorway. "What's to say?"

"You're leaving," Elana said.

"There's nothing for me here," she was dry-eyed now but her eyes were red; she had been crying. "I will take some money and leave tomorrow. Chares has a cousin who will look after me for a fee while I have my baby. You said it will be a girl. After that, I will make a life for myself and my daughter far away from here."

"Kynane, your friends are here. The Amazónes need you. This is your home, Hakeem loves you," Elana said.

"He says he does. He did, I think," Kynane said tiredly. "But it's you he really loves, he never stopped loving you. While you were dead, I had a chance. But just look at me! I was only at best a second choice!"

"Kynane, Hakeem would never marry you as a substitute. You must know him better than that!"

Kynane looked at Elana coldly. "We didn't sleep together afterwards, so there is no marriage. He only has one wife, and that is you."

"Kynane, Hakeem and I have not slept together either. Not until we can sort this out," Elana said.

"Well, you don't have to worry about me. I don't want to see anyone from here again." Kynane raised her voice to a shout. "Do you know how foolish I feel? It was my wedding day, Elana. For the sake of all the Gods, did you have to come back on my wedding day?"

Elana bowed her head in guilt. Tears started to run down her cheeks.

"Kynane, I wish we could be friends," she whispered.

"We cannot!" Kynane snapped, turning away.

"Æloðulf took me to a terrible place and tried to break my will." Elana looked up at her, her face a mask of pain. Anyone could see that the experience had aged her. Her hair was coarsened and her face was weathered and tanned. "I expected to die in that dreadful place. For two years only thoughts of Hakeem and my daughter helped me to endure. Do you hate me for that? I came back too late, I'm sorry for that. I will not see you again and I'm sorry about that too. I wished things could have been different between us, Kynane. Please don't think too badly of me."

"My Lady!" Kynane turned back angrily.

But Elana was gone.

* * *

Kynane could hardly sleep that night and by the time she woke, the sun was well up. She could hear the noise of the novices training outside but otherwise the women's quarters seemed empty. She told herself she liked it that way, so she could leave quietly. It was a lie. So many dreams she had had here, so many hopes.

Best to get this finished.

As soon as she stepped outside she noticed the elf guards had gone.

"Where is everybody?"

"Seléne and her escort left at first light, my Lady," Alba replied. She had been crying.

"But I would have said goodbye! They should have woken me! Do they think so little of me already? I will speak to Hakeem about this!"

"It was for the best, my Lady," Alba said. "Hakeem didn't say goodbye either. You'll find him sitting by the steps."

Kynane was shocked. Hakeem didn't say goodbye! How could that be? Then she felt a touch of fear.

Something was wrong, far, far wrong.

She found Hakeem sitting staring blankly into space. Asha had her arm around him. He looked like he hadn't slept for days. For the first time, Kynane felt a surge of compassion for the man. She knew that she loved him still.

As she approached he looked up, his face was haggard.

"Please don't leave me, Kynane." His voice was husky. Kynane felt awful to see him in so much pain.

But she had a growing sense of dread.

"Hakeem, what is happening?"

"She has gone," he said simply. "They left early. I could not face her to s-say goodbye, not again."

He began to sob.

"Hakeem, what have you done?" Kynane felt frightened.

"Elana came back too late. We couldn't do that to you."

"Hakeem!" Kynane screamed. "She was ill! She had gone through hell!"

"She is with her sister, Kynane," Hakeem said dully. "The elves will look after her."

"You can't do this!" Kynane had a feeling of panic. "You will hate me!"

"Kynane, this is nothing to do with you," Hakeem said. "It was between me and Elana. I love you, I said that. I promised to love you and treasure you always. You are having my baby. Elana returned too late. There is nothing we can do, it is our karma."

"But this will destroy you!" she shouted, aghast.

As Hakeem looked up at her, his mouth working wordlessly and she realised the truth of her words.

"Elana and I agreed," he said, standing up. "We will not talk further on this."

"Hakeem, I never meant for you to do that! Go after her! Bring her back!"

"It is too late!" He walked away.

"Asha, we must do something!"

"And what would that be, my Lady?" Asha asked her coldly.

"Why bring her back, of course!" Kynane said.

"And what then, my Lady, you will lcavc?"

"Why, yes I will leave. Hakeem loves Elana, I've never met a man so devastated by the loss of his wife and now she is back."

"And he has lost her again!" Asha said. "Don't you understand, Kynane? He had to choose!"

"I never meant ..." Kynane stood, fixed to the spot, appalled.

"Leave it be, Kynane. It's hard enough on the two of them without dragging Elana back. Why would you do such a thing? Do you hate her that much? They understand you would have to leave if she remained. No one blames you for that. They made the only decision they could. Hakeem won't see Elana again."

"Did Elana leave for Hakeem's sake?"

"Of course not, they love each other!"

"So all that time in hell, thinking of Hakeem, loving him and she would give him up for me? Why would she do such a thing?"

"Don't you know?" Asha asked. "Hakeem can only love a woman who is truly exceptional. He pledged to you in good faith, Elana wouldn't come back and take him away from you."

"Alba! Anastasia!" Kynane shouted out. "Take some women and bring Elana back here!"

"My Lady, she will not come!" Alba said, hurrying up.

"Say to her, if she does not come, I will ride after her myself, despite my pregnancy, and I will beg her to return! If she will not come, I will drag her back myself, no matter how pregnant I am!"

Alba and Anastasia didn't have to be told twice, they broke out into grins and scrambled for the stables shouting for the women who were to accompany them.

Kynane waited, pacing.

The royal party had an hour's head start but would be travelling slowly. It seemed to take forever before she saw the small cloud of dust returning. She strained her eyes, trying to pick out the features and the number. As they got closer, she could pick out two male elves and a woman in white with fair hair.

As the women entered the gate and rode up, Elana and the two elf guardsmen didn't dismount. Elana sat on the horse listlessly, her head averted. Eventually Alba encouraged her to get off. She stood in front of Kynane with her head bowed; her shoulders were slumped in defeat.

"What would you have of me?" she whispered harshly.

Kynane couldn't speak, she realised in awe the agony Elana and Hakeem were prepared to endure for her sake. She started to cry uncontrollably and gathered Elana wordlessly into her arms and hugged her.

Elana looked at her in surprise. Hope was starting in her eyes.

"Now I know," Kynane said. "Hakeem loves us both."

Kynane knew at that moment that neither of them could leave. In the end it would only destroy all three of them.

"Elana, it will be hard for me ... But I think we can become friends. If not, we will destroy the man we both love and then ourselves."

Elana looked at the large woman and nodded.

"Yes," she said through her tears. "I think I could easily love you."

Kynane held the elf for a long time.

"Should we go and tell Hakeem?" Elana asked.

"No," Kynane said firmly. "Let someone else carry that message. The two of us will spend time getting to know each other before we face him."

Elana bowed her head humbly, "Yes, Kynane, and thank you for giving me this chance."

"Thank you for your offer to leave. I am a little in awe of that, but I think we almost made a terrible mistake. Do you think we can make this work?"

Elana nodded. "I would like to be your friend. Hakeem wouldn't love you unless you were very special."

"Asha said something like that, but she was talking about you. I think she is right."

Elana and Kynane withdrew into the women's barracks and asked not to be disturbed. They needed to form a friendship before the hundred and one complications and pressures intruded, especially before they dealt with Hakeem!

Kynane expected Elana to be alien, proud and difficult. She had been the Queen of the powerful Eastern Elves! To her surprise she found her shy and humble, down to earth and impossible to dislike.

Elana was worried Kynane being a female warrior would be coarse, but she reminded her so much of Jacinta that at times it brought tears to her eyes.

Elana had gone through a terrible experience which had almost destroyed her, and she was almost mad with worry over Jacinta. She desperately needed a friend. Kynane felt very protective of the elf and Elana was very grateful.

Kynane after the manner of women asked how Elana and Hakeem first slept together.

Elana laughed. "Hakeem really loved me, I knew. But he is so stiff with his Shantawi honour. He was driving me crazy. He would never have made a move. I had to grab him with both hands."

Kynane laughed, delighted.

Elana looked at her in surprise, and then it hit her! "Oh, no! You too?"

Kynane nodded, unable to speak for laughing. Then the two grabbed each other and laughed and laughed. When they stopped they excitedly began to compare notes. It broke the final ice between them as the two settled down to smile in fond amusement with the antics of the man they both loved.

* * *

"I have finally managed to locate two of her three friends, Great One." Vanâra bowed. "It took a lot of searching. They have separated from her at Hamgmatāna and are headed back east." The acolyte looked tired. "They are a couple. I think they are returning to Qori, the man's home village."

"Don't we have a friend in Arys, not far from there?" Tishari asked.

"Menna, the Aígyptoi? He worships the Goddess 'Anāt. I thought you despised him."

"Say what you like about Menna, but he and one of his acolytes trained with the brotherhood of Set. He is very strong, strong enough for Jess. I might forgive his devotion to the Goddess version of our God if he kills her. If he can't, then Jess will have saved us some work."

* * *

It was the third day and Elana and Kynane were enjoying spending time together. Elana was explaining to Kynane the times before, when she wanted to be one of two wives. The first was with Philip the Grey and his wife Eugenia. The second was when she realised she was barren.

"Elana, are you jealous of me and my child?"

"Kynane no, truly. Hakeem should have children. He will be a good father. I just feel happy it is you to give them to him. It will always be your child, but if you allow, I would like to be like a doting aunt, that's how I think I'll feel. To be honest I have been through far too many things to worry about being barren." Elana shyly touched Elana's stomach and smiled at her.

"Elana," Kynane took her hand and gently kissed it. "You are a remarkable woman. I am privileged to have you as a friend.

There may still be some hope for you to have children. You have been under so much stress it may be with some rest you might conceive."

Elana shook her head sadly. "That would be nice but the infection when I lost Philip's baby isn't the only reason, you see ..." Elana stopped mid-sentence. Then her face began to transform into an expression of wonder.

"Kynane!" she said excitedly. "I am dead!"

Kynane looked at her in shock. She couldn't imagine all her new friend had endured. All that had happened, all that she had been through. It had finally caught up with her.

She stood up. "Elana, please rest. I am going to get Alba. She has some knowledge of healing."

"No, no!" Elana said excitedly. "Can't you see, I am dead! I could go and see my own grave! Isn't it wonderful?" She started to laugh. "Of course ... I am dead!"

"Of course you're dead," Kynane said, placating the elf. "Now as I said, I will just get Alba and she will make you some herbal drink and you will feel a lot better, I'm sure you will."

"No, Kynane," Elana was laughing hysterically ... and she was thoroughly frightening her new friend.

"Hakeem said that it could work out and I never believed him!"

"What could work out?" Kynane asked, perplexed. "Your death?"

"No, Kynane, let me explain. I cannot have children because in the Prophecy I am the last of my line. Even if I had resigned as queen, I would still be a royal elf. Any child or grandchild would have to die before me."

Kynane nodded, she followed so far.

"Under elf law, I have died. I can challenge that ruling but until I do so I am seen as a different person. I am no longer a royal elf. Queen Elana is dead and her line is ended. If I bear children the Prophecy doesn't apply!"

Now Kynane understood! "You intend to give up being the elf queen?"

"Gladly!" Elana laughed with a small shudder. "Even if I didn't have children I want nothing to do with it. I already told Seléne that. She makes a better ruler in the peace and recovery than I ever could and she is welcome to it. All I want is here with you and Hakeem."

Kynane chuckled. "I am no longer a princess."

"And I am no longer a queen!" Elana laughed. "We are the two wives of one minor noble who was once one of the most powerful men in all the Middle East. And I for one couldn't be happier," Elana whispered.

"Welcome home, Elana, dearest sister-wife."

* * *

Hakeem, Father Lazar, the senior Amazónes and Elana were having a meeting to discuss what had happened to Jacinta. Their worry was like a black cloud of misery, hanging over everyone. Elana especially was looking worn down and exhausted.

She sat between Hakeem and Kynane. Hakeem was holding her hand in both of his and Kynane's held her tightly, one arm around her shoulders. Eirene had just asked her about the daimôn realm and the Illvættir War.

"Jacinta joined Ba'al, which put her on one side of that war and I was Æloðulf's captive. He was on the other side. To understand how the Illvættir reached the daimôn realm and the events just before my rescue, you have to know something about daimôns." Elana took a deep breath. "The first thing you need to understand is how daimôns bind to each other. Daimôns spawn; daimôn newborns are mindless and hungry. They are very small and grow slowly by absorbing energy from the blistering sun and from each other. As they mature they can form bonds with each other which get stronger the more mature they get.

"They do not form groups based on blood-kin like we of this realm. The most important groups are led by a senior daimôn who adopts younger daimôns who show promise. This bonding is very powerful. It is something that involves deep mutual responsibilities and is one of the most important aspects of daimôns. It is what allows daimôn summoners to bind to daimôns in a similar but slightly different way. When a daimôn summoner dies, their soul is absorbed into that daimôn. It is not destroyed, it is absorbed, and that is the second crucial thing to know.

"Absorbing human souls is a very rapid and powerful way for daimôns to become smarter; the ones that do also become human-like, they became daimôn lords. When the Illvættir died, though, most of them managed to retain a part of themselves inside the daimôn. They took over the daimôn like a parasite from inside, taking over a host. They ended up with the power of both a daimôn and an Illvættir and they carried the madness of the Illvættir."

Hakeem gasped. "So much power and so dangerous."

"Indeed, when Ba'al and his allies found out what was happening they began to fight back but they were badly outclassed and other daimôns were slow to join them. Daimôns, due to the nature are very tribal and insular within their 'families'.

"Æloðulf bonded with a daimôn but he betrayed it, forcing it to become a double for him, under his control. It was that that Jacinta killed in the final battle for Elgard and it was Æloðulf who attacked me just after that and took me to the daimôn realm. He had learnt to travel between realms like Ba'al can. Ba'al and Jacinta followed to rescue me. When Ba'al had gathered Jacinta inside himself to transit, you had thought he had killed her."

Elana looked up to see if they were all following.

"Æloðulf and the Illvættir never understood daimôns and that was their final undoing. They assumed they were evil. While only the most senior daimôns would understand what we would understand as evil, daimôns have their own codes, especially the smarter ones. Æloðulf betrayed a daimôn he was bonded to. For a daimôn, such a thing is completely inconceivable. He could not have done anything worse."

"So when a šamán or another one of power binds with a daimôn it is similar in some ways to their family bond," Hakeem said. "And Æloðulf betrayed something that was sacred to the daimôns."

"Exactly," Elana said. "But we are thinking like humans or elves. To call bonding sacred to daimôns is an understatement. As the news spread, all free daimôn lords flocked to join Ba'al. And once bonded they will never go back. That single event has changed the face of the daimôn realm forever."

"So it's over?" Eirene asked.

"I don't think so, not so easily at least. The Illvættir are still very powerful individually, more powerful than all but the greatest of the daimôn lords, but for the very first time they had lost a major battle. Ba'al and his new allies had struck at Æloðulf's great fortress. I was held deep below the ground but the lesser daimôns around me told me what was going on. They were still bound to the Illvættir, but they didn't like them anymore. As his stronghold was about to be overwhelmed, Æloðulf sent one of his daimôn lords to kill me. The lesser daimôns that were looking after me gave their lives to protect me." She began to cry. "Daimôns are not reincarnated, so when they die, that's it, but they didn't even hesitate. I feel so unworthy of what they did."

She paused. "I became angry and I felt myself change and fight back but against a daimôn lord it wasn't enough. Then a small female daimôn appeared. Female daimôns are not common and I've never seen a daimôn move so fast. She managed to hold off a full sized daimôn lord long enough for Ba'al and Jacinta to arrive in a crash of thunder. He fled but as we were beginning the transition back to our world he appeared again and attacked Ba'al. Ba'al couldn't finish the transition carrying the two of us and fighting the other daimôn lord at the same time. That was when I felt Jacinta leaving."

She bent her head and began to sob. Kynane pulled her closer and began to stroke her hair. Hakeem lifted her hand to his mouth and kissed it.

* * *

Vanâra sat outside the fortress, trying not to show his fear. Tishari had described Menna as an ignorant heathen from Aígyptos, but the man and his acolytes had gained considerable power in a short while. Of course, this sort of thing had happened all throughout the region the Hun had conquered. In desperation the people turned their backs on the faith that had failed them. The worship of the old, powerful Gods and Goddesses had returned.

Menna's chief acolyte, *Rameses* (son of 'Ra') appeared over the battlements, smiling down on him. "Well, we *are* honoured." He laughed. "A visit from an acolyte of mighty Aēšma, no less."

He lost his smile. "Put your bows down, men, and open the gates. We are certainly coming up in the world."

Vanâra was given a tour of the desert fortress. He expected it was all for show: the heavily armed men, the temple with its oversized bronze statue of *'Anāt* wearing an Aígyptios crown and wielding an axe, and the murals of her covered in blood, killing her enemies.

Written by the side of the statue on a great marble tablet was a fragment from the famous Assyrian Epic.

'Then 'Anāt appears, fierce, wild and furious; wading in blood, striking off heads, cutting off hands, binding the heads to her torso and the hands in her sash. Driving out the old men and townsfolk before her with her arrows, her heart filled with joy.'

Nonetheless, there was no doubt that these disciples of 'Anat were doing much better than Tishari's group. Admittedly Tishari was trying to establish himself in the enemy heartland, the region still controlled by the Persis.

Eventually Vanâra was ushered in to see Menna. The man was bare to the waist with a simple white linen *shendyt* (Aígyptios kilt) belted at the waist. His hands were painted with Henna, and eyes outlined with black kohl. Red ochre mixed with fat was smeared on his lips. He had a thin wispy chin-beard like a goat. He was balding with a sloping forehead and back-set ears. Above the waist of the kilt he had a paunch. He was sweating in the heat and reeked of perfume from Aígyptos.

He was a remarkably ugly man. Vanâra wondered yet again why his Goddess would favour him with such power. Likely she did not have many followers, especially this far east, but then why didn't the great Aēšma match the gifts that 'Anāt, that forgotten Goddess, had given to Menna and his acolytes?

"Salaam alaykum, Holy Menna; a thousand blessings on you and your people."

"Ah, Vanâra isn't it? As you can see, we are doing well here. With blessed *'Anāt* on our side we have been able to raid our neighbours, take their herds, their gold, their women and children. None can stand against us. We enslave whomever we want and our numbers are growing every day."

"My heart is full of praise, Great One, blessed is your cause."

Vanâra felt like spitting on him; he bowed low instead.

"Well, you must stay and dine with me."

And be poisoned?

"I must humbly beg your indulgence, Great One. I am on a matter most pressing otherwise it would be an honour beyond my worth. If I could be permitted, I would mention a trifling matter. You may know that we encountered some difficulties in Margu."

"I heard you had to run for your lives."

Menna threw his head back and laughed. Then he stopped as quickly as he started. He leaned forward, the smile wiped from his face; there was no sign of banter now.

"You tried to kill a sorceress and found out you couldn't, even though you had her in chains. Is that what this is about?"

Menna may be many things, but he was no fool.

Vanâra coloured. "We were unable to get her to join us." He felt his face burning.

"What a shame, but why is this of interest to me?"

"There is a soon to be married couple returning to Qori. They are under her protection."

"And where is she in all this?"

"She cannot be seen through far sight."

"Oh Ho." Menna's smile became wolfish. "A worthy adversary then, and you want me to kill her I presume. I will want something in exchange."

"We will concede this fortress and all the land one day's travel by horse in any direction. All of it for the Goddess 'Anāt."

Menna thought that was hilarious. "We already have that!" After a while he stopped laughing. "Very well, I will agree. How much trouble is she capable of causing me?"

"Remember Horkan?"

"That was her?" Menna asked, somewhat sobered by the news. "Well, well, well. You people have really made a mess of things, haven't you? Didn't you realise she was *sent*? And what did you do? Why you tried to get her to join you, were you really surprised when she refused?"

"She is a changeling," Vanâra warned.

"Don't worry, I know what to do. I won't be making the sorts of mistakes you did."

                              * * *

The contractions were becoming stronger. Kynane stopped her pacing and lay down so Elana could feel her belly.

"That seems to be all right. Hakeem!" she called out to the back. "Can you come here now and monitor the baby please?"

"Elana," Kynane whispered desperately. "I think I just wet myself."

"No love, your waters have broken. Don't worry, the fluid is clear, the baby is healthy."

Alba helped Elana lift Kynane's hips and they slid clean towels underneath.

"How much longer?" Kynane asked.

"At least two turns of the glass, but you are doing well for a first child."

Hakeem climbed onto the cushions behind Kynane and took her in his arms. He kissed her hair, and tears of joy came to his eyes.

* * *

Kynane lay back, exhausted, her body covered with sweat.

She smiled tenderly at her new daughter when Elana cut the cord and placed the baby, glistening with fluid, onto her chest.

"Aren't you supposed to give her a smack?" Hakeem asked.

Elana giggled. "It wasn't needed. She cried and is breathing already. Look, she has a full head of hair!"

Elana moved around to kiss her fellow wife and kiss Hakeem. "You two make good babies."

Elana and Alba busied themselves delivering the after birth, while Eirene whisked the new baby away for her first bath.

Chapter 17: The Parting

Aryānā, also called 'Ērān' or 'Persis', was the centre of the known world. It became obvious as soon as they passed through the old border region of the Koppeh Dagh Mountains to the great city of Tus, the crossroads of trading routes that spanned thousands of miles. The fortress walls were 8-9 m thick and protected by 43 rectangular towers.

It seemed that everywhere they went from there on had enormous, gorgeously decorated buildings, shrines, libraries and universities, sculptures, marble, gold, ivory, and ceramics ... and of course gardens, lots of gardens.

They started on the Great Northern Road heading west. The Great Southern Road rose to meet it and the two formed the Royal Road which led all the way to Sardeis in Anatolē.

These were the greatest trade routes across the greatest nation on earth. They had been there for thousands of years. For many hundreds of years now they had been built and rebuilt with one purpose only: to speed the traffic on them.

They were all hard-packed gravel and cobble stones. Embankments were reinforced by stone. Stone bridges crossed smaller streams and culverts. Through many large towns the road was up to an incredible six metres wide. The route was dotted by regular inns and guard posts and the posts of the famous Persian message-relay riders, the fastest message service in the known world.

Jess sold the camels and bought a spare horse for each of them. Compared with their travel across the desert they began making incredible time past the dazzling cities and prosperous towns. And still Jess couldn't shake a growing sense of urgency.

As they reached western Aryānā, a cloud began to hang over the hearts of the hurrying travellers. Too soon the time was approaching when Iraj and Rohana would have to turn back and Jess and Pandora would have to ride on.

They had planned to part company in Kermanshah but it was in the ancient city of Hamgmatāna, not far from the old border, that Jess and Pandora went shopping for surprise gifts for Rohana and Iraj.

For Iraj they bought an exquisite purple *khalat* (caftan) made of silk, embroidered with leaves and flowers.

"If you are to become a wealthy herder you will need something to wear for formal occasions." Jess laughed as they made him try it on.

Pandora and Jess gave Rohana a small silk pouch each. It was considered bad form to open gifts in front of the people that gave them, but Pandora would have none of that. "Go on, open them," she insisted with an excited grin.

From Jess, Rohana received a silver pendant of *lāžaward* (lapis lazuli) stone well-polished, showing intense blue with white calcite flecks and pyrite looking like flecks of gold. Pandora gave her a matching silver ring.

"These are absolutely exquisite!" Rohana held them to her in delight. "They must have cost a fortune. But why are you giving us gifts?"

"You have been vomiting the last few mornings, though you are trying to hide it," Pandora said.

Tears came to Rohana's eyes. "It's true, I think I'm pregnant."

"Can I check?" Jess asked.

Rohana nodded and Jess took her wrist. Even before Jess opened her eyes again she broke into a broad smile.

"Congratulations to both of you, it is too soon to tell but I think it is a boy."

Pandora squealed in delight and hugged and kissed Rohana and pulled her across so she could hug Iraj at the same time.

"Daddy," Pandora kissed him and then gave him a light punch.

Iraj looked happy but shy.

"We haven't gotten you anything!" Rohana complained.

"We aren't the ones getting married, silly," Pandora said. "We are just sorry we can't be there for the wedding."

* * *

The four friends stood outside the city gates, talking softly. The time had come for them to part.

Hamgmatāna lay in the foothills of the *Harvant* (Alvand) Mountains. They were part of the large fold of mountains, the great Zaqros Mountains, which characterised Western Aryānā.

Civilisation in this part of the world was *old*. The elves believed that much of human agriculture came from here. The hills and plains all around still teemed with wild varieties of stable foods: wheat, barley, lentils, pistachio, almond, walnuts, apricot, plum, pomegranate and grapes.

Beyond the Zagros lay the plains of Mesopotamia. Pandora and Jess would now travel on to Baghdad, that great river port on the Tigrā (Tigris River). There they would travel up-river by shallow draft boat as far as Mosul (across the river from the ruins of Nineveh). From there they would head over the highland country to the Kilisian gates that lead to Anatolē.

Rohana and Iraj were returning to Iraj's home, a few days from Āmul. There they would get married, Rohana would have her baby, and she would become the wife of a modestly wealthy shepherd.

From where they stood, they could see the great mountains; they had little snow this time of the year. The forest was dominated by oak trees, green with the late spring in the mountains. The road, headed west waited for them, winding down to the valley below.

"It is time for us to part," Jess whispered to her friends.

"Almost," said Iraj.

He took his belt knife, rolled up his sleeve and cut his forearm, not far from the old scar.

"Iraj!" Jess and Pandora cried out shrilly.

Oh no, not again!

He looked at Jess levelly as he passed the knife to Rohana.

"In Chandyr I lost one sister, but I gained two others. I will always carry my love for both of you here." He struck his chest with his other fist. "Within my heart."

"I was dead and my life was over," Rohana said as she made a cut in her forearm and the blood started to trickle down. "You and Pandora came to take me. You loved me and you gave me my life again. My life, my happiness, my wonderful man, my baby, everything: I owe it all to you. Jess, you told me you have no family. That is no longer true. Iraj and I are now your family in blood."

Pandora made a cut on her forearm and her blood began to flow. She pressed the handle of the blade into Jess's hand as she pressed her wound against Rohana's in the time honoured elvish blood oath.

"Sister," she murmured.

"Sister," Rohana murmured back.

Jess couldn't see for her tears. She couldn't see her friends, she couldn't see the knife, she couldn't even see her forearm. She had to do it almost blindly.

"I will never forget you," Rohana said.

It set Jess crying even more.

"Brother," Pandora whispered as she pressed her wound against Iraj.

"Sister," Iraj whispered.

Rohana came over to Jess and reached up to take her and kiss her on her lips.

Jess couldn't stop crying.

"Sister," Rohana whispered to her as she pressed their wounds together.

"Sister," Jess replied through her tears.

Then she felt rather than saw Iraj approach and take her and kiss her and press their forearms together. They refused to let Jess heal them. She was only allowed to bind their arms.

Then it was time to truly part. They hugged for a long while and clung together. Rohana and Iraj stood arm in arm to watch them go. Jess and Pandora turned to mount, leading their spare horses on to the west and whatever their destiny held for them in Anatolē.

Chapter 19: The Troad

"Aaaa!" Jess sat up, and looked wildly around, hand on the hilt of her knife. It was the middle of the night and the camp fire had burnt down. Pandora grabbed for her.

"Jess, love, what's wrong? You were dreaming."

Jess shuddered. "I don't know, I honestly don't know."

She got up and put some wood on the fire for something to do. "Why don't you try to get some sleep?" Jess suggested. "I'm going to stay awake for a while."

"What, after you almost scared me out of my skin?" Pandora shook her head. "What can you remember of the dream?"

"It wasn't all that scary, really. I was riding a horse and next to me was a big man, a desert tribesman on a great white horse. It had a light grey mane. It was all so vivid."

"Hakeem."

"Yes, Jacinta and Hakeem," Jess said. "As I get closer to where she lived, I am getting more memories from Jacinta and I'm feeling increasingly jumpy. I think she is sending them to me as some sort of message, but I don't understand what it is she is trying to tell me."

Jess sat down next to Pandora and Pandora put her arm around her and kissed her on the cheek. Jess's cheeks were wet with crying.

"I feel so scared," she said. "Scared of what I am going to find in the Troad. Thank you, Pandora. I bless the day I ever met you."

"I have an idea." Pandora gave Jess a coy smile.

Jess laughed. "Lover, you really always have the best of all ideas."

* * *

Iraj kept glancing again and again with pride at the beautiful woman riding by his side. Rohana loved him so much that she would bear his child.

Soon they would be united in love as man and wife.

Rohana grinned back at her handsome man. He was strong and muscular and yet he was so gentle and loving. He had a deep warm voice and a smile that made her tremble all over. Jess had described him as a wonderful man, so long ago. Little did Rohana think back then that one day she would be riding proudly by his side.

After they parted from Jess and Pandora, they had discovered a small bag of gold and a note amongst their luggage. It was addressed to Rohana. How Jess snuck it into their luggage they never found out, but when Rohana read it, it set her crying.

'Dear, dear Rohana. This isn't much, but a bride as lovely as you deserves a dowry from her family. We are your family. This is a part of my share from Dilkor. They stole your money and they stole two years of your life, so Pandora and I think you should have it. I don't know if fate will allow us to come your way again but know that you and Iraj always hold a piece of our hearts. You sisters in love, Jess and Pandora.'

They finally crossed the Oxos where Iraj had to buy small presents for *all* his family. Even small presents added up to a big load, piled on their two spare horses. Then they headed mainly east but slightly north to the village of Qori, Iraj's home.

They had to pass through the village to reach his family home. People came running and shouting out from everywhere, Iraj had returned!

They marvelled at his four horses, his bulging saddle bags and all his luggage. And he was so well dressed! And who was the beautiful Indoi lady by his side?

Rohana stayed on her horse, overwhelmed by all the attention, while Iraj hopped down to greet his friends. But then he caught her eye and gave her that smile that made her feel warm all over.

They stopped at a *bazaar-cheh* (mini-bazaar) for Rohana to buy the traditional flowers for her prospective mother-in-law, after which it was only a short ride to his house. The news of their arrival had preceded them, especially the news that Iraj had arrived with a woman and that he looked prosperous.

Everyone was already waiting outside: his parents, his younger brother Peshana looking for all the world like a younger version of Iraj, his sister Esther and her husband Usmanara and their two young children. His youngest sister Asabanâ and one of his young female cousins waited a little behind.

Iraj hopped down but before he even greeted his parents, he turned and helped Rohana from her horse and held her possessively in front of him. As a woman, she would be introduced to his mother, the senior woman of the house, first.

"Mother, please meet the *jāné del-am* (life of my heart), Rohana, the girl I wish to marry."

Oh no! Iraj had said it in front of everyone even before they had a chance to get to know her. What would people think? Rohana went bright red and fell at the feet of her prospective mother-in-law. But Iraj's mother, Humâyâ, grabbed her by both arms and lifted her up into a hug.

"Iraj, she is very beautiful." To Rohana she said, "Rohana, arūus (daughter-in-law), please call me mâdaršowhar (mother-in-law) already! Be welcome to our house."

Iraj's father, Mayu, echoed the greeting with a broad smile. "Arūus, be welcome. Your presence lightens our day."

Rohana's eyes teared it was such a wonderful warm greeting, and then the rest of the family gathered around to greet her and be introduced. Of course, a family that had produced Iraj could be nothing but absolutely wonderful, just like him!

Iraj had a small gift for each member of his family and then they all gathered around to drink tea and chat and eat cakes to welcome Rohana and welcome back Iraj.

The house had been built by Iraj's father's father. It was a one story stretched out house in the shape of an 'L'. It had more than enough room for an extended family and several servants. An 'L' shaped wall the height of the house completed an enclosed rectangle so that in the Persian style the rooms opened into enclosed gardens with seats, a well, cobblestones, and fig trees, pomegranates and grape vines.

Rohana was given a large room to share with Iraj's youngest sister, Asabanâ. She was fifteen, a head taller than Rohana and wouldn't stop talking.

"I just know we will be good friends. Iraj went searching for poor Katin. Then he visited to tell us he was working for a wealthy black woman and now he turns up without warning with a bride. Usually nothing happens here. It was always so dull until our poor Katin ran away!"

Rohana smiled, feeling a bit breathless with the conversation.

"Where did you meet?" Asabanâ asked.

"I was a prisoner of slavers at Dilkor. It was Iraj that led the rescue of that whole town."

"I heard of that, was that my brother? He is a hero!"

Rohana laughed gently. "He is all of that."

"Did you fall in love with him, then?"

"A little," Rohana admitted. "I remember thinking he was very handsome."

That evening they held an impromptu outdoors feast, which somehow grew to involve the whole village. Iraj's family killed two goats and several chickens but they wouldn't have had enough if their neighbours hadn't cooked as well. It seemed everyone brought something. There was a lot of wine consumed and even some white milky tea made from the hemp so loved by the Skythians. It grew well here.

It was the first time people from the village got to meet Rohana and their reaction was everything she could have wished for. Iraj played the veena to show off his new skill while Rohana beat her drum and they sang together before others finally took over. It didn't finish till late in the morning.

* * *

After the ritual bath and drink of pomegranate juice, Rohana emerged with a prayer cap and only the loose white trousers and shawl to cover her nakedness. Her mother-in-law to be, Humâyâ, as the eldest woman in her new family, circled the egg three times over her head and then dashed it to the ground to remove any lurking evil. Then she formed up a small honour guard of Iraj's sisters and female cousins to lead Rohana to the waiting priest.

She had to repent her sins.

"That's a short list, Arūus," Humâyâ hissed.

Rohana struggled to keep a straight face as she recited the short prayers Iraj had taught her. Then she made her pledges in front of the whole village:

Astuye humtem mano (I pledge my thoughts to good thoughts), *Astuye hukhtem vacho* (I pledge my speech to good words), *Astuye hvarashtem shyaothanem* (I pledge my actions to good deeds), *Astuye daenam vanghuhim Mazdayasnim* (and I pledge myself to the highest worship of our God).

After this, they took her behind a curtain where the women helped her put on the small cotton vest the like of which she would wear as an undergarment for the rest of life. It had a pocket against her chest for symbolically collecting her good deeds. She had to think of what it might contain (or not contain) before she judged or criticised anyone else.

Then she gathered the shawl around her shoulders again and wound the *Kusti* (cord) around her waist three times (one time each for good thoughts, deeds and speech) and then knotted it. The priest placed a red dot of paste on her forehead, indicating the spiritual eye.

Then it was done.

The priest recited a blessing, her future mother-in-law put a garland of flowers around her neck and kissed her. Then the people from the village sprinkled her with rice and rose petals for good fortune.

Rohana was a *Behdin* (Zoroastrian).

She had converted to the good religion.

Now they could celebrate.

* * *

Jess preferred to grip her sword with her right hand bare. But she wasn't sure if wearing one glove like an Amazóne would be a good idea once she reached the Troad. Out from Sardeis she finally found a glove maker who sold her some soft leather gloves in her size that seemed to solve the problem. They were designed for a swordsman; the palm was suede for grip and the back lightly padded for protection. Now she could feel comfortable wearing two gloves.

Sardeis now lay behind them. They forded the Hermos River and finally sighted the Mediterranean Sea. Whatever had been driving her only seemed to feel stronger as they both turned their horses to the Troad.

"I feel I could travel this way blindfolded," Jess said as they passed Myrína. "As I get closer I am getting more of Jacinta's memories. Somewhere in them is a clue as to what happened to her and how to find her."

* * *

Elana brought the crying baby out and cast around for her fellow wife.

"Such a fuss, such a fuss." She laughed as she passed the small baby to her friend to feed. "Just like her father, she loves her food, and just like her mother she has a loud voice."

Kynane smiled as she took her daughter and moved over to sit in the shade. She pulled one breast loose from her chiton and guided the tiny mouth to her nipple.

"She feeds so well." Elana sat beside her and put her arm around Kynane and kissed her, smiling down at her tiny child. She gently began to lightly massage Kynane's shoulder and upper back. "That's not distracting is it?" she asked.

"Not with you doing it," Kynane murmured. "It feels good."

She felt the tingling feeling in her breasts as the milk let down. The baby's hungry sucking slowed as it didn't have to work as hard. Elana passed Kynane a cloth for the other breast which had started to drip and moisten her dress.

"You're good at this. You're like an old cow." Elana laughed.

Kynane giggled.

She realised how happy she was. She had the love of a wonderful man and had this adorable new little person settled in her arms so full of love and trust. She was surrounded by the sisterhood and companionship of her Amazónes and she had Elana, dear Elana, so gentle and loving, still tentative and lacking in confidence which was not surprising after all she had been through.

She was the sister Kynane had never had. Did her mother have this with her father's other wives, at least before Olympias came?

Theirs had been an arranged marriage and yet Audata seemed content with whatever Philippos gave her. It had been an easy relationship, more like friends.

They had named their baby Audata to honour the grandmother that she would never see. As she thought of her mother, she felt a stab of grief. Having her mother around at this time would be the only other thing she could want but that had been stolen from them.

* * *

"Are you sure you don't mind visiting the Troad before your own family?" Jess asked as they trotted their horses deeper into the Troad.

"Jess, I'm not deserting you now! Besides, when we search for my family I want you with me."

"Pandora, I don't think I can tell you enough how much I love you." Jess's eyes teared. "Now that I am here, I feel scared. It all seems to be building up into a climax and I just don't know what I will find."

It was late in the afternoon as they followed the dirt road around a curve in the Skamandros River and the mud brick and wooden fort came into view. Jess had no memories of Hakeem's fort. Jacinta had never been there. There was rich farm land all around and a pleasing amount of livestock. They turned their horses towards the nearby village along the main road leading to the fort.

"It looks prosperous and restful at least," Pandora remarked.

BANG!

It sounded like lightning hitting a tree. It echoed back and forward across the valley. A great daimôn lord blinked into existence across the meadow leading to the fort.

"Oh, oh," Jess gasped in fear. "So *that's* why I had to hurry."

Jess let go of her spare horse. She turned her horse towards the daimôn and snatched for her gorytos.

"Stay here, Dora. It looks like we are about to see if I can fight daimôns. If not, it will be a brief and very one sided fight. Well, I may as well start with a daimôn lord, I suppose!"

* * *

"My Lord, my Lady Kynane! A daimôn lord has appeared and is making for the fort!"

Hakeem took the steps three at a time up to the walkway and looked where the lady sentry pointed. The gong was sounding frantically. The light was starting to fade but they still could see a huge red daimôn at least nine feet tall, shambling towards their fort.

Between it and the fort was a black woman. In a display of expert horsemanship and archery, she turned in her saddle and began firing arrows back at the daimôn behind her. They were having no discernible effect.

"Who is that lady and why is the daimôn chasing her?" Elana yelled, appearing at Hakeem's elbow.

"I don't know who she is, my Lady," the scout replied. "She galloped across to intercept it, as if she was trying to prevent it reaching us here. Whoever she is, she has courage to the point of madness, but I fear it will only earn her her death."

Hakeem clenched his jaw, willing the woman's horse to gallop faster.

"This daimôn isn't friendly."

"I'm afraid not this time, my love," Elana replied next to his elbow. "It is the one that Æloðulf sent to kill me, the same one that attacked Ba'al. I fear it has followed me here."

The stranger holstered her bow, abandoning her attempt to shoot the daimôn. At the bottom of the hill she jumped off her horse and grabbed at a shield, slapping her horse's rump hard with her sword. Then she began jogging up the winding road to the gate.

"Hakeem," Elana shouted. "Get everyone out. It is me it is after, I can delay it."

Elana's eyes were glowing yellow. She gave a low growl as she watched the approaching daimôn.

In an impressive demonstration of endurance the female warrior ran the entire slope up to the fort carrying her sword and shield. Outside the barred gate, she turned, bent over panting for a moment and then crouched, ready, hefting her sword and shield. The gate opened slightly and a great hand stretched out to catch her by the back of her leather armour and drag her to the temporary safety of the fort.

Jess found herself pulled into the embrace of two bearlike arms and squashed against a muscular chest. A handsome face smiled down at her.

"Umph!" she said.

A part of her felt like staying exactly where she was!

"You must be Hakeem, but you're married aren't you?"

Hakeem looked at her, a little puzzled. "I have two wives, yes, but who are you?"

What a pity, of course he would be married!

"My name is Jess! We can talk later; if we live. I am a changeling and my other form is a daimôn. If you promise that none here will kill me because of it, I will try to fight this thing for you. I think that is why I have been brought here at this time, from a place far away."

"I would never permit any hurt to come to you just because you are a changeling."

"Thank you, Lord. Please get everyone else away. Can you help me with this wagon?" She ran over to push a wagon against the gate.

"Will it help?" Hakeem asked.

"I don't think so. You should have reinforced your mud bricks."

"I'll remember that next time," Hakeem said as they overturned the wagon against the gate.

"Lord, get everyone else away!" Jess repeated.

Hakeem shouted to the remaining Amazónes. He had to shout angrily to make them obey.

"Now you too, Lord!" Jess insisted. "You cannot fight this thing. If I have to try to protect you too, it will only get me killed."

"I don't need you to protect me."

Jess glanced around and saw Kynane standing ready, holding a javelin; she could see the power swirling over it. "Lady, you are breast feeding. I can smell it on you. What do you think you are doing here?"

"Jess, my name is Kynane. I am the best here with javelins."

Jess nodded. "Kynane, try not to use it. If you kill a daimôn its energy will come to you and kill you."

Just then the daimôn hit the gate with a deafening crash and Jess saw Elana.

"I know you!" Jess said in recognition. "You are the queen. You are Jacinta's mother. You bear the mark of the daimôn realm."

"I was held captive there for two years," Elana replied.

"Well, are you ready to fight this thing, my Lady?" Jess quickly stripped so she only had a sash; she pushed her knife in it and took off her gloves. Her left hand glowed faintly in the failing light. "Maybe this will work for daimôns as Jacinta's did."

Then she transformed.

"Jez!" Elana shouted excitedly. "It's you! Hakeem, this is the small daimôn that came to protect me. It's her, it's Jez!"

"Well Lady, now I have the answer as to what I am." The daimôn spoke thickly. "It is bitter news. I am a daimôn who has managed to take human form! Try to save yourself. You are with child, it is a boy."

Elana cried with joy. "Now I will make sure I will live!"

She began hurriedly to take off her clothes.

Hakeem wondered what it was with these women taking off their clothes before battle.

There was a mighty clap like thunder. The ground shook and cracks appeared in the nearby wall.

"This one has great magic!" Jez shouted. "It is all coming back to me. Its name is Mot, which means 'death'. All of you! Run! Mot is a match even for Ba'al himself!"

Elana was now in daimôn form; she just bared her teeth in a snarl. Hakeem and Kynane merely grinned back at Jez.

Fools! Jez thought, shaking her head. *I have come all this way to find a land of fools!*

Then another explosion rocked the fort. A section of the wall near the gate crumbled. There was dirt and dust billowing up everywhere.

"Mot!" Jez threw her head back to scream in challenge. "This is not your world. Leave now before you are destroyed."

"Jez, good!" Mot laughed. "Time I destroyed Ba'al's little lieutenant!"

He didn't wait to tear down the gate. He leapt over it, his shoulder crashing into the entrance hall as he landed. The whole fort shuddered and more buildings began collapsing.

Mot rose up to his full height, his huge red body shimmering with power, his tail knocking rubble aside. Jez ran at an angle past him to distract him.

"Jez, no!" Elana screamed.

Mot threw a bolt of power at Jez, which exploded as it hit. Jez appeared to the side rolling and scrambling to her feet.

By all the Gods, she's fast!

Mot tried again but Jez shot between his legs. She tried to bite at his leg but he laughed and kicked her behind him. She twisted her body to land on her feet. Elana snarled as she ran at him from one side.

"Bitch of an elf, there is no one to save you now."

He swivelled to meet the small yellow haired daimôn. But he screamed in rage and pain. Jez had grabbed his calf with her left hand.

"It works!" she screamed in triumph. "It really works!"

Nothing these puny beings did *should* be able to hurt him, but his leg burnt like fire.

He spun to confront Jez but she was gone, running back towards the gate. Elana hit him from the other side and raked her claws across his thigh. He turned to deal with her when Kynane appeared from nowhere and threw the last charmed javelin. He took it full in the chest.

"Run, Kynane!" Hakeem screamed.

Kynane ducked around the corner as the daimôn sent a burst of power after her. She was lost to sight as the building wall collapsed, dragging the roof over with a load crash. A dense cloud of dust went high into the air.

Broken tiles sprinkled down everywhere.

The daimôn pulled out the javelin and looked at it, perplexed. It was dark with small sparkles through it. He could feel a burning cold spreading from where he was struck. What evil magic had Ba'al taught these humans?

He was weakening.

For the first time he felt fear.

This was a trap!

Well, he would take all of these beings with him. He sent a burst of power at the yellow haired daimôn but a black blur collided with it just as the blast struck.

Jez felt like a house had fallen on top of her.

Elana was in better shape and trying to climb out from underneath her. Jez looked at her hand. It was shining with silver light and silver sparkles were running all over it. The daimôn blast had fed it power!

Could she transfer the power to her knife blade as Jacinta had done with her javelins? She carefully moved her knife across and clutched the blade in her left hand. She was struggling to get off Elana at the same time. Hakeem appeared at her elbow.

"No time," she gasped. "We have killed it but it is slow to die. It will destroy us all first."

She pushed the handle of her knife into Hakeem's hand. The blade was dark with strange sparkles like stars running through it.

Hakeem looked at her in awe. "Who are you? What are you?"

Jez merely shook her head weakly. Her body was in agony and she was trembling with cold.

"Cut his hamstring while he is distracted!

"Elana, if you want to keep the tiny baby you carry, run now! There is nothing more you can do."

Hakeem ran forward and stabbed the daimôn in his calf. Mot screamed, a terrible wailing sound, and kicked him into a corner. Jez managed a teetering run and with the last of her strength threw herself on top of Hakeem to shelter his body. Mot lunged after her but only ended toppling towards them.

Jez held her left hand out. It had to be her that had killed him, anyone else would be destroyed. Her hand pushed deep into his chest, sucking his power into her body.

Then the universe exploded around her.

* * *

Jess struggled weakly in terror. She felt a hand pushing her back onto the bed as someone leant over to kiss her.

"Jess you are safe. It's me, Elana."

"I'm a daimôn, I know that now," Jess protested feebly. "Don't trouble yourself with something like me, Great Queen."

She realised she was wearing clothes. "Someone has touched my body; they must have found it disgusting. Better to have left it were it was."

"Jess! Don't you dare talk like that, or you will make me really angry with you!" Elana kissed her again. "You have saved my life twice. You have saved Hakeem and Kynane and so many more that I love. You are more than our friend, you are part of our family!"

"You would say that?" Jess was overcome. She looked at the elf queen through a sheen of tears. "You would say that to such as me?"

Jess was too weak to sit up but Elana bundled her up and hugged her, tears were running down both their cheeks. "But you are a queen, you know the thing that I am."

"I know exactly what you are, Jess. You are a dear and true friend who happens to be a daimôn. I have a daughter who is in love with a daimôn lord, don't you forget it!"

"She's awake!" she called over her shoulder.

Hakeem and Kynane came in from another room and hugged and kissed her. All Jess found she could do was to cry.

"Where's Pandora?" she asked eventually. "Please tell me she is safe."

"Your friend tried to stay awake the whole time. Eventually she collapsed and is now fast asleep. She is not the only one who waited by your bedside," Elana said with a smile.

Jess tried to stifle a yawn and was fighting to keep her eyes open.

"Why am I so tired?" she asked.

"That would be my fault," Hakeem said with a grin. "You changed back to human form but you almost died defending me and were in really bad shape. I had to heal you. I was frightened I couldn't heal a changeling but it was no different in the end. You will feel tired for many weeks!"

Jess didn't hear him, she had fallen asleep.

She had a contented smile on her face. She had never known a home. Finally she was home surrounded by friends.

* * *

The voice in her mind woke her. "For a moment I thought you were Jacinta, who are you?"

An image of the red haired elf seeress came to Jess.

"No, I am a daimôn who works for Ba'al. I know you, you are Sophie!" Jess called out in delight.

"You know me?" The child seeress asked. "I just arrived by boat at Abydos. You really are a lot like Jacinta."

"Elana thinks it is because I formed a daimôn bond with her. I am hoping to get Jacinta back but," Jess yawned, "I will have to recover my strength first and then find out how."

"Well, I have come to help. Can you get Kynane to send an escort to pick me up? I have two novices with me."

Chapter 20: The Search for Jacinta

Pandora, Sophie, Kynane and Elana had gathered around Jess's bed to talk about looking for Jacinta.

"It is an area of nothingness from which reality is created," Jess said. "I want to search there, but I don't know how."

"It seems to be easier and safer for daimôns to move in that place than those from our realm." Sophie warned them.

Even at thirteen she remained small for an elf, but she was the most powerful priestess of the Great Earth Mother. Perhaps she was second in power to Maerwen whose soul she was linked to and who established that same order so long ago.

"It still sounds dangerous," Pandora said.

"I don't care," Jess said. "Jacinta has this wonderful family that love her; it is my job to get her back. Ba'al might know. If only I could get more of my own memories!" she felt like screaming in frustration. "I am starting remember some of the fight to rescue you, my Queen."

"What I can't understand was how you were rescuing me at the same time you were travelling here with Pandora," Elana said.

Jess ground her teeth in frustration; for her the rescue was a couple of years ago, before she ended up in the desert. For Elana it was recent, just before Ba'al brought her back to the Troad. Everything seemed to be going around in circles and she felt *so* sleepy and it was so hard to think!

"If you are a daimôn, can you be in two places at the one time?" Kynane asked. "Or maybe the same place at different times?"

"Only if she is one of the greater gods," Sophie replied.

"So I am a god now?" Jess giggled. "First a changeling, then an angel, then a daimôn, and now a god."

"Mot said you were Ba'al's lieutenant," Sophie said. "And you are faster than other daimôns. That's why you were sent to defend Elana till Ba'al and Jacinta could get there. You must have been there when Ba'al tried to transition and he was attacked. The energy he was using must have misfired onto you. It sent you back in time and half way across the world."

"So where is Jacinta?" Jess asked.

"Jacinta will be trapped in the region of nothingness while ever you hold the energy that was supposed to transport her," Sophie said softly.

Jess looked at Sophie in fear. "So while I exist here, Jacinta cannot return."

Sophie suddenly realised what she had said. "No, Jess! That's not what I meant."

"That is why I have been getting her memories." Jess looked to Elana. "All that has to happen is for Hakeem to kill me and you can have your daughter back."

Pandora and Elana cried out in unison, "Noooo!"

Elana turned on Sophie, in a fury.

"Get out of my sight, you witch! How dare you say such a thing to Jess?"

The little elf girl went pale, her eyes teared. "I never meant ..." and then she turned and fled.

"My Lady, don't be angry with Sophie. What she says makes sense," Jess insisted. "I had a bond with Jacinta as Ba'al's lieutenant and I am here instead of Jacinta. That is why I resemble her so much. But I am a daimôn. If you can find a way to kill me, you can have your daughter back."

"Jess!" Elana went red with anger. "Don't be a complete and utter fool! Jacinta would never want you to sacrifice yourself, even if this was true!"

"I don't belong on this plane." A tear ran down Jess's cheek. "I don't think I can ever find my way back!"

Pandora was horrified. "Jess, I love you. Doesn't that count for anything?"

"Jess, don't you talk like this!" Elana added. "*We* are your family."

"Thank you both. I'm sorry," Jess said. "Maybe I'm just too tired to think clearly."

"Do you want me to sleep in this room?" Pandora asked, alarmed at her friend's mood.

"No, my love." Jess smiled at her reassuringly. "I can rest better if I am alone, I'll be all right, really I will. I just got a little silly for a bit, that was all."

Elana and Pandora stormed out together, in search of Sophie. Once they had left, Jess got up and carefully closed the door. She knew what she had to do.

She began to meditate, deeper and deeper till she found a certain staircase inside herself. After that her weariness was gone. She lit a candle and quickly wrote a note to her friends. She stole some food from the kitchen. Out of habit she almost took her sword and her bow but then she laid them aside. Her knife was all she needed for this.

Then she went to the stables and saddled her horse and led it to the gate. The sentries challenged her but she said Hakeem had sent her on an errand. With a joke about Hakeem and his strange requests she walked her horse to the bottom of the hill. When she could no longer be seen from the fort in the light of the half moon she mounted and encouraged her horse to a trot.

Sophie couldn't sleep.

She burned with shame and felt more than just a little battered from her encounter with Elana and Pandora both together. She thought for a moment that they were going to physically attack her.

She shot up straight in bed. That was it!

She knew what had happened to Jacinta!

She had to tell Jess immediately! Of course! It was so obvious, why couldn't she have seen it before?

She went hurrying towards the room where Jess had her bed. As she passed the common room, she paused to see Elana sitting there. Elana glowered at her but Sophie was bursting with excitement.

"My Lady, did Jess have anything with her when she arrived here?"

Elana was puzzled by the question. "She had a pendant! It was strange — of metal, like bronze. I had meant to ask her about it."

"About two inches long, covered with red marking?" Sophie asked, thrilled.

Elana nodded. Sophie was grinning uncontrollably.

"The answer to everything was right under our noses! Now I know what happened to Jacinta. We need to wake her!"

"You will explain to me before you dare test any more of your cursed theories on that poor girl!" Elana said coldly.

Sophie nodded. "Jess is like Jacinta in so many ways, now I know why!"

Elana looked at Sophie suspiciously. Was this another crazy theory that would hurt her Jess?

"Her pendant is the magical svartálfar key! It is the key to the room that exists in 'No Place'! Of course it is and of course Jess was wearing it!" Sophie said excitedly. "The room can be used to travel great distances. It exists in that region without time and space; the region that lies between our realm and the daimôn realm. What did your daimôn servants call you?"

The question surprised Elana and for a moment she smiled at the memory.

"Only the bigger daimôns can talk like us. The smaller ones called me Ee'la." Then she looked at Sophie in shock. "You can't mean it!"

"I do mean it!" Sophie said excitedly. "What would the daimôns call Jacinta?"

"J'ezz!" Elana whispered, her hand to her mouth in shock. "They would call her Jez!"

"Jacinta stepped out into the region without time and space," Sophie said breathlessly. "Somehow she found her way into that room that exists there. She somehow used it to travel into the desert but she arrived a couple of years in the past. All of what happened to her affected her memory!"

She continued, talking rapidly. "You never saw Jess and Jacinta together, did you?"

"It was all confused," Elana said, casting her mind back. "Ba'al's army was attacking Æloðulf's fortress. Æloðulf' had set up protection spells but it seemed that the whole of the universe trembled. Æloðulf suddenly appeared near me with Mot. Æloðulf was badly hurt and I could tell almost at the end of his strength.

"The Illvættir had lost. I felt joy but also terror. Æloðulf was my jailor but he was also my protector in that terrible place. I think he really did love me. For all I knew these new daimôns would kill me or worse.

"Æloðulf said he was *sorry*. He said he didn't want the other daimôns to get me and told Mot to kill me. Then he sort of faded. It was the last I saw of him.

"The daimôn world is a brutal place but the Illvættir saw daimôns as evil, which they are not. Mot never liked me but when he tried to kill me, the lesser daimôns rushed to my defence.

"I felt so angry. I transformed into a daimôn for the first time then but Mot was too powerful for me." Elana gasped. "Then Jez was there. She was no bigger than me but she was faster than any daimôn I had ever seen. Soon after, Ba'al appeared with a noise like thunder and grabbed me up. Jacinta was there *then*. No, I never saw Jacinta and Jez together. Before we could get away, Mot appeared again and attacked Ba'al.

"I could feel Jacinta step out, sacrificing herself, but had no way to grab her!" Elana closed her eyes in pain with the memory. "But the Jacinta that was with me didn't look like Jess."

"My Queen!" said Sophie intently. "You absorbed some daimôn substance even though you were far from the surface. Your features are different now, it made you a changeling and it affected your memory. Jacinta arrived in the realm already with daimôn substance inside. She travelled the surface and killed scores, maybe even hundreds of daimôns for all I know. She absorbed their substance. It doesn't affect daimôns this way but that must have been overwhelming that part of her that was human. Being a paladin, she was able to resist for a time, but not forever. She probably knew it was happening but refused to leave until she had found you. In the end she was losing her memories and control of her daimôn side.

"Think of Jez, black skin and a large jaw line. Think of your daughter as you last saw her. Now add just a little bit of Jez and what do you get?"

"I get Jess!" said Elana, leaping up with joy. "Jess is Jacinta! Of course she is! Why couldn't we see it?"

They lit a candle each and ran to Jess's room, bursting in together.

"She is gone!" Sophie cried out in horror.

On the table there was the key to the room that existed nowhere. To Sophie/Maerwen it was unmistakeable. Underneath was a letter.

Sophie started to read and then gasped, ashen. "What have I done?"

She almost dropped the letter. Elana snatched it from her.

'Great Queen Elana,

I now know my existence in this world is all that is preventing your beautiful daughter from returning to you. This must stop now, while a chance remains.

I hope you know I never meant to steal the life of another. It must be the reason why I am becoming troubled by the memories that belong to your wonderful daughter.

I had thought it would be best for Hakeem to kill me, but I realise this might put him at risk and maybe my body would poison the very ground. I know now how this must be done.

Tell Pandora I love her. I cannot stay with her being what I am I hope she understands that.

I hope she will find her way home. Home is something that is forever lost to me. I only knew you all a short time. Despite what I am, know that I love you all very deeply. For a time you helped me feel like a person rather than the thing I really am.

I go now to gladly give the one thing I can give for my friends. I have travelled far for an answer as to what I am, I have travelled here to help bring your daughter home. Now it is only a short journey.

I hope, despite knowing what I am, you will remember me a little and know I loved you all,

Jess'

Elana crushed the letter to her and screamed in agony.

"NO! DEAR GODDESS NO! NOT JACINTA! NOT LIKE THIS!"

From the hallway came the sound of running feet.

* * *

"Jess!" a voice sounded in her mind.

"Sophie! I'm sorry. You know I don't just seek death, as my substance will poison the ground. I am getting Jacinta's memories and it has given me the answer. I hope she gets her own memories back when I am gone. This is painful for me. It is surprising that one such as I would feel so much pain at the thought of my existence ending. It feels lonely to die without a friend by my side and so far from home. I have no right to ask this but please think of me sometime. I am putting up a barrier against you now. I must do this alone or my courage will fail!"

"Jess!" Sophie shrieked in desperation, "Jess!"

But she was blocked.

The fort was in turmoil. People were rushing everywhere to join the search and groups of mounted women were still assembling. They had found Jess's horse not far away but the trail was cold in the darkness. Elana and Kynane had rode back to give the news to the other searchers.

Sophie came running out of the house with tears streaming down her cheeks. "Lady, she refused to listen to me."

"Haven't you done enough, Sophie?" Elana said with cold fury. "Just let me search for my daughter. Pray to the Goddess we can find her in time."

"But my Lady, she said something," Sophie insisted. "She is starting to get her memories but she doesn't think they are hers. She said, 'You know I don't just seek death as my substance will poison the ground.'"

"What's that you said?" Elana froze looking at Sophie.

"She talked not of dying but of ending her existence."

"Sophie!" Elana yelled. "I may forgive you yet. If you wish, you may come but no one can wait for you. We must ride as if the *Erinyes* (furies) themselves ride at our very heels. Do you think she can get past our elves undetected?"

"I'm coming too!" Pandora demanded, leading a saddled horse.

"What does it mean?" Kynane asked, confused.

"Jacinta isn't just going to kill herself. She plans to cancel her existence and destroy her very soul! She is making her way to the ruins of elvish Troia. It's where she hid the book that cannot be read. She hopes to use it to destroy herself," Elana said. "Don't you understand? She will be gone without any hope of redemption!"

Kynane went pale in horror to hear such a dreadful thing. "We must stop her!"

Sophie had leapt onto a horse and the stable hands raced to shorten the stirrups. Pandora was already mounted, waiting and looking very frightened.

Kynane was shouting orders to her Amazónes and a small group of her six favourites led by Anastasia joined the four of them. The women were bearing torches and were about to light them when Sophie started to mutter harshly and they were surrounded by a glow that allowed them to see in the dark.

The horses were unsettled by it and took a moment to settle and then they were off, galloping to elvish Troia.

* * *

Jess smiled as she approached the ruins of elvish Troia.

Clever Sophie! Clever Elana! They were here before her!

Jess was fast and slow to tire in her daimôn form but she couldn't outrun horses!

She felt deeply moved to think her new friends would try to stop her. It made her hesitate. They thought she was worthy of saving despite the dreadful cost. They had roused the elf camp.

She had no intention of harming anyone even if it ended in her capture. The elves have good night vision but nothing like what she had.

Can you sneak through a camp of elves, you sneaky little daimôn?

Half way up the hill, she froze. She smelt an elf in hiding. She had to back-track a little and circle around. There were several elves guarding but they were too confident.

Typical elves! They didn't realise in the dark she was infinitely better than they were.

She deliberately by-passed the entrance to the excavation and found a back way in. There was a pulley to lower goods. She secured it and rapidly let herself down. In the impenetrable darkness the keenest eyed elf would have difficulty seeing a black figure making her way down the long rope to the bottom.

Even for Jess it was a long and difficult climb. Half way down her arms and back were burning.

Silly little daimôn! Did you really think you could lower yourself all the way with only your arms? She twisted the rope around her legs and arms so she could rest. She grimaced and blocked out the agony as much as she could. Still, it was as if her body cried out in torment. It would be a great irony if she fell and killed herself only to desecrate the holiest sanctuary of the elves after all her efforts!

At the bottom she crouched in agony. For a moment she couldn't move, couldn't straighten. She felt like she had been pounded by iron bars.

* * *

"Lady Elana!" The elf guard Homeros pointed to the tracks. "See she managed to get past our guards and has entered the catacombs."

Elana was dizzy with terror. Once Jacinta made it into the catacombs, there was no chance to stop her. As fast as they could, they scrambled down the ladder. At the bottom, Elana paused in despair.

"Where to from here?" Kynane asked.

"Only Jacinta knows!" Elana said, feeling desperate. "We have to follow her tracks!"

"That's no good, the tracks are too confused!" Kynane shouted.

Sophie muttered under her breath. A series of glowing foot prints appeared on the floor.

"Sophie, remind me to take you on my next hunt!" Kynane gave her a crooked smile.

"Let's go!" Elana shouted urgently.

"I don't think we can catch her, she is too fast," Kynane said.

Elana merely flashed a frantic look and disappeared, carrying a torch borrowed from the elf guards. Even the Amazónes with all their training couldn't keep up with the desperate elf.

Up ahead, Kynane could hear Elana screaming.

"Jacinta! Please, no! Jacinta!"

They were too late.

The elf was huddled up against the rock, pounding on it weakly with her fists, her torch hissing on the floor. The way was barred. There was a figure of Silver standing in front of it looking at them angrily.

"You cannot pass!"

"You cannot pass!"

It was repeating it over and over.

It was a projection.

Sophie stared at the unbroken surface of rock, dismayed. "The way is sealed to all but Jacinta."

"Who's this?" Pandora pointed to the projection of Silver.

"Her name is Silver. She is the last of the *svartálfar* (dark elves)," Elana explained tiredly. "She sacrificed herself to be the guardian of the book. She was awoken when the daimôn fire triggered the book's defences the first time."

"It was she that saved Jacinta when one of the spells attacked her," Sophie added.

"Will Silver recognise Jacinta and help her?" Kynane asked.

"I don't know," Sophie said. "She may see the daimôn side and see her as too dangerous. Guarding that book is far more important than even Jacinta's life. Silver will not take any chances with it."

* * *

Jess was moving rapidly through the darkness towards where the book was concealed. Up ahead, she saw a slender beautiful woman with a pale complexion, soft silver hair and elfin ears. She was dressed in an exquisite dark blue gown.

Incongruously she was sitting casually on a stone coffin. She had to be some sort of projection.

"You are Silver, the guardian of the book." The memory stirred for Jess. "I'm glad to meet you."

"Are you?" Silver asked acidly. "Are you really? Well I'm most certainly not glad to see you! What I am is disgusted and angry! How dare you come here? And you bring an army of followers trailing behind you! Now we will have to move the book again! This book has enough power to destroy heaven and earth! It is not your play thing, girl! Don't let me think I made a mistake selecting you! Now explain to me this complete idiocy about killing yourself! How can you be so *stupid*? Tell me that!"

Jess was taken aback.

She felt hurt.

She had come here to not only end her life but to destroy her very soul. Surely that wasn't a trivial matter and Silver was treating her like a naughty child!

"Silver," Jess tried to explain. "I am not Jacinta. My name is Jess. I am a daimôn and I have to destroy myself so Jacinta can return."

"So Jess, as you call yourself! You are supposed to be chosen for your wisdom, not for your stupidity!" Silver's lip curled in disgust. "Sophie suggested you needed to kill yourself to save Jacinta. That was never true. Did you weigh the evidence? Did you stand strong, as you were meant to do? Did you face what your God has asked you to bear? No! You jumped at the chance to kill yourself. And do you want me to tell you why? It is because you are a coward! And you expect me to welcome you with open arms?"

Jess bowed her head and tears were starting. "Silver, I am a daimôn!"

"So what?" Silver sneered. "Oh Silver, pity me! I am part daimôn and I don't like it very much! How would you like to be the last of a race that has brought so much evil into the world?"

"But I am so ashamed!" Tears blurred her vision.

"Is that all, Jess?" Silver asked, her voice softer. "*Shame.* That is what your God has asked you to bear. Is it such a terrible thing?"

"I am a thing!" Jess cried out in agony. "I am disgusting!"

"What you are, *girl*, is supremely arrogant!" Silver pointed at her. "How dare you see yourself that way?"

Jess looked up in surprise. She didn't think she was arrogant!

"You are loved by so many. They see you as beautiful and wonderful, but you are so arrogant you say *they* are wrong and *you* are right! You only choose those opinions that fit with yours.

"They *need* you! What will it do to Pandora if you kill yourself? Have you even thought of her? What would have happened to her without you? And Elana or Hakeem or Kynane? They all want to love you but you won't let them. All you want to do is hurt them, wound them in a way from which they can never recover. And why? Because you can't bear the shame of being a daimôn! You have been sent by a God! The Dastur explained that to you, don't you remember that? You know it is true. If a God chose a daimôn or a changeling, how dare you say you are unworthy? Do you think you are even greater than your God?

"You have ended much evil already. Those shepherds, those devil worshippers, those bandits; you destroyed Mot. And your task is not finished. Would you defy the will of your God by ending your life and running away?"

"Aach!" Jess fell to her knees, her head in her hands.

"You are right," her voice was harsh.

Her God had asked, he had demanded, that she carry her shame! It was the final lesson in humility.

It was shame that had driven her to become a better person than she could ever have been. She had been given incredible power and she would be given more; almost enough to challenge a god.

It would become as much a danger to her as to her enemies. It needed to be balanced by humility and so she was given shame, it was supremely painful but it was also a gift.

Why was it that shame was so hard to bear?

Well, she had to find a way.

But that left one problem.

"I wish to bring Jacinta back for her friends and family!" she said. "But I don't know how."

"You have to accept your true nature, only then can Jacinta return."

Jess smiled ruefully at the irony. "I was prepared to destroy myself for Jacinta and my friends. That was selfish. I hated myself and that was arrogant. Now you ask me to not destroy myself but to accept myself, so Jacinta can find her way home?"

Silver nodded, she looked very weary.

Jess formally bowed to Silver. "I think what you ask is much harder than you imagine. I will try but I will need a different kind of courage to what I am used to. I need to love myself despite things about myself that I hate and am ashamed of. There is something I can do for you, isn't there, Silver? You look weak and tired."

"Jess, I was woken. I have lived too long," Silver said. "I am fading."

"You need something which I have in abundance. I will give it to you gladly ... and don't say you are unworthy!"

Silver smiled. "I was not willing to ask! It is life force I am losing. If I just take a little of your daimôn essence I can change it into all I need and much more. I will feel reborn."

"You are afraid it will diminish me?"

Silver nodded.

Jess laughed. "Daimôn substance? I have so much it feels like it will overwhelm me again. Must I say more?"

Silver reached forward to touch her face gently.

Jess felt a dull pain move over her jaw. As she rubbed at it, her jaw and face felt different.

Silver passed her a mirror, as clear as water.

"See Jacinta in the mirror and know where she is."

Jess sighed. "That really is Jacinta? It's what she looked like in my dreams. Is this real?"

"Yes Jess, *you* are Jacinta." Silver nodded. "You stayed in the daimôn realm too long and absorbed too much daimôn substance. As a paladin you fought it, but when you got lost in the realm of nothingness the daimôn part of you had to take over or you could not have survived in that place.

"You lost the human part of yourself and lost your memories both of the daimôn world and your life before that. Since then you are slowly reasserting control and your memories are returning."

The Jacinta in the mirror smiled at Jess and Jess began to laugh. Once she started it was hard to stop. Silver looked at her in surprise, she didn't see any humour in it.

"I journeyed half way across the world to find who I was. I was prepared to search the realm of nothingness to find Jacinta. All I had to do was look in the mirror. The Gods *do* have a sense of humour! I wondered before but now I am sure."

Silver chuckled. "When I drained some of the daimôn substance to renew myself I also took that part that altered your appearance. It won't last, but you are a changeling, eventually you can learn to change your appearance at will."

Jess nodded. "I had to go on a long journey to face something that was inside myself all this time."

"Before you go," Silver insisted.

She conjured the key that Jess had left at the fort.

"You will need this for the next part of your journey. It is the key to the room that exists in no place. You can use it to travel quickly from place to place. I will refresh your memory of how to use it. There is an invisible door here, and there are other doors to match the great cities of that time. When you came out in the desert you arrived where a city had been long ago."

"How do I know where I am going?" Jess asked.

"You don't remember this but there is a dial and a lever, a screen and pictures."

"It can also be used to travel in time," Jacinta said.

Silver shook her head, "The displacement in time happened while you were in the realm of nothingness. You're lucky much more didn't happen to you. We deliberately did not design the room to travel in time. If you really understood, you would never play with time or any of the worse things you could make the room do. Remember reality was created out of that region!"

"You had the power to destroy the Illvættir."

"Yes we did, but we didn't use it."

"To fight the Illvættir, that was why you made the elves, wasn't it?"

Silver hissed.

Her hands flew to her face in shock.

"The elves were never the eldest, were they?" Jess pressed her.

"Of course not!" Silver said. "How silly of the elves to say that, and so typical of them! They believe the eldest were the best, so it had to be them. Humans were the eldest, all other types of men descended from them. The elves were the youngest and they were magnificent! They were the best thing that we ever created." Silver smiled at the memory.

"The Illvættir had caused unimaginable slaughter and the war continued. Dwarves and svartálfar lived to great ages but we had few children. We could not win. Some humans helped us but humans are either too weak or too unreliable. Humans can be great. They can be wise and brave and good but then they tire of greatness and become evil or cowards or fools; especially when you put them in groups."

"So you made something better than the svartálfar and more reliable than humans but it is running down now?"

"Yes it is, it was slow at first but the elves are declining and the humans with their ten paces forward and nine paces back and with their good and bad will eventually pass them," Silver admitted. "The world can ill afford to lose the elves! Only if they combine with humans will the decline be arrested permanently."

"That was how you made them, didn't you?" Jacinta said softly.

"Jacinta, you scare me! How can you guess so much? Not me but yes, yes that was done. We svartálfar did not want to create another Illvættir to rule the world."

"Did you think you were Gods?"

"Jacinta, we *were* Gods! We had all the power of Gods but none of their wisdom! It was lucky we were few!"

"And hence, my mother and Seléne's task: the union of humans and elves! And that is why Ælward had to destroy the elvish magic, to cause the elves to fall, so they would be so weak they would have to unite with humans before all was lost! That is horrible, so much death and suffering."

Silver bowed her head. "Yes, but we paid our price too. Æloðulf thought he could reverse what was happening to the elves. He didn't understand there was only one way."

"Through love," Jacinta whispered.

"Yes, through love between elf and human. No one must know this!"

"I will not speak of it. I wish I didn't know it myself. I will help you hide the book now and I will come to visit you again one day, if I may."

"That is not needed," Silver said. "I have told you all that I will."

"I know it must have been you that helped me when I was lost," Jacinta said evenly. "You have saved me four times now: after the battle with the daimôn, after I accessed my life force to heal my hand, when I was lost in the realm of nothingness and now you have saved me from myself. I owe you much and I love you. There, I can say such a thing more easily now if I can only accept myself. And I know that you are lonely."

"Jacinta, is there nothing you cannot guess? I asked the room to call to you." Silver smiled. "I do not want to know myself how to search in that region. It is something I could maybe learn, but for me I think it is best not to know."

"You could become like a God!" Jacinta stared at her levelly.

"I could be like a God if I wished, but I do not. We svartálfar only became wise when it was too late."

Jacinta moved forward. To her surprise she found she could touch Silver; she kissed her on the cheek and hugged her gently.

"I need to give you one more thing," Silver said, smiling.

"What's that?" Jacinta asked.

"Jess, you are naked. I will give you the illusion of clothes that you can conjure when you need to. For a changeling, you might find it ... convenient."

* * *

Out of the darkness, a large woman in a short silky apricot shift emerged. Her legs were bare and she wore no shoes. She carried a knife in a black band at her waist. As she got closer they could see the features of a Gypsy. Elana threw herself at her and collapsed uncontrollably into tears. Jacinta held her and cried along with her. The other women gathered around in relief. Jacinta tried to hug them all at once.

"Mother, it is coming back to me," Jacinta murmured into the elf's hair. "I followed you to the daimôn realm and I lost who I was. For you I would do it again and again and again. I have had to travel half way across the world and reach the depths of despair to find out who I really am. If I was a little smarter I would have looked in a mirror."

Elana clung to her daughter. "You came for me, thank you, Jacinta! It was a terrible place."

"Mother, I was there," Jacinta said grimly. "And there were things I saw ... I'm glad you never saw them. Yet sometimes even the daimôn realm has a power and a beauty all of its own."

"I thought I would lose you."

"I am so sorry to you and everyone, please forgive me."

Finally Elana was comforted, though she refused to let go of her daughter. Jacinta then turned to Kynane. They were a close match in size.

"Kynane, if you permit, I would wish to call you mother and if you agree I will call your daughter Audata my sister. But you must understand one thing."

Kynane waited.

"I am easily your better at the javelin and I long to show you!"

Kynane threw her head back and laughed.

"Well, daughter of mine, I will look forward to making you eat those rash words." She pushed Jacinta playfully and then grabbed her and hugged her fiercely.

"And Sophie, dear, dear, Sophie." Jacinta continued on to the red haired elf girl. "You passed a thoughtless remark but it was a small thing. It was like a pebble thrown on the mountain-side that starts an avalanche, it was what was inside me that almost made it a tragedy. You are blameless. I had to face something about myself that I was refusing to accept."

"And Pandora! I have hurt you, wounded you, deeply. To say I am sorry cannot express how badly I feel. A madness overcame me. I will have to work to earn your forgiveness."

She grabbed Pandora and kissed her passionately on the lips.

"Jess! Not in front of these people, what will they think?" Pandora blushed in the torch light.

Jacinta laughed. "You know, Pandora, I don't care! I hope you don't mind, I'm not as black as I was and my real name is Jacinta."

"I liked the black," Pandora said, still shaky from almost losing Jess. "But give me a chance to check the new Jess out. I'm sure I can adjust." Then Pandora beamed at another thought. "You're a legend, Jacinta! My girlfriend is a legend!"

After a moment Jacinta took a deep breath and addressed them.

"And now we have much to do, all of us! How many know I am Jacinta?"

"Us here and only a few more," Elana said. "There was no time for explanations."

"A few more will need to know, but for the moment we need to be quiet about this. Please call me Jess and think of me as Jess," she said. "Soon I will have to go to kill Gansükh. To be an assassin Jacinta is just a little too famous by half. It would be too much to hope that a šamán like Gansükh and those around him won't know that someone is coming to kill him, or try to, but the less they know about me the better."

* * *

It was the evening of the next day, Sophie was sitting sideways on Jess's lap and Jess had her arms wrapped around her. She was discussing war axes with Kynane. Elana and Hakeem were sitting next to each other and talking softly.

Pandora was about to enter the room but she hesitated.

"Sorry." She coloured. "I didn't mean ..."

"Pandora," Jess said. "Please come in."

"But you are spending time with your family and I'm ..."

"Pandora, you *are* part of my family."

Hakeem got up and dragged the embarrassed Greek girl into the room.

"This must be awkward for you, Pandora. You have already met us, and we suddenly transform into Jess's family. We are overjoyed to have her returned to us but we did not mean to exclude you. Let us start again with you not as a guest but as part of our family." He hugged her and bent his head to kiss her cheek.

"You don't mind that we, that is I, we are, you know, both of us?" Pandora sputtered.

"I think she is asking if you are angry with her because we are lesbian lovers," Jess suggested helpfully.

"Uggh!" Pandora went crimson and wished she could disappear into the floor. She could have cheerfully strangled her girlfriend. It wasn't like Jess at all to say something like that!

"I don't care even a little about you being a woman and not a man," Hakeem said. "My daughter loves you. Thank you for loving her and be welcome in our house."

"Thank you, Kyrie," Pandora said shyly.

Elana appeared at Hakeem's side and moved forward to kiss her cheek. Sophie and Kynane came forward to greet her as a new family member.

"Jess is only trying to embarrass you," Hakeem said. "Did you know she is ticklish? She was worse when she was younger."

"No, I didn't," Pandora said. *How could I have missed something like that?*

Hakeem and Elana circled around to come at Jess from either side.

"HEY!" Jess ended up writhing around in the chair till she slid, laughing helplessly, to the floor. And they had hardly touched her!

"That's not fair."

* * *

"Awwk!" squawked Jess.

She went sailing through the air to hit the mats with a thud and a loud "oohpf".

Pandora, who was watching from the sidelines, winced. Pandora wasn't used to seeing Jess being beaten in combat, but today her girlfriend was definitely having a bad day! Hakeem and Kynane were testing the gaps in her abilities and they weren't going gently!

Early this morning Jess tried her hand at throwing axes. Kynane explained about axes to Pandora while she was supervising Jess's practice. Pandora never knew there was so much to know about axes.

Apparently battle axes are lighter than axes used for chopping wood and generally have a smaller blade. "That is because a block of wood doesn't dodge and try to kill you back," Kynane explained.

The point of balance of a sword is close to a handle but the point of balance of an axe is in the head so they can't be used like a sword for defensive parries. In fact, using an axe leaves you more open to counters. They must be used with a shield.

In single combat, as long as the shields are still intact, they are no good against an equally skilled opponent with a sword, but they are cheap, easy to make, easier to learn and better for penetrating armour and destroying shields.

And it doesn't matter as much if the quality of the metal is poorer or the edge not as sharp. They can still do a *lot* of damage ... and a skilled axeman can use them to hook a shield, arm or weapon.

So a battle axe, a *kopis* (machete) or a spear are the popular weapons for rustic peasants, which might explain the popularity of axes in Illyria.

Axes can be thrown as well but need to be of better quality and very sharp. They need to rotate once in flight and hit with the axe head. Some are made with a larger blade to make it easier but that can make them cumbersome.

The target Kynane used for novices was soft wood and novices wore leg guards and arm and body protection. They used axes with wooden handles, a narrow single head and the back was blunt like a tent hammer. It reduced serious accidents, but not by much.

Jess's first axe bounced off the target, narrowly missing the spectators, getting them all to move back. The fourth attempt brought her axe practice to an abrupt end by hitting her on the shin guard. It gave an impressive bruise.

"Could be better, I think," was all Kynane said as she bandaged Jacinta's leg and helped her up. After a bit of limping around, Jess faced her father in unarmed combat. An opponent wouldn't stop trying to kill her if she was injured.

"Stay there, Jess!" Hakeem commanded before she tried to get up and come at him again.

"You're trying to overpower me with your strength!" Hakeem said, walking over to her. "Have you forgotten about using *my* strength against me?" He helped her up and steadied her as she favoured her sore leg.

"Not bad, though. You could use the practice against a more skilled opponent. Do you want to rest now?"

Jacinta nodded. "I promised to take Pandora to the river for a picnic, o patéras ... er, I mean Kyrie. I'd like to start tomorrow with the axes again and fighting in formation if we are doing that."

Hakeem hesitated and Jacinta grabbed him and hugged him and kissed him on the cheek. "I'm still your daughter and I still love you desperately," she whispered.

Hakeem didn't answer but he coloured and his eyes teared.

They took a picnic basket and two horses the short distance to the Skamandros River. Jacinta wanted to show Pandora the swimming hole some of the girls used. It was a lovely day for it, warm and sunny but Pandora seemed unusually quiet on the ride out.

"All the locals are respectful of women bathing here," Jacinta said. "Or else, I suppose."

Pandora gave her a wan smile.

Jess spread a blanket and began unwrapping small parcels of cheese, meat, bread, olives. Pandora sat on the edge of the blanket and looked out over the river while Jess worked.

"I don't know about you, Dora," Jacinta said, "but I'm really hungry."

Pandora merely nodded and continued to stare, out over the river.

"I can help you search for your family now," Jess offered.

Pandora didn't turn around.

"Jess, when you go to Āzar Pāyegān," her voice was flat and distant, "I want to go with you."

"Pandora," Jess said softly, reaching out to her. "Love, you can't! I'm going there to kill someone. Gansükh is a šamán. He has surrounded himself with beings of dark power, maybe I will be facing blood priests again and they almost killed me last time. He has an army of something like forty thousand men and he has likely arranged for his daimôn to appear if there is any threat to him. This is a daimôn lord we are talking about."

"And how will you be, without me there?" Pandora started to cry and angrily wiped at her tears. "Jess, you tried to kill yourself! I was losing you and you weren't even going to say goodbye! What if you need me again?"

As Pandora said it, Jess felt herself shrinking inside. Her heart felt like a lead weight in her chest and her face was burning with shame. Pandora began to sob. Jess put a tentative hand on her shoulder.

"Dora, Dora, Dora," she said and then wondered what she could say. "Never again, I will swear an oath on it." She took a deep breath. "Being in the daimôn realm ... the time in the desert when I lost my humanity; it made me more than a little crazy I guess. To say I'm sorry ... I just don't know what I can say or do to make it up to you. I love you with all my heart. If it wasn't for you I would be even more crazy than I am."

She risked a teasing smile.

"Then I am going to Āzar Pāyegān with you?"

"Pandora, no." Jess took her in her arms. "I am a very special assassin, trained by a God. I have to do this alone."

"Will you stop all this *'poor me, I hate myself'* nonsense." Pandora giggled and relaxed a bit.

Jess laughed. "Pandora, I will try."

"What about that dwarf city? That will be your next task."

"Yes, it leads on to a battle with Æloðulf. I have to admit I fear that even more than Āzar Pāyegān."

"Then I will go with you there."

"Maybe. Can we talk about it later? You never give up, do you?"

"You know I don't." Pandora laughed. "I am going to join the Amazónes."

"Dora, that simply won't work!" Jess said. "I won't take an apprentice into danger in Āzar Pāyegān."

"Kynane has accepted me."

"What?" Jess looked stunned. "Oh all right, I will take you as an apprentice but you will have to wait till I am back."

"Jess, I don't want you training me."

"AND WHY NOT?" Jess sat up straight. *I'm the best, after all.*

"Jess, I love you. I want to go wherever you go, but I don't want to be a warrior like you. I want to help Asha. Someone has to look after you warrior girls."

"Dora, Dora," Jacinta laughed. "You are right. We do need looking after, at least I do. But let me eat some of this food before I start eating you out of hunger."

"You want to eat *me*?" Pandora giggled. "That sounds like fun. We had better have a swim first. I want to be tasty and not all sweaty."

* * *

Jess and Pandora took the back road to Abydos and then joined the coastal road to Bithynia.

Jess would have loved to show Pandora Troia but until Gansükh was dead she didn't want for 'Jess' to be too widely known. The less Gansükh knew about Jess the better.

The port city of Astakos lay at the end of a narrow gulf in the Propontis. It was an ancient colony of Meyara, that early rival of Athens, and was most famous for its fishing. It was named after the Astakos, the local lobster.

They finally found her old house. Pandora nervously approached the front door and knocked. She called out for her mother, her father, her sister. A stranger opened the door, a small crack.

"Excuse me," Pandora asked. "Do you know what happened to the family that used to live here?"

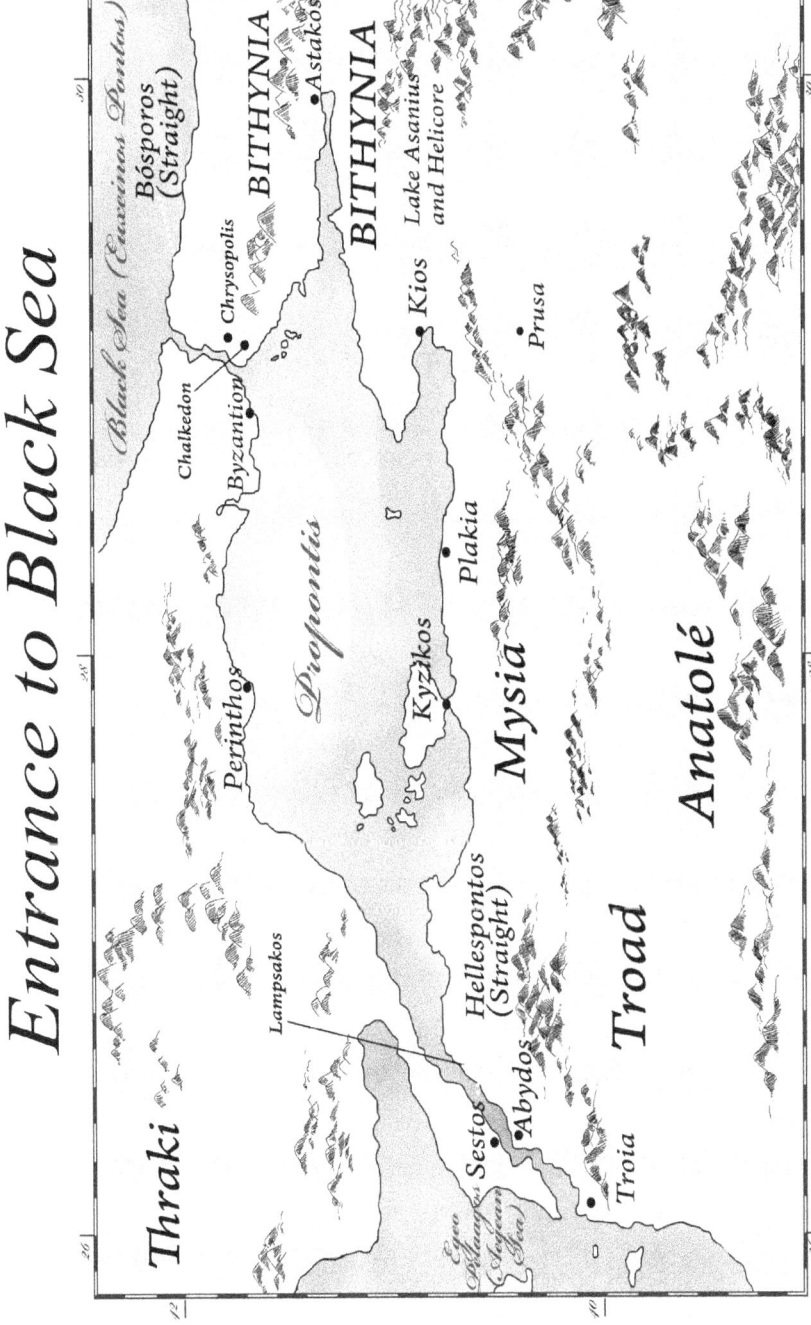

Entrance to Black Sea

Thraki

Black Sea (Euxeinos Pontus)

Bósporos (Straight)

BITHYNIA

Astakós

BITHYNIA

Chrysopolis

Kios

Lake Asanius and Helicore

Prusa

Chalkedon

Byzantion

Perinthos

Propontis

Plakia

Kyzikos

Mysia

Hellespontos (Straight)

Lampsakos

Sestos

Abydos

Troia

Troad

Anatolé

Egeo Pelagos (Aegean Sea)

"I can't help you. A lot of people disappeared in the war. You're not going to make a claim on our house, are you? We aren't going to move. The Lord Parmenion said that anyone living in these empty houses could stay. "

"I don't want your house," Pandora said through her tears. "I just want my family."

"I can't help you, I'm sorry."

The lady shut the door.

Pandora sat down on the step and Jess sat next to her.

"I don't know what to do." The tears began to run down her cheeks.

A door across the street opened and an old lady shuffled out to squint at them near sightedly.

"Pandora? Is that you?"

"Oh, Myrrine," Pandora leapt up and brushed at her clothes. She rushed over to hug the old woman. "Jess, this was one of our neighbours. This is Myrrine."

"I thought you were all dead," the old lady said. "Come inside. Let me offer you some tea."

They went inside. It was a shabby one bedroom house, empty of most furniture. They had to sit on the floor. She had had to sell her possessions, Jess realised.

"I wish I had some cake to offer you but it has not been an easy time for us old ones, with the war and all," Myrrine said as she sat them down. "I'm better off than most, I have a niece so I don't have to beg on the streets, but she has her own family. What happened to you? You disappeared, all of you, five years ago when the Makedónes first came."

Pandora sighed. "The enemy had breached the walls. They were burning the town and killing people. You remember we had lost a brother and a baby sister to the fever. There was just my younger sister Ambrosia who was twelve and I was fifteen. My mother and father hid us under some rubble and wood. They said she would come back for us but they never did.

"I said to my sister to stay there while I went searching for some food and water. One of the soldiers caught me. I was frantic to get back to my sister but he was very strong and kept hitting me until I stopped struggling. Then he tied me up. I became a captive and then a slave; I never saw my sister again."

"There were lots of stories like that." Myrrine's voice became harsh. "The Makedónes punished us for resisting."

"What happened to your son, your daughter-in-law and your grandchildren?"

Myrrine wordlessly shook her head.

They said nothing for a while.

A cat poked its nose through the open door and meowed.

"It's not my cat," Myrrine said. "But I feed it sometimes. Just don't let my niece know I go without to feed a cat."

They didn't stay long. There was little left to say. They left some money, it was the least they could do.

They stayed at Astakos three full days, camping just outside the city walls; searching the city for news of a missing girl named Ambrosia who was twelve at the time of the war.

It was fruitless and disheartening. All the stories they heard about others caught up in the war only made them feel worse. So many people died and had gone missing. Pandora was very morose as they rode back to the Troad.

"I guess I knew my parents were dead or they would have come back for us. I just couldn't bring myself to believe it. All those years as a slave, I kept getting the same dream. I would be outside my home with my sister. She would be twelve and I would be fifteen again somehow. I would knock and my parents would push the door open wide for us. They would be standing there waiting and smiling and holding their arms out. They would be so pleased to see us.

"Jess, why is it so great to kill people? Why is war is so glorious?"

* * *

They needed some time together, just to stop for a while.

At Abydos Jess found a room available for short term rent. It was owned by a middle aged widow, Agathe, and she was prepared to cook and wash and repair their clothes.

It was in a house on the hill side. They had a view of the harbour and the promise of an evening breeze. It was very comfortable inside and had its own private entrance through a garden shaded by olive and cypress trees. The house itself had a tiled bath room.

It was free for six nights and Jess booked it for the whole time. It wasn't cheap, so Jess didn't tell Pandora how much. For once she didn't even ask.

So they just relaxed, walking down into the town to do a little shopping, watch the fishing boats and have a swim together, or a drink and a snack or taking time to explore the nearby hills. Of an evening they would eat home cooking with lots of delicious sea food before retiring to make love.

After their first love making, Jess wrapped a light wrap around her nakedness and moved to the window to watch the tiny lights of the squid fishermen in the water. "Dora?"

Pandora lay back, drowsing on the bed. "Mmm."

"There is someone I would like to see here."

"Jess," Pandora gave a yawn. "You know you can't contact anyone from your past. It is you that wanted to keep your identity secret."

"I wasn't going to meet with him." She coughed with embarrassment. "I just wanted to see him."

Pandora sat up slowly. "You mean you want to spy on a *man*, without him knowing who you are?"

Jacinta nodded in the darkness. "From a distance, like."

"Jess, is this an old boyfriend?"

If Jacinta could have blushed, she would have.

"He's just a friend. He was an *Anthypolochagos* (junior lieutenant). It over a couple of years ago now, almost three, since I last saw him; longer for me of course. Still, he's probably forgotten about me by now."

"I doubt that." Pandora leaned forward with a wide grin. "Jess! You must tell me everything! Have you slept with him? Did you love him?"

"Yes, I did love him, once. No, I didn't sleep with him."

"But you wanted to."

Jess sighed. "Pandora, I wasn't joking about being a virgin before I met you and you know it's you I love. But I like men too, and Akhilleus was my first true love. He said he would wait for me, though of course they all say things like that."

Pandora laughed. "Jess, of course we have to see him. I have to see what he looks like."

The very next day, they went to the barracks to enquire about Anthypolochagos Akhilleus Kleiniou. Pandora seemed to find it hilarious that Jess was just so nervous.

"I'm sorry, *Kyra* (Lady)," the duty sergeant apologised. "He is in Kyzikos but he should return in a few weeks. Should I say you were looking for him?"

"Oh, he wouldn't know us," Jess said. "Kyra Pandora here is a distant relative." Pandora favoured the man with a smile. "It was suggested we look him up when we were in Abydos."

"Disappointed?" Pandora asked as they walked away.

"Yes, more than I expected I would be." Jess sighed.

"I have an idea." Pandora tugged at her arm. "A swim; then some *dakos*, you know barley rusk topped with chopped tomatoes, feta, goat's cheese, olives and all those wonderful Greek herbs. I saw a shop selling it. Then we can go back to our room."

"What will we do when we get there?"

"We'll think of something."

"That's three ideas, Pandora. You said you had an idea."

"Two ideas, I hadn't thought about what we might do when we got back to our room."

That got a laugh and a kiss. "You're a liar, Pandora!"

* * *

It was their last night in Abydos. They had fallen asleep in each other's arms.

Something woke Pandora. The candle had burnt out, the moon had risen but it only cast a faint glow, hardly penetrating into the room. Jess was lying beside her but Jess didn't sleep much, she would probably be awake.

"Jess, can you tell me about the Deepest?"

Jacinta turned in the dark. "It was the last and most powerful of the three dwarf cities. I think by that time it was Æloðulf alone who attacked it. They say it took a long time to fall. They were so strong they shouldn't have had anything to fear. He didn't use daimôns that time. I don't even know what he used, but whatever it was is still down there somewhere."

Pandora trembled in her arms.

"Do you still want to go with me?" Jess whispered.

"I want to go with you, yes. I just don't want to go *there*."

Jess kissed her on the lips. "My brave Dora, after all you have been through, you would do that for me."

"Your time in the daimôn realm has gotten you ready for what you have to face," Dora said, thinking. "Did you love him?"

"What?" Jacinta sat up in bed.

"Ba'al, who else would I be talking about? Were you in love with him?"

All Pandora could see was the shape of Jess in the darkness.

"Yes, I was in love with Ba'al. Ba'al and I were, we still are, as close as two daimôns can ever possibly be."

"Jess, were you his wife?"

"Pandora!" Jess made an exasperated sound. "Male and female doesn't mean the same thing to daimôns. There are very few female daimôns."

"Then how do daimôns do, er, you know?"

"It is considered very poor form to talk about." Jess said stiffly.

"Jess, you must be joking with me!" Pandora snorted, sitting up. "Did you ever have sex with Ba'al or not? Or whatever it is you daimôns do?"

"Mix essences," Jess said coldly. "You girl, are obsessed. And the answer is yes. It happened when he carried me inside him. We loved each other and we couldn't have stopped it happening even if we wanted to. Dora, I don't ask you about any of your previous lovers. I don't see why you need to know about mine."

"Me and another woman or even a man, that's hardly the same thing as with a daimôn!"

"Pandora, I am part daimôn. I am permanently bonded to Ba'al, in a way you could not understand. We fought a war together. It is something, he is something, I will never regret or forget. But he cannot return to live in this realm for hundreds of years and I can't return to the daimôn realm. If I do I stand to lose every part of me that is human."

* * *

The great bronze statue of 'Anāt, virgin daughter of Ēl, the great father God of the Semitic people, sat on an elaborate marble throne.

She was very slender and wearing a kalasiris (an Aígyptios sheath dress) held by two shoulder straps and stretching from just above her breasts down to her ankles, on her head was an Aígyptios crown. In her right hand, over her head, she held a great mace. In her left hand she held a spear and shield which she rested on the floor.

Keresaspa wondered, not for the first time, how she was expected to fight looking like that, but of course she was a Goddess or more correctly, this was just a statue of her. She was the Assyrian War Goddess but the statue was from Aígyptos and the Aígyptoi were very stylized with their art. A sheath dress was their sign of feminine nobility.

Keresaspa touched his head to the floor before HER image. Then he walked back to where Menna, the high priest, waited for him. He was seated behind a marble table and motioned for Keresaspa to sit. "Our Goddess has a task for you."

The air was heavy with incense. Menna sprinkled some seeds onto coals in a tiny brazier on the table. It gave off a cloyingly sweet smelling smoke, thick and greyish-white. Menna leaned forward to inhale and motioned for Keresaspa to do the same. Menna showed no reaction but Keresaspa's head began to spin, his mouth went dry, his eyelids felt heavy, and a strange echo seemed to fill the room.

"Blessed is our lady of war," Menna intoned. "You must go to the village of Qori. I will give you directions. Find a Hindu lady there known as Rohana and bring her here to me."

Keresaspa's heart filled with joy and love for his Goddess.

"It shall be as you wish, Holy One." He bowed deeply.

Menna knew that to destroy this changeling sorceress he would have to lure her into a specially prepared room.

And it was ready now.

* * *

They stopped in the afternoon to camp by the Strymōn River in the Troad. Tomorrow they would be back at the fortress: Pandora would enter the dormitory for novices and their time together would become limited.

"Jess, when will you leave for Āzar Pāyegān?" Pandora asked.

"I need to visit Daniel and Sophie at Elgard and learn as much about magic as I can," Jacinta said. "I expect it to take quite some time and I'm not going to hurry it. I'm not going to Āzar Pāyegān until I am truly ready."

* * *

Iraj had gone to a nearby village to buy breeding stock and would be gone two nights. He was starting to build his flock. Our flock, Rohana smiled at the thought. She was going to be the wife of a shepherd, albeit a modestly wealthy one.

She had slept most of her life alone, and now she found it hard to sleep without her man! The warmth of his body, his gentle strength wrapped around her, the soft sounds of his breathing. In the day she ached for his smile, his touch, the wonderful way he kissed.

They had been married six weeks. If this is what marriage was doing to her, what would it be like in thirty years?

She lay with the waning light of the moon coming faint through her window and thought about the ceremony: the tying of the knot, the egg and water to capture any evil and the fire to symbolise the hearth fire; the rice they threw at each other for good fortune (now that was fun) and the blessings, the prayers and the songs.

She was definitely showing the bump of her pregnancy now and her new family were delighted. She hoped it would be a boy; she would like to have a boy for Iraj.

She was loved here, not just by her wonderful husband. His whole family had been so welcoming. It was nothing like the family she had been born into. She hadn't really felt loved since her father had died. Her mother could not bring herself to love a heart cripple.

It made her think of Jess and Pandora. Had they reached the Troad? Had Jess found out the answers she had sought? Had Pandora found her family?

A stealthy figure passed outside her window. And then another.

Rohana slipped her feet out of the bed. She gathered herself to run and yell and wake the house when a scream split the night.

Chapter 21: 'Anāt

Iraj finally fell into an exhausted sleep.

In the small hours he tossed and turned, his body soaked in sweat. In his dreams he screamed out. "My parents! Rohana!"

"Iraj?"

"Jess! Is that you? Am I dreaming?"

"Yes you are, but you have reached me. Tell me what happened."

"I went to buy sheep. While I was gone raiders came in great numbers but they only attacked our house. They killed my parents and our man-servants. They took the rest of my household: my younger brother Peshana, my sister Asabanâ, my sister Mehrak and her husband Usmanara, their children, two women servants ... and they took Rohana. I think they are from Arys, it is two days hard riding from here. They have turned to raiding and slaving. No one from here will go with me.

"Jess they tortured her. They cut off Rohana's finger and left it with the ring I gave her still on it. Playing her veena is her life."

"Iraj, slavers wouldn't do that."

"Who would do such a horrible thing then?"

"Who would capture innocents and torture people? I think your slavers have a new religion."

"Aēšma's blood priests?" Iraj moaned in agony.

For Jess, it felt like her heart had stopped. Rohana, her dear beautiful, gentle Rohana captured by blood priests!

"Iraj, this is a trap designed for me. They must know you are my friends."

"Where are you? What are we going to do?"

"I am in the Troad but I have a way of travelling fast. I will come and spring this little trap that they have set for me."

"We can't go against them just the two of us."

"Not all at once, no," Jess said. "I may not be able to reach you through dreams again. Don't do anything until I get there."

Jess threw her blanket off and walked to the window to look out. It was almost dawn. She sat down to pack.

She dressed as an elf scout. She looked at the chain mail armour in agony of indecision. It was elvish design, light and strong but dull bluish in colour, good for stealth, but would she be doing a lot of sneaking around in human form or would it be in daimôn form? She had better take it. Seléne had only recently sent it to her.

She checked her weapons for the umpteenth time, even the concealed knives in her boots and the throwing axes. Then she felt for the key hanging from her neck.

She couldn't put it off any longer. Time to say goodbye to the others! She cautiously poked her face out of her door.

"You took your time coming out!" Pandora said.

Jess almost jumped ten feet in the air with a guilty start.

Pandora was sitting, dressed for travelling. Her booted feet were kicked up on a stool.

"Where under the sun do you think you are sneaking off to, daughter?" Kynane was sitting next to her, dressed for war.

Hakeem wandered in from the next room to join them. Several Amazónes followed. Jess recognised Alba, Eirene and Anastasia. Everyone was dressed for war.

"Sophie!" Jess slapped her head in realisation.

"She said you were shouting in her head," Hakeem confirmed. "How many of us can fit in that room of yours?"

"With horses, weapons and armour, a score," Jess said. "That is if we keep other gear to a minimum, but the trip is almost instantaneous."

"A score of our best women and you and me," Hakeem decided. "You didn't think you were going all by yourself, did you?"

"Not at all," Jess said. Her eyes blurred with tears.

"I didn't think that for a minute."

* * *

The bodies of Iraj's parents and their four workers were sponged with Gomez, the sacred disinfectant made from consecrated bull's urine. They were placed on clean linen sheets so people could come and pay their respects. A small fire of wood soaked in frankincense burned in the corner and a dog was brought in twice a day to frighten the daēva of corruption away.

The elements: earth, water and fire are sacred, so dead bodies (which carry corruption) cannot be burnt or buried. On the second day they were conveyed to the *dakhma* (Tower of Silence) which lies open to the sky so the birds of the air can pick the bones clean.

Iraj and his cousins said prayers for three days, the time that the *urvan* (soul) remained on earth. On the fourth day, the souls of their loved ones ascend to *Chinvat* (Bridge of Judgment).

If they had been wicked, the bridge would appear narrow and the daēva Vizaresh will emerge and drag their soul into the druj-demana (Hell, the House of Lies). If a person's good thoughts, words and deeds in life were many, the bridge would be wide and the deana spirit (angel) would appear and lead their souls joyfully to ascend to the House of Song and into the presence of their God.

Iraj's parents had not been wicked. His mother had been a saint and his father would never hurt anyone.

Iraj ached from silent crying. Not everyone came, mainly cousins and the closest of friends. Many from the village were too ashamed ... and too afraid. The house had been targeted by the blood priests. Maybe if they visited they might become a target too.

On the morning of the sixth day, a heavily armed party rode through the village on the path leading to Iraj's house. There were twenty-two of them in all. Their leader was a large powerful-looking man dressed in flowing robes of an Aramaic tribesman. The rest were female warriors, dressed as elf scouts, wearing leather armour and looking very grim. Each of them, barring only one, was wearing a glove on their left hand. They were the famous Amazónes of Troia.

The people were amazed. No one here had ever seen any of the Greek Amazónes. They lived half way across the known world. Then they remembered, it was said that Iraj had worked for a powerful sorceress. That large black woman riding amongst them! Was that her?

It was said that she had fought blood priests before. Had she come to help them fight the evil that had come to their land? Had she brought warriors from the other end of the world in only a matter of days?

It would not be enough, but one look at these women showed they were proper warriors. And who knew what else the mysterious black woman could do. Many of the villagers remembered their courage then. They began to call to their neighbours to go to Iraj and offer their support.

All the family and visitors from the house crowded outside to wait for the arrival of these strange visitors and many people came running from the village to be there when they arrived.

Hakeem led his small war band to the gates of Iraj's parents' house. He stopped and leaned forward in his saddle to survey those present.

"My name is Hakeem. I am the Warlord of the Shantawi. These are the Amazónes and their leader Kynane. More fighters are on the way. We have come to share your loss and give you our pledge: we will stay here until we have stopped this evil once and for all and returned your loved ones to you."

* * *

There were too many for the house so they had to meet in the enclosed garden. Most of the women looked relaxed, talking quietly amongst themselves, but they rarely smiled and their hands never strayed far from their weapons.

Jess, Thaïs and Eirene had set up a small fireplace in the corner and were making tea and breakfast for everyone. Hakeem and Kynane were conferring with Iraj, his cousins and some men from the village. Hakeem could speak Sogdianē so he translated for Kynane. There was a steady trickle of men offering their help.

First up, Hakeem had some bad news for Iraj.

"We will be getting more people as soon as we can. But until such time we can't carry out a frontal attack on their fortress. I'm sorry, but that is how it is."

"They have cut the finger off my wife's hand!" Iraj reminded him.

Jacinta averted her eyes. Her heart burned at the thought of leaving her gentle friend in the hands of those monsters. She could only guess what it must be like for Iraj.

"This is a trap," Hakeem said heavily. "A score and however many you can take from the village will not be enough against two hundred inside the walls of a fortress. A failed attempt would be lives given for nothing. It would only lessen our strength and cause the captors to go even harder on their prisoners. The prisoners will be safer if we don't attack until we can win. Despite the torment in your heart, if you wish to ride with me, you will obey my orders just like everyone else."

Iraj looked at the big tribesman who stared back at him, unblinking. Eventually Iraj nodded. "You have the right of it, I know, and yet my heart is on fire."

Pandora moved across to put her arms around his shoulders like a sister. He took her hand and kissed it.

Hakeem softened. "We cannot rescue the prisoners yet, but we haven't come all this way just to sit around. Jess!" he called to his daughter. "You are in contact with Sophie, what else is happening?"

Jess scooped up soft cheese made from ewe's milk onto a large piece of fresh unleavened bread and knelt to offer it to Hakeem.

"Sophie has my key." Jess didn't say which key. "They have set up two camps of senior novices; one in the Troad and one six days journey from here. There are five more Amazónes and three elves on the way but unfortunately that is all the seniors we have and the guard on elvish Troia is not large enough for them to spare any more elves. We have sent messages to Abydos and Troia. Shame we can't bring men from Elgard or Karsh."

"Abydos? Troia? Elgard? Karsh?" Kishpi, the head man of the village, was incredulous. "Are you really the Lord Hakeem come to help us? But this will take months."

"It will be two weeks, not much more. As Iraj reminded us, we do not have time to waste," Hakeem said. "Iraj and Rohana have powerful friends, ones they didn't know they had. We don't want to draw the attention of the Hun but we *will* take this fortress and we *will* end this threat; that we can promise you."

Then Hakeem gave them his second piece of bad news.

"With a score of warriors we cannot protect all the points which the enemy can strike. Many of you have herds, this is dry country and there are many scattered settlements and small villages. Our enemy has the man-power and freedom of movement. If I stayed here, they will simply attack elsewhere.

"All I can do is to try to limit their freedom of movement and to do that I plan to attack their scouts, any smaller patrols and raiding parties. The sooner I do that the better, but I can't prevent another attack here in force. In fact it is likely once we start to give them trouble, and it will be before more reinforcements arrive."

"So, for a time, we are on our own," Kishpi said. "We have three dozen fighters, only one in three are seasoned. We have relatives amongst the nomads, but it would take time before they can come."

"If you are attacked, I will try to get back in time to help, but I cannot guarantee it."

"Should we bring some senior novices?" Jess asked.

"No," Kynane shook her head firmly. "We have brought Pandora. I will not put any other novices in danger."

Hakeem glanced at Kynane and slowly nodded, then he turned back to Kishpi. "I suggest you send anyone who can't fight to Parap, until this is over. Abandon the lower and outlying houses and fortify and provision the upper ones as best you can."

"But these are our homes!" one of the men protested. "And I have to look after my sheep."

"Not if you are dead," Hakeem replied. "The greatest danger I believe will be in the next few weeks."

"We will send as many as will go to Parap," Kishpi decided. "Maybe some of the surrounding villages will send some men."

No one said anything; they wouldn't, they couldn't.

"I hear they have a powerful sorcerer," one said.

"Leave him to me," Jess said.

Hakeem looked at her. "Jess, they wouldn't be doing this if they didn't believe they could fight you."

"Leave him to me," she repeated quietly. "They can fight me, yes, but can they win? We will have to see."

"Pandora, you will join the defenders of the village."

"But I want to go with you!" Pandora protested.

Hakeem stared at her in stony silence.

"Remember your place," Kynane reminded her.

Jess looked embarrassed.

"But I swore an oath to Rohana. She is my blood-sister," Pandora said softly.

"Kyrie," Jess said quickly before Hakeem could reply. "May I have your permission to explain?"

Hakeem hesitated and then nodded.

"Pandora, this is not about how any of us 'feel'. It is a military matter. Hakeem is the best I know at this sort of thing. He is in charge, no argument and no debate. If you want to comment on his decisions, you must ask his permission first. If you can't follow orders, you can't be one of us."

Pandora went pale and tears came to her eyes.

"I'm sorry. P-please forgive me."

"Apology accepted," Hakeem said gently. "Pandora, you are an infantry archer. From what Jess tells me, you are a good one but you don't know about fighting in the open or on a horse's back or how to kill by stealth. Allow me to place you where you are of greatest use to me, and that is here."

"Yes, sir. Thank you, sir." Pandora bowed her head. "I won't disappoint you, sir."

"Pandora, I fear for all I am leaving here. I really do. May our God watch over you."

Then he turned back to the rest of his plans.

* * *

Pandora stood, watching as her friends rode out of sight.

She twisted a lock of her hair over and over and chewed at it.

"Hello," a small boy's voice called from beside her. "You must be Pandora Khánum. Why aren't you riding out with the rest of them? Are you any good with that bow you are carrying?"

Pandora grinned down at the small boy, maybe seven.

"I am Pandora, as you have guessed. I can use the bow well enough but haven't been trained to fight on horseback or a dozen other things that will take me years to learn. Is there anything you *don't* want to know?"

"They call me Adharsh because I am always asking questions."

"Well Adharsh, perhaps you can help me find Kishpi, your head man, unless you have work to do."

"I have jobs, but my mother won't complain if I am showing you around."

Adharsh kept up a constant running commentary as he showed her his village. It was a pleasant village. The main settlement was centred on one hill with a small spring at its base. Even in the drought the spring had not dried up. There were palm trees giving shade to the crops. There was a number of goats, fat tailed sheep (sheep that stored their fat in their rear, away from their bodies for the summer heat) and of course, chickens.

A lot of the irrigation was by simple muscle power but the people of the village worked hard and they were proud of what they had achieved.

As always the houses had been built above and away from the precious irrigated land. The lowest houses on the hill were the oldest part of the village. They were poorer, crowded together and made of simple mud brick and palm thatch. A few were derelict.

Those who could afford larger houses were forced to build on vacant land higher up the hill or (like Iraj's grandfather) a little way out from the older, main part of the village. That had cost Iraj's parents and their servants their lives.

The highest houses stood along a terrace overlooking the main road winding up from below. They were two-story, the flat roofs were sun dried earth supported underneath by wooden frames. The roofs had low walls around them that could serve as make-shift parapets.

The men were busy blocking windows and doorways, erecting obstacles and barricades on the road, filling sand bags, gathering rocks and stones for throwing and for slings, assembling ladders and storing supplies of food and water.

It was easy to find Kishpi, he was up at the top. He directed her to look around the village and then stay with those women that had remained.

There were four families that had remained and they would share the final house on the terrace. They were the ones who could not afford to leave. They had no servants or donkeys so the women collected their water in pots balanced on their heads and trudged all the way up the hill. They tended their chickens, watered their crops, milked their goats and spun their wool. They sewed and cooked and did a hundred and one jobs as well as look after their men at night in all the usual and varied ways that men and custom demanded. Life, for poor women of the village, went on much as before.

Pandora was the only woman who was armed, beyond those with belt knives. She did her best to help and tried to be an unofficial guard; taking her gorytos slung over her shoulder wherever she went.

One of her tasks was helping Adharsh with his family's poultry. Adharsh's mother, Fedrî, had four red hens, descendants from her wedding dowry. Her husband had recently bought a young rooster from a nearby village hoping they could breed chickens.

The new rooster was certainly a fine specimen. He stood tall and proud, with sleek red feathers over his wings and dark blue-black shiny feathers over his tail, his chest and his underneath.

He had cost a lot of money, for a rooster.

And he was certainly convinced of his own magnificence. He loved to crow, flap his wings and puff up his chest just to show how important he was. He also thought his four new hens were especially lucky to have such a handsome rooster in charge of them. So Fedrî had called him 'Siramarg' (Peacock).

In truth Peacock was very attentive to his hens. Apart from his obvious duties as their rooster he was constantly scratching around industriously, searching for the tastiest morsels for them and making clucking noises to call them over.

Adharsh's family had lived in the outer part of the village so they had to move Peacock and his small feathered harem to a shed on the upper hill; this was achieved by locking them in their new home for two days. After that, they knew to return there at night to roost. In any case, they always came when called, it meant a handful of wheat or even two.

It was quite a nice new home for them: dry and airy with nice laying boxes, filtered light and plenty of fresh straw. There were even several benches for roosting.

When Pandora arrived, it was time to let them out. Moving them was going to prove the easy part.

The first problem was caused from a rival flock of three hens led by the older rooster Zumrud (Emerald). When Peacock saw the other flock he saw it as intruding into his new territory. It didn't seem to occur to him that this was really Emerald's territory.

Peacock crowed loudly at his rival, flaring his hackle feathers and lowering his head threateningly. Emerald wasn't at all impressed. He just flared his neck feathers, flapped his wings and crowed right back.

They began to edge cautiously around each other. This was followed by mutual wing flapping, heads held high, chests puffed out and then a half circle dance.

Soon they were flying at one another, jumping over the top, pecking and slashing with their spurs. Feathers were raining down everywhere. Adharsh and Pandora had to race to intervene.

"Just like a real cock fight!" Adharsh laughed.

"Yes, but your mother and the others will kill us if one of these birds gets hurt," Pandora said.

The war between Emerald and Peacock settled into a series of regular skirmishes which kept Adharsh and Pandora constantly on edge. On the second day Pandora chased Peacock away from his bird wars, thinking murderous thoughts but as she trudged back up the hill, she heard him calling to his hens delightedly. She spun around to see what he was doing.

Oh no! She had accidentally chased him into someone's vegetable patch.

The lookout put his ram's horn to his lips. Hakeem and ten of their women riders were returning to the village early.

Something was wrong.

Pandora left Adharsh to look after Peacock and his hens, lifted her gorytos and scurried up a ladder to a nearby roof. She strained her eyes but it was only a blur in the distance. One of the three elves, part of the recent arrivals, appeared next to her.

"They are leading one of the horses," he said, peering at the distance.

Without any conscious thought she jumped and slid and started running, scratching her arms and legs climbing over the obstructions, raising a dust cloud in her hurry till she finally waited, heart pounding and breathless, at the base of the hill.

Please, don't let it be Jess!

One of the riders saw her waiting and kicked her horse towards her. Jess threw herself off and ran to her. Pandora flung herself at Jess, hugging and kissing her fiercely, her tears wetting her shirt.

"I saw the horse. I was so afraid." Pandora kissed her again.

Jess broke away to stare at the slender body tied over the horse.

"We came against them sooner than we expected; a group of over thirty, none had armour. We had total surprise, they were completely outclassed and we were cutting them down quickly but some of them fought back. It was my fault; I just couldn't get to her in time."

"It was *my* fault, daughter," Kynane dismounted and spat noisily onto the ground. "If only I taught her better."

"Both of you!" Hakeem shouted angrily. "I will hear none of your nonsense. It was no one's fault, not even Alba's."

"Alba?" Pandora remembered the young woman who seemed to be so full of life.

"Alba," Jess whispered, tears in her eyes.

They watched as the others gently lifted the body down.

"She has a sister, Meliboea. They were the first to join me. Now she is the first to die. Her sister will never see her again."

For Hakeem's party, there was no time to grieve. He picked up the extra fighters, the last for a while, and some supplies, and turned back.

Alba was a *juddin* (a non-believer) but she had given her life to help the people of Qori and they would honour her with a Mazdayasna funeral. Pandora was left to stand in as the only representative of Alba's family and friends.

* * *

Menna's initiates watched wordlessly as the head man of the village stormed past them.

Menna thought what a shame it was that the head man was Utana and not Keresaspa. That gave him an idea which brought a smile to his lips, but it would have to wait.

"The raiding party that has not returned, have you found them?" Utana demanded.

"No, we haven't, but it is you that have lost them, not us."

Menna tried to sound disdainful and not show his fear. He didn't want to frighten Utana any more than the man was already frightened.

The response of their enemy had been terrifying. She was hidden from his far sight but he knew that she passed into Mesopotamia heading west a couple of months ago. She should have been very far to the west. Within a week of the raid, a dark cloud passed over Qori, heading their way. It was impossible that she could travel so fast, and yet she had.

Thirty men all at once was well beyond the power of a changeling. If she had used arcane power, he would have heard and felt it from here. So it left one terrifying possibility. She had the power to bring enough helpers to handle thirty men!

Menna knew he couldn't find the missing thirty men because they were already dead.

"I thought you were confident of handling her."

"I still am, and you must also have faith in our Goddess. As I said to you before, if I can get her to attack us here, we will have her. You are our leader, think for a change! If she attacked your raiding party, that means she is not alone. She has enough helpers that she can attack thirty men, but she doesn't have enough to attack the fortress.

"We have one of her friends here and there is another in the village of Qori. What we need is a large attack on that village, hit and run. Kill as many people as you can and do as much damage as you can and then leave quickly before she can return with whatever force she has.

"After that she will come here."

Menna passed him a small parcel wrapped in a bloody cloth. Utana looked at it with distaste. "Once our men have returned from the village, we will be ready for her."

Menna knew that a confrontation with this sorceress had always been inevitable. If he had it on his terms he still expected to win. But the speed and power of her response had him wondering. Had he underestimated her power?

He would soon find out.

* * *

Hakeem expected them to send scouts searching for the missing party. He wanted to be back in time for that. After midday the next day their lookout's bronze signal mirror blinked: six short flashes. It meant six men.

Hakeem was not in the habit of giving his enemies any chance he didn't need to. The enemy scouts would find out they were riding into a trap when the arrows were already flying in the air.

* * *

Emet, the leader of the scouts out of Arys, signalled for his small group to stop. In the near distance, by the road, they could see a man's body, lying face down, facing in the direction of the fortress of Arys. It looked like one of their own. Maybe he had died on his way back to bring them news.

He scanned the surrounds. The ground was uneven: gullies, boulders and hillocks. It seemed empty but it was a good place for an ambush.

The worship of 'Anāt, the Assyrian Goddess of War, had made Arys strong. They could raid at will. They always won and their casualties were always light. Now one of their raiding parties had failed to return. Nothing like that had ever happened before.

Emet led his men, walking their horses, slowly closer to the body on the ground. They had arrows nocked, scanning their surrounds. He nodded for two of his men to check the body while he waited on his horse, on guard, with the other three men.

The two men lay their bows down and awkwardly turned the body over, trying to touch it as little as possible. They were no longer Mazdayasna but the old taboos remained.

"He's one of ours; dead a couple of days."

Emet instinctively nudged his horse forward to look at the dead man's face and see what wounds he might have. Every eye for a moment was on the dead man. No one saw eight women stand up behind Emet, well spread out to choose targets. A soft woman's voice called, "Now."

The two men had been feeling more than a little sickened by the state of the dead body. They couldn't see the women hidden by their friends' horses. As their friends began screaming and falling, they stared for an instant, frozen. A riderless horse spooked and galloped away. Then they leapt for their bows. As one of the men straightened, fitting an arrow, and peering through the chaos of milling horses, he got hit from another group who had stepped out of cover off to one side.

"Put down your weapon."

The last man stood up, looking very pale. He dropped his bow and held his hands above his head.

"You are going to tell us all you know."

* * *

Eirene finally finished the charcoal sketch on papyrus to her satisfaction and used a mouth atomizer to give it a fine coating of shellac dissolved in pure brandy spirit. She held it up to their captive as it dried in the air.

"That's just right," Gaomant, their captive, said, admiring her work.

It was a detailed drawing of the fort with barracks, headquarters, slave quarters, the new temple of the blood priests, stables, warehouses, kitchens and individual housing.

He looked tired. There had been a lot of questions. Chara, one of the smaller girls, was just behind him, seemingly looking over his shoulder.

"You have been very cooperative," Kynane said with a smile and gave an imperceptible nod to Chara.

Gaomant smiled back a little uncertainly. He didn't expect to be attacked by a girl Chara's size. The first he realised it was when he felt her grab his collar to jerk him back, off balance.

He screamed in agony as she stabbed him in the right kidney, making him arch his back. She used his falling weight to drive the knife in deep, supporting her arm with her hip and thigh. He continued to fall, twisting away from the pain of the knife. Chara used her thigh and body to take some of his weight. She snatched her knife out as she nudged his body further to the left.

With superb power, speed and control she grabbed his jaw with her left hand in a firm grip, exposing his throat and used his falling weight to give her depth and penetration as she sliced her knife across his throat.

Then she shoved the body clear. It was done in seconds. He made a gurgling choking sound, clutching at his throat as his body continued to thrash in the dirt.

"Chara, that was very neat." Kynane gave her a delighted smile. "It was perfect!"

A few of the veterans murmured their approval.

Chara looked more than a little sick.

"Jess! You always use brute force, you should learn from Chara. Use a sudden severe pain; the shock of it paralyses your enemy for a few seconds. They are frozen in pain so they won't resist you. Then use their own weight to give force to your attack. Do it quickly and —"

All the colour had drained from Chara's face. Jess dove for the girl as her eyes rolled up in her head and she crumpled. She managed to awkwardly grab her one handed and Chara fell against her to vomit noisily over Jess's boots.

"— and humanely," Kynane finished.

Jess only barely managed to grab Chara with her other hand, by the back of her armour, so she could stop the girl from falling face down in the dust and her own vomit. Chara hung limply and then her body convulsed as she vomited over Jess's trouser leg.

"Help me get her down and get her feet up," she called to Eirene.

They carried her to some softer ground and rested her feet on Eirene's pack while some of the other girls used their bodies to provide shade.

"I'm sorry." Chara's eyes fluttered open, her face chalky.

Jess had dampened a cloth and squatted to wipe the vomit from the girl's mouth and hair. As Chara recovered, she got her to sit up and blow snot out of her nose and drink some water.

"Ohh," she moaned and gave a cough. "I have just managed to make a fool of myself in front of every single person in this world that I admire."

"It's easy enough to say we won't take prisoners," Jess said, rubbing her back. "But the first time killing with a knife is horrible. You didn't hesitate and you didn't make him suffer; that is the main thing. It hit you afterwards. After the pirates I ended up in bed for a day and a half."

"I know you are Jacinta. It's just that I never thought of you as being like that." Chara grinned. "Your fight with the pirates is rather famous you know."

Jess smiled back. "Well, let me tell you I was absolutely terrified the whole time."

She hadn't known Chara from before but she realised they could become good friends.

"I think we are getting some bad news," Jess murmured as she helped Chara up and gave her a quick hug and slap on the back. A single very long flash was being relayed from the lookout, repeated over and over.

A hundred fighters had left the fort.

All they could do now was hide, until they knew where they were going. If the enemy was making for the village of Qori, there was little they could do to stop a hundred riders. Even tracking them was going to prove dangerous. In a few turns of the glass it would be dark.

* * *

Pandora climbed to the roof like she did every morning to look out. Adharsh joined her. Adharsh's mother, Fedrî, had made them dumplings from *maza* (coarse barley flour) with honey, cheese and olives. It was delicious, reminding Pandora of one of the dishes of her childhood.

A family of nomads was herding their sheep far out from the village, dirty white and black in the distance, the sound of dogs barking carried faintly on the breeze. There wasn't a cloud in the sky. It was going to be another hot day.

Being locked up didn't stop Peacock from crowing loudly, almost as if he was telling them to hurry up and open the door. No sooner had Adharsh let him out than he crowed several times more, flapping his wings, clucked to his hens and then ... launched himself into the air.

Pandora checked her gorytos and went running to help, but before she and Adharsh could grab any of them, most of the small flock was in flight, headed for the vegetable patch!

"I'm going to wring your neck and cut your wings!" Pandora yelled after him as she ran down the hill. She didn't know what she would do first.

While she charged down the hill after the airborne escapees, Adharsh was trying to herd the one remaining hen back up the hill. It was squawking indignantly and flapping its wings in a determined effort to dodge past him and join the others.

"Don't scare it, Adharsh," Pandora yelled over her shoulder as she careened down the hill, "It'll stop laying."

She ducked between two houses and almost ran into two foreign men crouched there. They were as surprised as she was, but it wouldn't be for long.

She clutched her Gorytos tightly and kept running, ducking into a doorway well below to string her bow and fit an arrow.

She saw them higher up, searching for her. They needed to stay quiet and keep out of sight of the lookout high above. She wanted to alert the lookout but it was most unlikely there were only two in hiding in the lower part of the village. If she yelled out now, she would get herself killed.

She just might forgive Peacock. He might have saved the village, but now she needed to find a way to give the alarm without getting killed. Maybe she could fire an arrow; that would do it.

Adharsh appeared, near the vegetable patch. When he saw one of the raiders, he began to scream. The two men tried to chase him. One ducked low to enter the garden and found a small red ball of angry feathers flying at his face. Pandora stepped from cover and fired at the other man. He staggered a few feet and then collapsed. The other man was trying unsuccessfully to catch the rooster when another flying rooster attacked him from another direction.

"You leave them alone!" Pandora cried savagely.

She sent an arrow at short range into his chest as the lookout began to blow his horn. Adharsh ran to Pandora and she smoothly shoved him behind her as she crouched. An arrow went whizzing by her ear.

The alarm was raised but they were trapped, cut off from the rest of the village, and the enemy was all around them.

* * *

The camp fires were cold and burnt out. Thaïs signalled to the nearby woman and they circled around, moving closer. Stealth wasn't needed, the campsite was deserted.

"They have moved to the village under the cover of darkness," Thaïs told her. "I think we had better hurry."

At a signal from his scouts, Hakeem led his small force at a fast trot to the village. As the hill came in sight they could hear the horn sounding over and over.

Jess swayed on her horse. "Pandora!" she gasped.

She turned to Hakeem. "Father, they got warning but are badly outnumbered. The enemy has too many bowmen against their slingers. They have captured the first roof and the villagers cannot hold out much longer. There are ten attackers on the first of the two-story roofs and seventy on the road. You should catch them in the rear if you hurry. Pandora's trapped and cut off near the bottom."

"Daughter, go to her, quickly," Hakeem said. "We will attack the rest."

Jess didn't hesitate. She kicked her horse to a gallop. She was almost there, riding hard when a voice in her mind screamed in terror, "Jess!"

"I am almost there, Pandora. Try to hole up somewhere."

"Jess, there are four of them."

"Pandora," she screamed as she kicked her horse for extra speed. "Just stay alive!"

A terrible pain cut through Jess's chest but she knew it was not her pain. She slowed her horse.

She was too late to save her friend.

* * *

A pall of nothingness was flying across his far sight.

"Get out of there," Menna screamed in Keresaspa's mind. "The sorceress is coming for you and I don't know what else is with her."

Keresaspa signalled urgently for everyone to leave. The men on the roof began to quickly climb down and some men went hurriedly to help their wounded. But some on the ground hadn't gotten the message or didn't understand why they needed to withdraw while they were winning. They milled around in confusion. Then they heard the sound of horses and shouted orders as the women dismounted.

"How many are there?" Keresaspa called out.

"It's only women," Janara, his second in command, called back, "and there's not too many of them."

The raiders were crowded on the roadway out of the way of the defenders above. Now their retreat was cut off, and before they could act they were hit by the first volley and it was almost immediately followed by the second. From the roof, slingers, a single archer and anyone who could throw rocks joined in.

The counter-attack from the roofs was ineffective, but the raiders were villagers and shepherds only. They had had some basic training with weapons but they did not know even elementary battle tactics and discipline: flanking, moving your vantage point to catch your enemy in crossfire, penetration of the centre, concentration of force, or anything about strong and weak points.

They scattered, looking for cover from a two sided attack, and another volley hit those that were too slow. They were unaccustomed to facing skilled and determined resistance. They fought as individuals while many of the women took to the roofs and fought as a team. And the raiders couldn't even approach the individual skill of the Amazónes.

They were caught. The screams of men in anger and terror carried through the village over the 'phtt' of bows releasing and the wooden clatter of arrows being drawn.

A dark figure scaled a vertical wall. She called up and then joined the village defenders on the roof, carrying several spare quivers with her; when they were empty she drew her sword and slid down, darting through the rubble searching for any enemy left alive.

* * *

Menna sat for a while in stunned contemplation. He had been able to look into Keresaspa's mind before he died.

Amazónes! It seemed impossible. The big man leading them could only be one person. He was perhaps the greatest warrior of an age. But why under all the Gods was he here? How had the sorceress summoned someone like him?

There seemed so few of the women and yet each fought like a lioness. He suspected few if any of their men would escape. He had not seen a changeling but there was a dark woman of extraordinary skill. That would be her.

Menna had been trained in the ancient magic of the Aígyptoi. He was a master of Heka, the magic that underlies all reality. It was more powerful than the Gods. He was up against something the like of which he had not faced before, but still he knew what he had to do.

He wouldn't tell Utana what had happened to his raiding party. It would make the man near hysterical. He already knew to prepare for an attack and that was all he needed to know; it just would be sooner than they had expected.

It was difficult having his far sight blocked but the enemy were few, they didn't have enough warriors to attack the fortress. Hakeem had to see that. Or if he didn't, he would be making a mistake. No, it left them only one choice, to send her in at night. They might lose some men, but once he had her inside his room he would kill her.

                                  * * *

Hakeem and Iraj had to walk past dead bodies and step over one to get through the doorway of the small hut near the base of the hill. There was another dead man in the room.

The boy that Pandora tried to save by covering him with her body lay face up in the corner. A fly feasted at the corner of his eye, another buzzed onto his lip to inspect his mouth. He had been opened up, his guts spilt on the floor, attracting more flies.

Jess had dragged Pandora's body up against the wall and was hugging it to her, soaked in blood not her own. Jess herself seemed to be asleep but her eyes opened as they entered.

"Isn't she beautiful?" She kissed her hair. "I always loved her hair, dark like coal and so soft and shiny."

Pandora was very pale. The wound had bled out before she died.

"I'm sorry, Jess," Iraj said softly.

Pandora's eyes were staring sightlessly. Jacinta seemed to only notice then. She closed them and kissed the lids.

"I loved so many things about her, but it was her laugh I loved the most. She will never laugh again." She looked up at Iraj. Her cheeks were tear-stained. "You know, I told her not to come with me. More than once I told her. I told her I would only get her killed. That is what I do. Rohana, Alba, Pandora, I get my friends hurt or killed. It is me they want, not Rohana, and they will have me."

"Jacinta, no." Hakeem breathed. "Fight this cursed madness that is within you."

"I'm sorry, Father, I love you. I will always love you. But when I came back from the daimôn realm, I was not the same. I had stayed too long." She looked straight at Hakeem, her eyes shone yellow in the shadow. Her mouth had widened and was filled with fangs, her speech was thickened. "I will go there, Father, it is my karma to do so. They will let me in because they want to trap me. But they cannot even imagine what I can do."

"Don't go there for revenge," Hakeem said.

"Revenge, no. But they must die now, because we have run out of time. They came for Pandora because she was my friend and they left this on her body."

She held up a small bloodied parcel.

Hakeem stared at it for several moments before he would take it. His face was unreadable. He held it gently and reverently before he passed it, unopened, to Iraj.

Iraj let out a moan of anguish as he took the small parcel and held it to his heart. Hot tears came to his eyes as he kissed it and slowly, tenderly, unwrapped it.

"I couldn't protect her from this." He whispered in horror.

It was another of Rohana's fingers, the one bearing the ring that Pandora had given her.

"We will all go," Hakeem said. His eyes looked dangerously cold. "We have hurt them badly enough now. We are protected, you and I from far sight but if they know anything about us they will be expecting an attempt at rescue, not a full assault, not yet. Let us give the men and women a little time to sleep, and eat. You and I need to ease their hurts."

"I will do it, Father. I know how to not make them tired."

"After that we will all go, all the Amazónes and all the fighters from the village." Hakeem said. "With their defeat here, we can gather more on the way."

"Dark is best," Jess said. "Father, give me the three elves. With them, I can get you all inside."

"You know this is what they want."

"And I will certainly not disappoint them."

"Jess, they may not fully know what you can do, but neither do you know what they can do, remember that. One thing you must agree on Jess, you too Iraj," Hakeem said grimly. "We destroy them first. Only when we are sure they are beaten do we search for family and friends."

Iraj nodded, he feared what else they might do to Rohana but this would be a fight they had to win.

"I can find your loved ones, Iraj. As soon as I can, I will search them out," Jess said.

Hakeem stared at her in silence. *What has my daughter become?*

* * *

Dinsha tried to stifle a yawn. He hated the third watch most of all. It was always hard to sleep before-hand. You had your normal day duty before. You have a late start but still had to work the next day so you had to try to sleep, but no sooner were you asleep than you had to wake up and dress for duty.

The third watch, between midnight and three a.m., was the time when those awake are least vigilant and those who are asleep are hardest to wake. It is the best time for a night attack.

Their raiding party had not come back from Qori yet, they would probably come tomorrow. So they only had half their force at the fortress, less with their recent losses.

He looked out into the night; there was no moon and the stars were obscured by a light cover of cloud. Had something moved out there? Hakhamanish, his fellow guard, paused beside him.

"Is something wrong?"

"I just thought I saw something moving out in the shadows." They both searched the darkness. It was as black as pitch.

"There! Can you see it?" Dinsha pointed.

There was an animal snarl somewhere out in the darkness. Hakhamanish laughed and clasped his friend on the shoulder.

"Our men are not the only ones hunting. It is a good omen for their success."

As Dinsha and Hakhamanish turned to resume their pacing, a dark figure detached itself from the shadows and ran to shelter by the wall. It paused to make sure it wasn't seen and then it scaled the wall, going up it as if going up a ladder. It slipped over the parapet onto the walk-way and cast its head around and sniffing the air. It squatted for a moment, whining in frustration, its eyes glowing yellow. A low growl rumbled in its throat — too many things to hunt.

Its claws formed into hands and it carefully secured a rope to the parapet and lowered it over the outside of the wall. Then it stayed crouched, keeping guard till the first elf climbed the wall. He fitted an arrow to his bow as the dark shape melted into the darkness.

Hakhamanish glanced back to find his friend. The torches on the sconces must have burnt out. Strange that two had done so at the same time. He couldn't see Dinsha. He must have gone to replace them.

He also didn't see a dark shape rise up behind him. He only felt a cruel grip like a vice around on his throat. He opened his mouth to scream but a hand clamped over his mouth. He was thrown backwards as a hand gripped either side of his head. At an exact moment muscles bulged with inhuman strength and twisted as the weight and momentum hit his neck. There was a crack and the black shape lowered him gently, almost lovingly, to the ground and disappeared into the night.

* * *

Utana couldn't sleep and had called for some servants to be woken. Asabanâ, Iraj's youngest sister, had been sent. She placed cheese and dates and watered wine on the table and turned to go. She was fifteen and slender but very beautiful with long silky hair and it was the middle of the night.

Utana leered at her as he moved to block her way. She tried to slip past but he caught at her wrist and forced her body up against the wall.

"Leave me alone!" She spat and struggled.

A real spit-fire.

Utana just laughed. She was a bit young for his taste, but he liked to feel her fear. He would play with her ... for the moment. He rubbed his hard cock against her through their clothes. She shuddered in fear and disgust.

"I will have you later, you know that, and there is nothing you can do about it."

Pleased with his game, he let her go. Asabanâ flung the door open but what greeted her outside made her freeze in fear.

"Where are all the lights?" she asked. "They have gone out. And where are your guards?"

There were always two guarding the chief's house, and guards on the wall.

"*Madar Ghahbe!*" he whispered in horror. "She's here! Close that door!"

There was nothing playful about him now, he sounded scared. Who was '*she*'? He was buckling on his sword.

"Put out those lights!"

He got the young girl to hide behind him as he picked up a cross bow and stepped on the leather loop at the end to cock it. She hadn't latched the door and it began to swing open. Utana raised the cross bow, aiming into the darkness. Asabanâ could see a vague shape moving, a shadow against the faint light.

Utana released. There was the meaty sound of a cross bow bolt hitting a body and something dropped, but there was no outcry.

"Ha!" he shouted in satisfaction.

He passed his tinder box to Asabanâ. "Let's see what we have got; quickly now."

By touch Asabanâ opened the tinderbox and crouched near the fire place. There was flint to strike sparks off a 'D' shaped ring of iron that fitted in her fist and some easy burn char-cloth. She deftly struck the flint across the edge of the iron to give off little sparks. It lit the char cloth immediately. She blew gently and fed it with a little straw and then small sticks in the fireplace.

In the dim flickering light Utana bent over the figure, muttering in consternation. It was Vaumisa, one of his guards, and there was a rope around his neck.

Behind him a dark shape appeared. Asabanâ opened her mouth to scream but found she couldn't speak.

The figure grabbed him with terrible speed and strength, jerking something across his throat. It held him till his struggles weakened, finishing with a convulsion. As it lowered him to the floor, in the flickering uncertain light, Asabanâ had a glimpse of a creature from out of hell: all black; crouching half human and half panther; yellow eyes; broad face with fangs.

She blinked and it was a black woman in a short apricot dress. It made her wonder what she had seen.

"Are you Asabanâ?" she asked. "You smell like a female version of Iraj."

Asabanâ still couldn't speak for terror.

"Stay here, you will be safe, it's not over yet."

Asabanâ looked at the bodies with dismay.

"Oh, I'm sorry, give me a minute." The woman went to Utana's bed and grabbed blankets to cover them.

Asabanâ stared at the two bundles. Not much better.

Was this horror from hell her 'rescuer'?

"Don't worry, I am a friend. My name is Jess, Iraj must have told you about me but there are probably a few things he didn't mention."

Asabanâ's mind felt sluggish in shock. "You can see in the dark."

"Yes I can, that is one of the things."

"Was it you that killed the shepherds that killed Katin?"

"Yes, it was. I killed them all, and now I'm going to kill the men who have done this to you and your family."

She picked up the cross bow and the leather pouch filled with the quarrels made of iron and wood.

And with that, she was gone.

* * *

They left their horses under guard and waited outside the fortress. A desert bird called from the battlements. Hakeem hooked his two smallest fingers in either side of his mouth and repeated the call.

The door swung a quarter open. A pale figure could be seen moving through it and waiting for them just outside. It was one of the elves. Iraj felt as if his heart was burning as he followed the small force through the gates. All he wanted to do was run and find Rohana. But he had promised. He had to trust Jess.

He gave a lop-sided smile. If he wanted to find Jess, all he would have to do was follow the trail of dead bodies. He could feel very little sympathy for her victims normally. Tonight, he felt none at all. His parents were dead, his family had been taken, he had lost several dear friends including Pandora, and his wife had been tortured.

Jess would say that revenge was not the point but, no, he wouldn't feel sorry for any of their enemies tonight.

Well, first things first.

They had all memorised the map. Six villagers would lie in wait in case anyone came to close the gate. Kynane led a group of Amazónes with some of the villagers and nomads, hurrying in the direction of the barracks. They would prepare a fire against the door and a lethal trap for any who came running out. With smoke and fire at the only exit to the barracks, any prepared to surrender would be allowed to.

Most of the warriors lived in the houses rather than the barracks and Hakeem and Iraj led a larger group of archers quickly into position. They would set up on roof tops and along the walk way looking down over the houses.

Both groups lit fires in small pottery containers for fire arrows. The defenders would be outlined by fire while their attackers would be mostly in darkness.

Eirene, Chara, Anastasia and Thaïs had to be in position near the slave quarters. They had a rough estimate of how many captives they would find, it would be a greater number of women. Eirene's group were to protect them and keep them well out of the line of fire. In a way, her group had the most dangerous part; they had to penetrate into the heart of the fortress.

Hakeem waited till Eirene should be in position or near to it and then he raised a fire arrow and shot it high into the air.

* * *

Jess could smell Rohana's blood even from here and feel the traces of her energy. At least her friend was still alive.

Behind her she could hear shouting, screaming, the sound of running and the clash of weapons. She could see dancing fire, getting stronger. Her father had arrived.

Jess's route took her via the slave quarters first. Four guards had taken up position around the entrance. Where was Eirene's group?

Something had gone wrong.

She paused to lift the cross bow to her shoulder and release. She could see in the shadows as if it were daylight. The first man spun to meet her but too late. No time to arm the cross bow again, she dropped it and ran to his body to grab his short sword and shield. She could hear the shouts and screams and the rising tumult of battle behind her.

The three remaining guards raced across to where she was. She watched warily as they spread out to box her in. They had her forced back up against a wall. She had no room to run, no room to dodge and they were going to come at her from three sides.

She was in big trouble.

And she was in a hurry to find Rohana.

She noticed the men were holding their shields in front of their bodies, square on to her.

Are you men joking with me?

That's what you do in formation, or against archers.

In single combat or mêlée you attack with the shield but these were light wicker shields, reinforced with raw hide. They only had a simple strap stretching from top to bottom for gripping.

They were nothing like the tall shields of the Persis that sat on the ground you fought with those differently ducking behind them and swivelling them back and forward on their axis. And they were nothing like the Greek Hoplon (heavy infantry shield), you could hold them face on and bash with them. With a light shield in the mêlée, you had to attack with the edge.

Not what they were doing.

She lifted her shield as if to cover her face from a high attack from the wall behind her. Its edge was pointing to the man on her left with her sword at waist height, pointing forward.

Now that's how you use it.

She lunged in, attacking with the edge of her shield against the inside edge of his. The edge of her shield hit the side of his and flipped it out of the way and she rammed both shields to the side with her shoulder.

The two shields ended up both edge and to one side only his blade was on the outside of the shields and hers was on the inside. He was completely open to her sword.

Who had trained these men?

She thrust deep into his abdomen and desperately spun to try to disengage her shield and get it around in time to block the man coming from the front. He hadn't waited for her and was already charging in. His technique was just as sloppy but it didn't matter, she couldn't get her guard around in time.

He bashed her with his shield and there was a sharp pain in her side. Jess was only saved from a fatal wound because she had twisted away but she was badly hurt. She cried out in anguish and stumbled backwards, falling over one of the dead men and ended up helpless on the ground.

She tried to pull her shield across to guard her body but it caught against the dead man. The two men grinned at each other and crouched over her, swords getting ready to thrust.

‘Phtt!’ ‘Phtt!’

Anastasia came running up with a third arrow knocked. Satisfied, she put her bow aside to make sure all the men were dead.

“Jess, are you all right?”

“Thanks to you, I am. Where are the rest of you?”

“Just Eirene and me and she’s badly hurt. We ran into six men and they were onto us before we knew it.”

Eirene staggered around the corner to sag against a wall, panting and clutching at her chest.

Jess let go of her shield and staggered up. She stumbled towards Eirene, trying to heal herself as she ran. Anastasia had lifted her bow again with an arrow fitted and was scanning the roofs and alleyways.

Eirene knew she was dying. She couldn’t breathe, she couldn’t go any further, but she was worried. Thaïs and Chara were already dead and Anastasia couldn’t rescue the prisoners on her own. She slid to the ground, darkness was falling across her vision but her fear for her friends wouldn’t let her die yet.

She didn’t see Jess fly to her side and bow her head in prayer. She had lost all awareness. The next thing she knew there was a blinding flash of light, an explosion in her head and the feeling of being hit by lightning. She jerked up, wide awake.

“Ha, wha. What did you do to me?”

"I'm sorry," Jess apologised, "very dangerous, but this is an emergency. Can you fight?"

"I don't think so," Eirene said, gingerly getting up. "Er, maybe, I can walk at least. Did you two get rid of the guards? Let's get these slaves free."

"What happened to Thaïs and Chara?" Jess asked.

"I'm sorry, Jess. We were delayed and had to detour. Then six men came flying around the corner, running flat out in our direction. They had swords and shields, we had bows. Thaïs was at point, she had no chance at all. Chara killed one before he raised his shield; she showed a lot of promise, that girl."

Jess grimaced, nodding.

"I got one in the thigh on my second shot. They weren't full sized shields and the men weren't using them properly. They should have kept behind them and came at us crouched low. I then shot one in the side when he turned to kill Chara. I didn't think either one was dead but they were out of action at least.

"Anastasia was behind me and we both turned and ran then, back into an alleyway. The remaining three men were close behind. Anastasia kept hold of her bow and killed one there. I took my knife in my left hand, over-hand, and used my axe right handed to hook their shields. The last one got me. If they had used their shields properly and stayed in some sort of formation it would have been a different story."

So Thaïs was dead, another of her first group. And Chara, she had liked her.

Jess collected as many of the spare weapons as she could find and passed them to Anastasia.

"Is it worth getting more weapons?" She asked.

"Not much," Anastasia told her. "There will be less than a handful of the captives I would describe as warriors. I'm setting up on the roof next door which is defensible. Do you know which way the battle is going?"

Jess got a faraway look. "We have taken the barracks and Kynane's group are taking prisoners already. Hakeem and Iraj have taken over the greater part of the village and have the majority of the people trapped or hiding in their houses. And you have the slaves. There hasn't been any real organised resistance. If we can keep this up we will win, but this side of the fortress hasn't been secured, so be careful. I really have to go. I have a promise to keep."

Now Jess moved cautiously, following Rohana's trail. Her heart was beating rapidly with fear. The greatest remaining danger was the sorcerer and his acolytes. What might they do to Rohana now?

Up ahead there were four men in brown robes, clustered together, chanting.

Hello, a reception committee.

One man pointed an ivory wand to the ground, drawing a protective circle. The man next to him had a garishly painted face and body. He began stamping and yelling, making threatening gestures and banging a rattle and a drum. Jess lifted the cross bow to her shoulder and fired. He died mid yell.

The man next to him pointed the wand at her now, his chant rising to a crescendo. She stepped on the leather loop, cocked the cross bow and scrambled to load it before he could finish the spell.

After she hit the second man an agonising pain shot through her right arm, causing her to drop the bow. One of the two remaining men was holding a small black wax figure. He shoved another needle through it and Jess was blinded by pain. She began a lurching run to reach him. Half way there her leg gave way and she skidded face-forward across the cobble stones.

Bleeding and dazed, she staggered up, doubled over and limping as he rammed another needle into the middle. She was almost there now and snatched at her belt knife left handed. In a panic he dropped the doll to grab at his knife but she was already onto him, stabbing him in his guts and waving the blade around with her wrist.

The last man that had been chanting stopped and drew his own belt knife. Jess kicked him in the knee with her riding boot and stabbed him as he stumbled. She picked up the doll, it was already losing its magic but she made sure of it by pulling out all the pins.

The man who made the doll moaned. She reached down with her blade almost absent-mindedly and drew it across his throat. *Now let me see.*

Rohana was in the building in front of her. She could detect one other person in there with her and the coppery smell of blood, a lot of it. The house had an open window high up; that would be safer than the front door.

She changed back to her daimôn form and leapt, scrambling with her claws to gain purchase on the window frame. With some difficulty she squeezed her bulk through the narrow gap and looked down.

There was a man at the end of the room, legs folded, sitting on the floor chanting in a strange language. He wore a short linen skirt; otherwise he was naked to the waist. He looked like he was from Aígyptos, and he was ugly.

Rohana was huddled, in chains, in the corner. It was hard to tell if she was conscious. The smell of blood was overpowering. It was painted in symbols on the walls, there was a large circle painted on the floor, decorated in arcane symbols with a five pointed star with candles at each point.

Jez pushed off the ledge and landed front feet first, like a cat.

The man made no response, he continued to chant in his harsh guttural tongue, it was as if he had not seen or heard her. *Well, this will be easy then.*

She moved forward to cut his throat, but all that happened was she staggered around in a circle, ending in the same spot. His chanting seemed to get louder in her ears. With a growl of frustration she stopped, squatting on the floor, panting. She tried to walk more slowly but the blood circle started to move again.

Jez whimpered with confusion. The more she tried to walk in a straight line, the faster it seemed to spin. A noise started like a wind, getting louder and louder till it was painful. She could feel some sort of pressure seeping into her mind. She dropped onto her stomach, whining, and tried to crawl out of the circle.

"Well, well." The man finally stood. "My name is Menna and you have kept me waiting."

Jez tried to change into human form, and she found she couldn't.

"You are a changeling all right, but I've never seen anything remotely like you." He started to walk around her, keeping outside the circle. "Tell me your true name and I will let you go."

"True name?"

"Ah, you can talk in my mind. You are strong and intelligent and powerful, but you don't know much, do you? Is it because you are very young? I had planned to kill you but I see that is not needed. You will be more use to me alive. Your true name; that wouldn't be so bad would it? A fair exchange for letting you go."

Jez tried to crawl away from him but things were spinning so fast that her paws buckled under her. If she were in human form she would have been helplessly throwing up.

I need to learn about the magic of Aígyptios.

I don't think this is the best way.

"Don't pretend or I will just have to give you pain." He sighed, clutching at an amulet around his neck. The candles flared brightly.

Jez howled as agony shot through her body.

"Perhaps I should just hurt your friend." He looked across at Rohana.

Jez sprang. It was awkward, her claws scratching for purchase, her rear legs not quite coordinated with her front ones. It felt like she hit a stone wall at the edge of a circle.

Menna scampered back hurriedly.

"Someone is outside. I imagine it will be one of my assistants."

I very much doubt that.

"Perhaps they can help me to tame you. Then I can get you to attack your friends. You won't be able to hold out against me for long, you know."

I'm fairly sure 'true names' don't apply to the daimôn realm, what supernatural creatures is he used to dealing with?

* * *

They were raiders of undefended villagers, unused to a hotly contested fight. They had been poorly trained and woken in the middle of the night to fire and smoke and confusion. Most were more interested in running and hiding than fighting.

Their leaders were killed early. They had the numbers but it had done them little good against what were mainly highly trained warriors, disciplined and fighting as organised units.

Now their attackers were calling out for them to surrender, herding the survivors and women and children into the stables. For the attackers, next came the dangerous undertaking of flushing survivors, out of their houses and hiding places.

Kynane was good at that. Call for surrender. Tell them they wouldn't be harmed. She had found some of the prisoners that could be trusted to call their friends out. Kynane had no intention to lose any of her girls in the clean up operation.

If she did have to send her girls in, she sent some of the prisoners in front, their hands bound, but mostly she had fire and plenty of hay. She didn't want to set the whole fortress on fire but the houses were mostly mud brick, wood was too expensive.

* * *

Just follow the trail of dead bodies, Iraj thought.

Hakeem led him and two Amazónes, Aoide and Chloe, to Utana's home. They found Asabanâ hiding in the dark, almost hysterical but otherwise unharmed.

She flung herself at Iraj, clutching at him and refusing to let go. She was still young and after being rescued by a daimôn she had been hiding in the dark with two dead bodies. She could see fire and hear the sounds of a battle but had no idea what was happening or who would come for her at the end of it.

It was only once she heard that they still had to find Rohana did she bravely quelled her sobbing enough for them to lead her to where the slaves were and reunite her with the rest of the family. Apart from Rohana, the family hadn't been seriously hurt any further. They received the news that Rohana was being held in a room near the temple.

Jess had been at the slave quarters, Iraj could tell. Just follow the trail of dead bodies. Most on the way to the temple had been killed in the conventional way. Some their throats cut, some shot by a cross bow.

"Stay close to us," Hakeem said to Aoide and Chloe. "There are no women and children amongst the dead at least."

"Jess wouldn't do that sort of thing," Iraj said.

Hakeem looked at him for a moment and then nodded.

"Have faith in your daughter," Iraj reminded him.

The house where they thought Rohana was being held had a light flashing behind the door. Nearby was a small pile of dead men in brown robes, two had been shot with a cross bow.

Just then they heard a howl like an animal in pain.

"Jess!" Iraj ran to the door.

"Don't!" Hakeem warned.

An explosion of power took Iraj off his feet; the two women coming behind tried to catch him. None were badly hurt.

Hakeem looked at the sword clutched in his hand. It had been made by the dwarves and infused with their *Dweomer* (Dwarf Magic). While it didn't work against daimôns, it concealed him (and those around him) from far sight, like the small tattoo they had given Jacinta on her buttock.

Let's see what it will do with this.

He touched the door with the tip, tensing and screwing up his eyes. Something invisible tried to push the sword tip away. There was a bright flash and he felt the spell suddenly gave way.

It was still bolted from inside. Hakeem squared himself, raised his knee and gave the door a powerful snap-kick with his booted heel. On the fourth kick it gave way, and he shouldered in to find Jez was curled up on the floor in agony.

"Don't step in the circle," she managed.

Freed by his presence, she was able to change back into Jess.

"Who is your big friend with a sword?" a man in the corner cried in glee. "I know what to do with him, don't I?"

He gestured and a bolt of power shot at Hakeem.

"Look out!" Jess tried to struggle up.

Rohana screamed.

Hakeem stood there, unharmed, his sword glowing white.

"I had forgotten about that sword," Jess whispered in awe.

Hakeem ran over to where the wizard cringed and struck him across the neck almost hard enough to take his head off at his shoulders. *I would have liked to ask him some questions,* Jess thought. *I won't be doing that now. Too dangerous to keep him alive, I suppose.*

Then Iraj staggered in, making an unsteady path to his wife.

"They hurt me," Rohana said as he took her in his arms. "They cut two of my fingers off."

Iraj couldn't see her as he hugged her, he was crying too much. "There were too many, we couldn't get here any sooner. I'm so sorry."

"And yet you came, I didn't think you could," Rohana said. "I see you had some help. Did you know Jess is a changeling?"

"Yes, I have known all along, and now we know she is Jacinta after all. This is her father, Hakeem, and two of the Amazónes, Aoide and Chloe."

He didn't mention Pandora. There would be time for that later.

Hakeem had to lift Jess up. All she could do for a moment was shiver violently and cling to him.

"He caught me, Father, he was hurting me and I couldn't change back. It is one of my worst nightmares: I dream I am trapped as a daimôn and I can't change back."

Eventually she was able to stand and she stumbled over to where Iraj cradled Rohana and dropped to her knees, tears streaming down her face. "I'm sorry, they used you as bait for me."

She reached over and took Rohana's injured hand and kissed the bandage.

"You can't —" Rohana asked.

"No, I can't, not regrow fingers; not that you could use anyway. Your baby is fine though, he really is a boy."

"Are any of the bad men left?"

"What, the ones that hurt you?" Jess smiled. Rohana noticed her fangs were still there and her eyes still glowing yellow.

"I suppose not." Rohana gave a shaky laugh.

Chapter 22: The Šamánka

"Jess, you have the power to appear in dreams!"

"I do, Holy Father!" The woman in the dream bowed low. "I have found out that I am a šamánka, amongst other things."

"What you are is God's holy warrior." The Dastur smiled in his sleep. "Did you find Jacinta?"

"Yes I did, Father. God, it seems, has a fine sense of humour. I am Jacinta, I always was."

The Dastur chuckled.

"I need you to find Tishari for me, please. My friends aren't safe while ever he lives."

"There is another group at Arys."

"Not anymore there's not. I am at Arys now. They hurt Rohana badly. They killed Pandora and many others just because they were my friends. I made them regret that. I have two great tasks with no real expectation of surviving them but I want to deal with Tishari first."

"I sense great grief inside you, do not throw your life away because of it."

"I will never try to do that sort of thing again, Father, but after Gansükh I have to kill Æloðulf. To fight him I must wear the armour hidden in the Deepest.

"There is a cost to wearing it and it has a name: 'the drinker of souls'. It has taken one person already that I know of."

"Then I will pray for you, my daughter. I would wish that we would meet beyond this world."

"It would be a great honour for me, Father, but I don't think that can happen for me. I have been warned that this journey will take everything I have to give."

"I will pray for you nonetheless, and many others will also. You are the only hope for the free world. Always remember, prayers are no small thing."

"Thank you for that, Father. We need your help with Arys. We have taken the fortress but don't know what to do with it."

"I will pass a message to the Dastur of the fire temple at Parap. The Hun won't interfere with the religion of their subjects which means they won't take our side against the blood priests, but the local Noyan at Parap has been more than just a little annoyed with Arys for killing off his villagers. He probably would have attacked Arys before if it wasn't for their sorcerer. It will take nothing at all to convince him to send a garrison there. I think he would be more than happy to allow some of our priests along to cleanse the place."

"That would be good! I have to sleep now. I am very weary. Thank you once again, and don't forget about the blood priests."

The Dastur smiled again. "That won't be likely. I will let you know as soon as I find them."

* * *

Jess said her goodbyes to Chara, Thaïs and Apama, the three Amazónes who fell in the capture of Arys. They were to be farewelled in a ceremony the next day with the others who died at Arys, both friend and enemy but she wanted to get back in time for the final prayers for Pandora.

Iraj and Rohana wanted to come too, so Iraj's family and Jess left at first light. They had the horses belonging to the fallen

Amazónes and Jess and they drove two carts, for the family members and for Iraj and Jess's share of the loot. They expected to be in Qori late the next day.

Something in the battle with Menna had affected her. She felt weak and couldn't keep warm. It reminded her of her recovery from the battle with the daimôn below the ruins of elvish Troia, but this was different though she didn't know in what way.

Hakeem couldn't help her then and he wasn't able to help her this time and she wasn't up to healing anyone else, let alone herself.

She instinctively knew it would be a serious mistake to try to access her life energy and she wanted nothing to do with accessing daimôn energy to speed her healing. So she rode in the back of the cart with Asabanâ and Mehrak's two children.

Asabanâ was very kind to her, feeding her and making sure she drank enough, but Jess was feeling too miserable to care.

Rohana was supposed to ride in the cart too but it was just like Rohana to take one of the horses and ride alongside (despite only being rescued from captivity and torture the night before)!

* * *

As the day wore on, Jess got rapidly worse. She became feverish and began to talk to people who were not there. Once or twice she seemed to be reliving being trapped by Menna.

 Finally she had lapsed into a coma.

They had stopped early by the small township of Mubarek. Iraj had thought to camp there to let Jess rest but as soon as he saw how rapidly she was fading, he realised she needed special care and it would not wait.

"What can I do?" Iraj asked Rohana, pacing back and forwards.

Rohana was sitting next to her friend, sponging her brow. Jess had gone a muddy colour and showed no response though her eyes remained open, staring. She would occasionally shiver though her body felt burning up.

"What is wrong with her?" Mehrak, Iraj's sister, asked.

"Jess got trapped by the blood priest in a circle made of blood. Hakeem had to release her."

"A circle of power!" Usmanara, her husband, whispered, appalled. "We need to get her to a maguš without delay."

"Iraj," Rohana said, tears in her eyes. "We are losing her. After all that Jess has done for us, she is dying."

"It seems their cursed evil has not stopped with their deaths," Usmanara said. "Take her, Iraj, make for Parap. They have a fire temple there. Take two spare horses, we will continue on to our home."

"I know a route to Parap from here," Iraj said to Rohana. "I will make it. If I have to kill the horses to get there, I will make it."

As he got ready, they could see a small group of horsemen hurrying along the road towards them. The women of Iraj's family were all archers and everyone reached for weapons.

"Roua?" Rohana called out as they got closer. "Roua, is that you? Iraj, this is the Hun leader we met in Āmul. What are you doing here?"

Roua was in the front of his arban of cavalry as they trotted up. Better yet, wonder of wonders there were two *Mazdayasna* priests. They had brown coats over their white vestments, and padan masks hanging from their turbans.

"Is this a miracle?" Rohana asked. "*Ahu* (lord high priest), what has brought you here?"

"My name is Yamshed," the head priest said. "I am here because your friend has been screaming out for help. I am almost surprised you couldn't hear her as well. We were on the way to Arys, so we made a detour."

Iraj quickly introduced his family and took Yamshed to where they had lain Jess. She seemed more peaceful already and her eyes had closed. "It seemed like she was dying."

"Not quite, what she faced is incredibly powerful. She is fighting back hard, the Dastur Dångha has been telling her what to do. She tried to do it all on her own. She really should have thought to pray. Now that we are here, we will help her."

"Can you?" Rohana asked. "Out of doors?"

Yamshed laughed. "Once *all* our rituals were out of doors, didn't you know that? I'm sure we will manage somehow."

They prepared their sacred fire in an urn, surrounded by an offering of fruit and flowers they had bought at the village. They cleansed themselves and then began the chant.

* * *

The people of Qori and the surrounding villagers erected a tropaion, a monument. It was fashioned in the shape of a great cross and made of oak from the Oxos forest. It was an ancient Greek tradition to celebrate a victory.

In the past it would be simply dressed in the armour of the defeated enemy but now it was carved and polished as a memorial to the victory and to the fallen.

Near the bottom were the names of the villagers who had fallen carved and painted in black lettering with a tribute to them.

Above this was the date, the names of the five Amazónes who had given their lives and the villagers' tribute to their rescuers.

"In a time of trouble, a great evil stretched its shadow across the land. Unlooked for they came, riding out of legend. Not counting the odds they stood with us and spilt their blood unstintingly. They will never be forgotten. May the one true and uncreated God bless them forever."

They had a small ceremony to mark the occasion. Kishpi gave a speech and then Hakeem thanked all that came to help. Kynane finally gave a speech outlining the life and achievements of each of the fallen Amazónes, even Pandora, who was the newest member.

Jess sat there, hunched forward in misery with a blanket over her shoulders and Rohana's arm around her on one side and Eirene's on the other.

For Jess who had been lost in time, it was longer ago than it was for Eirene, but it reminded both of the women of a very similar ceremony. Back then it was to mark the first battle of the fighting women of Troia when they had defended the manor house.

That was the first battle to involve the newly formed Amazónes. This time Pandora was dead, and Alba and Thaïs and two Jess had been given no chance to get to know: Chara and Apama.

Dora, are you really dead? Jess began to get flashes of Pandora laughing or giving her a loving glance or her grin so full of mischief. She could scarce breathe; it felt like a sword had been thrust into the centre of her chest.

Jess could not afford to pause; she had to kill Gansükh before he raised more daimôns. *But Dora it is so hard, going on without you!*

After lunch Hakeem and Kynane bid them goodbye with most of the Amazónes, they had to get back to the Troad. Anastasia and Eirene would travel with Jess once they were sure she was sufficiently recovered.

Jess was meditating and communing with her God several times a day to make sure she continued to recover. *How stupid could I be?* Jess wondered. She had never thought to try *praying* when she was attacked by the dark magic. *A child would know to do that.*

That evening some of the young men of the village had their own ceremony to give honour to the dead. A small fire was lit and they performed a special Skythoi rite. They made a small *mya* (tepee) not much taller than four feet high and sealed it with felt cloth, no smoke hole. Inside they placed red hot rocks on a dish in the ground. And they made a small pile of hemp seeds on a leather cloth. Each of the men in turn would poke their head under the felt cloth and sprinkle hemp seeds on the hot rocks and sniff the acrid white smoke inside the tent.

It was the Skythian version of a wake.

Jess had asked Anastasia and Eirene to give her a few minutes alone. She didn't need any time alone, but nothing was helping. She was stuck with an empty aching hole inside.

"You should try it," Iraj said to Jess. His eyes were bloodshot and he had a silly look on his face. "It helps with the grief."

"Don't let him talk you into it," Rohana warned, bustling past carrying a plate of food.

"How do I do it?" Jess asked him when Rohana had gone.

"Just take a small handful of seeds, stick your head in and sprinkle them on the hot coals."

Rohana walked back to catch Jess with her head stuck in the tent and Iraj squatting next to her shouting instructions.

"Iraj! I told you not to let Jess get in there! She has been sick and she sometimes has funny reactions to drugs."

Iraj looked up at her and giggled. He slapped Jess unsteadily on the back. "I love this girl. She's a good, she's a good ... she's all right."

"How long has she been in there?"

"Longer than any of the rest of us," one of Iraj's friends said, giggling. "She really is a strong girl."

Rohana kneeled down.

"Jess, are you all right in there?" she called. "You've been in there too long."

There was no answer, no response.

"Iraj!" Rohana glared at her husband. "How much did you tell her to use?"

"Just a pinch."

"Well, help me get her out!"

Rohana tried to ineffectually tug at the big girl while Iraj and his male friends giggled and fell on top of each other trying to help.

Eventually she managed to get them coordinating well enough to drag her out, AND roll her on her back rather than to keep dragging her on her face through the dirt.

Jess's eyes couldn't focus on her; she had dust all over her face. She gave Rohana a broad dreamy smile.

"Pandora," she breathed.

* * *

Jess found herself on her back. It was dark but the stars seemed to be moving. Hold on, she was being dragged across the dust. Her muscles felt weak, her mouth dry, her eyes stung. She felt dizzy, and paradoxically hungry. At the same time she was drifting and full of nervous energy.

"It affects people differently," the young form of Jacinta told her.

"Lover," Pandora said. "You definitely shouldn't take drugs. They have strange effects on you. I have been trying to attract your attention for some time, but you were too sad."

"Dora!" Jess cried out excitedly and then she burst into tears.

"Sit down before you fall down," Thaïs advised her, laughing.

"Hey, I'm not standing," Jess said.

They were all floating in the air and they weren't anywhere near the tent.

Chara, Alba and Apama gave her smiles and they waved casually. The younger Jacinta had disappeared.

"I found my parents and sister. She died of the fever early during the time of hunger," Pandora told her. "And Thaïs here found her Drakon."

Jess tried to float over to kiss and hug Pandora but she didn't know how. She settled back and grinned at her instead.

"Your parents?" she asked. "Haven't they moved on in their next life?"

"Why of course they have, and so has Drakon and my sister. It is important to let them go, you know that, but we the dead inhabit a realm created by the echoes of the past."

So the human soul has more than one part to it. Ghosts are a different part and can be left over after each reincarnation.

"Jess, I'm sorry I left you, I was given no choice. I'll watch over you as much as I can."

"Pandora, I need you now! I need you so much!"

"There is more for you to face, be strong for me."

"I have to be ready to give my life, my love, my very soul, everything I have," Jess said, remembering what the dead had told her at the manor house, so long ago. "Tell me we will be reunited in death."

"Oh, Jess, there are things I can't tell you. Just know that we here love you."

"Jess." The young Jacinta had appeared again. "I'll show you how to clear the poison from your blood, you took far too much."

"Jess?" She was back near the tent and Rohana was trying to help her sit up.

She sat up, unsteadily.

"I'm going to kill my husband when he sobers up, would you like to help me?"

Jess thought she must have looked a mess, red eyes from the drugs and crying, and swaying as she sat.

"If you like, but I'm all right," she told her. "I saw Pandora."

"And that's supposed to reassure me that you are all right? I'm sorry, Jess. I feel she gave her life for me."

"Funny, I feel the same way. I feel it was my fault. I suppose I should stop thinking that way, I'm not a god after all." She giggled, was it the smoke still making her giggle?

Iraj was right, it helped with the grief.

"Don't even think that you brought the problem of Arys down on us." Iraj was sober for a minute. "We would have had to face them sooner or later. It was best to face them while we had your help. I'm sorry about the kánnabis, but with all that has happened I really needed it."

Jess was sobering rapidly with her young alter-ego's help. Drugs were definitely something she definitely planned to avoid in the future.

There was one thing she had to ask.

"Rohana and Iraj, I feel embarrassed to ask this, I really do. I don't think I will survive what I have to face but if I ever get a home for myself I would like Pandora's remains to be close to me."

"It will just be bones, but we will have a casket made," Rohana promised. "No need to feel embarrassed. We will look after her, till you have a home of your own. She was our blood sister and she gave her life for us. We will pray for you every day. Do you think we will see you again soon?"

"I would like to, especially to see your new baby," Jess said. "I don't think it will be possible though. Things are moving too quickly now and I need to learn more about magic. I have made a lot of mistakes through ignorance.

"And killing Gansükh has just become a lot harder. People will know about Jess after Arys and the fact that I don't take too kindly to dark magic. It will be easy to guess what I am, why I am here and that I will be coming for Gansükh."

* * *

They were in Elgard and Jess was having one of her first lessons on magic.

"This world is an illusion," Sophie explained. "Some magic imposes its own illusion on the illusion of reality, other magic relies on ignoring the illusion and some relies on what is hidden beyond the illusion. Are you following me, Jess?"

"Not at all," Jess admitted, shaking her head. "I need to know what happened to me and what I could have done about it."

"Let me try," Daniel offered. "Jacinta, everything is not as it seems because we are trapped in this illusion we call reality. From what you say, Menna tricked you into stepping into a circle of power. It contained stolen energy from people he had murdered, his incantations and the power of his will. The Aígyptoi have powerful death magic and he may also have called on 'Anāt, the blood thirsty Assyrian War Goddess, in fact for that sort of power I think he did. Even after Menna was dead, you were attacked. It was only through prayer that you were saved."

"How could I fight it?"

Sophie giggled. "Did you try?"

Jacinta sat back and thought about it. Then she began to chuckle softly.

"No, I guess not. I didn't even try prayer, some paladin I am. I tried to resist it with my will alone but that wasn't enough."

"The human soul is very powerful but if you find you can't simply resist magic then you need to learn how to fight it," Sophie agreed.

"The magic of the paladin and of the šamánka," Jess said, nodding.

"And of the daimôn," Daniel reminded her.

Jess shuddered.

She remembered the long fight to become human again. She remembered the feeling of being trapped in her daimôn form by

Menna. It felt as if the daimôn part of her was always lying in wait for her, ready to take over.

* * *

Jess's voice steamed in the frigid air. "Where am I?"

She was sitting in a conical-shaped tent. She had moccasins and an *irnauti* (fur coat) draped over her but underneath she was naked. A small fire burnt in the middle.

Two men and a woman sat across from her. Their black hair was sprinkled with grey. There were two of those gorgeous fluffy white dogs being stroked by a young boy. One dog walked across and sat down next to her. She automatically reached down and patted it.

"Kako Vesako (Old Man Kako)!" she cried out in delight. "Am I really here this time?"

"Put your hand in our fire little šamánka and you will know soon enough." The old šamán suggested.

Who had such power to bring her to this far place?

"It is you that travelled here, part of you has remained in Elgard. Though we had to help, it is a rare power you have. You know from where you got it."

My time in the daimôn world.

"This is my pupil, Nyalku." He indicated a long haired youth. "I will not introduce my companions, they are only here as witnesses. You are becoming great in power but not in knowledge. For me to teach you, you must first agree to be bound by the law of the šamán. You must work towards maintaining balance and never abuse your power."

"I would gladly agree to that," she said.

"Then come, you will be our warrior-šamánka, our champion."

Jess stood up and cast her furs aside. All that was left was moccasins on her feet.

She tried not to shiver as she exposed her naked flesh. Kako and his assistant began painting her body with lines of power: her forehead, her cheeks, her neck, swirling lines around her breasts, her abdomen, down to the fur of her feminine parts, her inner legs, her inner thighs, down her back and her buttocks. It was white against her dark body.

They got her to repeat the words of the šamán oath and then they wrapped her up again for the few steps outside to the water. Nearby the *mya* (the Siberian version of a tepee) a wooden carving stood: head, breasts and torso only.

That's me!

Yet somehow not her, it had an other-world quality to it. It was a carving of her soul when it wandered.

Next to the wooden statue was a tree decked with small pieces of coloured cloth, prayers to keep her safe. Kako began chanting as he broke the thin layer of ice from the surface of the river with a fishing spear. He gestured for Jess to step in.

Are you kidding me, Kako? You don't seriously expect me to get in there, do you?

She cast off her furs and kicked off her moccasins. A light breeze was blowing. The cold hit her like a physical blow. Her feet began to burn as they touched the frozen ground. She began to shiver uncontrollably as she stepped into the water.

Aiyee! It burns!

He grabbed her head and forced her to sit and then lie down, finally pushing her face under the water. Pain shot through her.

She stopped shivering. She lost the strength to sit up. Her body began to feel warm and numb and her mind became drowsy.

Hey! Have you forgotten about me?

Suddenly she felt a sensation as if she was hurtling between the stars. Her eyes snapped open. Ba'al's handsome face was looking at her in shock.

"Jacinta, what are you doing here?" He was speaking in her mind.

She threw herself into his arms. Could they merge, maybe just for a little while, maybe just this once?

Probably not.

"I thought I would surprise you."

"You have grown much, my dear little daimôn. Thank you for ending the existence of Mot, it finished much evil."

"I can't stay. I'm in the middle of being initiated as a šamánka. Can I destroy Gansükh, without fighting his daimôn lord, Namatar?"

"I don't think so."

"Having to kill Namatar is the last thing I want." Jacinta grimaced.

"Assuming you can. Gansükh is not worth the loss of Namatar. You must find a way to weaken Namatar, get him to disappear for a while and then you can kill Gansükh."

"That doesn't sound easy. Can Gansükh train others to summon daimôns?"

"No." Ba'al looked grim. "We are killing any šamán whose soul he sends here. But be careful, Æloðulf can summon other beings, not just daimôns, and Gansükh has surrounded himself with others of great power. In a dream I saw a woman, a warrior-šamánka like you, standing by his side. You will have to kill her first and she is very dangerous. She has lived in the daimôn realm."

"Kako Vesako didn't warn me about her."

Though he can be a little vague at times.

"You will know her from the healing touch and a heart of ice. I will send you some help. You are definitely going to need it."

She was already speeding back.

Jacinta woke surrounded by Sophie, Daniel, Eunike and two novices. She was shivering violently, they had bundled her up in blankets and they offered her warm milk and honey.

"That *was* impressive," Daniel said. "All that was left here was a shadow."

"Argh," was all Jess could manage.

"You need rest."

But she was already asleep.

* * *

"The Enemy Within"
Book 5 The Paladin Chronicles

"An enemy at the gates is less formidable, for he is known and carries his banner openly." Marcus Tullius Cicero.

Chapter 1: Mohini

Āzar Pāyegān (Azerbaijan) means 'keepers of the sacred fire'. The name of the capital, *Ateshi-Bagavan* (Baku), means 'God's place of sacred fires'. It is famous for mineral-oil and gas.

In many places oil issues from the ground. It is shipped all over the known world for fuel for lamps and to make an ointment for 'the itch'.

Gas issues from vents in the rocks in many places. One of these fuels the eternal flame within the second most important fire temple in all of *Mazdayasnaism* (Zoroastrian faith).

It seemed that the one and uncreated God, Ahura Mazda, had made this place especially holy, but it has not saved its people. When the Skythians of the Transkaukasos lost the war, their government collapsed. At first their new masters were more interested in looting and stealing rather than governing. Gangs ran free, sanitation broke down and people lived in squalor. And now with the drought, the wars and the trade embargoes hunger rules the streets of what was once a wealthy city on a major trade route.

The Transkaukasos

Greater Kaukasos

Likhi Mountains

Msndr

Kaspiian Sea

Tarki

Black Sea

Phasis

Kutaisi

Dariel Pass

Darband

Elgard

Phasis River

Lesser Kaukasos

Mt'k'vari River

Ateshi-Bagavan

The new Šâh, Gansükh, has brought many evil men and men and women of dark power to the city. His hands are stained with the blood of hundreds of thousands of men and elves. The people cry out under the weight of a terrible oppression.

* * *

The young man's muscular body was sleek and shiny with sacred oil. His wrists were tightly bound behind him and tied to the stake hammered deep into the earth. His head was slumped forward, drowsy from soma and herbs. Four old men surrounded him. All the five in the small stone room were men and all were naked. The smoke billowing from the sacred fire was thick with acrid smoke.

"Do you freely agree?" Their leader asked loudly.

"Yes, I freely agree." The young man nodded in the flickering light of the fire. He was also a maguš and this could only be done if he agreed.

Then their senior, started.

"I call on Mithra, protector of covenants. Reward those who are righteous and punish our wicked and sinful enemy. Protect us this night."

The man on his left continued. "And I call on Varuna, great God, keeper of the underworld and the law. Reward those who are righteous and punish our wicked and sinful enemy. Protect us this night."

The third man started, "And I call on Indra the mighty one. Reward those who are righteous and punish our wicked and sinful enemy. Protect us this night."

The last man chanted. "And I call on Agni, the fire God, the messenger, the destroyer of darkness and daēva. Reward those who are righteous and punish our wicked and sinful enemy. Protect us this night."

They needed strong deities to protect them. For the one they would now call was a Daēva, a false Goddess. Chanting her mantras were very dangerous, she was very dangerous.

Her name was *Kālarātri* ('black night'). Amongst the Hindu she was also called *Mahākālī* (great Kālī) or sometimes simply Kālī. In her statues Kālarātri is depicted as blue skinned with eyes red with rage. She has multiple arms to carry several sharp swords and holds a severed head with a skull cap to catch its blood. Strapped about her body is a garland of the heads and she wears a skirt of severed arms. To the Hindu she is the consort of Siva the destroyer but to the Magoi she was far darker and far more dangerous.

This was a ceremony older than the Prophet Zarathustra and he had been dead for these last thousand years. It was strictly forbidden, but some amongst the Magoi preserved the old ways in secret.

The powerful protection that they had drawn did not extend to the young man in the centre, for he would leave himself open to the Daēva-Goddess.

The enemy had crossed the mountains far to the east. They conquered the place where the prophet had been born and died. Then their hordes crossed the *Rā* (Volga) and they had swarmed down from the north. They should not have succeeded but they had used the horror of daimôn fire to destroy the great city of Darband, the mighty fortified gate standing across the entrance to the Transkaukasos.

Now the blessed lands of Kohestan and Āzar Pāyegān were groaning under the occupation of the evil šamán Gansükh and his Hun. The royal family lie murdered in their graves with only Princess Azarin the last of the old royal family in hiding.

Endlessly the people of the city have prayed for justice and delivery, but it seemed all their prayers were unanswered. Finally there had been a tetrad: four blood moons (lunar eclipses) in a year and on the last one there was a great comet. The meaning was obvious; it was the sign of an assassin.

But who was he and what did it mean? Strangely now, all divination failed. It was as if a veil was drawn across the future. So now, more in desperation than hope they turned to Kālī, the destroyer, the Goddess of Assassins.

They would ask her to make sure the assassin killed Gansükh. But for this, one of their number must be offered.

Nothing less would do. They only hoped it would be enough, for Kālī had no reason to love them.

As their chanting reached a frenzy they drew their knives. The young man looked up and smiled. He clenched his teeth so as not to cry out. This was not to kill him but it was his blood from which the arcane symbols must be drawn. As the forbidden symbols were drawn on his body, the young man slumped and a darkness filled the room.

"Kālarātri, hear us, answer our prayers." The four men chanted in turn.

The eyes of the young man snapped open, they were blood red. The voice of the Daēva hissed from his lips and his face was twisted with hatred.

"For a beginning there must always be an ending. For creation there must be first destruction. For life, there must be death. I tried to teach you but you did not understand me; you only wanted soft Gods." She snarled. "You called me false. You turned away from me and now you find you need me. Why should I help you now?"

"An assassin is coming. Can you get him to kill Gansükh? " The head mage asked.

"She comes for reasons of her own, not in answer to your prayers and she is more dangerous than you can possibly imagine. You will know her by her heart of ice."

"We offer you this living sacrifice, will you will help us?"

Kālī laughed. The man began jerking at his bonds like a maniac. His eyes reflected murderous rage. Blood began dripping from the rope cutting his wrists. His mouth showed fangs and spittle flew from his lips.

"Your sacrifice is useless. She has her own Gods, equally as ancient as I."

"But will she kill Gansükh?" The senior Maguš insisted. Daēva were devious and untrustworthy. He had to be sure.

"Do you even understand the impossibility of what you ask? If anyone tries to kill Gansükh his daimôn lord will appear." Kālarātri for the moment talked more softly and let the young man stop struggling.

"A force I have not seen before has clouded my vision. I cannot even see the Assassin. I see Azarin's body, her blood on the Assassin's hands, or is it Gansükh's? She helps one or is it the other? I cannot tell, it is all confused."

"So, can you give us no answer? Is our sacrifice in vain?" The leader of the Mages was appalled. It was all for nothing, the young man was already dead. Out of the darkness came the faint echo of laughter.

* * *

As soon as they had settled into their rented house, the three young women set out to explore the city on foot. They were dark even for *Dravidians* (southern Indians) with a faint dark blue metallic tinge to their skin.

Their leader, Mohini, stepped out confidently in front. She was tall, dressed in a bright crimson *sattika* (sari) decorated with gold thread. She had chosen a matching gold and crimson sun umbrella made from silk on lacquered bamboo but she didn't bother to open it, just twirled it over her shoulder as she walked.

Mohini was the name of the divine enchantress and her two companions bore the names of Goddesses: Aranyani, the elusive Goddess of the forest whom the Greeks would call Artemis; and Astártē, one of the many names of the Goddess of love.

Aranyani and Astártē were dressed in saffron silk pants and tunics. Over their shoulders they carried bows, on their broad hips they had quivers and large knives. Tucked into their waist bands at the back were two throwing axes each. They were only a fraction shorter than Mohini but they looked exactly what they were, her body guards.

Today was hot and humid but the women showed no discomfort.

"Great Lady, do you want a guide?"

Mohini eyed the small Saka boy, with obvious distaste. He was eight or nine years old. His grey woollen pants were two sizes too small, stained and frayed at the knees. Over the top he had a faded brown jacket with splotches of mud and dirt. He wiped his nose on his sleeve and grinned up at her hopefully.

"I certainly don't think so."

Aranyani drifted forward. "Mistress, perhaps he can show us where we might hire a cook."

"We *had* a cook." Mohini reminded her dryly.

"And I think he is still running." Astártē giggled. "All he could do was look at our bodies and make snide remarks. Aranyani had to have that talk with him."

"The one that involved holding a knife to his throat?"

"You want a cook? Nîjara knows a cook!" the boy said revealing a mouth full of crooked teeth.

Mohini sighed. *Now why do I think I am going to regret this?*

"Very well, show us your cook."

Aranyani gave him two *pašîz* (copper coins). He took it and examined it with delight. Waiting to see if they were following him, he ducked down a side street.

The road was narrow and dusty, lined by tiny mud brick houses and stalls, covered with thatch and palm leaves. No few were abandoned, roofs collapsed from neglect. Piles of rotting rubbish, animal and human manure seemed to be everywhere.

Mohini gave a disgusted snort and lifted the hem of her sari. She pulled out a perfumed cloth and held it to her nose.

"Boy!" She called. "Slow down, this is not a race, you know! What is this awful place you're taking us to?"

At the far end of the street, a woman ran out of one of the small shacks.

"Help me! My daughter and her baby are dying!"

She looked around wildly and then caught sight of Mohini looking rich and confident in the distance. A life time habit of servitude made her run the whole length of the street and collapse at her feet. Her cheeks were marked by dust and tears. Her hair uncombed. Her feet were bare and dirty.

"Please, Great Lady, please you must help me." She cried out.

"You! Stop your wailing." Mohini snapped her fingers at her. "Why *must* I help you?"

"My daughter and the child she carries are going to die, do you know anything of healing?"

"Healing?" Mohini looked smug. "More than you can possibly imagine; but why should I care what happens to your daughter and her child?"

The woman burst into tears.

"Oh alright," Mohini's lip curled in a sneer. "I will have a look at this worthless daughter of yours. Just stop your dreadful noise!"

The woman almost fainted with relief. She went to grab the hem of Mohini's sari but Mohini swatted her away with her umbrella. "Don't touch me!"

She strode down the street and then pushed her way through the growing crowd, her umbrella held out in front like a weapon. "Get out of my way! Don't touch me!"

They were poor people, trained in making way for someone dressed in fine clothes. Soon she was in the woman's shack where she found a young woman, barely older than a child herself, covered with perspiration and straining in labour. Two women were wiping her brow. The mother followed Mohini in wringing her hands.

"I felt a foot and it's not Frênay's time."

A footling breech! Mohini gasped in horror.

She spun into action, old training taking over. There were only minutes left in which to save the baby. "Bring a mid-wife, now!" she snarled. "If you cannot afford her fee, I will pay, I don't care. There is no time to lose."

"The mid wife is dead, my Lady. None have the craft for this."

Oh no!

"Well get ready for the baby and the after birth, then!" Mohini yelled throwing the loose material of her sari over her shoulder and pushing the short sleeves of her silk *choli* (blouse) higher to bare her arms.

"I need water and soap, now! Warm water, the hotter the better, don't worry I can take it hot." She pointed to a man standing around looking confused. "Someone get this man out of here!"

"My Lady, it is our *maguš*."

Mohini took a deep breath and exhaled, sending a prayer of thanks to the gods.

"My apologies, Lord. We have a footling breech and I was just about to feel for the cord."

"Emre, my name is Emre, and what are you talking about?"

Mohini looked at him, incredulously. "The midwife is *dead* and you are going to tell me you don't deliver babies?"

"I'm a man!" Emre seemed offended by the very thought.

"Who let this fool in here?" Mohini's eyes swept the audience as if to find who was responsible. Then she looked back at him in distaste. "If you are not going to help why did you come, *Emre*? Did you come just for your entertainment? Alright, whatever you call yourself, at least relax the mother for me." She saw the direction of his gaze. "No, not her! She's the grandmother, you idiot. I mean the one having the baby!"

Emre blushed deeply. "I'll bring my herbs!"

"Oh, for the sake of all the Gods!" Mohini almost spat in disgust. She reached over and put her palm on the mother's forehead. Emre felt a great surge of power. The girl relaxed back with a silly smile on her face.

Someone came bustling in with a bowl of steaming water. Mohini washed her hands with soap and water with great care and dried them on the cleanest part of the towel. She turned the girl's pelvis on the side, lifting her smoothly into position. It was a surprising exercise of strength and balance, quietly done.

"How did I get myself into this?" she muttered.

"Alright," She said to young maguš. "A woman would be far better, I agree. But you are the local healer and if there is a problem delivering babies you are all there is; so get a woman assistant by all means but you are going to have to learn. Babies can come out head first which is best, sometimes they come chin on their chest, or they can come bum first. Foot first isn't one of those ways. It doesn't form a seal so the cord can drop."

She eased her hand inside the woman's' vagina as she talked, feeling for the cord, pulsing in time with the woman's racing heartbeat.

"That puts pressure on the cord and the baby has minutes to be born or it will die or at very best be born stupid." Her face became a mask of anxiety and concentration. Her breathing was coming rapidly. Her face began to dot with perspiration. "This baby is not ready, it is small and that's partly why it's breech. There is no damage to it, *yet,* thank all the Gods. I stopped the labour but we don't have much time."

She felt inside the woman and pushed, grunting a little. "No I can't ... I thought I could get the leg back up and try to turn the child but it's impossible, the womb has already dropped too much. Oh no! The womb is contracting again. I will just have to get the second leg down and deliver the baby."

"Here, Emre wash your hands and you feel!" She moved aside to let Emre have a quick feel. It was taboo for a man to touch a woman that way but Frênay was too far gone to protest and the other women were too scared of Mohini.

Mohini felt yet another contraction starting and she spat a curse. She lifted the woman onto her back and seemed to be doing something inside her and then a smile of satisfaction spread across her face.

"I have got the second leg down! Good! The cord is back inside, and I have the pelvis!" She began laughing with relief and triumph. She had one hand inside and the other pushing up against the woman's bulge.

"Are you a healer?" Emre asked.

She shot him a look of pure and utter contempt, but it was all she had time for.

"I will have to get the arms down or the head won't fit I think. How can I get an arm down? Twist the body gently ... then hook it forward with a finger I suppose." She was talking to herself and working quickly.

"Good! Now the head, that's critical. It's turning to the back that seems right...

"Get ready!" she shouted to the others waiting. The feet had emerged.

Next minute she slid the baby out smoothly catching its back with one hand and passed it to the mother's mother who gave the baby a smack. It took a shocked breath and its arms spasmed out in outrage. Then it cried, its whole body red with indignation.

Mohini massaged the cord towards the baby. "The child is small. A bit of extra blood will do it no harm," she muttered. Then she tied the cord quickly and deftly. "The after birth should be easy."

She signalled to one of the waiting women to take over while she washed her hands again.

"Thank you! Thank you!" The mother tear's flowed freely down her cheek. Her face was beaming as she held her grandchild "You saved my daughter, you saved her baby. And it's a boy! A healthy boy, may God bless you!"

The smile dropped from Mohini's face. She stared at the woman as if she was a cockroach.

"Do *you* think *I* want your gratitude? What use are you to me?"

"But you saved my daughter and her child." The mother's face paled, tears of hurt and disbelief came to her eyes. "We don't have much money, but what we have you can have it, all of it."

Mohini laughed in the woman's' face. She gestured meaningful at the one room house. "Do *I* look as if I need *your* miserable pittance? Your daughter's problem interested me, or I would have walked on."

The mother was aghast. "What…what are you? Are you even human? Will you steal my grandson's soul?"

Mohini snorted with amusement and spoke almost kindly. "Don't be so stupid! Your daughter and the child are without blemish. All I used was harmless seeing-magic. I *dislike* death-magic. Any that say otherwise, insult me. I will know of it and will return to punish them."

"You talk as if you don't care," the woman said.

"Then we understand each other, woman. All I care about is power. I have learnt something from your daughter. That is a gift you have given that is infinitely more valuable than you and all your neighbours possess. I am content, you owe me nothing."

The woman looked at her anxiously, uncertain. "My neighbour has a grandson."

"And you suddenly think I have nothing better to do with my time?" Mohini laughed with derision.

The woman looked like she had been struck. "He has the fever and is close to death."

"A simple matter, then. I suppose I will have to wait while I send one of my servants to bring me clean clothes." She gestured at her beautiful sāṛī covered with blood and liquor fluid and looked meaningfully at Aranyani. Aranyani bowed acknowledgement and left, running.

Mohini raised her voice. "Show me the way, *woman*, but no crowds. I detest crowds." She turned to the man before she left. "Coming Emre? This won't take too long."

She studied Emre out of the corner of her eye as the woman led them to her neighbour. "Emre, you are not a šamán, you trained as a maguš then?"

Emre bobbed his head in agreement. "I only had three years training before my magoi master died but I learn all I can from any who would teach me."

She gestured at her fine clothes covered in liquor and blood. "After this, I will need to clean up. And I need some information; perhaps we can agree on an exchange."

They ducked their heads to pass into the house of the neighbour. It was little more than a hovel. An old woman stood just inside. She stared at Emre with a haunted look on her face.

"You are too late, maguš. My grandson is beyond help, he already walks with the spirits. He goes to join the rest of my family. I will be alone."

"Get out of my way, you stupid, stupid, woman!" Mohini shoved the woman out of the way. "I can tell from here that he's not dead. It will be more difficult than I had thought, that is all, nothing more."

Emre signalled to the old woman to hold her peace.

Mohini walked into the one-room shack as if she owned it. She gazed down at the pile of rags. Inside was the thin figure of a boy, maybe twelve. The smell of sickness and incense filled the room.

"He needs fresh air," she announced and drew the rags the woman used as curtains back from the window.

"But Lady, you say he is not dead but if not, then he is dying." The grandmother looked perplexed.

"You have no money for meat." It was an accusation.

"There is no money." The old woman shook her head. "All the rest of my family is dead."

"How under the sun do you make any money from these people?" Mohini asked Emre.

She reached into her sārī and passed the woman a silver coin.

The woman looked at it as if it was the first coin she had ever seen. "Great One, what is this?"

"Are you simple? It is a silver coin." She placed two more on a small table. "Your grandson needs meat and barley broth. Do you wish to waste my time here? Surely you don't want me to bring you the food as well? Perhaps you want me to wait on you like a servant!"

She raised her voice to the crowd that had gathered outside.

"Not one sound, any of you, while I concentrate!"

She knelt by the bed as if to pray. She closed her eyes and placed her hand on the boy's forehead. She seemed to stop breathing.

Time passed. A drop of perspiration ran down her face.

How could she hold her breath for so long? People outside were becoming restless. Then she began chanting under her breath in a strange language.

There was a surge, a powerful drawing feeling, as if Mohini was taking something into herself. The boy jerked up in surprise and sucked a huge breath in and coughed long and hard.

"Who?" he asked, his eyes were unfocused.

"Uspasnu, you have wandered far," Mohini whispered. "There is someone here who has been waiting for your return."

She turned and helped the old lady up and led her to the bed. The old woman collapsed wailing and hugging her grandson and praising Mohini.

Mohini bent closer to the woman's ear.

"Thick broth, add meat of any sort, or an egg a day, two eggs for the first week is even better. Do this for a full moon-cycle if you can. He will be very tired and weak for two whole moons but he is young and still strong. I have had to draw most of the infection into myself so I could fight it for him. That is no easy thing. If he weakens again send for me immediately. Do you understand me? I will not be angry to be disturbed, but I *will* be angry if there is any delay. I don't want my work spoilt by carelessness or stupidity."

After pausing in thought, she added two more coins and turned to leave.

"Can you people get out of my way? This place stinks! Leave the door open."

Some of the crowd wanted to touch her garments or kiss her hand or bow down at her feet or thank her. She looked supremely irritated.

Then all of a sudden she relaxed and threw her head back and laughed. "I go from an evil death-maguš that will steal souls to a 'holy one' in just minutes."

Aranyani came running back, carrying a bundle of fresh clothes.

"I am not the saint you seek," Mohini announced loudly to the people. "I am just tired and I need to talk to this maguš of yours. Do not follow me, do not wait for me."

"Well, maguš." Mohini gave him a dazzling smile. The blood and liquor was becoming stiff as it dried on her clothes. "I will clean up and change at your house."

Emre blushed again. No woman would invite herself to a strange man's house, let alone to bathe!

Mohini looked around for the small boy, Nîjara. He had disappeared. "That's just typical!"

"This isn't the one we came for!" Aranyani murmured as they made their way to Emre's house. "Though he *is* rather handsome!"

"Huhh?" Mohini grunted absent-mindedly.

"It's not like you not to notice, my Lady!" Astártē smirked.

"You're right, Aranyani!" Mohini laughed as she eyed Emre speculatively. "he is not the one but this is better, you will see. Emre! Now that I have come to this city, I will wish to meet Gansükh. If I help you with your work then he is bound to hear of me. It will be *he* that wants to see *me*, rather than me arriving like a supplicant at his door! Besides, I wouldn't mind practicing my healing skills. It's been far too long and I need to keep in practice."

"Have you delivered many babies?" Emre asked her, as he led the way through winding streets.

He certainly doesn't live in a wealthy part of the city. Mohini noted.

"I have delivered just one baby and it was today. I always wanted to learn, though." Mohini gave him a smug look. "I have certain, *advantages.*"

Emre felt a chill of fear as he got a sense of her power. Since Gansükh had come to this city, many of great power had come to seek him out.

"Are you human?" his tongue asked before his brain could give it any thought.

"I once was," Mohini said. For a moment she sounded almost sad. "Am I still? I'm not sure. It seems a long time ago."

"How old are you?"

She looked barely twenty. She was so beautiful with silky black hair held at the back by a brooch. Her eyes were strangely hypnotic eyes and the colour of amber.

"Where I used to come from, it was rude to ask a lady her age." Mohini laughed. "My age has no meaning in human terms."

When they reached his house, Mohini and her companions disappeared with the lady that came to help Emre during the day. The small wood fire underneath the tall copper urn had burnt out but luckily there was still a lot of hot water left.

When Mohini emerged, clean and perfumed, she was wearing a simple shift of expensive white cotton from Aígyptos, with brilliant blue embroidery along the collar, sleeves and hem.

It was split at either side to reveal her thighs and cut low to show the upper part of her breasts. She was large for a woman, having the muscular body of a dancer and she moved with a dancer's grace. The skin of her arms was dark but it had a bluish sheen he had never seen the like of before.

She gave him a confident, intimate smile, a flash of shiny teeth against her dark complexion. He felt flushed by the sensuous heat she radiated. He tried to remind himself how dangerous she was.

His thoughts were interrupted by his servant complaining loudly that Mohini had forced her to take a silver coin for helping her, on top of giving her the ruined dress to see if she could salvage the material; she was feeling overwhelmed.

Emre was astonished that she spoke courteously.

"Auntie," she said respectfully. "That dress is no longer of use to me so I am giving you nothing. You have been very attentive to me when you didn't need to be and money is something I have."

"Why did you speak nicely to my maid?" Emre asked as the woman left for her home, looking very pleased.

Mohini shrugged. "She didn't annoy me."

"Mohini, why are you here?"

"Gansükh destroyed Darband, he almost destroyed the elves, and he gained a large kingdom for himself in the process. Now that is real power! He is offering rewards to those with power if they join him, so this has become a good place for me to live. Someone very like me is coming to kill him if she thinks she can do it. I can solve that problem for him if she comes. Perhaps I will be rewarded."

"He has a daimôn lord to protect him."

"Jess has destroyed scores of greater daimôns. We are a good match, her and I but I know how she can be killed."

She turned to her two servants. "What do you think me against Jess?"

"Now that would be worth watching." Astártē smiled.

* * *

Nîjara ran as fast as he could to find his sister, Fedrî.

He could run well over short distances and duck and dodge. He was nimble and smart and the best boy in his gang for climbing. He could rob fruit trees in the gardens of the wealthy and spot where the birds nested. He could steal their eggs better than anyone else and he knew where the rats nested and where to set his traps.

But he was a small boy for ten and not good at fighting boys bigger than him. So he went via the tower, panting up the slope past the iron-wood and hornbeam trees before he reached the cluster of wooden and mud brick shacks hiding from the winds in a small dip. Most were empty due to the war and famine.

"Fedrî?" he called.

His blood ran cold. Fedrî was curled up on a pile of rags, naked. She had been bleeding and her skin was discoloured from a beating. As he dropped to his knees, she rolled over to greet him. Her face was swollen, her lip was split and she had been crying. At least she was alive.

"Who did this?" Though he could guess.

"Peshana offered me two oboloí because I had never been with a man."

Two oboloí for them was a fortune. His sister was thirteen but some old men like Peshana the butcher would pay if it was a girl's first time.

And they needed the money since she lost her job.

"Pâzinah came later with three men," Fedrî said. "He took it off me and the little money we had. Then they beat me. He said if I wanted that sort of work I had to give him two shares out of three. Why? He doesn't do anything?"

"I will kill him!" Nîjara threatened, but he wouldn't.

He showed her the coppers. "This will get us a little of that stale bread that the baker puts aside. I will check my traps; as long as someone hasn't stolen what I have caught we should have a couple of rats to eat. Oh, and I might have gotten you a job as a cook with a wealthy lady."

"I can't cook." Fedrî pulled at her lip in thought. "Is she nice? Maybe she will be patient while I learn."

Nîjara didn't think she would be, but he wasn't going to tell Fedrî that.

* * *

"Why are you wasting your time with that half trained maguš," Aranyani asked as they walked back to their house.

"You will see." Mohini said smirking.

"Dearest sister," Astártē said to Aranyani. "You have no sense of romance."

"Romance?" Mohini looked at her.

"Astártē is the Goddess of love, don't forget." Aranyani groaned. "To her everything is romance."

As they passed by the entrance to a side alley Mohini paused.

"What's that?" she asked, pointing.

There was a body lying in the corner of a step covered with a dirty bundle of rags. The three women walked down the alley to examine it. It was a woman's body, a beggar, with dirty yellow hair.

"She's still alive." Mohini whispered.

She was lying on her side, unconscious. Her legs, arms and hands were crippled. They had been broken in multiple places and healed poorly. She probably couldn't walk and had to crawl and drag herself. She had sores over her body. One leg was swollen with pustules over it and was red and shiny right up to her groin.

"She is dying." Aranyani said.

"Yes, she is dying," Mohini squatted down beside her. "She is malnourished and the infection has reached her blood. Her body has stopped fighting it and her organs are failing. I have only just learnt how to draw another's infection into me. It will be a good to practice again."

She closed her eyes and stopped breathing. An impossibly long time passed. Mohini opened her eyes and almost pitched over with dizziness. Astárté had to grab her.

"Her mind is cloudy." Mohini panted. "I could tell she is named Tabiti, after the Skythian Goddess of home and the hearth." Mohini slipped some small denomination silver coins into a small pocket in her rags and got up to walk away.

"Can't you do anything for her?" Astárté asked.

"What do you think I just did?" Mohini looked at her as if she was stupid. "It may not be enough though. Her body is very weak. You want me to do more? But should I? Did you see her closely? She has calluses on her right hand but not on her left.

She was once a swords-woman. She has been stretched on something and there are old scars on her back from a hard flogging, nothing unusual so far.

But then someone has systematically broken her long bones and also the bones of her hands and feet with sledge hammers. None of that could be done too close together or she would have died.

"This lady has been systematically tortured." Aryanna said, in understanding. "It was over many months and then she was thrown into the streets to starve. If she was just a bad soldier or a common criminal they wouldn't have done that. If what she had done was so bad normally they would have just killed her. She has earned the spite of some great lord, maybe even the old Šâh, someone so far above the law that he can do as he pleases and then leave her here as an example to others."

"Can we make use of her?" Astárté asked.

"Astárté!" Mohini was shocked. "She is thoroughly broken. I have helped her all I can. Maybe she will survive, probably not. I am not here for this sort of thing!"

"Ha!" Astárté laughed. "You can't do it, can you? The great Mohini can't do it. Admit it, you can't fix her."

Mohini looked down at the broken woman in dismay.

* * *

Thank You

Thank you for reading Book 4 of the Paladin Chronicles. I hope you have enjoyed reading it as much as I have enjoyed writing it. Feel free to email me: paladin.chronicles@gmail.com for comments, or visit me at neilport.com to be on the mailing list for advance news or news on the next book. All author proceeds from this book and the other books in the series go to charity see http://donationstocharityfrombook.blogspot.com.au

Please consider posting a review

Star rating is a major determinate of book sales. I am very grateful for any reviews that you might post at the site you have bought this book from or on Goodreads or book likes etc.: https://www.goodreads.com/author/show/7079650.Neil_Port.

You don't know just how much they help. The descriptive part doesn't have to be too extensive. I would recommend only a few (short) comments. Amazon suggests for their star ratings: 5 Stars I love it, 4 stars I like it, 3 stars it is OK, 2 Stars I don't like it, 1 star I hate it.

Current Books in the Paladin Chronicles Series

Paladins are religious knights sent by their God, they dedicate themselves to their God and the task they are given. There has never been more than one and the last one was three hundred years ago, now there are two.

See http://www.amazon.com/Neil-Port/e/B00A7NTWW2

Book 1: The Elvish Prophecy

Book 2: The Defence of Troia

Book 3: The Gathering Storm

Book 4: The Assassin's Quest

   Future Books in the series (as at 9.7.15)

Book 5: An Enemy Within.

Book 6: Lost City of the Dwarves

Book 7: The Daimon War

www.ingramcontent.com/pod-product-compliance
Lightning Source LLC
Chambersburg PA
CBHW051933020726
47501CB00001B/110